Jackie FRENCH

Miss Lily's
Lovely Ladies

Angus&Robertson
An imprint of HarperCollins*Publishers*

Angus&Robertson

An imprint of HarperCollins*Publishers*, Australia

First published in Australia in 2017
This edition published in 2018
by HarperCollins*Publishers* Australia Pty Limited
ABN 36 009 913 517
harpercollins.com.au

HarperCollins*Publishers*
Level 13, 201 Elizabeth Street, Sydney NSW 2000, Australia
Unit D1, 63 Apollo Drive, Rosedale, Auckland 0632, New Zealand
A 53, Sector 57, Noida, UP, India
1 London Bridge Street, London SE1 9GF, United Kingdom
2 Bloor Street East, 20th floor, Toronto, Ontario M4W 1A8, Canada
195 Broadway, New York NY 10007, USA

A catalogue record for this book is available from the National Library of Australia

ISBN 978 0 7322 9854 8 (paperback)
ISBN 978 1 4607 0194 2 (ebook)

Cover design by Lisa White, HarperCollins Design Studio
Cover images: Woman by Richard Jenkins; Chinese peony, Redoute Flower Illustration by istock.com ID:514108261
Author photograph by Kelly Sturgiss
Typeset in Sabon LT by HarperCollins Design Studio
Printed and bound by CPI Group (UK) Ltd, Croydon CR0 4YY

Chapter 1

*... that was when I realised that war is as natural to a man as
chasing a ball on a football field. War is a scuttling cockroach,
something that a woman would instinctively stamp on. Women
bear the pain of childbirth, and most deeply feel the agony of their
children's deaths. Could one marshal women to fight against the
dreams of war?*

But women have no power, except what they cajole from men.

Miss Lily, 1908

FLANDERS, 12 JULY 1917

'Stop!' yelled Sophie.

She peered out of the car window through the night and gun
smoke at the huddled mound on the bomb-scarred track.

The blob became a dog, large and lifeless, its dark fur almost
invisible in the smoke. The dog's blood showed red and vivid in
the headlights. Beyond them, the big guns echoed like a singer
trying to be heard over the orchestra: the constant rumble and
belch of the front line.

Three years of war had taught Sophie this: if blood flowed,
the patient was still alive. This dog lived.

Tomorrow yet more men would die, even more horribly. But
how could she leave a dog?

Only a minute, she thought as the driver pulled on the brake.
She pushed open the door.

'What the damnation are you doing?' They were the first
words the driver had spoken since he had greeted her politely
again outside the French hotel, opened the rear door for her

and the picnic basket, then driven, hour upon hour, in resentful silence, through the afternoon, through yellow smoke-lit dusk, and now through the night.

She'd hoped desperately he would say something about her quest, about her reappearance in his life, ask *why* she had been in a hotel bedroom with a half-dressed French général. He hadn't. Now it was her turn not to answer.

Instead she stumbled out of the back seat, into the darkness. The moon crouched on the world's dark ceiling above her. The land on either side looked frozen into shattered glass. Flat land. Black glass, mud and soot, a flash of orange perhaps a mile away, giving a sudden glimpse of tangled barbed wire draped with what Sophie hoped were rags, not flesh.

This world was dead. Everything here was dead, except for the two of them. And, just perhaps, a giant dog.

She kneeled and touched its fur. The dog opened its eyes.

'Good dog. It's all right, you're a good dog.' She spoke automatically.

'We're in France, in case you haven't noticed. I don't suppose this mutt understands English.'

She hadn't heard him come up behind her. His face was white, his hands clenched in fear or anger.

The dog lifted its head, trustingly, and laid it on her lap.

A gun boomed to their left, louder than the ones before. She was beginning to make out the sounds of the different explosions now.

The dog made a small noise. It almost sounded like a plea.

'There's blood on its shoulder,' she said. 'Maybe it's been shot.'

'Things do get shot in war.'

'Help me carry it back to the car.'

In the darkness, the man didn't move. 'You're worried about a dog? You might have thought of *my* chances of survival before you had me ordered here.'

'Fine. I'll carry it myself.'

'You wouldn't get a dog that size two yards.' He bent swiftly, then cradled the massive animal in his arms. 'You don't seem to realise that every second we spend here is dangerous. Open the door ...'

He laid the dog on the leather seat, beside the picnic basket Madame had packed for them. Sophie pulled out the Thermos. She knew you shouldn't give a dog coffee, but this would be mostly chicory, and it needed fluids.

She pooled a little into one of her hands. The dog raised its head and lapped. She unwrapped the chicken and pulled off most of the breast meat. The dog swallowed it in three gulps, then licked her fingers, wanting more, and gulped down the bread she offered too.

She looked at the man in the front seat, who was peering at the road. Yesterday she'd loved him, had thought he loved her.

Hannelore had said love between a man and a woman was illusion, bright colours to disguise the necessary distributions of power involved in mating. But Miss Lily had once whispered, 'Oh, yes, there is love.'

Would Sophie see Hannelore or Miss Lily again? Perhaps she'd die here. Perhaps Miss Lily and Hannelore were already dead.

The car swerved onto another track. She leaned forward. 'Are you sure we're going the right way?'

The man at the wheel didn't glance back. 'No.'

'I told you, this is *urgent*.'

He shot her a look. 'I'm doing my best. Do you think there are maps of battlegrounds?'

'Yes,' said Sophie.

His lips quirked into a reluctant smile. 'You're right. But I don't have one.'

'I should have asked the général.'

'I doubt the général had a map with him when he lent you his car and my services earlier. It's not the sort of thing one takes to a seduction.'

'I don't suppose it is.' She tried to keep her voice light. The dog slobbered gently on her lap.

The ground beside them exploded. Dirt and pebbles rained down onto the car. For a few seconds the windscreen was black, then the dirt fell off.

'Holy hell.'

She had never heard a man swear before. Not at home in the paddocks — not even the men they'd nursed in the past few years.

Sophie swallowed, trying not to sound afraid. A man doesn't like to hear fear in a woman's voice, Miss Lily said. Fear is an accusation that he has failed in his duty to protect you. You may sound apprehensive, but never shrill. 'That came from nearby.'

'Too near. They're firing at us. They'll fire again as soon as they reload.' He peered at something through the smoke.

She tried to see what he was looking at. A farmhouse, she realised, or at least its walls, the rubble of its sheds, about twenty yards away.

He swung the wheel towards it suddenly. 'When I say so, get out. Run behind the nearest wall.'

She heard the next explosion in front of them an instant before she felt it. He wrenched the car onto the farmhouse cobbles.

'Move!' He leaped out as the car jerked to a stop.

Another shell ripped across the cobbles, from a different direction this time. Sophie flung herself out of the car and behind the farmhouse wall, landing hard on her knees.

The edge of the wall exploded. She shut her eyes till she thought the debris had stopped falling, then checked her arms, her deeply inappropriate silk dress, her shredded stockings.

Stupid. She would have felt wounds or a burn before she saw them. Instinct had taken over.

Instinct is what drives the world, Miss Lily said. Use it, enjoy it, but never let it take control.

Sophie peered through darkness that was more dust than night. The car was intact. The dog lay unmoving on the leather seat. Two steps and she had it hoisted like a sack of potatoes over her shoulder. She staggered under its weight.

'*Sophie!* Get over here!' His voice came from what looked like a fireplace, set deep in the wall.

Once — a year ago, a world ago — this had been a kitchen. Some French farmwife had scrubbed the hearth. Stews had bubbled here, and pots of strong coffee for the men to dip their lumps of sugar into. Now it was two walls and a patch of sagging roof, with a bird's nest up in the rafters.

'Hurry!'

It took a second for her to realise that the fireplace would protect them from the shells.

Perhaps. For a while. Until the German soldiers followed with their guns and bayonets. But perhaps, Sophie thought desperately, they would be English, French, even Australian ...

Two more shots. The picnic basket, still in the car, shattered behind her. Madame's roast chicken hung in an incongruous crucifixion on the steering wheel.

She tried to run under the weight of the dog, felt his arms grab it, then pull her into the safety of the chimney as more shells ripped the air.

'You should have grabbed the picnic basket, not the dog.' But he laid the dog down gently as he said it, at the back of the chimney where it would be safest.

The dog sat up and stared from one to the other.

The driver rubbed its long, fluffy ears. 'Sorry, old boy, no more chicken for either of us. How's the motorcar?'

'Intact. They shot the basket, though.'

'Probably by accident. They want to kill us, not destroy the car. They'll want to use it.'

'The whole German army can't escape in one car.'

He shrugged, causing a small cascade of soot from the chimney. 'There aren't many out there, I don't think. Two groups shooting at each other. Might only be half a dozen men. Patrols, maybe. Lost like us. We just happened to get in the middle.'

Except you're here because of me, thought Sophie. This man had loved her. But he was here because of orders, not love. 'So one lot are our chaps?'

Another shrug, more careful this time. 'Maybe. Or the French. I don't know this part of the line. We won't know who's shooting who till one lot takes this place, or till another gang rolls up to help them.'

She glanced out into the shadows. One lot of shots had come from what she thought might be a hen house. The return fire had come from a crumpled barn. 'When do you think that will be?'

'Tonight. Tomorrow morning. A decade's time. That's what we've been doing for the last three years, us and the Boche. You capture a few yards of mud, hold it for days or weeks or months. Then you die as the other side takes it back again.'

'And now we're in the middle.'

With difficulty: 'Sophie, I'm sorry. I must have taken the wrong turn in the dark. The front should still be a mile from here.'

'Maybe it moved. It's not your fault.' Suddenly she began to cry, trying to swallow the sobs.

He put an arm around her tentatively, then, when she didn't shrug it off, hugged harder. 'Sophie ...'

The dog whined. It laid a bearlike paw on her silk skirt. She bent down and hugged it, savouring its warmth, its doggy smell, like the sheepdogs of Thuringa, even its slobber.

'I'm not scared. Not for myself.' She peered up at his face in the grimy darkness. 'But men are going to die if I don't do something.'

He sat too, his back against the chimney wall. 'Men are already dying. Have died. Will die. This is war.'

'I don't mean die from being shot. Worse. Impossibly worse.'

Another blast — a rocket, this time — hit the ground outside.

He waited till the ground stopped shaking, till the cracked tiles no longer fell around them. 'I've seen men hung on the barbed wire of No Man's Land who took three days to die, their eyes pecked out by crows, screaming all the time. I've seen myself hanging there, in nightmares. Tell me one thing you've seen in your drawing rooms that is worse than that.'

I've seen a woman scream in childbirth for two days, then die as her blood drained from her body, she thought. I've seen a man try to make a life with no eyes left, and half a face. But he was right. This was his world, not hers. And he *had* tried to protect her.

She wiped her eyes, feeling the sting of soot. She knew she needed food, though she wasn't hungry. 'I don't suppose you have anything to eat?'

'Chocolate.' He took it from his pocket and passed it to her.

A big block, she saw gratefully. The dog shoved its furry face towards her. 'Oh, no you don't. You just ate bread and chicken.' The dog sat back, drooling reproachfully. 'You don't have a pistol in your pocket too?'

'No. There's one in the car. But I was dressed for an afternoon off at the hotel, not war.'

'I do. But then I wasn't at the hotel for the same reason as you.' She reached into her own pocket and pulled it out. Somehow the pistol seemed smaller here, with the massed armies of so many nations around them.

He stared at it. 'Where in damnation did you get that?' He reached for it.

She pulled the pistol back. 'I can shoot a 'roo a hundred yards away.'

'I can shoot a grouse. They're smaller.' He hesitated. 'Keep the pistol.'

She had been going to, but suddenly the meaning of his words hit home. The Germans out there would kill him. But they might spare her. For a while, until they'd finished.

'What else have we got?'

He reached into his pockets. 'My identity card. Francs. Pen knife. It's got tweezers and a nail file.'

'Just what I need right now, a nail file.'

'What about you?'

'Francs, pounds.' A *lot* of English pounds, but she didn't tell him that. 'Four diamond rings.'

'You brought diamonds into a war zone?'

'Diamonds are easier to carry than money.'

She broke off six squares of the chocolate, then handed him the rest.

He shook his head. 'Keep it.'

'Forget gallantry. You need to eat. If there's any chance of getting away from here, we have to keep going.'

'For heaven's sake, why? What's so important that you would risk our lives to get to the front line?'

The comfort of the chocolate vanished. 'Why didn't you ask before?'

'I was angry.'

'You're not angry now?'

'Three hours ago I found the woman I thought I loved in the bedroom of a French général.'

A small hole ripped in Sophie's heart. But she had known already. How could any man still love her after what she had done today?

He looked at her steadily through the erratically gun-lit gloom. 'I'm probably going to die on this expedition of yours, and that makes me angry too. But you know what makes me angriest? You haven't even had the courtesy to tell me *why*.' His gesture took in the chimney, the silent dog, the thousand shades of yellow, white and red from the explosions beyond them.

You could have asked me, she thought, instead of sulking as you drove.

Then she glanced at him, his face white in the flashes of shellfire. She had been wrong. His silence had been fear, not pique. She had misjudged him, badly.

'The Germans are going to try a new weapon. Worse than guns or chlorine gas.'

'Another sort of land engine?'

'No.'

'Then what?'

She hesitated. Could she trust him? He might even refuse to keep going if he knew what was ahead of them.

What would Miss Lily advise now? More tears, whispered Miss Lily.

Sophie glanced at the poor helpless dog, its eyes closed, faintly panting. This shouldn't be a dog's war. Now the tears were real.

'I ... I can't tell you.' She pulled out her handkerchief and blew her nose.

It worked. He put his arm around her again. His voice was gentler now. 'You think Miss Sophie Higgs can stop the enemy?'

'No. But I can warn our officers in the field to get their men away. I tried to speak to someone with authority back in England, but I couldn't manage it. Not in time.'

'So you're going to try to speak to whoever is in command at Ypres? Even if we survive, you won't get past the first sentry post.'

You have no idea what I can do, she thought. Sentries are only men too. 'I will be in the général's car, with a decorated English officer driving. And I've got a letter.'

'One letter? Who's it from? The King?'

'A German princess.'

He stared at her silently. But it wasn't silence; there was no silence here. Even the earth vibrated with the shelling a mile away. Every few minutes another rocket screamed outside.

His voice was wary now. 'A Hun? How exactly did you get a letter from a German princess in wartime? How do you even know one?'

She was suddenly impossibly weary. 'The letter came via Switzerland. I met the princess through Miss Lily.'

The wariness was as thick as syrup now. 'Who's Miss Lily?'

'She's the cousin of the Earl of Shillings.' Another lie. But still the easiest explanation. 'She ... taught me all that matters.'

She could sense his suspicion growing. 'Is she a spy?'

'No.' Though she was no longer sure if that was true.

'Why couldn't Miss Lily help you herself, then? Or the earl?'

'I couldn't contact the earl in time. I ... I don't know where Miss Lily is.' If she said that Miss Lily had vanished at the beginning of the war, he would assume that Miss Lily was a spy, and that Sophie was a spy too. But there was no quick way to explain Miss Lily.

A shadow flickered past the door. German, she thought, recognising the helmet. The soldier gave a cry as blood blossomed on his uniform. He fell onto the cobbles, spasmed twice in the light from the rocket fire, then lay still. The dog shivered, its head in Sophie's lap as if to say, 'I am a sheep-herding dog. Dead men are not my business.'

Sophie stared out at the body in the flash-lit darkness. Last week I'd have tried to help him, she thought. Or at least wondered if I should. But my life isn't mine to risk just now.

She felt the warmth of her companion's hands as he pulled her further back against the inner wall of the chimney. He unwrapped another square of chocolate, broke it into halves and gave her one, then pulled her into his arms again. For warmth, she thought, feeling the chocolate's sweetness melt on her tongue. And then, No, he's trying to cover me so that if someone shoots us they'll hit him, not me.

Is he doing it because a man protects a woman, or because he loves me, in spite of everything?

The dog looked at them, considering, then clambered onto Sophie and lay down, curling as much of itself as possible on top of her. Its fur was warm, as comforting as the arms around her.

'I don't know you, do I?' he said at last. 'I never did.'

'No. I'm sorry.' She wasn't quite sure what she was apologising for: for bringing him here, or for failing to tell him the whole truth. Maybe it wasn't even an apology. She was just … sorry. For him. For herself. For the giant blood-spattered dog across her lap. For the whole bloody mess of war. And that isn't swearing, she thought. Just truth.

The guns had hypnotised her. That, and his warmth so close to her. She had faced this burden alone all week. Would he understand? And if he did, would he still try to help her?

He stroked the dog's furry back. It put its head on its paws, slobbering again, and reassured.

'By tomorrow,' he said quietly, 'we may be dead. So eat your chocolate and tell me about Miss Lily. Tell me about yourself — all of it, not just the bits I knew before. Tell me everything.'

'My whole life?' asked Sophie.

'We have time.' She caught a glimpse of a half-smile in the growing dark. 'And if we run out of time, we will be dead. How did an Australian girl meet the cousin of the Earl of Shillings?'

He had risked his life for her. She owed him the truth. 'It started with corned beef,' she said.

Chapter 2

Never try to manipulate a child. Children sense false smiles.
Speak to them honestly and they'll like you, which is the best way
to charm their mothers too.

Miss Lily, 1913

SYDNEY, 1902

The most important problem in life, decided Sophie, was how to spoon up the last of the ice cream and caramel sauce from the silver dish before her. When you are seven and three-quarters, and visiting the Quong Tart Tearooms, leaving a spoonful is a tragedy.

Scraping the edges of the dish would make a noise that was unladylike. Other patrons might hear — the women in the feathered hats that only other women would appreciate, their bodies erectly corseted; the girls in their frills and white muslin dresses, eating with as much greed as she was, though politely, of course. A lady must always be polite.

Here at the Tearooms, where men were a rarity — Quong Tart was a Chinaman, so he somehow didn't count — female gluttony was allowed in a pact unspoken by any of the patrons. Plump scones damp with melted butter, piled with raspberry jam or thick with dates; apricot jam on pikelets with cream ... the servings were lavish. A woman who moved food gracefully around a plate in front of men could eat with visible pleasure here.

The Quong Tart Tearooms also made The Best Ice Cream in Sydney. Sophie knew that for certain, because her father employed The Best Cook in Sydney, like he bought the best of everything, but Mrs Cleaver's ice cream was like toffee. It stretched. The Tearooms' ice cream was like frozen clouds. Perhaps the ice cream at home was intimidated by the portraits on the wall: Papa in his best waistcoat, holding the silver chain of his watch; Mama looking like the angel she now was.

'Sophie, have you finished?' asked Miss Thwaites patiently. She was a tall woman, with a face like a friendly cow.

'Yes, thank you, Miss Thwaites,' said Sophie.

Miss Thwaites was no Gentlewoman in Reduced Circumstances, who taught girls a deliberately cultivated ignorance. Miss Thwaites's father was an English vicar, and her mother had been 'an honourable'. Miss Thwaites had even attended Somerville Hall at Oxford on a scholarship — though not gained a degree, of course. Women couldn't be awarded degrees, even at The Best University in the world.

It was good that Miss Thwaites was Sophie's governess, especially now that Mama was an angel. She had never known her mother, but she loved Miss Thwaites. Miss Thwaites was also the most interesting person she had ever met, even more interesting than Papa. If Miss Thwaites hadn't had four sisters, she might never have had to become a governess, never have come to Australia, never have joined the Women's Suffrage Association. Sophie was pretty sure Miss Thwaites had single-handedly got Australian women the vote.

She clicked the heels of her white patent-leather shoes against the chair, earning a frown from Miss Thwaites. She stopped kicking — not because Miss Thwaites would lock her in a cupboard when they got home, like one of the Suitable Friends whispered her governess did, but because she liked Miss Thwaites. Instead she looked around the Tearooms while Miss Thwaites finished her scone.

The ladies all looked much the same, in their silks and feathered hats, their big drooping sleeves that almost — but never quite — trailed in the jam.

The waitresses were more interesting, like the one who limped, as Papa did, but only as she approached the doors to the kitchen, just like Papa tried to limp only at home and not in the street. The limping waitress always gave Sophie two wafers in her ice cream too, standing up like tiny sails.

Would ice cream float like a paper boat? wondered Sophie. Miss Thwaites would say it wasn't done, even if Sophie were willing to risk her treat.

'But if I do it, then it can be done,' Sophie had said once.

'Don't be cheeky,' Miss Thwaites had replied, but she'd said it with a smile. Miss Thwaites was iron under her grey silk, but it was warm iron, like the stair railings on a sunny winter's day.

Miss Thwaites finished her scone, dabbed her mouth with her napkin and looked up, a signal to an attentive waitress that they were finished.

The not-quite-limping waitress came with their bill, and a pen and ink well. Miss Thwaites signed the bill in her sloping handwriting, pushing the nib neatly up the paper like a mob of ants pushing a stone up a pyramid. Papa kept an account at the Tearooms, and at David Jones and Anthony Hordern's Palace Emporium and Percy Marks the jewellers and any other place Miss Thwaites might need to take his daughter.

There's no point stinting when you have only one chick, Papa said. Whatever Sophie wanted she should have, and he didn't want to be bothered at work by a governess asking for five pounds for a new bonnet and some ribbons.

'My dear Miss Thwaites! And little Miss Sophronia Higgs, isn't it?'

Miss Thwaites looked up, but didn't stand, which meant that this woman must be Encroaching. Lots of people Encroached, Miss Thwaites said, when your father was the richest man in New South Wales. Miss Thwaites's smile diminished, from Friendly to Just Barely Polite.

The woman noticed. Her own smile widened. Definitely Encroaching: either a governess or a recent widow. Governess, Sophie decided — a recent widow couldn't eat scones at the Tearooms, and a widow of longer standing would wear silk and jet jewellery like the Dear Queen used to, not shiny poplin.

The boy at the woman's side was a few years older than Sophie, his blond hair neatly oiled and wearing a dark blue velvet knickerbocker suit. He looked at her curiously.

Suitable Friends came to afternoon tea every Tuesday and Thursday — daughters of other businessmen, and sometimes their brothers too. This boy was not one of the Suitables.

He might even be interesting.

'Do sit down,' said Sophie, in the tone she had heard one of the Suitables' mothers use.

Miss Thwaites's top lip tightened, but she couldn't draw back after Sophie's offer. 'Please do. Sophie, this is Miss Wilson. And this must be Master Malcolm Overhill?'

Sophie looked at the boy even more curiously. The Overhills had Warildra, the property out at Bald Hill, next door to their own Thuringa. Mr Overhill was the local Member of Parliament. But she had never met the Overhills. She was vaguely aware that many people thought the Overhills Most Suitable Indeed, but Miss Thwaites said that Australian squatters were just jumped-up sheep farmers. Sophie imagined the squatters in their moleskins, jumping over sheep. Miss Thwaites said that a man like Papa, a man who had made his own fortune, was worth a thousand sheep farmers.

The Encroacher sat. The boy — Malcolm — sat too. 'I hope you don't mind, Miss Thwaites,' said the Encroacher. 'It has been so long since I spoke to anyone from home ...'

Sophie looked at the boy.

'Hello.'

'You're the corned-beef girl.' The boy gave a slight snigger.

'What's funny about corned beef?' demanded Sophie coldly.

The boy smirked. 'Gentlemen don't own factories.'

Definitely Unsuitable. And stupid. Sophie sought a weapon. 'Why don't you have a tutor? Only *girls* have governesses.'

Malcolm flushed. 'She's my sister's governess. She's just taking me to buy a new school uniform.'

'I think she's really your nurse,' said Sophie flatly.

Malcolm reddened. 'She's not!' He lowered his voice. He glanced at his governess, but the woman was intent on trying to interest Miss Thwaites, one gloved hand resting on the other woman's unwilling one. 'You're the girl whose mother vanished.'

Sophie stared. 'My mama died.'

The boy shook his head. 'No, she didn't. She just vanished. But Mama says she probably *is* dead. There was an article in *The Bulletin* a few months ago saying the case has never been solved,' he added with relish. 'Didn't you read it?'

'No,' said Sophie. 'My mama would never vanish. My father wouldn't let it happen.'

'She vanished six weeks after you were born. Policemen from three states were looking for her! There's a reward too. It's never been claimed. Mama says that's why our family doesn't meet yours. Your father might be a murderer. *And* he makes corned beef.'

Sophie gave him a sharp kick under the damask tablecloth. He winced. She moved her legs so his retaliation missed.

'My papa is the most wonderful man in the world! *Everyone* wants to meet my papa!'

'Not my family.' Malcolm glanced at his governess. 'My mother is going to be cross when I tell her Miss Wilson made me sit with you. But Miss Wilson is leaving at the end of the month, so maybe she thinks it doesn't matter that you are Not Acceptable.'

It was a lie. It all had to be lies. Mama was an angel in heaven and Papa was the best man in New South Wales. Sophie narrowed her eyes. She couldn't pinch Malcolm, not in public.

'If it wasn't your father, then maybe white slavers took your mama and —'

'Malcolm!' The Encroacher seemed to suddenly notice her charge. 'What have you been saying?'

Sophie stood up. 'Silly things,' she said. 'We need to go now, don't we, Miss Thwaites?'

'Indeed we do,' said Miss Thwaites. She stood too, and bowed slightly. 'How nice to meet you, Miss Wilson.'

'We must meet again,' said the Encroacher, desperately. 'I ... I will be seeking a new situation soon. I wondered ... perhaps tea next week?'

'We will be out of town next week,' said Miss Thwaites coolly. 'May I recommend Miss Sorrel's Agency? It is in Macquarie Street. Come along, Sophie.'

The boy smirked. He knows that there's nothing I can do about his lies, thought Sophie. For they had to be lies, surely.

One day she'd get even.

Chapter 3

Is there any such thing really as a happy childhood? Children must
be taught to be who they are expected to be — which is usually
very different from who they are. Childhood is a time of moulding.
Adults only pretend that it is pleasant.

Miss Lily, 1913

FLANDERS, 12 JULY 1917

Darkness clung around the ruins of the farmhouse. The guns
thrummed in the distance, but there had been no shots from the
sheds nearby for the last ten minutes. The dog seemed asleep.

Were all the soldiers in both patrols dead?

No. Waiting.

Sophie should be terrified — for herself, for the men who
would suffer unimaginable horror if she were to fail.

No, not unimaginable. She had seen too much not to imagine
it all.

But she didn't feel terrified. Instead she felt alive, as though
the last shell of Sophie Higgs from Australia had cracked and
fallen away. The only rules in this landscape of burned trees
and shattered farms were those of war.

She was free. A chuckle rose, impossible to suppress.

'What's so funny?'

She wished she could tell him there was no need to hide his
terror. But that was another rule: men were brave, and soldiers
were braver. 'Rules. The ones we never speak about. Even when
I was small I knew there were rules ladies had to obey but never
talk about. Men too.'

'I obey army regulations because I have to,' he said stiffly.

'And you think army regulations are the only rules you obey without question? Would you stab the Kaiser?'

'What?'

'If he were here now. And if you had a bayonet. Would you stab him?'

'Of course not.'

'You see? You'd end the war if you did. But it would be unsporting. Not following the rules.'

'This isn't a game of football.'

'Isn't it? It's just bigger. Anguish instead of bruises. But still the same stupid rules.'

He sighed. 'Go on with your story. I don't know what to ask about first. Did your mother really vanish?'

'She vanished when I was six weeks old,' said Sophie flatly. 'I found the article in Dad's desk in the library. Cuttings from other newspapers too.'

'People don't just vanish. Were her clothes there?'

Sophie looked at him in the dimness. 'People vanish every day. Thousands of them. Don't you read the papers? Missing in action ...'

'But that wasn't wartime.'

'No. And, yes, her clothes were there. Her jewellery. Nothing taken, except the nightdress she'd been wearing.'

'She can't have gone far in that. The servants saw nothing?'

Sophie shrugged. 'If they did, they didn't tell.'

'And there was never any clue? What about her family?'

'My mother was an orphan. English. She'd come to Australia via India as a governess. My father had a thing for governesses. Still has, I believe.'

'Miss Thwaites?'

Sophie smiled. 'Miss Thwaites spends every Sunday afternoon with him. I was fifteen before I realised.'

'You said she had a face like a cow!'

'She did. Does. But a friendly cow.'

'But your father ...'

'My father is rich enough to have a beautiful mistress?' She frowned. 'I think that beauty intimidates Dad. Or maybe it reminds him of my mother. Anyway, as far back as I can remember, he and Miss Thwaites were close. We'd all play with the model trains at Thuringa. Dad loves model trains; he's got one whole room filled with them. Miss Thwaites and Dad share the controls. They never shared a bedroom though, even at Thuringa.'

'One doesn't marry a governess.'

She smiled. 'You forget — he already *has* married one. But he can't marry anyone now. Not unless my mother is declared dead.'

'I admit I ... I've never thought about that sort of thing.'

'Why should you? The next of kin has to apply to have someone who is missing declared dead. My father never has.'

'Why not?'

'In case of more gossip, I suppose. Raking it all up again. Maybe he's always hoped that she might still be alive. I don't know.'

'Sophie ...' He hesitated. 'It must have occurred to you ...'

'That my father might have killed my mother? Other people thought so. He could have bribed the maids to assist, the coachman to take her body. Men as rich as Dad can buy many things. But I know he didn't kill my mother.'

'Because you love him?' His voice was gentler now. Good, she thought. The terror seemed to be easing from his body.

'I suppose I do. But I know he didn't do it.'

'Why? How can you be so sure?'

'Because I asked him,' said Sophie.

Chapter 4

Some men want children desperately, often those who don't like children much. To men like that, a child is an extension of who they are. Sometimes I wonder if they ever truly see their child at all.

Miss Lily, 1913

SYDNEY, 1902

Sophie let Nanny Jenkins change her clothes after the tearoom visit, then obediently lay on the bed for half an hour with *The Girl's Own Annual* stories Miss Thwaites had sent from England. But today even the adventures of two schoolgirls in ancient Egypt could not grab her.

Why had her father lied?

She let Nanny bathe her, then changed once more to dine with Miss Thwaites on chicken salad and strawberry jelly, a meal that would shock the mothers of the Suitables, who fed their children mince and tapioca, the tasteless mush deemed proper for a child.

At last it was time to see her father. Mr Jeremiah Higgs dined by himself each night in the library, not in the dining room with its table that sat forty, used only on the few occasions he had guests. Miss Thwaites would always act as hostess on such occasions, even though she was just a governess; the fact that she was the daughter of an honourable made it different.

Sophie's father didn't believe in cutlery, except in company, which was one of the reasons why he preferred to eat alone. Fingers before forks, he said. Sophie assumed for years that this was because he was from New Zealand — that New Zealanders, for some reason, avoided cutlery. Only a careful study of Cousin Oswald's use of knife and fork convinced her otherwise.

Mr Jeremiah Higgs's lunch was a slab of bread and cheese at his desk at the factory or in the library on Sunday — the only day of the week he didn't work — with a slice of apple pie and still more cheese, every day of his life. (A pie without cheese is like a kiss without whiskers, he'd said once, while stroking his moustache.)

Dinner was served when he felt like it, and 'no palaver about it', in his armchair facing the library fire in winter, or the vase of gum leaves that occupied the fireplace in summer.

Till she was five, Sophie had imagined he ate the same meals as she and Miss Thwaites: lamb cutlets, roast chicken or squab with baked potatoes. But one night she had interrupted his meal to show him the pen wiper she had finished (finally) for the church fair.

It was as close to guilty as she had ever seen him look. She'd found him with his pocket knife in one hand and a slab of roast beef in the other, slicing off bits to put on the bread on his lap. A bowl of mustard sat on the table within easy reach.

Sophie and Miss Thwaites ate dinner at five o'clock, with milk from their own cows out at Thuringa, for her father didn't trust town milk: the dairymen added chalk dust to make it thick and white, he said. Sophie was allowed to see her father only at six o'clock, for an hour in the library, after he had changed from the clothes he wore to the factory, and both of them had bathed — as though we have washed away everything we have done during the day, thought Sophie. For her father, she wondered if it was to wash away the smell of corned beef.

Today she had changed into the loose white cotton gown suitable for a girl to wear to see her father after work. She wore a pink sash, and pink ribbons too, even though she hated ribbons flapping at her cheeks, but because her father liked her to wear ribbons. And she loved him.

'Good evening, Papa.'

He smiled at her from his armchair and held out his arms. They were short arms. Sometimes her father reminded her of an ant: a bull ant, in charge of all the other ants. The top of his head reached only to Miss Thwaites's shoulders. 'And how's my princess today?'

Jeremiah Higgs had never tried to turn his New Zealand accent into mock upper-class English, as most wealthy Australians did. Sophie was glad. Papa wouldn't have been Papa if he spoke in any other way, though Miss Thwaites ensured that Sophie's own accent was impeccable.

Sophie willingly participated in tonight's hug. Her father wasn't good at hugging, but she knew he liked it and so did she. He was older than other fathers, his hair white at the temples and sideburns, which made him special. He had told her once he'd decided not to have a wife or child until he could 'do right by them', which meant a big house and money.

She sat on the stool by his feet. The brocade didn't match the green velvet curtains or the dark wood of the library. It had pink roses on it and golden tassels. Papa never put his feet on this stool. It was hers.

'I can do long division now.' Miss Thwaites had snorted, just like a cow, when one of the Suitables' mothers had said that mathematics stunted girls' bodies and made them unfit for motherhood.

'What about your piano practice?'

'I don't like piano,' said Sophie.

'All ladies play the piano.'

Sophie considered. 'I won't,' she said.

He stroked her hair. He was better at hair-stroking than hugging. 'You'll be the finest lady in Sydney.'

'Then I won't *need* to play the piano. Piano playing is ... repulsive.'

'Is that your new word?'

Sophie nodded. 'It's a good word. We went to the Tearooms and met a boy. He's repulsive too.'

'Why's he repulsive?'

'Because he said a stupid thing. He said Mama vanished.'

Her father became still.

She watched him. 'You said Mama had died.'

He chose his words with care. 'That was easiest for a little girl to understand.'

'Then she *did* vanish?'

'Yes.'

'Why didn't you find her then?' Sophie's voice was fierce. Her mother was *hers*. She'd have felt as protective of a lost doll.

'Sophie love ...' Papa's accent changed when he called her that. 'Have I ever failed to give you what you've asked for?'

'Yes. I want a proper horse, not just a pony,' said Sophie promptly.

'You'll get that horse when you're fourteen years old. What else?'

Sophie pondered. There had been Rufus, who had died. But dogs did die when they got old; Papa had explained that. She wasn't allowed to play with sail boats in the fountain either, because girls didn't; nor was she allowed to have bare feet like all the boys around Thuringa. Even Papa wasn't able to change the rules set down for ladies.

'No,' she said at last, cautiously, not wanting to give him too much credit. If he usually gave her what she wanted, sometimes it took a lot of arguing to convince him *not* to give her things she *didn't* want, like piano lessons and cod liver oil.

'If I could have given your mother back, don't you think I would have?'

He was speaking the truth. Sophie always had a pretty good idea if someone was speaking the truth.

'Why did she go?'

Her father hesitated. That means he is wondering how much more to tell me, she thought.

The thought didn't anger her. Adults usually considered what bits they should tell children.

'I can't tell you why she left, Sophie.'

'Did ... didn't she like me?'

He smiled at that. 'Everyone loves you, Sophie.'

That *wasn't* true, but he probably thought it was.

'Was it because of corned beef?'

'It was not. She knew about that when she married me.'

Sophie took a breath. 'Was it because you don't have a leg?'

He stopped breathing for a few seconds. 'Who told you about my leg?'

'No one.' She wished she could swallow back the words.

'Then how'd you know?'

'I went into your room when you had the influenza last year. Miss Thwaites wouldn't let me in, in case I caught it, but I wanted to see if you were all right. You were sleeping.' He sat there watching her. 'It was by your bed. It looked like a leg, but with straps on. And I could only see one foot under the bedclothes.'

He still looked at her, considering. 'Yes, I've a wooden leg. Lost my real one in the wars on the Indian North West Frontier when I was a soldier. But your mother knew that when she married me too.'

'How did she go missing?'

'You want a story then?'

'Yes,' said Sophie. Sometimes Papa told stories of when he was a little boy back in New Zealand, of how Greymouth was grey, just like its name, and he'd been so poor he'd warmed his feet in fresh cow droppings. Other times he described how he'd seen Thuringa after it rained and looked green and lush, then when it dried out he'd thought that it was ugly till one day he saw the golden hills and fell in love with it again.

'This one's not a nice story, Sophie love.'

She shrugged. She liked stories in which heroes ripped off giants' heads better than nice ones. 'Tell me.'

'All right then. Your mama was sleeping down the hall, recovering after your birth. I went down to breakfast that day and asked the maid how her mistress had slept. The fool said she'd taken her dinner and breakfast up, and when she wasn't in the bedroom either time, nor the bed slept in, she'd just brought the tray down again — eaten it herself, most likely. She said she

24

thought your mother might have spent the night with me. But she hadn't. I ran up the stairs ...'

'And then?'

'I searched. The police searched. I hired men to search. There's still a grand reward for finding her.'

'Papa ... did someone kill her?'

'I don't see why they would,' he said heavily. 'She were ... she was a girl everyone liked. No one'd want to kill her. How could they, in her own house, with servants downstairs?'

There was something he wasn't saying. 'Was she kidnapped by pirates, to pay a ransom, like in *Treasure Island*?'

'I'd have paid it,' he said gently. 'No one ever asked.'

'White slavers?'

She was pretty sure she wasn't supposed to know what white slavers were. But he just said, 'White slavers take girls who don't have families to care for 'em. Nay, Sophie love. Whatever happened, it weren't that.'

'Then what could have happened?'

I should be crying now, thought Sophie. That's what a heroine in *The Girl's Own Annual* would be doing. But she just felt a dawning excitement.

Other girls had mothers. She had a mystery ...

'I wish I had an answer for you,' he said.

She thought for a moment. 'Papa?'

'Yes?' he asked, a little warily.

'Can I see your wooden leg now?'

He laughed, his face breaking up into a hundred tiny wrinkles. She could see his worn-down bottom teeth, all yellow. 'Yes.' He reached down and pulled up a trouser leg.

She looked at it, disappointed. It still looked just like a round of wood, vanishing into his sock just like a real leg would.

He hesitated, then pulled his trouser leg up further. The knee was more interesting, hinged like the legs of one of her dolls.

'Is it heavy?'

He let the trouser leg fall. He was smiling. 'No more than a real leg. You get used to it.'

'What was the war like?'

'Now you're just trying to keep me talking instead of going to bed.'

'No, I want to know. Were you a hero?'

A hero would make up for corned beef.

'No. I was just there. It was hot and dusty, then it was freezing and dusty. Too many were killed and even more wished they had been. War isn't a good story, Princess. You don't talk about wars, not when you come home.'

He touched her cheek. He had never done that before. 'Sophie love, if you ever hear gossip about me, about our family, come to me about it, as you have tonight. You promise?'

'I promise.'

He kissed her on the forehead then, which was her signal to go to bed.

Almost by magic — or as if she'd been listening — Miss Thwaites arrived to take her upstairs. Sophie heard the library door shut behind her.

One day she would find out. Maybe not soon — she was realistic about how much she could hunt for a missing mother with Miss Thwaites as her constant shepherd, not to mention piano lessons she still had to convince her father she didn't need. But one day she would find out what had happened to her mother.

Chapter 5

To some men an opinion from a woman is like mustard on their egg: unthinkable. For others it can be opening a window to let clean air into a crowded and stuffy drawing room.

Miss Lily, 1913

FLANDERS, 12 JULY 1917

The dog drooled gently on Sophie's lap. 'What sort of dog is it, do you think?' she asked.

'Sheepdog, I think.'

'What? I've known sheepdogs all my life. This one is bigger than a sheep.'

'A Spanish sheepdog.'

She ruffled her hands through the woolly fur. 'What on earth are Spanish sheep like then?'

He ignored the question. 'Which regiment was your father in?'

'Only a man would want to know that. I never asked. My father came out to Australia after his time in the army, because Australia has more cattle to be turned into corned beef than New Zealand has, and more people to sell it to and ships to export it in. That's all he's ever told me.'

Gunfire suddenly rattled from what had been the barn. A man called out, a warning perhaps. The dog's ears twitched.

'German,' said Sophie.

'You speak German?' The suspicion was back in his voice.

'Only enough to recognise it. Could we make it to the car?'

'No. Both sides will be watching it. Both probably want it.'

'We could run away in the darkness then ...' She paused. 'No. We need the car too.'

He didn't disagree. Another shot cracked from behind them almost at the same time as the first volleys of gunfire crumbled more of the wall in front. 'Stalemate,' he said. 'Neither side dares move in case the other sees them.'

'So what happens now?'

'They'll try to take each other by surprise. Or if there's an officer he may order some of the men to advance and take out the other side, even if it means the poor duffers die in the attempt.'

'We might get to the car while they're fighting each other.'

'And we might get shot if we try. We can only wait, Sophie. That's what war is mostly about. Waiting to die.'

'You think we're going to die?'

'I've known I'm going to die in this war for the last two years. It's a case of when, not if. But a girl like you shouldn't even be thinking about death.'

Sophie was glad it was too dim for him to see her face.

'Let's talk of something else,' he went on. 'So, did you ever find out about your mother?'

'A little, over the next couple of years. My father moved house six months after she vanished, I suppose to get away from people who pointed and said, "That's the house where that woman disappeared." We moved again, a few years after that, to an even grander house. But I found a trunk of my mother's clothes in the attic. They must have been brought with us in each move. And I found two people who had known her.'

'Mothers of the Suitable Friends?'

'No. The women who had known her weren't really friends of hers. They had just dined with my parents fairly often, as you do without being close. My mother had only lived in Sydney for a little over a year, so no one knew her well. One said my mother was pretty, another that she had a lovely laugh. Both were sympathetic and slightly excited by the mystery. As you are.'

'I'm not ... Yes, I am. But only because it doesn't seem to have hurt you.'

'It did hurt,' said Sophie slowly. 'It still does. I know it seems odd to miss something you can't remember. When I discovered she'd vanished it was like the house suddenly had an empty space I hadn't seen before, a voice in far-off rooms, a shadow in the corridor. I kept staring at her portrait. Somehow her smile seemed to say, "I know, but you do not."'

'Hard to grow up without a mother.'

'I suppose that depends on the mother.'

'Did you find out any more when you were older?'

'You do pick up on things. I think I did,' she added slowly, 'when I met Miss Lily.'

'I wondered when we'd get to Miss Lily,' he said dryly.

'Not yet. We haven't even got to my twelfth birthday.'

'Was that birthday important?'

'Very. My mother was just a story. Knowing about the mystery didn't really change my life at all, though it explained some things I'd sensed, as children do. But my twelfth birthday was when I ...' she shrugged '... began to be the Sophie Higgs I am today.'

Chapter 6

We are all hungry. Those with a hunger for food need their hunger fed more urgently.

Miss Lily, 1913

SYDNEY, 1907

The birthday cake was three tiers high: lots of tiny icing roses surrounding the twelve candles, in the middle of each tier a layer of yellow butter cream.

It was an impressive cake for a twelve-year-old. The Suitable Friends who had been invited to share it, however, were boring. Miss Thwaites's impassioned descriptions of Socrates discussing philosophy with his friends were far more interesting than comparing cats and new dresses.

Today's birthday afternoon was made worse by the absence of Sophie's father. Mr Higgs was at work, of course, but he wouldn't be home tonight either. There was a Dinner; the capital letter meant it was a meal with business benefits beyond the food.

Sophie wasn't sure she loved her father *properly*. The love children gave their parents in Dickens or the Suitable novels didn't seem like what she felt at all. But her father was *interesting*, with horizons that weren't restricted to tearooms and tennis courts.

Finally the Suitable Friends melted away to their carriages; one to a motorcar. Mr Higgs had not yet bought a horseless carriage, saying he preferred to rely on transport with brains: if his driver was a fool, then the horses would still see him home.

Miss Thwaites was upstairs, superintending the turnout of Sophie's winter wardrobe. Sophie looked at the cake. The lower, largest tier had not been touched. And it was her birthday.

Sophie pulled the bell.

'Tell Rogers to bring the carriage round,' she told the servant. She nodded at the cake. 'And ask Mrs Cleaver to put the cake on a fresh plate, with a cake knife, please. I'm taking it to my father.'

'Shall I call Miss Thwaites?'

'Don't bother Miss Thwaites. She's busy.'

The carriage was at the front steps by the time she had fastened on her hat, pale straw with white netting in a swirl, a new one. All her hats were new.

'To the factory, thank you, Rogers.'

Rogers jiggled the reins. The horse began to trot.

She expected the horses to head out of town. A corned-beef factory needed cows, and cows lived in the country. But instead the carriage turned into a side street, and then another, and then began to climb.

Another turn at the top of the hill. The houses were strange here. Small, like dolls' houses. No, not like dolls' houses — those were small editions of big houses. These were squished together like layers on a cake, with grimy choko vines and ivy instead of butter cream, and a smell recognisable as what Miss Thwaites described as 'pooh' — familiar only because Sophie was familiar with the smell of her own from the few seconds before she flushed the water closet.

A child with a naked bottom and a tatty singlet squatted on a doorstep. A woman with lips and cheeks and hair coloured the wrong clashing reds glanced hopefully out of a window at the carriage. Otherwise the street was deserted.

Dirty air, heavier than smoke. A fine layer of soot on Sophie's white sleeve already, just from the open carriage window. Dirty houses, with layers of grime streaked by rain and then more grime on top of that. And then a corrugated-iron building taking up a whole block, burping dense black smoke from too many chimneys to count. The sky seemed an eternal grey, as if it had never known blue.

How could this exist in the same city as proper houses and the Tearooms?

The carriage stopped.

Sophie knocked on the driver's panel, then spoke as it slid open and Rogers's head peered in. 'I asked you to take me to my father's factory.'

'This is it, miss.'

'Oh. Thank you, Rogers.'

She let him help her out. He handed her the cake.

There were no stairs, just a doorway in the corrugated iron. She could feel the heat as she stepped through, like a hot, soapy towel clapped over her face. It smelled of hot tin, steam and smoke, not meat. Light came through a gap between the walls and roof. Dirt floor, greasy machinery, long metal benches, faces …

So many faces. White faces, smudged faces, women with lank hair or greasy scarves — girls too, her age or younger, much younger, all turned to her, their hands suddenly idle.

Someone barked an order. Most of the faces looked away. Only one came closer. It belonged to a girl, five years old perhaps at first glance, ten at a second. She was wizened like a monkey, or like the woollen coat the washerwoman's helper had shrunk. She wore what was left of a dress, enough to cover a rabbit-boned body. The rags, like her face, were bleached of colour. Bare feet on the dirty ground. Red hands, so thin the skin seemed to be painted on her bones. One hand reached forward. A finger touched the cake.

An icing rose fell off.

'Look what you done now!' A man stepped closer, in a rusty black suit, shirt greasy at the collar. 'You're for it, you are. Sorry, miss.' He gave a clumsy bow. 'You're Mr Higgs's daughter, ain't ye?'

Sophie nodded. The child shrank back.

'Not her fault. She ain't seen nothin' like that afore.' A woman with hair like a worn-out mop and an even greyer face, presumably the child's mother, carefully didn't look up from the bench, her swollen hands picking up a corned-beef tin, dipping a label, slapping it on, putting the tin down, taking another. The small girl still stared at the cake.

'Would you like a slice?' It was automatic: that was what you said, when there was cake.

The girl glanced up at the man, then nodded at Sophie quickly.

Sophie used the silver cake knife to cut a wedge. She held the plate out to the girl.

The child grabbed it, stuffed it in her mouth, swallowed, then licked her fingers carefully, looking at her dress in case there might be crumbs.

There weren't.

Sophie stared. She had never seen anyone eat like that. Like one of the farm dogs, gobbling its food.

The girl still stared at the cake. No, thought Sophie. At food. The child had gulped too fast to even taste the cake.

'Mind yer manners. Say thank you to Miss Higgs.' The woman kept working, her tone apologetic. 'She's hungry, see. I'm sorry, Miss Higgs. I learned her better. But things are tight just now.'

'Tight?'

'With our Bennie not working, and her dad took bad.'

Hungry. The peasants during the French Revolution had been hungry, Miss Thwaites said. Marie Antoinette had said, 'Let them eat cake', when they couldn't afford bread. Miss Thwaites had made it clear that Marie Antoinette should have given them bread. Jesus had fed the five thousand with bread too, which was also admirable.

This seemed an excellent chance to be admirable too.

The girl bent down and picked up the fallen icing rose. But she didn't thrust it into her mouth. Her fingers traced the petals. Perhaps, thought Sophie vaguely, she didn't know you could eat something shaped like a rose.

So many mouse-like faces glancing at her, at the cake, then down. Shadowed skin that might be discoloured by dirt, that she'd remember years later and know was the colour of hunger, of tuberculosis, and of the slowly eroding diseases of poverty that sucked away life but left you still able to pack meat into cans.

There wasn't enough cake for them all.

She thrust the plate onto the bench next to the woman. 'Please. Take it home.'

The woman put her hands on the girl's shoulders, perhaps to stop the child from grabbing it at once.

'Are you hungry too?' Sophie asked.

The woman's eyes were stained with loss. 'I'm always hungry, miss. Can't eat if the little uns need it more.'

The man in the rusty suit shoved himself between the woman and Sophie. 'If they don't brings their lunch, then that's they's fault if they get hungry. Now, you step this way, Miss Higgs. I'll take you to your dad.'

'Yes. I would like that,' said Sophie.

Chapter 7

Most people only ever understand one world: their own. You need to learn that every person feels things much like you. That isn't meant to be sentiment, my dear.

I am not a saint, asking you to bleed with those who hurt. Imagine the world is like a machine. To use it properly you must understand how it works. Our world is other people. Understand them, and you will begin to know how you can move the world.

Miss Lily, 1913

FLANDERS, 12 JULY 1917

The dog snuffled softly. The front-line guns were muffled now. There had been no shots nearby all the time Sophie had been talking, almost as though the soldiers out there had been listening to her story too. But of course they were too far away to hear anything but a mutter of voices.

'What happened then?'

'An argument. My father was angry because I'd gone out alone. I was angrier because … because it was another world, one he'd never let me see. I'd felt bad down on the factory floor, and hadn't liked it.'

'And then?'

She shrugged in the sooty darkness. 'I demanded he send out for bread for them. He liked giving me what I wanted. A pony for his daughter, crumbs for the ducks, bread for the factory workers. Not much difference. The coachman brought back loaves and loaves, one for every person. I watched them eat while

Dad stood next to me, his hand on my shoulder. I made him promise he'd give them bread every day. Some of the women called out to thank me as I left. One even called me "a little saint". They got all the bread they wanted to eat at the factory after that, and could dip it in the liquid from the corned beef — and if they stuffed some in their apron pockets like Dad had said they would, well, it showed their families needed it.'

'Did he keep his word?'

'Oh, yes. Even told me a year later it had been a good idea, he was doing it in all his factories. It hadn't occurred to me he *had* other factories till then. He said he'd discovered that people worked better with full bellies. And at Christmas time I insisted every child got a ball and an orange. I preened myself for so many Christmases thinking of those balls and oranges. One day off a year,' she said softly. 'Christmas Day, and I gave those children a ball. Maybe they played with it then, though I expect they slept. I was so proud of myself.'

'Lady Bountiful?'

'I didn't know that term then. But, yes.'

The moon was rising, its light shining through the shattered walls. Strange to think that same moon stared down at war and at the peace back at Thuringa, had floated above Dad and Miss Thwaites only hours before. And above Miss Lily perhaps, wherever she was.

'So did you go on playing the Lady Bountiful? Was that why your father sent you to England?'

'No. I think Dad half liked my being interested in the factory, even if women aren't supposed to know factories exist. Dad even liked arguing with me about increasing the wages. I was about fifteen then, and had finally worked out why the factory women couldn't buy their own bread. It seemed such an easy way to do good with no inconvenience to myself.'

'I think you may be being hard on yourself.'

'No. Doing good can be deeply self-centred. I thought I was being Lady Bountiful again, but really I wanted to show Dad I could make useful suggestions about the factories. If well-fed workers are more productive, then give them enough money to buy their own food.'

'Did he actually increase the wages?'

'No. He told me he couldn't. If he did, the other factory owners would be pressured to do the same. His wages were already on the high side, and if they went higher he'd be ostracised. They'd make him pay, one way or another. Factory inspections, pressure on suppliers. Money-makers belong to a club, he told me. The only way to get into it is to make money. The only way to stay in it is to obey the rules. They're not rules that are written down, but everyone knows them nonetheless. Stupid rules — like not killing the men who begin a war, only those who fight it.'

'And not paying your workers a decent wage is one of the rules?'

'He said so.' She smiled, reminiscing. 'I called him a coward.'

'No wonder he sent you to England.'

'No. That was because of a man.'

'Ah,' he said. 'I wondered if we'd get to that.'

'Or a boy,' she added slowly. 'He was just a boy then, and I was a girl.'

'Sounds like the beginning of all the best romances.'

'It was,' she said. 'For a while.'

Chapter 8

Love? Love all you want, my dear. But love makes a very
inadequate meal by itself.

Miss Lily, 1913

SYDNEY, 1912

It was a blue and gold day: blue shadows and blue trees, and
infinite possibilities. The light was gold. Timber cantered along
under the trees: a perfect horse, playful enough to challenge a
nearly seventeen-year-old girl who had been riding since she was
four, but a horse with all vices scrubbed from her equine soul.
Lady Jane ran before them: ostensibly a cattle dog, but Sophie's
ever since a swaggie had carried a red and black puppy to
Thuringa in a billy and swapped her for a forequarter of mutton
and a pound of tea.

Nine years earlier a boy had insulted her. Back then she had no
idea how very Suitable indeed the Overhills were, despite Miss
Thwaites's disdain. Today Sophie Higgs was going to enchant
Mr Malcolm Overhill, partly to show that she could.

One of the Suitable Friends had mentioned a month back
that Mr Malcolm Overhill was in the same college at Oxford
in England as her cousin, and had sailed back for the Christmas
break. The only risk to Sophie's plan was if the young man had
brought friends home with him. If he had, though, they weren't
with him today.

Moonbeam Joe, the head stockman on the property, was
supposed to accompany her, but he had wrenched his back

working cattle a week ago and his formidable wife had informed him that he was not to ride till he could stand straight again. Sophie had told Miss Thwaites truthfully that she was riding to the river as usual. She hadn't mentioned she planned to ride along it, past Thuringa's boundaries.

But they were still on Thuringa land — just — when Lady Jane barked as she saw the other rider.

'Hello!' Sophie carefully let Malcolm Overhill hail her first, pulling at Timber's reins as he cantered up to her. His horse was good, a big black gelding. He rode it well. Lady Jane sniffed at the horse's fetlocks before deciding it was acceptable too.

'I'm sorry. Am I trespassing?' She smiled at him from under her white hat. 'I'm Sophie Higgs, from next door. We have met, you know. Years ago, at the Tearooms in Sydney.'

'I say, Miss Higgs, of course I remember you. Astonishing we haven't met again.'

It wasn't, and they both knew it. Malcolm's family were the upper class in this society, while the Higgses were Trade. The chasm was too wide to breach.

This year that would change.

Sophie waved the flies away with a gloved hand. 'I *am* trespassing. I'm so sorry. It was just so lovely here by the river.'

'I think I may be the one who's trespassing. But you're right — it's a cracking ride. Look here, may I accompany you home?'

'Of course. We might even offer you a slice of Coronation cake.' She smiled again. She knew she was beautiful, except for the two front teeth that crossed slightly, but which you didn't see if she smiled in a certain way. Even if she hadn't been beautiful she might have believed she was, flattered and sheltered by her father, Miss Thwaites and the Suitable Friends. She knew that too.

'How can one resist Coronation cake?'

The horses began to amble along side by side, both riders keeping their pace as slow as possible, talking, as the young mostly do, of themselves and each other, with Lady Jane panting behind.

That was the beginning.

It was only years later that it occurred to Sophie that Malcolm had ridden that way to meet *her* too.

She meant him to fall in love with her, of course. It seemed reasonable. She was used to being irresistible, in every sense of the word.

She hadn't meant to fall in love herself.

It began with corned-beef sandwiches. Ridiculous to fall in love over corned-beef sandwiches.

They rode together every morning after that. Not by themselves, of course; even Sophie couldn't manage that. But Miss Thwaites, after consideration, allowed her to go out escorted only by Moonbeam Joe as long as she was back by mid-afternoon. (Miss Thwaites didn't ride herself.) The young man was eminently respectable, after all, and out in the country the chaperonage rules were relaxed.

They rode to the Bushranger Cave one morning. It was only a few metres deep — a crevice where a young man had waited, damp and scared, for the troopers to find and shoot him, with a colony of bats that fluttered out in panic as soon as Lady Jane nosed inside, instead of a chest of gold coins.

'Maybe he buried it,' said Sophie hopefully.

Malcolm laughed. It was a good laugh. 'Not in the cave. It's all rock under the dust. See? If he buried it out there ...' his hand waved across the hills '... a hundred men could dig for a year and never find it.'

Yet it was still a day of sunlight and cicadas, the horses meandering under tree dapples, bark crunching like toast under their hooves, their breath hot, their sides sweaty. Collecting fallen branches to light a fire, with a twist of last week's *Sydney Morning Herald* to get it going; boiling the billy that had once held plum jam; drinking the black tea Sophie disliked, but drank because you couldn't drink lemonade from a billy ...

Moonbeam Joe had let them light the fire. He accepted his mug of tea as though he hadn't made many thousands of fires, a hundred times more expertly than Malcolm Overhill, and retired to drink it by the horses near the stream. Sophie sat, her back against a tree, hot as the billy under her silk and whalebone stays, her bloomers, her thick serge skirt and high-necked cotton blouse, envying Malcolm in his open-necked shirt and trousers, and unwrapped the damp damask napkin that held her sandwiches: scrambled egg with shredded lettuce, and chicken with grated carrot, pickled beetroot, lettuce and mayonnaise. Lady Jane sat at Sophie's feet, waiting for her share.

She glanced at Malcolm, vaguely curious about what the Overhills' cook would have given *him*.

It was corned beef. Plain corned beef, on buttered bread. He bit into the first sandwich while she stared. Plain corned beef, without even pickled beetroot or mango chutney ...

Had he meant it as a taunt? No. The smirking boy back in the Tearooms might have done it, but not the young man flirting with a girl he obviously admired. He mustn't have thought about it at all.

Corned beef was never eaten in the Higgs household, even below stairs. Every can of corned beef opened in England or India or Hong Kong, spilling out its fatty gelatinous goo before you came to the thick, veined, still-pink meat more suitable for spooning than slicing — every single tin meant a few more pennies to be transformed into Sophie's dresses and hats, or cans of caviar to adorn the family's hard-boiled eggs. But that was its only role in the Higgs household: to bring wealth, not to be eaten, or even, when possible, acknowledged.

How could a family be so confident of its status that it would eat corned beef? Not even dressed with pickles? Even as Sophie stared, Malcolm threw Lady Jane a crust. The dog snapped it before it had time to fall, then looked back, waiting for Sophie's chicken.

And suddenly she saw him more clearly than she had ever seen another person. His arms were tanned darker than the tree bark, his hat pushed up off his forehead to let the sweat dry. Behind them the horses cropped the tussocks.

He was beautiful. The whole day was beautiful, every part of it. And because you couldn't love a day, that left Malcolm himself to love. Malcolm, with the sunlight on his face. Malcolm, who could carelessly eat corned beef.

He caught her glance and smiled, then held her gaze a moment longer. Both of them automatically turned to Moonbeam Joe, eating his slab of fruitcake, so obviously there to prevent anything more than glances.

But they both knew that something more than glances had already happened.

They met at church the next three Sundays, sitting through the service with their respective families, Malcolm with his father and mother (his father a grey-moustached man who hiccupped well-bred snores during the sermon), Sophie sitting further back with Miss Thwaites and the Thuringa servants behind them — her father came to church only on Christmas Day.

But afterwards she and Malcolm talked, while Mrs Overhill and Miss Thwaites carefully managed not to engage in conversation, no matter how long their carriages were kept waiting.

They talked of Oxford, city of spires and young men in black students' gowns who climbed over the wall to get into college after hours, and of London with its creeping fog that tasted of coal. If she hadn't loved him before, she'd have loved him then, speaking of the world beyond gossip and corned-beef factories, so unlike the talk of the Egberts, Cyrils and Alberts, the possible suitors who now so Suitably adorned the Higgses' dining table.

Malcolm spoke about home too: how he'd like to put the river flats into lucerne when his studies were over; about shooting rabbits by lamplight down by the river — the animals were a plague on both properties. She didn't tell him her father took her shooting as well, rabbits and even quail that burst out of the knee-high summer grass, or about Jeremiah Higgs's pride when his daughter shot eight rabbits with ten shots, so that for a few moments she felt almost as good as a son.

She didn't tell Malcolm about her father's model trains. Malcolm might laugh at model trains. She didn't talk about the Suitable Friends, who would not have been Suitable for a Mrs Malcolm Overhill.

By the time Malcolm sailed again for England, Sophie was hoping he'd write.

He did.

Each week she waited for his letters, afraid he'd find an English girl — an honourable, perhaps — far more fascinating than a colonial Miss Sophie Higgs. But around once a week, depending on the ship's timetables, the letter would be there. *Dear Miss Higgs* ... for although he called her Sophie now, you couldn't do that in a letter Miss Thwaites might read ... and signed *Yours truly, Malcolm Overhill.*

'Mr Malcolm Overhill is a most reliable correspondent,' observed Miss Thwaites, looking up from her boiled egg.

'It's so interesting. He's been to a Friday-to-Monday; he calls it a shoot.' She glanced down at the letter. 'He bagged thirty-four pheasants. The old chapel of the house has a ghost.'

'Thirty-four pheasants and a ghost as well. Impressive.'

Sophie frowned, then stopped. Ladies weren't supposed to frown. Frowning gave you wrinkles. Ladies could smile, look impassive, or give a little laugh. Hearty laughs, like frowns, belonged to men. 'Don't you think it's interesting?'

'Extremely interesting. It's just that I have never known a young man to write so regularly. Correspondence is usually between women.' Miss Thwaites nodded to Bates to pour her more coffee. 'Could we have fresh toast too, please, Bates? In my experience,' she added to Sophie, 'men add postscripts to women's letters. *PS John sends his regards and says the weather has been foul.* But perhaps the men in my family are simply poor letter writers.'

'He likes writing to me,' said Sophie defensively. 'He likes *my* letters too. I tell him about Warildra and Thuringa. He misses home dreadfully.'

'Despite the pheasants and the ghosts. No, I agree with him entirely, my dear. After all, I chose to come to Australia, and stay here too, as did your father.'

Sophie looked down at her letter again. By mid-1913 Malcolm would have graduated, would be home again.

The weekly letters continued.

Meanwhile there was life in Sydney. A dance at the Higgses', with Suitable Friends and the Alberts and Cyrils; dances at their homes too; the small and stultifying world of commercial Sydney's social life, far away from the stories of debutantes and balls and the London season in the English papers. These were delivered each morning so Jeremiah Higgs could read his business news, and the political news that might impinge on business, and were perused by Miss Thwaites from nostalgia and a hunger to know about the world beyond Sydney and the Higgses' drawing room.

Sophie was hostess at the Higgs dinner table now. Miss Thwaites sat in the middle of one side. Factory owners, an omnibus king and a newspaper owner brought their sons to dinner, younger sons who might charm a corned-beef princess, and also prove their ability to manage the corned-beef empire after her father's death.

And Cousin Oswald.

Cousin Oswald was from Canterbury, which appeared to be a more desirable part of New Zealand than Greymouth. He had become an accountant there, had applied for a job with his cousin (twice removed) in Australia, and now, five years later, was deputy manager and came to dinner once a month: a family dinner, just the four of them. Cousin Oswald was perhaps an obvious contender for Sophie's hand. Sophie had made it plain, however, that even though he was worthy and admirable in all ways, she would not consider him. She had not admitted that she was also deeply jealous of her father's confidence in Cousin Oswald. A life spent as Cousin Oswald's wife, kept on the sidelines by a husband instead of a father, would be insupportable.

'We've gone as high as we can go with the existing market,' said Cousin Oswald earnestly that evening, forking up lobster gratin as if it were fish and chips. 'What would you think of a luxury tin, Mr Higgs, with a painting of a maid presenting a can on a silver salver in a drawing room? We could charge two shillings for a can like that.'

Mr Jeremiah Higgs looked with resignation at his despised cutlery, and at the lobster, then took a mouthful. 'No pretty picture on the lid will change corned beef into a luxury. No, lad, we need to come up with a way to make 'em eat more of it, that's all.'

'Don't other countries like corned beef?' Sophie had already finished her own lobster.

'Australians can only sell in the Empire, Sophie love. Canada doesn't want Australian corned beef — they've got their own farms — and Higgs's has already got the contract for the Indian army. But England is our best market. Always has been.'

'Can England sell to other countries?'

'Of course.'

The idea seemed obvious. 'Then why can't we export to England and have an English company that would sell it to, I don't know, France, maybe?'

Miss Thwaites smiled. 'I doubt the French would care for corned beef.'

Mr Higgs chewed his bread roll absently. 'If the Frenchies are going to war again with Germany, their army could use corned beef. If it's good enough for our troops in India, it's good enough for them. What do you say, Oswald?'

'An English subsidiary might open up many possibilities,' he admitted cautiously.

'It might indeed.' Jeremiah Higgs reached over and patted his daughter's hand. 'You've got a good head on you, Princess. If it works out, you'll have a diamond necklace. What do you say to that?'

'Pearls,' murmured Miss Thwaites. 'Much more suitable until she's married.' She nodded to Sophie to rise, to leave the men to port and cigars and business discussion. She heard the men's animated voices discussing English managers and possible markets, as Bates closed the dining-room door.

Sophie felt a small tide of anger rise in her. It had been *her* idea, yet she was banished to the drawing room. At least when I am married, she thought, I will be in charge of when the ladies must retire. And when Dad discusses business with my husband I will insist that I be there too.

The year passed: winter at Thuringa, away from the cold southerly winds of Sydney; then back to more dances, more musical evenings with Suitable Friends and the Reginalds and Ernests who never looked beyond Sydney Heads.

Malcolm wrote of his friend who had joined the Sussex Territorials, determined to show the Prussians that England too had a backbone of military might; of a London ballroom where he'd danced with debutantes, *but none half as beautiful as you.*

It was the first time he had called her beautiful.

The first Sunday in December at Bald Hill Mrs Overhill smiled at Sophie after church, adding, 'A charming hat, Miss Higgs', before climbing into her carriage. Her husband raised his hat and followed her.

Sophie stared. For seventeen years Mrs Overhill had taken great care not to be introduced to her. Was seeing each other at church for seventeen years the same as an introduction? Beside her, Miss Thwaites frowned.

Two weeks before Christmas the invitation arrived, gold edged, to the Overhills' New Year's tea party.

It included Miss Thwaites too, who had somehow become companion rather than governess now that Sophie was older; her grey silk was now trimmed with lace, and she had put the schoolroom in Sydney under dustcovers. The invitation also included her father, though Sophie guessed her hostess would hope, even expect, that Mr Jeremiah Higgs would send his regrets.

'The white silk, with the yellow roses,' said Sophie, while Annie the maid waited patiently to lace her stays and slip on whatever dress they settled upon, to draw on Sophie's stockings and put on her shoes, to curl her hair with the hot irons, as she would wear it down for a country afternoon, not up.

Miss Thwaites shook her head. 'Mrs Overhill will find white muslin more acceptable.'

'The one with lace panels, then.'

'If you insist.' Miss Thwaites hesitated. 'Sophie, there have been reports that Mr Overhill has suffered losses on the share market; that Warildra is heavily mortgaged.' 'Reports' meant that Mr Jeremiah Higgs had made it his business to find out.

Sophie considered the information only briefly. Her father had more than enough money, after all. And Malcolm loved her, despite the corned beef and his mother's earlier disapproval.

And she loved Malcolm. She also loved the idea of a future in which she would be Mrs Malcolm Overhill. A Malcolm Overhill was as suitable for a Sophie Higgs as the Higgs fortune was for Malcolm Overhill.

Miss Thwaites, even her father, must feel the same.

The dress was white, the two panels of floral lace from shoulder to hem made by French nuns.

And she was overdressed. She knew it as soon as the coachman handed her and Miss Thwaites down from the carriage; saw the girls in plain muslin dresses scattered around the gardens, playing tennis on the court, most definitely not in French lace. Miss Thwaites had been right.

'Miss Higgs, and Miss Thwaites, how good of you to come.' Mrs Overhill's large yellow teeth flashed a smile. Her husband muttered something, and peered for just slightly too long at Sophie's bosom.

Miss Thwaites stationed herself in the drawing room with Colonel and Mrs Bronte, who kept hens to eke out a military pension, but had still made Mr Higgs sit on the verandah instead of in the drawing room when he returned the Brontes' afternoon visit the previous year, to ensure that the social superiority of army over trade was made clear.

Sophie wandered, ostensibly to see the gardens, across the fine green grass that no sheep would ever have a chance to eat. Mrs Overhill hadn't introduced her to any of the young women. Over by the hydrangeas two unfamiliar girls turned their backs, raising their voices slightly as a barrier.

She was embarrassed, and angry too. She should go back and find Miss Hartley, the vicar's daughter. Mr Higgs contributed generously to the church, ensuring that Miss Hartley had become a Suitable Friend too. But she didn't want to pass the two girls again.

She headed behind the house, through the gravel courtyard, past the dogs barking on their chains. Then stopped.

Dark faces looked up at her. Dark faces like Moonbeam Joe's and his wife's and all their family, whom she loved. Five black stockmen crouched by the dairy, in worn moleskins and tattered shirts that had once been blue, chains on their wrists and ankles linking them together and attached to a steel bolt in the wall. She saw the whites of their eyes as they glanced at her, then looked away; they were so motionless as to be saying, 'We are not here.'

None of Miss Thwaites's lessons had told her what to do when faced with chained men. Nothing, probably. Like painted ladies, this was something a girl should pretend she didn't see.

And yet Sophie looked again, saw cracked lips. The courtyard glared heat. 'May ... may I bring you a drink?'

She wished she hadn't said it. She had no right to offer drinks at Warildra, even ask the kitchen for them. The black men must be criminals, might grab her if she came too close.

It was as though she hadn't spoken. They looked at the ground, not her.

She moved away, lifting her white skirt to keep it clear of the dust. She found a bucket at a rainwater tank with a tap. She filled the bucket, then handed it to the first man in line, who did not look at her; he drank four gulps only, then passed it along. She filled the bucket again, and then a third time, till she sensed their thirst was quenched, although still none had looked up at her, nor spoken.

Anguish tore at her, not at their chains, but at their resignation. These could not be criminals.

She put the bucket back. She had no words. It was as if the men here, and her action, did not exist. The world felt crooked. She turned, silent, and walked back to the garden.

She was passing the conservatory when she heard her hostess's voice. 'A sweet thing. Quite pretty. Overdressed, of course, but that can be fixed.'

'... her mother?'

Sophie stiffened. Was that the voice of Malcolm's married sister?

'If anyone remembers that old scandal, she'll be an Overhill, not a Higgs. No, it would work out quite well. I shall take her in hand, of course, to make her presentable, but she will scarcely expect a London season, as a girl of a better family might. Little Miss Higgs will be quite happy here in the country in a new house of her own. I am sure Mr Higgs would be delighted to provide it. Malcolm has no mind for politics.' Was there a ghost of relief in Mrs Overhill's voice at the thought of remaining at Warildra? Mr Overhill senior, whispered one of the Suitable Friends, had a mistress in Melbourne.

The voices vanished through the potted begonias.

Sophie absently wiped the perspiration from her palms onto her handkerchief. So Mrs Overhill expected a proposal, even encouraged it. She should be glad.

But she was angry, *angry* at this yellow-toothed woman who thought thirty thousand daggy sheep made her superior to fourteen corned-beef factories, who felt she had the right to plan Sophie's life. And she was shaken still by the memory of the chained men's faces, not so much hopeless as wiped of any feeling at all.

There was something else as well. For the first time, her future with Malcolm here, the seasons of branding, shearing, the roundups, sounded such a small life. Yet life in town with a Cyril or an Egbert would be worse, and surely as Dad grew older, she and Malcolm would have to be part of managing the factories, even if the day-to-day running were left to Cousin Oswald ...

And she was helpless. Her hem was dusty. Mrs Overhill and the sniggering girls would remark upon it. For once she did not care.

Later, in the carriage, she looked at Miss Thwaites. Miss Thwaites, who had been rereading Gibbon's *Decline and Fall of the Roman Empire* that morning, who must have been as bored as she had been that afternoon, these many, many afternoons, but never showed it. 'Miss Thwaites, do you sometimes feel like the world is closing in on you? Like there is something, anything, just past the horizon, but you can never find it?'

Miss Thwaites smiled, but there was a look of concern too. 'Frequently. But as the fourth daughter of a country parson, I was brought up to expect such an experience. My dear, a woman of intelligence rarely finds satisfaction in the company of other women, or even a husband. Women's lives must always be circumscribed. Husbands need relaxation when they come home, whether it's from overseeing property or running a corned-beef factory or defending the Empire. But there are always books, the infinite world of the mind. A woman of good sense finds her own interests and consolations. How did your hem get dirty, Sophie?' she added quietly.

'There were men chained up in the courtyard. Black men.'

'I imagine they've refused to work.' Her voice was cautious. 'Mr Overhill is the local magistrate as well as our Member of Parliament. He is probably sending them down to prison.'

'Is it against the law not to work?'

'It's ... complicated. Wild blacks can be troublesome but ...' She hesitated again.

'The blacks around here aren't wild!' Sophie thought of Moonbeam Joe, of his wife Bill, who made her Johnny cakes with syrup.

'I confess that much of what happens with the natives in this country makes me uneasy. But that is the law.'

'Laws can be changed. Like you got the law changed so women can vote.'

'There were tens of thousands of us,' said Miss Thwaites dryly. 'It took nearly two decades to achieve.' She glanced at

Sophie. 'It might also have cost me my career, if my employer had been less tolerant. Once a woman loses her reputation it is lost forever. Sophie, this is not an issue you should involve yourself in. A woman must limit herself to the causes her husband approves.'

Sophie thought of the men stumbling through the dust towards the prison. When Malcolm comes home, she thought, it will be different. Malcolm would never let men's lips crack with thirst in the courtyard. She would be Malcolm's helpmeet, just like missionary wives helped their husbands in darkest Africa.

Just for a moment she felt pity for Miss Thwaites, a single woman who had never been able to hitch her life to a husband's wider one.

She and Miss Thwaites were at Thuringa when Malcolm returned in mid-winter. She saw him first at church, even browner than before, with new mutton-chop whiskers, but so much the same that she felt her breath catch. He caught her eye, smiled, and suddenly his smile was on her face and hers on his, and she could feel his warmth even in the chill of the church.

After the service, the hatted Sunday-best crowd around them, he took her hand and bowed over it. It was the first time they had touched.

'I do hope you'll join us for luncheon tomorrow,' said Mrs Overhill, rigid beside him in corsets and satin, bestowing a yellow shark smile.

Luncheon. Brown soup. Grey meat. Roast vegetables. A shearing-shed meal, Miss Thwaites might have said, but didn't, sitting opposite Sophie, chatting amiably to the rector. As soon as they rose from luncheon, Malcolm took Sophie to see the camellias, her hand on his arm.

She was so nervous she shook. He smiled down at her, then looked past the bare English trees of the garden, the wilting camellia bushes, to the brown paddocks beyond. 'Gosh, it's good to be home. To smell sheep and grass.'

'What does England smell like?' Her voice sounded too high. A schoolgirl's voice.

'London smells sour. The fogs are ghastly. Yellow, so thick you can't see your hand in front of you.'

'You wrote to me about them. I ... I liked your letters.'

'I liked yours too. Look, there's an eagle! It'll be after the lambs,' he added. 'Wish I had my gun.'

Let him kiss me, she thought, partly because she wanted it, had even practised with the golliwog in the nursery (it seemed more appropriate than a doll), but partly because kisses — at least in the world of a Miss Sophie Higgs — were irrevocably linked with proposals of marriage.

The shadow of the eagle passed over them. 'Sophie ...' said Malcolm, and led her behind the camellias.

She had expected words of love first. Instead he drew her to him. She felt the heat of his skin, the press of his body, his nose against hers — golliwogs didn't have noses, she should have thought of that — so she couldn't breathe, but then all at once they seemed to fit and she felt his lips, and realised she wanted this warmth hard against her even more than she wanted to be Mrs Overhill.

The whiskers tickled. His hand held her waist, hot even through her stays. Sophie had grown up with rams, with stallions, and when told not to look had peeked through her fingers. She even had a reasonable idea what 'marital relations' might entail, though women seemed badly designed compared with sheep.

'Sophie,' said Miss Thwaites, coming suddenly around the camellia hedge, her voice expressionless.

Malcolm released her. 'I must apologise, Miss Thwaites. But under the circumstances ...' he smiled down at Sophie '... I hope that Mr Higgs will consent to giving me Miss Higgs's hand in marriage. I hope she will be my wife.'

It was only later, in the carriage, that she realised that in the eighteen months since they had ridden together she and Malcolm had exchanged perhaps six sentences in person, and three of those as he handed her and Miss Thwaites into the carriage. Had his smile perhaps been more self-congratulatory than joyful, the smile of a job well done? She would never have a young man kneel before her now, asking for her hand, suitable for a Chapter Nineteen. Had Malcolm moved her like a piece in a game of checkers: place Sophie behind the camellias and have her discovered by a vigilant governess, with guests nearby to whisper the scandal unless she agreed to marry him?

But she loved him. She looked at the pink camellias he had handed her as she stepped into the carriage, and imagined the house that they'd live in, above the river.

'No,' said Mr Higgs.

Sophie stared at her father, standing like a large square bat among the chintz flowers of the drawing room, in his dark suit, and his well-shined gold watch and chain. Malcolm had just had afternoon tea with her and Miss Thwaites — Coronation cake in memory of their first ride together — before his interview with Mr Higgs. Sophie had asked him to stay afterwards for a celebratory dinner, the champagne already cooling in the ice chest.

But Malcolm had left without coming into the drawing room to say goodbye.

'I don't understand.' It was impossible that her father had said no to Malcolm, no to something she wanted so badly, something that was so *right*.

Miss Thwaites looked up, startled, from her embroidery. 'Mr Higgs, you seemed pleased with the alliance when we told you last week.'

'That was before I met him. My girl can do far better for herself than that. Popinjay! I asked him if he felt any qualms about taking on the factories when I'm gone. Do you know what that whippersnapper said to me? "But of course I would sell them, Mr Higgs."' He mimicked the young man's smooth tones a little too well. '"You might even consider selling now, Mr Higgs. Rest on your laurels, Mr Higgs. Enjoy your grandchildren, Mr Higgs." Ha.'

Mr Jeremiah Higgs never yelled. But his hand trembled as he reached for a cigar.

'I'm sure Mr Overhill didn't mean —' began Sophie, then realised that would have been exactly what Malcolm meant. 'I'll tell him that I don't want them sold,' she said quietly. Impossible to imagine Jeremiah Higgs without his factories. 'You'll give permission if he says he'll keep the factories, won't you?'

'I will not. That monkey would never have asked you to marry him without my money. And he had the hide to demand I get rid of the source of it!'

'You don't understand a man like Malcolm. You've forgotten what love is like!' Her anger sounded like a child's: shrill and petulant. She felt she was battling cotton wool, suffocating but immovable.

'I remember all too well, Sophie love. Would he want you without your money?'

'The young man will have no power to sell his wife's possessions, Mr Higgs; I believe you must trust Sophie to make sure her affairs are managed properly,' said Miss Thwaites quietly. Miss Thwaites had explained the Married Women's Property Act to Sophie long ago, and how long and hard it had been fought for.

'She'll do whatever those Overhill biddies want her to.'

'I won't!' Sophie wanted to stamp her foot, run up to her room, burst into tears. But each of those actions would make her seem like a child too young to know her own mind. She hunted for another weapon, and found none.

'One lass can't stand against an entire family. Once I'm gone you'll be on your own, except for them.' The anger had gone, the red drained from his face. The unspoken 'If only I had a son' was almost loud enough to hear. He gazed at her, then seemed to come to a decision. 'If he wants you enough, he can wait till you're twenty-one!'

'I want to marry him *now*!'

'Why?' Her father's small green eyes stared at her. 'And don't talk to me about love, my girl. Love is all very well but it don't put cabbage on the table. It's not like you won't have more offers.'

'I want a ... wider life.'

He snorted. 'You think the Overhills will give it to you?'

No, thought Sophie. But I can take it from them. 'They dine at Government House! At Parliament House! I could chair committees like Mrs Overhill does. Do things!'

Her father gave the grunt that might mean yes or no. 'It only needs enough brass to start a committee and be its chair. You just need a bit more experience. In three years you can choose for yourself.'

'Few women are lucky enough to be able to choose their future, Sophie.' Miss Thwaites spoke quietly. She didn't add: 'And your governess wasn't one of them.' What would Miss Thwaites be, if she could choose? thought Sophie.

'I'm going to write to Malcolm! Tell him I'll marry him as soon as I'm of age!'

Mr Higgs stared at her. Sophie waited for words from the novels so beloved by the Suitable Friends: 'I'll cast you off without a shilling', or even 'Marry him and you'll be dead to me.'

But even if he had fourteen factories, Thuringa, a governess lover and a missing wife, her father had only one daughter. We're evenly matched, she thought. The only sure weapon her father could use against her would hurt him just as much.

Mr Higgs gave a sudden snort. 'My ma asked me when I joined the army, just fifteen, "Why do you want to do it, Jeremiah?" And I said, "I want to see things." I dreamed of a bigger world than Greymouth. And I found it too. You're your father's daughter, and no mistake.' He was silent a moment, then suddenly smiled. 'Mebbe I'd better write a letter myself, then.'

'To Malcolm?' Sophie asked, a seed of triumph in her voice.

'To someone I knew a long time ago. Mebbe I'll make it a wire instead. And I don't want any more questions.' He waved his hand. 'Off you go and practise your piano.'

She still didn't play the piano, and he knew it. She'd been dismissed.

Three whole years, thought Sophie as her father limped from the drawing room. How should she fill up three whole years?

Chapter 9

*The difference between a girl and a matron is how many
movements it takes for them both to rise from their chair. A matron
shoves and creaks; a girl rises in one smooth sweep. If you rise
in one effortless, swift action, you may still be taken for a girl at
eighty, at least until they light the candles.*

Miss Lily, 1913

Mrs Overhill arrived at the Higgses' Sydney house in puce and
ostrich feathers, carefully timing her visit to arrive an hour after
Mr Jeremiah Higgs's carriage had rolled down the cobbles to his
office. She patted Sophie's arm with a hand covered in a mauve
lace glove. 'I am delighted, my dear. Simply delighted.'

Sophie tried not to show her shock. Hadn't Malcolm told her
that Mr Higgs had refused his suit?

Mrs Overhill seated herself with a creak of whalebone.
'Your dear papa is quite right, of course. You need a little
more experience of the world —' the qualification '*our* world'
hung above the scent of toast from breakfast '— before
anything is announced. No formal engagement yet. Just an
Understanding.'

Who was supposed to 'Understand'? thought Sophie. The
creditors waiting for the Overhills' wealthy new wife? Other
possible suitors for her hand? She carefully didn't look at
Miss Thwaites.

'There is a concert at the Conservatory on Tuesday,' said
Mrs Overhill. '*Everybody* will be there. We will call for you at
eight.'

She, too, didn't glance at Miss Thwaites. Miss Thwaites

was not 'everybody'. Mrs Overhill had claimed the right to be Sophie's chaperone now.

'And a pantomime on Saturday — such fun ...'

Sophie wore pale yellow, Mrs Overhill in blue satin beside her, Malcolm with his back to the driver, elegant in white tie. On either side the new electric lights glowed along the Conservatory drive.

Sophie told herself that she was happy. An Understanding was close to an engagement, after all. If only she hadn't felt the family had put a label on her — *Property of the Overhills* — just like a label on a can of corned beef. If only, most of all, she'd been able to talk to this new, be-whiskered Malcolm alone. But private conversations, it seemed, were a luxury for after they were married. She had known him better, she thought, on those rides more than a year earlier.

She glanced at him, found him looking at her too, saw his smile in the flare of the electric lights, thrust aside again the question she couldn't ask, 'Do you really love me?'

Mrs Overhill surrendered her cloak — blue satin with fur trim — to the attendant; Malcolm took Sophie's ruched silk. They climbed the stairs, Mrs Overhill pausing on every fourth step ('My heart, you know', patting the ample flesh above that object), till at last they reached the Overhills' box.

And, as Mrs Overhill snored lightly after the first crescendo, above the shadowed heads of the audience in the stalls, with only the stage lit, they had the privacy she'd longed for.

'Malcolm?'

Malcolm glanced at his mother, her head back in her seat, then squeezed Sophie's hand. 'You look impossibly lovely.' He had said she looked lovely when he handed her into the carriage, but this was different.

'I ... I'm sorry about having to wait,' she said.

'Your father will come round.' He said it so easily that Sophie knew he believed it to be true, that Malcolm Overhills would always get their way with a Jeremiah Higgs.

'Malcolm, darling,' she tested the word, was glad when he smiled at it, 'do we really need to sell the factories?'

He looked genuinely startled. 'I should have thought you'd want to. Sophie, you must understand ...' His voice trailed off. Suddenly she wished he had the courage to say: 'The factories will demean you — and me — as long as we are associated with them.' Instead he said, more confidently now: 'There's no need to worry your head with business. Not now, and definitely not after we are married.' He smiled again. 'You'll have plenty to occupy you then.'

A household to run. Children. Perhaps his mother would even relinquish her role as patron of the St Anne's Ladies' Guild. Suddenly she thought of her own mother's vanishing. She would vanish into Mrs Malcolm Overhill. But that was exactly what she wanted to be ...

'Mother will call on your Miss Thwaites tomorrow,' he added. 'Miss Thwaites seems a sensible woman. Mother will ask her to intercede with your father. Explain the advantages of marrying this year.'

She wasn't sure what to reply. She nodded instead.

'I'm going to Warildra next week,' he added softly, below the surge of the violins. 'Shearing. It's time someone oversaw things there; the pater's hopeless. You'll be coming down to Thuringa in a month or so, won't you? I can't tell you how much I missed riding with you, all that time in England.'

She wanted to talk about the men in chains, the factories that were so much part of her father. Instead she said: 'I wish we had sheep at Thuringa. I love the way lambs' tails wiggle.'

He laughed, quietly, under the music. 'You can see them wiggle every spring when we're married.'

Perhaps her father was right, she thought suddenly. She needed the experience to ask the right questions before she would be ready to be a wife. 'I ... I saw some of your black stockmen in chains,' she attempted.

'Just some darkies refusing to work. It should never have got to that stage. Darkies need a firm hand. A touch of the whip will do it. The pater's away too much, lets things get out of hand.'

'Why don't you employ white men?'

'Less expensive. Darkies work for rations. Most of their families are on the reserve so it's really just flour and tea and tobacco. Mama won't have black housemaids, of course. Don't worry; she'll see we have suitable staff after we're married.'

He leaned over in the dimness of the box and kissed her. The world shivered, exquisite for long seconds. This was love. His hand still held hers, warm and tantalising through her glove.

The kiss ended. I have everything I ever wanted, thought Sophie, and wondered why the emptiness remained.

Mrs Overhill sat in the Higgses' drawing room, nibbling her scone with teeth the colour of her engraved notepaper, then stared at it, as though counting the size and regularity of the sultanas. She put it back on her plate. 'Of course Mr Higgs may keep the factories if he insists upon it.'

'I'm sure he'll be glad to know that.' Miss Thwaites was serene. She held up the silver teapot, specially made, larger than any pot Sophie had ever seen.

'No, thank you.' Mrs Overhill gave the slightest hint that the tea had not been adequate to tempt her into drinking more. 'Although I do think that Mr Higgs might consider his daughter's reputation ...' She looked down at her scone disparagingly. Sophie almost thought she was referring to the neat placement of sultanas when she added: 'Why not announce the engagement now? The marriage itself can wait, if Mr Higgs wishes it.'

'Mr Higgs believes eighteen is too young when a girl has seen so little of the world.'

'That is precisely my point. Please, let me be frank, Miss Thwaites. Dear little Sophie will see far more of the world — our world, the world she will be part of — once she is married. The longer she stays in her father's house the more she will be exposed to ... certain influences.'

Cousin Oswald and conversations about factories? Rumours that might be reawakened about a missing mother? Sophie glanced at her mother's portrait on the wall. What would her mother have thought of Mrs Overhill? She looked back at the scones steaming on their salver. They'd be cold by the time Mrs Overhill left, and she was starving. But a hearty appetite wasn't ladylike. Ladies must be restrained. Safer — especially with Mrs Overhill judging her every move — not to eat at all.

She would rather have Malcolm than a scone.

'More hot water?' asked Miss Thwaites. 'You are sure the tea isn't too strong?'

Sophie had never seen Miss Thwaites quite like this before. She's angry, she thought. She's angry for me. And for Dad too.

'I am sure you see, Miss Thwaites, that marriage will open many doors that are shut to a daughter of a butcher's shop.'

It was a mistake. The insult was too open. Sophie felt a flush of anger too. She pushed her hands under a cushion so Mrs Overhill wouldn't see them clench. This woman would be her mother-in-law, expecting to guide her daughter-in-law, just as Sophie would be expected to follow her husband's will. Marriage was supposed to be the culmination of a girl's life. Instead it might become a prison, with far less indulgent warders than Mr Higgs and Miss Thwaites.

The striped wallpaper of the room was closing in on her.

She realised Miss Thwaites was speaking, her voice like velvet over steel. 'I'm so glad you agree that Sophie needs to see more of the world, Mrs Overhill. Miss Higgs's father has been considering a finishing year for her in England. So important for a young girl, don't you think?'

Sophie stared. Why hadn't Miss Thwaites mentioned this before? Suddenly she realised that her guardian was angry enough to let information slip.

Mrs Overhill blinked, and then recovered. 'It is difficult to finish what was never started at all.' She glanced down at her scone again. A fly was crawling on it. She smiled, as though the presence of the fly were a personal triumph. 'Dear little Sophie is going to England? How delightful for her. Then she will be presented at court during the season?'

'A slice of fruitcake?' offered Miss Thwaites.

'I never eat fruitcake. Sophie will need the recommendation of two ladies who have been presented at court themselves.' Mrs Overhill took out her fan, and opened it with a snap. The fly abandoned the scone. 'I can be one of them, of course. I remember my own presentation well. The dear old Queen. How we miss her. I am sure one of my other friends would be glad to recommend Sophie too ...'

What was happening? Was she really going to London for a season? To be presented at the palace? And was this shark of a woman really glad for her? Did Mrs Overhill think a London season might help outweigh the factories?

Something even more than excitement began to wriggle up from Sophie's toes. The world she'd read about in the English papers, in *Country Life*. All of it hers for a season. Malcolm would come to England too, of course, with his mother, to escort them to balls, to parties; it would be quite proper if she were chaperoned, for Miss Thwaites would surely come as well ... She took a scone absent-mindedly, then took a bite and swallowed it. 'That's so kind of you ...'

A purse of the lips from Miss Thwaites silenced the speech of gratitude.

Mrs Overhill didn't look at her. This battle was with Miss Thwaites. The parchment teeth were shown briefly again. 'But I was forgetting. The daughter of a tradesman can't be presented at St James. A pity. Malcolm was invited to parties all through the season, of course. Such an exciting time — balls, breakfasts, pheasant shooting, the regatta. So sad that dear little Sophie won't be able to go to any of them. There really isn't much point in travelling, is there, if one isn't received when one gets there? Of course in a few years, as Malcolm's wife ...'

And after the factories have been sold, thought Sophie. She glanced at Miss Thwaites. Was this true? Was the English upper-class world denied to her unless Mr Higgs sold his factories?

'Sophie will stay with a cousin of Nigel Vaile, Earl of Shillings, at the earl's country seat. His lordship is an old friend of Mr Higgs.' Miss Thwaites spoke as calmly as if she were announcing that they would be revising French grammar this afternoon.

Mrs Overhill's mouth hung open, as though inviting the fly to enter. Sophie's scone crumbled into her lap. Was Miss Thwaites serious? Did Dad really know an *earl*? An earl who'd let a Sophie Higgs visit his family?

Impossible. But there was Miss Thwaites, brandishing her teapot. 'Do you know the Earl of Shillings, Mrs Overhill? One of England's oldest families, I believe.'

Sophie brushed the crumbs off her skirt, hoping the butter hadn't left a mark. She stared at Miss Thwaites, this suddenly new Miss Thwaites, holding the teapot as though it were a sword and she were Horatius guarding the bridge at Rome. Guarding me, thought Sophie. And Dad. This was the woman who had fought for the vote for women, who had sailed across the world rather than stay within the familiar genteel poverty of her family.

'I am not acquainted with ...' Mrs Overhill looked as though Miss Thwaites had slapped her face with a dead fish, as though she wanted to accuse Miss Thwaites of lying. But even Mrs Overhill couldn't do that.

'The earl's cousin — a lovely woman, I gather — will take care of everything before Sophie's season begins.'

'Her ... season? Miss Thwaites, you don't seem to understand.' Mrs Overhill tried to marshal her social forces. 'There can be no question of Sophie ... dear sweet little Sophie ... being presented at court.'

Miss Thwaites smiled. 'His lordship believes it can be arranged. So much depends on knowing the right people, doesn't it? If Malcolm is going abroad again, I am sure he will receive cards too. To some of the balls, at least. A colonial doesn't have the same entrée into society as a friend of the Earl of Shillings unless he has similarly high connections.'

Mrs Overhill's cheeks were purple. 'Malcolm is needed at home. It is not ... convenient for him to travel again so soon.' She still seemed incredulous. She'll call for her copy of Debrett's and the *Landed Families of Great Britain* as soon as she gets home, thought Sophie, to make sure the earl exists.

He did exist, didn't he? He hadn't just been conjured up from Miss Thwaites's anger? But Miss Thwaites wouldn't lie, not least because the existence of an earl was so easy to check.

This was impossible. Wonderful. Real.

'When Sophie returns,' said Miss Thwaites, too gently, 'we might ... discuss ... a possible engagement.'

Mrs Overhill stood up, still fanning. 'You will excuse me. The flies are so *bad* this afternoon.'

She is making it sound as though the flies are only at our place, thought Sophie, trying to focus on standing up politely too. She wanted to laugh, to hug Miss Thwaites, to dance around the room. But ladies didn't.

Was she really going to England? To stay with an earl? It was like something out of a novel, *East Lynne*, that was it: the poor disgraced heroine who had run off with an adventurer was the daughter of an earl.

Miss Thwaites stood too. 'Thank you so much for your kind visit, Mrs Overhill. Your husband must be wondering where you are. Bates,' as the butler appeared, 'do show Mrs Overhill to her carriage.'

'Mr Overhill is not —' Mrs Overhill stopped.

He isn't at home, thought Sophie. He's with his mistress in Melbourne. She'd overheard the Overhills' footman gossiping. Nor could the Overhills now pacify their creditors. Game, set and match to Miss Thwaites. And Mrs Overhill knew it.

She managed to wait until Bates had closed the drawing-room door. 'Miss Thwaites, can I really go to England? To stay with an earl?'

'Do you want to?'

'Of course!'

'Even without young Mr Overhill?'

She had read about love in novels. What she felt for Malcolm was exactly what they described. Her heart raced when she saw him. In church she had to force herself from staring at his neck in the pew in front. She even dreamed about him.

And she wanted to go to England. To stay with an earl, be introduced by his cousin ...

Why shouldn't she have both?

'Why didn't you tell me before?'

Miss Thwaites hesitated. 'His lordship's overnight wire only came this morning. Your father and I wanted to discuss it further before we talked about it with you.' Her gaze met Sophie's. 'I let Mrs Overhill anger me, and said more than I should have. Now I have made her an enemy. It wasn't well done.'

'She deserved it.'

'I ... I suggested to your father last year that you should spend some time in England, that I should accompany you. But he felt ...'

He didn't want to lose you, thought Sophie.

'He didn't want to lose you,' said Miss Thwaites. 'But after young Mr Overhill asked for your hand in marriage he reconsidered.'

'He wants me to marry someone who'll take over the business. Or oversee a manager, at least.'

'That's true,' said Miss Thwaites slowly. 'But don't underestimate him. He really does believe you are too young to marry. Your mother was so very young when *they* married ...'

'But ... but they were happy, weren't they? He loved her!'

'Yes. He loved her.' Miss Thwaites shook her head. 'I'm not putting this properly. Both your father and I would like you to grow and learn a little more before you decide on your future. No official engagement.'

'But we have an Understanding,' said Sophie stubbornly.

'If that is what you wish.'

That was enough. England, she thought. An earl! She grinned at the memory of Mrs Overhill's face. 'Miss Thwaites, how does Dad know an earl?'

Miss Thwaites hesitated. There is something she's not saying, thought Sophie. 'I believe your father and the earl were in the army together. His lordship hadn't come into the title then. It was long ago, Sophie. Before your father came out to Australia.' Miss Thwaites changed the subject. 'A year abroad is exactly what you need.'

'I ... I don't even know what to call the cousin of an earl. Is she Lady Shillings?'

Miss Thwaites paused, slightly uncomfortably again. 'His lordship neglected to tell your father the name of his cousin. But the cousin of an earl does not necessarily have a title. His cousin may be "the Honourable".'

'Like you?'

'A little more honourable, perhaps.' Miss Thwaites's voice was dry. 'I gather from his lordship's letter that his cousin often has young girls staying with her for instruction before the season. It is something of a ... hobby ... with her.'

'Hobby' suggested that this interest might be anything but. Did the cousin run an informal finishing school? Would she be paid for the friendship she appeared to be offering? Just like Miss Thwaites is paid to love me, thought Sophie.

Corned-beef money, once again. Suddenly — if it was — she didn't want to know.

Better to pretend she would be staying at an earl's house because Dad had somehow befriended him during the war. All men were comrades in war, weren't they? Staying at an earl's castle would rub out the stains of a meat-packing business. It would give her the status to become a proper Mrs Malcolm Overhill, who could say at luncheons, '... when I stayed with my father's friend the Earl of Shillings ...' She was doing this for Malcolm as well.

She hoped he'd see it that way.

'When do we sail?'

The shadow in Miss Thwaites's eyes grew deeper. 'Your father has suggested you sail in the care of Mrs Philpott. You met her at dinner here this year, if you remember.'

A faded woman who talked of children, cooks who couldn't make a soufflé, and the difficulty of getting nannies with the right accent so the children didn't pick up Australian vowels. 'Not you? Why aren't you coming?'

'You will scarcely need me as a chaperone in England. His lordship has also ... suggested ... that there is no need for you to bring a maid from Australia. His cousin will arrange for someone to attend you.'

Sophie tried to gauge Miss Thwaites's expression. How was she supposed to dress on board ship without a maid to lace the stays, do up the buttons, iron her clothes and set them out? She tried to imagine her hair undressed all the way to England ...

'Mrs Philpott's maid can attend to you both, with the help of the stewardess,' said Miss Thwaites, as though echoing Sophie's thoughts — almost as though convincing herself too. 'I have been too ... lax in many ways, I know. A lady's maid who knows how to do things properly will make English life immeasurably easier for you.'

A French maid, perhaps, thought Sophie. I will be Miss Sophie Higgs, ten thousand miles away from corned beef, with a French maid, and having dinner with an earl.

Miss Thwaites rang the bell. 'Annie, fresh scones, please. Mr Higgs will be back for luncheon today. And sandwiches, the ones with the strong cheddar cheese. And fresh tea. Indian, not Chinese.'

'Yes, ma'am.'

Sophie waited till the maid had left the room. 'Miss Thwaites, thank you. I have to thank Dad too. It is the most wonderful thing in my whole life.'

There was doubt in Miss Thwaites's eyes. 'I hope so.'

Chapter 10

Look how men sit, with their legs apart. It is a gorilla pose yelling:
'Look at me, I challenge you.' A well-bred woman must find
another way to assert dominance.

Miss Lily, 1913

The ship creaked below them, reminding Sophie it was a ship, despite its size. Mr Jeremiah Higgs was a tiny man, even in his black top hat, but his energy made the stateroom seem small.

He was prowling now, despite his limp. Making sure the water closet flushed, the bed was soft, counting the gold-edged chairs in her sitting room, checking that the basket of fruit on her table had a pineapple among its colourful contents, hefting the five-pound tin of chocolates in case it was short in weight.

'What do you think? Is she going to be all right?' It was the hundredth time he'd asked it, thought Sophie with affectionate exasperation. As though Miss Thwaites would suddenly say, 'No. Those chocolates are clearly only four pounds two ounces. She should stay home.'

'We need to go, let the stewardess unpack her cases. Didn't you hear them call "All ashore"?' Miss Thwaites looked at him sympathetically, as though she knew what he was feeling.

Mr Higgs snorted. It was a snort that said that if he wanted the ship to linger another twelve hours and wait for the next tide so he could say a proper farewell to his daughter, he could arrange it. Which he probably could, thought Sophie.

'Where is Mrs Philpott's maid, I'd like to know.' He looked around, as though expecting her to appear from the wood panelling. 'She should be helping Sophie as well as her mistress.'

'Second-class cabins are down another gangway. I told her I don't need her for a while.'

He blinked, his eyes suddenly bright. 'We should have arranged a maid just for the voyage over. Anything you want, little girl. Don't you stint yourself over there. A car, a driver, an ermine cloak. Diamond tiara.'

'Not a tiara,' said Miss Thwaites quietly.

Mr Higgs ignored her. The white in his hair had spread. He is getting old, Sophie thought with a shock. 'You've got the draft on Barclays Bank. Contact Mr Slithersole at our London office if you want anything.'

'I know.' She gave him a quick hug, which lengthened. It was only when she pulled back from the smell of bay rum and hair cream that she realised how much she would miss him, miss Miss Thwaites, Thuringa, even the house in town. Marrying Malcolm would have only meant moving next door. This was ...

Something of her own — not the same parties and shopping trips of Miss Sophie Higgs of Thuringa, or even the new ones of a Mrs Malcolm Overhill. This year was what she'd make it, alone.

She looked around the stateroom: a pink and grey striped sofa, a dark wooden sideboard, a matching dining table adorned with the fruit and chocolates from her father, as well as a basket of frangipani. She crossed over to the table, and read the card again.

Bon voyage. Love, Malcolm.

He hadn't come to Sydney from Warildra to see her off. It had only been a fortnight since Miss Thwaites's announcement, her father somehow wangling the first-class staterooms for herself and Mrs Philpott. There hadn't even been time for a letter to come from the earl's cousin in England, only a series of wires confirming when and how Sophie was to arrive. The lack of a letter — or a series of letters in the tradition of detailed feminine correspondence — clearly made Miss Thwaites uncomfortable. Mr Higgs, on the other hand, lived in a world of wires and quick decisions. And it seemed that speed was necessary if Sophie were to be prepared for next year's season.

At least Malcolm had sent the flowers.

A whistle blew, somewhere above them; a voice in the corridor yelled, 'Final call! Final call! All ashore that's going ashore. All ashore!'

'Come on.' Her father grabbed her hand. She followed him, fast despite his limp, out into the corridor, up a short flight of first-class stairs, Miss Thwaites behind them. The deck was crowded, with second-class and steerage passengers too, the only clear space leading down to the gang plank. He hugged her. 'You have a good time over there, you promise? All the frill-frolls and good times you can. Be happy, Sophie love.' All at once he looked strangely earnest. 'Promise me that you'll be happy.'

'I promise.' She had to wipe her eyes.

Her father hugged her again fiercely, his fingers digging into her stays. Miss Thwaites pressed her cheek to Sophie's, smelling of gardenias and rice powder.

Then they were gone, leaving a space that felt bigger than the ship.

She watched them walk down the gang plank — father and governess–companion waiting for her charge to return — pause halfway and wave, then make their way through the crowds to the edge of the dock. Water lapped hot and oily between them and the ship.

She managed to wriggle through the crowd to the rail. She reached into her coat pocket for the streamers the steward had given her and threw one out towards the dock. It fell short. She tried again, this time using the overarm bowling she'd seen cricketers use and hitting the woman behind her on the chin. ('Oh, I do beg your pardon, excuse me ...')

By the time she had finished apologising her father had caught it. A thin paper streamer linked them.

Another whistle, higher and longer now. The engines thudded under her feet. The streamer grew taut. They were moving.

She watched as the streamer grew tighter, to a long thin string. Then it broke. All around her streamers were snapping to hang limply against the rail. People were waving. She wondered how many others were crying too, but she didn't want to look away to see.

Then they were gone. She could have run to the end of the boat to try to see them again, but it wasn't done. Besides, Dad would be bustling Miss Thwaites back to the carriage, barking at Rogers if he were a second late opening the door, to hide the fact that Miss Thwaites would be crying too.

The ship glided past the rocks and green-clad promontories of Sydney Harbour. Suddenly she felt scared that she would love English trees better than straggly gums, that what had been the heart of her might change. She stood on the deck watching the coast turn blue then grey, then vanish till all she could see was a wrinkle of sea becoming sky.

Chapter 11

The way to a man's heart is not through his stomach, unless of course it is with a bayonet. But good food helps most situations.

Miss Lily, 1913

ENGLAND, 1913

A railway roast potato, looking crisp but actually soft when Sophie prodded it with her fork, six slices of brown meat, brown gravy over drab-coloured Brussels sprouts ... even the soup was brown: brown Windsor soup, the same colour as the drains when a stall was washed out at the Agricultural Show back home. The world beyond the windows glided in drabs of orange and red, with sudden shocks of gold when the stubborn English sun allowed itself a moment between clouds.

Mrs Philpott sat opposite her on the train, eating with the dedication of a woman who rarely dined without children vying for her attention, whose cook back home could stuff a shoulder of lamb but never had time to make brown Windsor soup.

Did the King and Queen drink brown Windsor soup when they dined at Windsor Castle? wondered Sophie, looking around the dining car. Her hat was bigger — a proper hat, a distinguished hat — and her furs more elegant than those of any other woman on the train. It had been exhilarating, ordering dresses without Miss Thwaites.

The gravy had congealed. Sophie sighed, and pushed the plate away. It was thick and white, with *British Railways* around the rim, and the same crest that was on the thick silver cutlery.

'Apple pie and crème anglaise, miss, or treacle tart?'

'Apple pie,' said Mrs Philpott.

Sophie smiled up at the waiter. 'Apple pie. Please.'

The apple pie was good. Sophie ate all but the last spoonful (left for 'Miss Manners' as Miss Thwaites had instructed her, back when the schoolroom had still been the nursery), and smiled again at the waiter as she followed Mrs Philpott back to their own carriage, carefully ignoring the red-faced gentleman and the two young men rising hopefully from their seats.

At least they had the carriage to themselves — two women, two travelling rugs, bricks to warm their feet (carefully changed at each station for fresh ones by Mrs Philpott's maid), a box of Russian toffee, Mrs Philpott's *The Lady* magazine and her own novel. Why do women who do nothing travel with so much more than men who are seldom idle? thought Sophie.

In another hour she would meet an earl! And the cousin, still unnamed. Plump and elderly, Sophie decided, and in reduced circumstances, which meant she must help colonials through their season. She had once asked Miss Thwaites how one reduced a circumstance ...

The train chugged through another tunnel. Mrs Philpott rose and closed the window, to keep out smuts. Sophie waited till the tunnel's darkness was passed, then opened it again, feeling the soft air on her face.

English air. Not just cold air, not just unfamiliar smells, but a different feel: moisture without humidity, air that stroked your skin instead of battering it.

'Shillings! Shillings!' It sounded like the guard was calling for money. The earl's house — *castle* — must be named after the town ... or the other way around. Sophie rose and Mrs Philpott folded her travelling rug.

Sophie felt guilty about Mrs Philpott. Mrs Philpott obviously minded enormously that the earl had suggested she accompany Sophie only to the Shillings railway station, and not to Shillings Hall itself, so that Mrs Philpott could catch the three-ten back to London instead of spending the night.

The Shillings railway station was small — a single platform, a low-roofed waiting room (just one, no first and second class), and a couple of stone cottages. The guard was already helping the porter load Sophie's trunks onto the trolley as Mrs Philpott's maid hurried up from the second-class carriage to offer a Thermos of tea and some oranges.

Sophie shook her head to both. 'I'm sure it won't be far.'

'Miss Higgs? I am Samuel, Miss Higgs.' The man might be either a driver or a groom. Sophie glanced through the waiting room. A carriage stood there, old-fashioned, black with a faded crest on the door. Two horses, perfectly matched bays. She looked at the man again. Fortyish, probably not able or willing to learn to drive a car. Either the earl was conservative or he was thoughtful enough not to let a chauffeur usurp this man's position. 'His lordship's carriage is outside, Miss Higgs.' He signalled to the porter.

'Are you sure?' began Mrs Philpott.

Sophie kissed her cheek quickly — she was afraid Mrs Philpott might not want to presume to give her a kiss. 'Thank you. You have been so kind. I promise I'll write to you tomorrow to tell you all about it. Goodbye.'

Mrs Philpott's maid bobbed a curtsey. 'Goodbye, miss.'

Sophie followed the groom out to the carriage. She stood by awkwardly as Samuel and the porter loaded her trunks. The driver opened the door for her, then held out his white-gloved hand to help her up the step. 'Thank you, Samuel,' she said.

Unexpectedly, the carriage seemed too empty. She had never, after all, been away from those her father trusted to look after her, except during the stolen hours at Thuringa and Warildra. 'Samuel?' she asked quickly, before he could shut the door.

'Yes, Miss Higgs?'

'You ... you've been with the family a long time?' It was the first thing she could think of to say.

'All my life, Miss Higgs, in one way or another.' He hesitated. 'It is a kind family, Miss Higgs. You will find them very kind.'

Kind. It was a strange word to use of an employer, but reassuring. 'Thank you, Samuel. You are very kind yourself.'

'Thank you, Miss Higgs.'

'Is it far to Shillings Castle?'

He smiled, as though he were glad he could give her a reassuring answer. 'Only about twenty minutes to the house, miss.' He shut the door for her as she sat down. Leather seats, old polished woodwork, a scent she almost recognised — lavender and roses, that was it. The polish must be perfumed with lavender and rose oil.

The last strap was fastened on the trunks behind. She heard the groom flick the reins. She took one of Mrs Philpott's Russian toffees out of her pocket. It was comforting. The carriage began to move.

The cottages near the station gave way to trees, with tall branches and leaves that were too flat, too yellow, as if only colonials would be brash enough to wear green. At least it smelled fresh here, away from the soot of the railway station and the stink of London; Malcolm had described it well in his letters: a combination of drains and coal smoke and unwashed clothes. Even at the Ritz the doorman had smelled of elderly underpants, the chambermaid of years of sweat stains in the armpits of her neat black uniform.

Those trees must be woods, just like in the poems. Poets never told the whole truth, said Miss Thwaites. You must never expect the world to be quite like it is in a poem.

Another street of houses, more substantial this time; a pub with *Shillings and Sixpence* on a wooden board hanging above the door. Fields and too-green grass, and Jersey cows, with the same brown-eyed resignation of Jerseys anywhere in the world, she supposed, even with grass well above their fetlocks here. They made her think of Miss Thwaites: well bred, calm, productive, captive in their green fields. Sophie stifled a giggle.

A church, a graveyard next to it, what she thought might be a tiny school.

The fields were edged with stone walls now. The walls by the road grew taller ... or rather the road sank, Sophie realised, the high banks on either side created by time, as well as men. This green tunnel was English history.

The carriage swerved around a corner, and met closed gates, wide, high wrought iron as if to ward off Cromwell's army. The carriage stopped as a man walked steadily out of the tiny cottage at one side, as though to say that opening the gates was his job but it didn't involve hurrying — or perhaps not unless the carriage contained someone more important than a Miss Higgs.

Then they were moving again. She had to force herself not to push the window down and crane her head outside. Clumps of trees, too even to be natural in the eyes of someone who knew how trees grew on their own, then grass, an avenue of trees, the house.

She had expected a castle, the sort the Prince might have taken Cinderella to. This was smaller and deeply plain — a flat façade of brick the colour of faded plums, not even stone. Two wings stretched back on either side. At least there was a portico, with pillars and broad steps to climb up to it. It was only when the groom had opened the door, and she had climbed the fourteen steps (she counted them) and looked back, that she saw that simplicity could have grandeur too.

The grass stretched endlessly, bordering a lake in the middle distance, edged by trees that turned to woodland on either side. The grounds flowed up to the horizon, the lawns sloping towards the pale blue sky.

No rose gardens. No statues. Just grass and trees and sky and water, but she was breathless.

The carriage had already vanished around behind the house. The door opened. A middle-aged man stood there in striped trousers, a stiff collar and a grey coat almost the same colour as his immaculate hair.

At first she took him for the earl. She wished she had asked Miss Thwaites or even the porter at the Ritz if you curtseyed to an earl.

The man gave her a short, stiff bow. 'I am Jones, Miss Higgs. Miss Lily is expecting you in the drawing room.'

Miss Lily must be the cousin. Perhaps the earl would arrive for afternoon tea. She must wear her blue frock to dinner ...

'If you will come this way, Miss Higgs.'

Somehow her coat was gone: magic, she thought, for she had no memory of taking it off, and had certainly not felt Jones's hands upon her person. She followed him across a hall — no, not a hall, for this space was larger than any room in any house she had ever seen, bigger even than the first-class dining room on the ship: a great vaulted ceiling and wood-panelled walls, tall doors on either side, a staircase branching in two leading up to a circular gallery above. Or perhaps this was a hall of the sort mentioned in poems like 'Lochinvar', big enough for the hero to gallop into on a steed.

Did the earl have horses? Not just horses for the carriage and to work the farms, but to ride. Impossible to live a year without horses ...

This door led to a more familiar sight: a proper hall, human sized, not made for giants or knights on horseback with those spear things — what were they called? Lances. Again wood panelled, the only light coming from the high windows above the space they'd left.

The butler stopped, opening a double door with a hand on each doorknob. 'Miss Higgs has arrived, Miss Lily.'

'Thank you, Jones.'

The woman who sat in the shadows of the sofa at the other end of the room didn't rise. Sophie supposed you didn't, not for a Miss Sophie Higgs, not when you were the cousin of an earl.

It was a beautiful room. Even at a fleeting glance, she could tell it was the most beautiful room she had ever been in. It was not just the parchment silk on its walls, the heavy drapes at the tall windows, not even the soft, faded silks of its carpets, the shine of floorboards and polished wood. It was more, perhaps the shape of the room itself, something that discerned everything that is needed in a room and said, 'This is perfect.' Or perhaps it was the scent, both floral and fruity, though there seemed to be no vases of flowers — those vases essential to Miss Thwaites and Mrs Overhill and every mother of the Suitable Friends — on any of the surfaces. A large but tidy fire burned in what Sophie supposed was a marble fireplace. She supposed this fireplace had had a long time to make fires do exactly what they should.

'Good afternoon, Miss Higgs.'

The woman in the shadows was tall, big-boned. Beautiful. Sophie had no idea why she was beautiful — it was actually quite difficult to make out her features, for her back was to the daylight. But even at first glance the beauty of the woman matched that of the room.

The glow from the firelight flickered on a dark blue dress, a dress that was just a dress, nothing fashionable about it, but that somehow seemed perfect for that afternoon, that room; and lit softly gold hair, pinned up in a swirl that was impossibly simple, impossibly elegant, just like the white neck gently touched by a silver chiffon scarf, the curve of the wrist and hand.

Sophie gave a small curtsey. 'Good afternoon, Miss Lily.'

'Whoever taught you to curtsey to your elders is two decades out of date.' The voice was gentler than the words suggested. 'Kind', as Samuel had said. This was instruction, not rebuke. 'Only servants or tenants curtsey now. Please do not curtsey again, except to royalty. Do sit down, Miss Higgs.'

It was difficult to tell her age. Forty, guessed Sophie, but maybe ten years more. Her upright back never touched the chair. Sophie edged forward in her seat.

The door closed behind them. The silence grew, broken only by the tick of the clock in the corner, the soft crackle of the fire and laughter from somewhere in the house.

Surely it was up to the hostess to speak, thought Sophie.

'Tell me why you have come here,' said Miss Lily at last.

'I ... I don't understand. I thought my father had arranged for me to stay here.'

The woman gave a wry but most charming smile. 'And I am asking why you have come.'

To stay, thought Sophie. And then, No, that's not what she's asking me. It was clear this woman — at this tick of the clock, at least — had no time for polite fiction.

'I ... I want to be presented at court, to do the London season. I am engaged — I mean there is an Understanding ...'

The woman failed to be interested. 'You want the glamour of a London season so you might outshine your prospective family?' Was there a tinge of disappointment in the voice? 'The young man is a colonial, I believe. His mother presumably believes her family is important. To anyone in England, it is not. I am sure your wishes are possible.'

'I thought I couldn't be presented, because my father is ...' she stumbled over the polite words '... in trade.'

'There are ways to do these things. A private introduction, luncheon perhaps down at Windsor.'

'Is that good enough, Miss Lily?'

'A private luncheon with Her Majesty is quite "good enough".' The voice was amused.

'If you didn't know what I wanted, why did you agree to help me?'

Sophie wanted to make this self-possessed woman with an accent that could cut glass admit that she was being paid. Instead Miss Lily laughed as though she were enjoying their meeting for the first time. It was a charming laugh. Sophie reassessed her age as forty at most, even thirty-five.

'I could say because my cousin's investments in your father's companies have been extremely successful. Don't look so startled, Miss Higgs — even the aristocracy need good investments, especially when the farms on their estates are in as poor a state as the ones at Shillings used to be. But that would only be a small part of the truth.'

'What *is* the truth?'

'All of it?' The voice was still amused.

'Whatever matters here.'

'A good answer. The heart of the truth is that I enjoy the

company of the young. I go very little into society these days. I prefer to watch my young friends venture into the world instead.'

'I ... I would be one of them?'

'Friendship isn't granted, Miss Higgs. It's earned.' The smile softened the words.

'His lordship doesn't mind your ... friends? Presumably their fathers are as generous as mine?'

'My dear child ...' To Sophie's shock, Miss Lily sounded delighted. 'It has been years since I have heard anyone speak quite so directly. To set your mind at rest: I neither receive nor need any financial recompense, and my cousin approves of my ... hobby. He spends most of his time in the East and is grateful for my occupying the house and liaising with his estate agent.'

'His lordship isn't at home now?' Sophie failed to keep the disappointment from her voice.

'I'm sorry if you were expecting his company,' said Miss Lily gently. 'You will have to make do with me.'

'I didn't mean —' Sophie stopped. There was something about this woman that pulled the truth from her. 'I apologise. I did want to meet an earl. Or at least be able to boast that I had met an earl. But if I had to choose, I think I'd prefer to spend the time with you.'

It was truth, neither kindness nor politeness. There was something fascinating about this woman; and not just her evident intelligence, her perception, and her lack of inhibition in showing both. She was at once almost familiar and deeply, intriguingly, unlike anyone Sophie had ever met.

Miss Lily regarded her. 'I think,' she said at last, 'that may be the most sincere compliment anyone has ever paid me. But we should move to specifics. I will arrange for a little ... softening, shall we say, of your accent, your manners, your French conversation, and your dress.'

'What is wrong with my dress?!' It had been the most expensive one in the salon the Ritz concierge had directed Mrs Philpott to.

'Lesson one, Miss Higgs. A young lady in her first season — any unmarried woman for that matter — is deferential, not questioning. A quiet "Thank you, Miss Lily" is an acceptable response.'

'Are *you* deferential?'

Miss Lily laughed again. She had found a way to laugh — properly laugh — and still be ladylike. 'No, very rarely. But then I do not go into society. Once you are married, you will have more freedom, which is why it is important to make a good marriage.' One exquisite eyebrow rose. 'You are now supposed to ask obediently, "What is a good marriage, Miss Lily?"'

'One where both people love each other,' said Sophie. She added, 'One where money and a respected social position are assured.'

'Why?' asked Miss Lily quietly.

'I don't understand.'

'My dear, let me be frank. You will never escape references to corned beef. But you can escape having it determine your social position if you have the determination to laugh it off, or at least pretend to. It is an art that anyone with any ... peculiarity ... has to learn. The first time a stranger meets you, you will be the corned-beef heiress. The second time, they will think, Ah, Miss Higgs, the corned-beef heiress. But if you are charming enough, by the third meeting, you will simply be that lovely girl, Miss Higgs.'

'I've never been charming.'

'Charm is something you learn, Miss Higgs. Like deference. After Christmas the relations of three of my friends will be here too: the Prinzessin Hannelore von Arnenberg, Miss Emily Carlyle and Lady Alison Venables.

'Lady Alison's parents are dead. Her grandmother — or stepgrandmother, to be precise — is a widow, the Dowager Duchess of Wooten, and one of my dearest friends. Her Grace the duchess will sponsor you into society at the same time as Lady Alison is presented. Her Grace will give a ball for you both, and arrange whatever needs to be arranged. Your father will pay for Lady Alison's season as well as your own. And that, Miss Higgs, is the only role your father's money will play, apart, of course, from making you a most eligible debutante, despite those cans of corned beef you despise.'

The graceful hands still lay unmoving in her lap. So I'm to be manoeuvred through society like a can on the factory conveyor belt, thought Sophie. And I don't despise them. Other people do, and I despise them for it. The thought shocked her. Despise Malcolm? Of course she didn't. But this woman did not despise corned beef, nor, it seemed, did the earl.

'Does my father know about the duchess and paying for the ball?' she asked at last.

'Of course, Miss Higgs.'

'Why didn't he tell me?'

'That is for you to decide.' The voice was gentle.

Sophie said nothing. Miss Lily moved slightly into the light. 'Tell me about your father.'

'Don't you know all about him already?'

'Do not raise your hackles, like a terrier. Tell me three things about him, the first that come into your mind.'

'Is this a game?'

'Of a sort.'

'He wears a watch chain made from linked gold nuggets. He had it especially made. He eats cheese sandwiches every day for lunch ...' She tried to think of a third. 'He's clever,' she said at last. 'People don't realise it. They think he was just lucky, saw an opportunity and took it. I don't know much about the business side — there is a closed door to business and only men are let through. But my father is fascinated by machines. He plays with model trains, but it's too serious to be really playing. He has conveyor belts installed in his factories.'

'I thought business happened behind closed doors?'

'Yes. But I've been to his factory in Sydney.'

'With his permission?'

'Not exactly,' said Sophie.

'And your father gives you what you want. Or do you manipulate him so that you get what you want, and not necessarily what he wants to give you?'

81

Sophie was silent. 'You make it sound horrid,' she said at last.

'No. What other power do women have? It's what women have done from time immemorial — Samson and Delilah, Caesar and Cleopatra — but men only write about the women who manipulated for evil, not for good. Do you admire your father?'

'I ... I think so. He grew up hungry. Corned beef isn't just a business to him.' It was the first time she had articulated it, even to herself. 'He wants to feed the world, the hungry part of it.' She smiled in memory. 'Even if he didn't notice his own workers were hungry till I pointed it out to him. He's not good at noticing the people around him much — he gets focused on things like, well, making money, or finding the grandest house in Sydney — but he makes sure his workers aren't hungry now. Only the rich can buy steaks, he says, but you only need a few coppers for Higgs's Corned Beef. I think that's why he bought Thuringa — that's our property. Everyone else sees cattle, but my father sees potential corned-beef sandwiches.'

Miss Lily laughed, with what sounded like true delight.

'It was only a cockie farm when my father bought it.'

Miss Lily raised the eyebrow.

'Cockie farms raise more cockatoos than sheep or cattle. My father bought up other neighbouring places all around during the nineties drought, when land was cheap. The Overhills are the only other big property owners around now, though they run sheep. My father doesn't like sheep. He says they remind him of too many men in the city.'

The laugh became a chuckle. 'Your voice comes truly alive when you talk about Thuringa.'

'Does it? I've spent much of my life there. That's where I'll live if — when I marry Mr Overhill. Well, in another house perhaps on the Overhill property ...'

'Which your father will build for you?'

How had Miss Lily known that she had already picked out the site on the hill, above the river, where they could watch the ibis fly down before night fell?

The door opened. 'Tea, Miss Lily.'

Was there a hint of a smile on the butler's — Jones's — face? Sophie felt suddenly reassured. Strange as all this was — and she suspected that even someone born to the world of earls and trees whose leaves so regularly changed colour would find this strange — Miss Thwaites said that a house where the servants smiled was a good one.

'Thank you, Jones.' Miss Lily waited as the teapot — small, not even with a crest — and the hot water pot and the cups were placed on the small table next to her. The cake stand sat on its own small trolley: tiny éclairs oozing cream and chocolate on the top tier, macaroons, what looked like a cherry cake and small sandwiches with their crusts cut off lower down.

Miss Lily poured the tea. The cups were thin, a parchment colour that seemed more to do with age than the potter's skill. 'Milk and sugar?'

'Yes, please. Two sugars.' Sophie looked longingly at the cake stand.

'Please help yourself.'

Sophie shook her head regretfully. 'No, thank you.'

Another smile. 'Your Miss Thwaites has told you that it is bad manners to be hungry?'

'Yes.'

'She is wrong. The only time you do not eat is in the presence of Her Majesty. You do not eat unless she eats. Sadly, she eats little. At court functions, knowledgeable dowagers secrete sandwiches in hidden pockets to see them through the night. Eat. The sandwiches are egg and cress. I recommend the cherry cake.'

Sophie took a sandwich, nibbled it, sipped her tea, then put it down.

'You are fond of your Miss Thwaites? The trick to eating and talking, by the way, is to take small bites, often. Never swallow before you answer. You will look like a turkey. Use your tongue to swiftly tuck the food into the gap between your teeth and your cheek. It only works if the amount is small. Try it, then answer my question. Do you like Miss Thwaites?'

Sophie nibbled, tucked. 'Yes. I *love* her too,' she added, even if it was not done to love a governess.

'Excellent tucking. Practise everything till you do not have to think about it at all. Interesting. Liking is often more telling than loving. You can love from duty, but not like someone at all. You like both your father and the woman who has been, I suppose, a mother to you. Usually at your age a girl likes one parent, distrusts or is frustrated by the other ... And your father let you come to England. Which means that he loves you enough to part with you.' A small smile lit the shadowed face. 'Or possibly he hoped that the newness of the old world might absorb your energies.' She shook her head. 'These self-made men. They expect their sons to inherit their energy then complain when their daughters inherit it instead. Do they really think that if they had been born in skirts they would have been happy with mah jong parties? You look surprised,' she added.

'I've never known anyone who talked like you. Is this what society is like in England?'

'Good gracious, no, child. Until you are married you'll be expected to say little more than "Yes" or "No" or "How interesting". Mostly the latter. Except with your friends, of course. But if you marry well — which is not quite what you think it is — you will find that a married woman's friendships can lead to a deeply fulfilling life. Are you good at friendship?'

'I ... I don't think I have ever really had a friend.'

'Yet you know that you haven't. So, Miss Higgs, you have at least the rudiments of an acceptable education — you notice I say an acceptable, and not a good one. You can speak French, presumably with an atrocious accent.'

'How do you —?'

'Because you will have been taught by an Englishwoman, not a French one. But your own accent is almost acceptable. I believe you have the capacity to learn enough to pass in good society by the next season. Why do you think your father has sent you to England? Does he wish you to be a conventional and appropriate wife to your Mr Overhill too?'

'I don't think so.'

'Is Mr Overhill a fortune hunter?'

'Of course not!'

'You answered that far too quickly, Miss Higgs. You have already considered it as a possibility. Or is your father doting enough to send you here simply because it is what you want?'

'No. I think he … he doesn't really know what to do with me. All my life he's selected Suitable Friends for me,' she noticed Miss Lily's smile at the evident capitals, 'but I do unsuitable things.'

'That is not a reassuring remark to make to someone who is about to launch your London season.'

Sophie found herself grinning, despite the authority of the ancient walls and portraits. 'Not too unsuitable. I was the one who made him give his workers lunch at the factory.'

'How noble of you, Miss Higgs.'

Sophie flushed. 'It wasn't. It didn't cost me anything.'

'A few pounds less for your inheritance?'

'Not even that. My father says it's made the workers more productive.'

'Oh, my dear.' Miss Lily dabbed her mouth with her napkin, possibly to stifle a laugh. 'I wish our vicar could hear that. So your father has sent you here to keep you away from his factories?'

'I didn't think of that,' said Sophie slowly. 'That might be part of it. But mostly he doesn't want me to marry Malcolm — Mr Overhill. Mr Overhill wants my father to sell the factories.'

'I profoundly hope he doesn't. My cousin receives an excellent income from his investment in those factories. Perhaps your father hopes you will marry an Englishman with a hankering to own corned-beef factories and move to Australia.' Miss Lily smiled. 'Perhaps he simply loves you, Miss Higgs.'

'Yes, Miss Lily.'

'Excellent, Miss Higgs. You sounded almost deferential then.'

She sipped her tea, watching Sophie over the rim of her cup. Sophie hesitated, then took a slice of cherry cake. It was the best she'd ever had, thick and moist, with the cherries precisely suspended. Its solidity said: 'I am the inheritor of hundreds of years of cake-baking.'

'Miss Higgs, I am going to be frank, which is not a custom you should emulate in society. You may not be comfortable with the other girls who are going to stay here. You might even prefer to attend a finishing school. Ridiculous phrase, isn't it? As if your life will be over once you have achieved a husband.'

Sophie flushed. 'Because of the corned beef?'

'If you see yourself as a product of corned beef, others will too. No, not because of the corned beef. Because your interests and theirs will not be the same.'

'How do you know?'

'Very well. Answer a few simple questions for me. What do you feel about female suffrage?'

'It's a good thing, of course. We've had the vote in federal elections since 1902 and in some state elections before that ...'

'Not in England. You didn't know that? Universal suffrage? Nearly half the men in Britain do not have the vote either, unlike in the colonies. You didn't know that either? What are your feelings about Home Rule for Ireland? Anti-establishmentarianism? The chances of the Liberal Party at the next general election? Would Serbian independence increase or decrease the stability of the Austro-Hungarian Empire?'

'I —'

'You neither know nor care. Your ambitions are focused on Australia, and your role in its society. There is nothing wrong with that, Miss Higgs. But the girls who will be staying here are interested in a wider world.'

'And yet you asked me to stay?'

Miss Lily laughed. It was a charming laugh, but again, genuine. 'You are trying to get me to say that I like you. Very well. I do. I also believe that Miss Sophie Higgs will find the wider world far more fascinating than she does Mr Overhill, or even corned beef. So, will you do me the honour of accepting my hospitality? You need only say, "Thank you, Miss Lily",' she added.

'Thank you, Miss Lily.'

'Very good, Miss Higgs. There is one other condition. It is deeply important, so do not agree without forethought. Do you promise never to mention my name except to those who know me once you are back in the world outside? To never mention these months with me, not even to your father, your Miss Thwaites or your eventual husband?'

'Why? I mean, why, Miss Lily? I know I am not supposed to ask questions,' she added. 'But how can I decide unless I do?'

'I didn't say you were not to ask questions here, merely that when you are acting the role of correct debutante — and in your case it will most definitely be an act — you will not question. There will be ... matters ... discussed here that women are not supposed to know about, much less discuss. And no, I will not tell you more until I know you. Nonetheless, I would like your promise now, as well as your promise that if you are ... bored ... and decide to leave, you will still keep your stay here secret.'

'But lots of people know I am staying at Shillings. Mrs Philpott alone must have told half of Sydney.'

'That was not what I asked. The world may know that you are welcome at the home of Nigel Vaile, Earl of Shillings. But the time with me belongs only to those of us who will be here.'

The fire snickered. This was ... odd. Yet Miss Thwaites, too, had indicated that men did not like women who understood too much of the world beyond their homes.

'I agree,' said Sophie.

Her hostess smiled. 'Of course you do. Well, we shall see. Now Jones will show you to your room,' she added. 'Your maid has already unpacked for you. Her name is Doris Green, but you will call her Doris, not Green, to avoid confusion with her older sister, who is my own maid. Doris is the daughter of a farmer on the estate. This is her first position, but she has been well trained by her sister. I trust you will be kind to her.'

The words of the groom came back to Sophie again. 'It is a kind family.'

Yet this was all far more than a Miss Sophie Higgs, daughter of corned beef, had any right to expect. Far too much …

A thought flashed through her mind and she blurted out: 'You're not my mother?'

Instantly she wished the words unspoken. How could she have claimed an earl's cousin as her mother, have thought her father would be part of a charade?

There was unmistakable kindness in Miss Lily's eyes now. She knows my mother disappeared, thought Sophie.

'No, Miss Higgs. I am not related to you in any way.'

Sophie stood. 'I hope I will be worthy of your kindness.'

Miss Lily sank back, into the shadows. 'I am sure you will.'

It was only much later that Sophie realised her hostess had shown no surprise at the question.

Chapter 12

Do you know the greatest privilege of all? It is being able to change your mind. Most poor creatures in this world must accept the life they are given. You need both money and the sense of privilege money gives to find that you can say, 'No, I think I'll go this way instead.'

Miss Lily, 1913

Miss Lily liked her.

Sophie followed Jones up the stairs, though somehow he was behind her and leading at the same time. Was only an earl's butler, she pondered, capable of that?

Miss Lily liked her.

Of all the emotions she was feeling, the joy and triumph were the strongest, but there were others too: excitement; exultation that this time Sophie herself had proved to be more important than the fortune from corned beef.

Miss Lily *liked* her.

She wished she could tell Malcolm, Miss Thwaites or even some of the Suitable Friends.

She also wished she hadn't left so much of the cherry cake behind. She was suddenly starving. She hoped it wasn't long till dinner. She glanced at her watch. Five-thirty. Another hour, then.

The hall upstairs was lined with dark wood, with a faint scent of mouse and rose. The hall runner was what the mother of one of the Suitable Friends called Persian carpet, but this looked more Chinese, with faint dragons winding their way along the hall.

'Your room is here, Miss Higgs. The other young ladies will have the rooms further along. The apartments through the end door are Miss Lily's. She prefers that her young guests stay on this side of the hall.'

'Thank you, Jones. Er ... where is the bathroom?'

'Doris will bring you hot water, miss, and everything else you require.' No bathroom, she thought. No water closet on this floor either, by the sound of it. She hated using chamber pots. Poor Doris, having to empty it.

Jones opened the door to the bedroom, then stood back. 'I will ask Doris to attend you, Miss Higgs. Will there be anything more?' He gave a polite cough. 'A little more tea, perhaps?'

'Please,' she said gratefully, hoping there would be food with it.

The door closed behind him. She looked around the room.

It was large, the same size as her room at home, but there the resemblance ended. The walls were covered in what looked like striped silk — she reached out and touched it. It was. There was a giant fireplace, with coals as well as flames. The fire had been warming the room since early morning, then. She was certain the sheets would be aired and warmed too.

Two armchairs and a window seat upholstered in patterned silk looked gently faded. She looked more closely and grinned. Tiny monkeys played among the greenery. It was a touch of whimsy and ridiculousness, something that Miss Thwaites would never have thought of, that Mrs Overhill might be shocked by. Just simply fun.

The bed was narrow. She felt vague disappointment it wasn't a four-poster. And, yes, there was a chamber pot under the bed, with a hinged top —

The door opened. Sophie jumped. She wasn't used to the way servants just came into a room here in England. Annie back home would have tapped on the door and called out first: 'You decent, lovey?'

The girl who entered was about Sophie's age, dressed in black, with a white apron and a small white cap. Her chin seemed to have been nibbled off at birth, making her look like a rabbit. 'Hot water, Miss Higgs?'

'Thank you. You must be Doris.'

Doris gave a bob. 'Robert is bringing up your luggage, miss. Would you like me to unpack for you now or later?'

'Now, please. Oh, thank you,' she said as another maid arrived with the tea, as well as a young footman, carrying her cases. She looked at the tray gratefully. Cheese sandwiches! Miss Lily must have ordered them for her specially. And more of the cherry cake.

'Shall I put it on the table, miss?'

'Thank you. Would you mind bringing another cup?'

The maid stared. 'Another cup, miss?'

'For Doris. I'm sure you'd like some while you unpack?'

'We have our tea in the kitchen, miss.' Doris looked slightly shocked.

Had she said the wrong thing? Annie sat gossiping with Sophie for hours when Miss Thwaites was busy elsewhere.

Sophie put up her chin. There was no backing down. 'Would you like a cup now?'

Doris's mouth hung open for two seconds. 'Yes, miss. Thank you, miss.'

Sophie nodded dismissal to the other maid and footman.

The door remained open. Jones appeared.

'Miss Lily's compliments, miss.' Did she just imagine the hint of another smile? 'Dinner will be at eight pm. Miss Lily keeps early hours in the country.'

'Early?' Sophie stared.

'She asked me to tell you that you will hear the dressing gong at half past six and then the dinner gong at ten minutes to eight, but wait five minutes before you go down. Doris will help you dress.'

An hour and a half to dress! 'Thank you, Jones.'

He walked out, looking down as though pretending nothing in the room existed. The manners of a perfect servant, thought Sophie. She wondered where he had learned to walk like that.

At least Doris would know what one wore to dinner with the cousin of an earl.

And no more food till eight o'clock. She grinned at her maid. 'You're welcome to the tea, but you're going to have to fight me for those cheese sandwiches ...'

Chapter 13

Food is usually prepared by women, and served to men. The more important meals are served by men, to men, and prepared by men as well. War, politics, men's clubs — wherever big decisions are made, the food will be under a man's control.

Miss Lily, 1913

A silver salver of fruit sat on the sideboard under the noses of the earl's ancestors and presumably Miss Lily's too. The dining room gleamed — not with the sunlight of Thuringa but with the glow of silver.

The furniture seemed to have absorbed centuries of firelight and candlelight and was reflecting it steadily, rather than with a single night's bright flash. Mahogany chairs with cushioned seats of green and gold, matching the brocade of Jones's waistcoat; a table that mirrored the candles in the three candelabra, except where the surface reflected flowers in tall silver bowls. Even the noses in the portraits gleamed.

Miss Lily sat at the head of the table, the candelabra behind her, so once more her face was in shadow, despite the brightness of the room; her elbows were neat against her body, her dress gold velvet, her evening scarf of gold and silver chiffon. She nodded as Sophie entered. 'I hope your room is comfortable. Please do sit down.'

Sophie sat. Only one other place was laid, to Miss Lily's left, so she lowered herself onto the chair, trying to keep her knees together and her back straight, two inches from the back of the chair.

Miss Lily took note of the knees. She smiled at Jones. Mrs Overhill and even Miss Thwaites had smiles for servants that never reached their eyes. Miss Lily's smile was warmly genuine. 'You may serve now, Jones.'

'Very good, Miss Lily.'

'Is anyone else ...?' Sophie said this really just for something to break the silence, complete now apart from the ticking of the clock on the mantelpiece above the unlit fire.

She stopped as Miss Lily gazed at her. 'Once seated at the table, you speak only after your hostess, or the most senior lady present, has spoken to you.'

'Yes, Miss Lily.'

'Now you may speak.'

All at once the mass of candlelight, diamond-bright and glinting from the table, the scent of daphne from the centrepiece and of furniture polish, the antique carpets on the polished floor flooded her brain. She could think of nothing to say. So she asked instead, 'What should we talk about?'

'Ah, an excellent question. Before you go down to dinner, find out what your dining partners are interested in.'

'How?'

'Never use one word, my dear. It makes you sound like a parrot or a fishwife yelling prices.'

'Yes, Miss Lily. How do I find out what will interest my partners? Or who they'll be?'

'You listen, you take notes; every hostess and every guest of distinction always has her "little book". You ask your maid, who will have heard the gossip downstairs — far more than we get upstairs. If necessary, you ask her to find out what you need to know. Your maid is a woman's most valuable tool, so it is worthwhile to be friends with her.' She smiled — again warmly. 'I hear you have already made a good beginning there.'

Jones, thought Sophie. 'Thank you, Miss Lily.'

'Good. "I hear you are a magnificent batsman, Mr Smith?" "I hear you love hunting, Mrs Green? How fascinating." After that you will find that conversation takes care of itself. Keep your gaze steady, look thrilled at every detail, and make noises of awe and wonder.'

'What if it's boring?'

'It probably will be. But someone who looks interested, who listens, will fascinate other people. Your face and your expression will attract those who cannot hear what is being said. Boredom is boring.

'You speak only to the person on your right or left. You change sides at each course. Never talk across the table.'

'What if there are only two of us?'

'Then you sit like this, side by side. The man, of course, at the head, and you at his right.' Her smile grew deeper. 'If your companion is an elderly woman, try, "You must have seen many changes, Lady Brown." No doubt she will have and will tell you of them. If in doubt, comment about the weather ...'

'Even if my companion is a man?'

'Oh, most especially ... But deepen your smile. "Tomorrow may be warm" can carry infinite suggestions. Cricket is useful too. I have found,' said Miss Lily, 'that the way to truly captivate many men is a light conversation about their bat and balls.'

Sophie blinked. Miss Lily couldn't mean ...

Jones entered again, followed by a maid in black, carrying a tray. The maid held the tray while Jones removed a bowl, white with a narrow rim of gold, and set it before Miss Lily. The maid stepped three paces, then Jones picked up the other bowl and placed it before Sophie.

Sophie looked at it. Soup. She was used to soup with lamb shanks and barley, or made from an old rooster if you were sick, brown soups or dull yellow.

This soup was green.

'Watercress,' said Miss Lily. 'But we won't speak of that. You do not speak of food, religion or politics, unless your partner is political or a bishop or a vegetarian or food reformist or anarchist, and then only if they bring up the subject. Few bishops want to discuss the Nestorian heresy over dinner, but a politician may want to speak of his own speeches; he may also seek approval of his policies. He may even, if you suggest it tactfully, consider moderating those policies. But that is best done in private. Most men can be influenced by a woman; few men wish to be seen being so.'

Sophie stared down at her bowl. She had never eaten watercress. Wasn't it a weed? She watched as Miss Lily picked up a rounded spoon, then scooped away from her towards the far rim of her bowl. Her spoon held perhaps a sip of soup. She tipped it towards her mouth, her lips opening so little that not even her teeth were visible.

The soup vanished.

Sophie copied her. The green liquid wrapped itself about her tongue. The taste spread, bitter at first then smooth and almost sweet. It was a world away from lamb shank broth, or the consommé royale on the ship. It tingled every sense, even her toes.

She blinked and smiled, then glanced at Miss Lily, afraid her reaction had been too blatant. But the soup had … everything. Richness, smell and taste and colour, bubbling English streams and too lush grass.

'The smile can stay,' said Miss Lily gently.

Sophie ate.

The next course was fish, a strange flat creature, covered with a dribble of green sauce — a different green from the watercress. Then roasted quail, tiny creatures that needed short, sharp surgery with the pointed knives, not the big blunt knife for spreading butter. ('Tear your bread, don't cut it,' said Miss Lily. 'A tiny piece each time. Place some butter on your plate before you spread it on the bread.' Miss Thwaites had already taught her that, but Sophie didn't mention it to Miss Lily.) Jones served potatoes with two spoons in his smooth white hand, then spinach, thick with cream, and then the next course, tiny brown strips on toast.

'Anchovies,' said Miss Lily, and smiled again. 'This is education now, my dear, not dinner conversation.'

'What's an anchovy?'

'A small salty fish. Or part of a fish. You know, I have never really considered the anchovy. But it is salty, and so makes an appropriate savoury after the meat.'

Savouries had never featured at home. A gust of longing swept through Sophie for paddocks and blue sky.

'I ate a fly once. Half a fly, anyhow. I thought it was a raisin in the pudding.'

The eyebrow lifted. Not appropriate conversation, thought Sophie. Are flies indelicate? Probably. Yes, she thought, Miss Lily is undoubtedly right. There is nothing attractive about flies.

Her back touched the chair. She straightened, checked. Yes, knees still together.

Another tray, its silver catching the candlelight. Glass bowls with a thin etching of gold, filled with a quivering white cream, a bit like jelly, but softer, sweeter, with a flavour that wriggled down to your toes. Vanilla, she thought, but a world away from the vanilla in Thuringa custards. Miss Lily left a third of hers uneaten, but it was impossible for Sophie to stop. She scraped around the glass with her spoon until the eyebrow lifted so far she thought it would vanish into Miss Lily's hair, coiled tonight about her head.

'I'm sorry. It was just too good not to eat it all.'

Suddenly a grin appeared across the table, a grin of so much charm and joy Sophie felt the hairs rise on her arms.

'You'll do,' said Miss Lily. 'Oh, yes, you'll do very well. Manners and ... technique ... can be taught. But sheer enjoyment of life ... no, my dear, that cannot be faked.' She lifted her napkin and laid it on the table. Crumpled, thought Sophie, taking note, neither folded nor scrunched tight.

Miss Lily stood. 'We will take coffee in the library. And I think your manners are sufficiently acceptable for you to dine with others. Just move slowly, slowly. Watch and learn. You are intelligent. Intelligent enough to know what you don't know and to be quiet and observant until you understand. No, don't push your chair back. You are not a furniture removalist. Stand and step sideways.'

'Is this right?'

'Perhaps you mean "correct". There is right, and there is left, correct and incorrect.'

'Yes, Miss Lily.' The evening suddenly felt endless. She wanted to sleep, to digest — not just the food, but everything that had happened. She needed to write to Miss Thwaites.

But she still had to learn how to drink coffee, not tea. She had never drunk coffee before, though it had been served aboard the ship. She had never known anyone who drank it. It seemed a small thing to learn, but she was already realising how large small things could be.

Dawn was a slim grey sliver of light between the curtains when Sophie woke. She blinked, working out where she was. There had been too many different beds lately.

The scent of pot pourri, the remnants of last night's fire — apple wood, Doris had said, a bit puzzled at her question. 'Apple wood to perfume the room, though we use coal down in the kitchen, Miss Higgs. Doesn't give a scent like this, but it's easier.'

A soft gong rang through the house. She counted the beats. Five am. The staff would be getting up, but it wasn't fair to Doris to ring for breakfast or even a cup of tea for at least two hours yet, much less hot water to wash in. She'd have other duties downstairs.

Sophie wriggled her toes onto the carpet by her bed — Miss Thwaites would have tossed it out years ago, it was so faded, but within these striped silk walls it looked beautiful — found a dress that didn't need fastening at the back, then pulled out the drawer for fresh underwear.

No doubt Doris would be even more alarmed by a guest who knew where to find her own underwear, who could even — at a pinch, after the weeks without a maid of her own at sea — lace her own stays, just tightly enough to be presentable, even if not to the accepted eighteen-inch standard.

The staircase was quiet, the wide hall too, though she could hear voices back towards the kitchens. She hoped — no, she believed — this was a house that allowed the staff a cup of tea and hunks of toast and marmalade before the dusting of grates, the setting of fires, the hall-scrubbing and stair-sweeping — all the jobs done before the household appeared. (Disaster if any gentleman were to realise that stairs didn't automatically clean themselves.)

Jones, or a footman, must have already unlocked the front door. Or perhaps it was never locked, as they were so far out into the country. They never had the door locked at Thuringa, though of course the front door of the Sydney house was always bolted at night and locked during the day. An intelligent burglar, though, would know to come around the back, where the kitchen door was open till 'locking up' at ten pm.

The air smelled of apple trees again — the fruit this time, not just the wood. A mist hung across the old stone walls, the first light sparking diamonds in the grass. Sophie cast a longing look towards the stables, but you couldn't just ride your hostess's horses without asking, at five in the morning.

Instead she headed through the gardens, or the scythed grass anyway, around one wing of the house — Miss Lily's wing, where visitors weren't supposed to wander. Its drapes were closed, the early sunlight turning them to sightless eyes.

At the far end of the house was a wall and a stone archway. Through that was an orchard, the source of the apple scent — she could even hear the bees in the fallen fruit — then a kitchen garden full of cabbages and Brussels sprouts and a manured ferny plot that might be asparagus, then she was into the trees. Light dappled as she walked among them, a thousand shades of gold and green. Suddenly she realised she could grow to love this country, that old stones and young grass might wriggle their way into your heart.

The grass was longer here, holding the dew, wetting the hem of her skirt, the trees arching above her. The path led to a mown area, the scythe marks gently curving, and ended at another small lake. Short grass to picnic on, she thought. Had children ever sailed their toy boats on this lake?

Miss Thwaites had shown her the earl in Debrett's lists of ancestors and titles. He was forty-six, and had inherited the title from his much older brother more than twenty years before. No wife, no children. A major, retired from the army at twenty-one. A major at twenty-one! They had looked up the earl's cousins too, but hadn't found any, which had worried Miss Thwaites a little. Was Miss Lily perhaps separated from her husband, and had kept his surname but gone back to 'Miss'?

The sun glinted through the trees now, the great golden beast of Thuringa looking curiously tamed here in England. Time for breakfast. She turned back. Smoke puffed from all of the house's six chimneys.

The curtains had been drawn back in one of the rooms in Miss Lily's 'unknown wing' — Miss Lily's room? She wondered if anyone was watching, and suppressed an urge to wave.

Definitely time for breakfast.

Jones looked startled when he found her in the hallway, damp skirt brushing at her shoe tops. She handed him a bunch of small pinky-purple flowers. 'Would you mind giving these to Cook? To thank her for the cherry cake. Tell her it was the best I've ever eaten.'

'Certainly, Miss Higgs.'

Did she see a twitch of his lips? No, good butlers never showed emotion. Or was that something she had to unlearn too?

'The breakfast room is through there, miss. Unless you wish to change first? I will send Doris to you ...'

'No, I'm starving. Thank you, Jones.'

'Thank you, miss.'

She frowned as he opened the breakfast-room door for her. There had definitely been a twitch of the lips that time.

It was a long room, smaller than any she had seen in this house so far, though still enormous. She supposed that in a climate like this, large rooms were the best way of discreetly saying, 'Look at how rich we are — we can afford to heat all this.' Unlike the other rooms, this had painted walls, a pale yellow. There was a fireplace on one side, the fire blazing, dark wood sideboards bearing covered silver plates, and a long table, set again for two.

Miss Lily sat reading a letter and nibbling toast, once again with her back to the fire so it formed a glow about her hair and tinged her skin with gold, while her face was shadowed from its drying heat. She glanced up.

'Good morning.' Her eyes flickered at the damp skirt, the pullover that — bother — had a thread pulled by a twig and a few burrs at one elbow, the shoes that had left a splodge of what Sophie hoped was only leaf mould on yet another faded carpet. 'I hope you slept well.'

'Good morning, Miss Lily. Yes, wonderfully, thank you.'

A ham with a clean pink gash across its top lay on a silver salver, next to what looked like cold pheasant, already carved. Sophie picked up a plate then lifted the covers. Steam rose from the hot water chambers. Porridge in a silver porringer. Lamb chops, with halved tomatoes nestling in their curves. A ghost of homesickness kissed her and passed on.

She picked up more lids. Scrambled eggs, poached eggs on rounds of toast, wrinkled oval kidneys in dark brown gravy, smelling like the bull pens at the Agricultural Show, bacon laid out neatly, a dish of yellow rice with hunks of what looked like orange fish decorated with slices of hard-boiled eggs. She sniffed. Curry. 'Is this kedgeree?'

'I believe so. You had better ask Mrs Goodenough, our cook.' Miss Lily's voice was dry. 'She will give you lessons, by the way. A lady needs to know how things are cooked, even if she never lifts a pan. Many a hostess has founded her reputation on secret recipes, as well as a cook who is loyal enough to keep them secret too. But please do not speak of recipes at the table.'

Another faux pas, then. She heaped some of the kedgeree onto her plate and sat down before she realised the butler was hovering, about to hold out her chair.

'Tea or coffee, Miss Higgs?'

'Tea. Thank you, Jones.' She added milk and two sugars, heaped her fork with kedgeree, then remembered and unloaded most of it and put the remnant in her mouth. The spiciness startled her. She tried another mouthful, then a lump of fish, decided the dish was strange, but good, then looked up to find Miss Lily watching her.

And that was definitely a smile.

'I've done something wrong again, haven't I?' she asked resignedly.

'Several things, none of which I am smiling at. I am simply enjoying your appetite.'

'Young ladies are not supposed to have appetites?'

Miss Lily laughed. 'The fashionable ones, no. Ethereal is still the rule. But I think, my dear, that your ... appetite will be seen simply as a charming foible. Which it is.'

Miss Lily spread marmalade on another tiny piece of toast. Behind her Jones accepted another rack of hot toast from a footman and placed it on the table, then stood back behind Miss Lily's chair, in case she needed anything, like more coffee in her tiny china cup, or defending from a lion.

Sophie took another mouthful of kedgeree. Decidedly good. Buttery. She sipped her tea — hard not to drink half the cup at once. The walk had made her thirsty.

'What were my mistakes, then?'

'Just now?' The smile was still there, Sophie saw with relief. 'Guests don't go wandering without the hostess's permission. No, you do not ask permission, you just don't wander.'

'In case you find the master dallying with the kitchen maid in the orchard?'

Had she gone too far? But Miss Lily simply said, 'Exactly. But if and when you do walk in a garden — secretly or by invitation from your hostess — you do not appear with leaf mould on your shoes, especially not if it is you who has been doing the dallying in the orchard. It takes only a few seconds to wipe your feet, to check for burrs. If you are unable to make yourself tidy, you go to your room, where your maid will have what is needed for a quick change and, under your guidance, remain discreet. If discretion is impossible, she will at any rate provide you with a change of clothes.

'Your maid will already have found out downstairs what activities are planned for the rest of the day and will have chosen the most suitable clothes. A random choice of clothes — such as you are wearing — reflects badly on the maid, and on her employer. Either ring for your maid as soon as you wake, or ask her to lay your clothes out the night before.'

Miss Lily sipped what smelled like coffee. Horrible bitter stuff that had made Sophie's heart pound despite her weariness last night. 'Understood?'

'Yes, Miss Lily. And I'm sorry,' said Sophie quietly. 'I had no idea how much I didn't know. How much work I'd be for you.'

Miss Lily smiled above the rim of her coffee cup, the lips slightly too perfectly shaped. Lipstick? Surely Miss Lily didn't paint? 'I have never had to tutor in etiquette before. The girls who come here need quite different lessons. But I am enjoying this, my dear. Far more than I could ever have imagined.' She smiled again at Sophie's look of doubt. 'Now, your second error ...'

Sophie waited to see what other points of etiquette she had managed to contravene.

'Wait for the count of four before you enter when a door is opened for you.'

She hadn't expected that. 'Why four?'

'Four seconds gives enough time to build up a slight sense of expectation. Any more is wearisome for the door-opener. Thirdly, make sure that when you do enter, to that sense of expectation, there is something to satisfy it.'

'How do I do that?'

'You already did, though I suspect accidentally. You were smiling as you entered. A smile makes your audience wonder for what — or whom — you are smiling. You may also look lost — a useful expression. I advise you to master it, as well as lonely, sad and furious. Never bored. Never irritated or cross. If something irritates you, solve it or forget it.' She stared at Sophie for long seconds. 'Tell me, what have you found the most interesting event in the world this year?'

'Coming to England, visiting here —' Sophie stopped as her hostess waved her hand again.

'Your own life is not necessarily important, Miss Higgs. Unless you think your visit here can change the world.'

Sophie tried to work out the most impressive possible answer. Something to do with the Balkans perhaps? Hadn't Greece annexed some country, or had another country annexed Greece? Or was it Bulgaria?

Her hostess was still waiting. Sophie grabbed at the perfect response. 'Stainless steel.'

Miss Lily looked startled. 'I beg your pardon?'

'Stainless steel. A man in America invented it, and one in Britain, and now they're arguing about who found it first. But it's going to change the world.'

'What exactly is this stainless steel?'

'It's a new process for making iron tougher. Iron rusts, but stainless steel doesn't. It's, well, stainless.'

'And why is that important? Less scrubbing for housemaids?'

'No, not at all. Well, yes, perhaps. I wasn't thinking about how it might work in a house. Saucepans, perhaps. But think of ships. I don't suppose stainless-steel ships would last forever, but they'd last longer than iron ones. You could make machines you could rely on because parts wouldn't wear through. Ploughs that wouldn't need to be rubbed with fat after use.' Sophie stopped, and flushed. 'I'm talking like a factory owner's daughter.'

'Indeed. And not a topic for the breakfast table, but that is my fault, not yours. Breakfast is a time for small talk as the household gathers the strength to start the day. No, Miss Higgs, what you said is fascinating. I am not easily fascinated. I can see how this "stainless steel" may well change the world. As I told you yesterday, you can't hide your background. If you try, and show you are ashamed of it, then you will be shamed. But speaking as you did now makes an advantage of it. Do you know what England's greatest product is, Miss Higgs?'

She tried to think of Miss Thwaites's lessons. 'Potatoes? Apples!'

Miss Lily laughed. 'Only one in five working men is a farmhand. But a third of the world's goods is shipped in British ships. That is England's real fortune, Miss Higgs. England can't feed herself, hasn't for years. We don't just import our coffee and nutmeg and wine, but most of the wheat for our flour these days too. Our guns are made in Germany; our cotton in India; and at least half of our electric motorcars are shipped over from the United States, not made in factories here. But we do have coal, and iron. And we make ships and sail them. So yes, Miss Higgs, you may possibly have nailed exactly what will change the next twenty or fifty years. And it is an English invention, not a German one, for which we should be grateful.'

Sophie decided not to remind her hostess of the American who had also invented it, not that she could remember his name anyway.

'You know, I was almost regretting my offer to your father until you arrived yesterday. You were not ... what I expected.' Miss Lily smiled. 'I am very glad you have come, Miss Higgs. I think we may be of considerable use to each other. But we shall see.'

She dabbed her mouth with her napkin, crumpled it on the table, then stood up as Jones moved to pull back her chair. 'This morning Madame Theron will arrive to instruct you in French conversation and to attend to the accent that I suspect will be your Miss Thwaites's version of how French is spoken. It is not enough to have a French accent. It must be the correct French accent. You will lunch with Madame. This afternoon Lord Buckmaster and Madame Ellery will attend to your wardrobe. I shall see you at dinner.'

Sophie stood too. 'Thank you, Miss Lily. Lord Buckmaster — I'm sorry, I don't understand. Surely a ... a lord doesn't sell clothes.'

'I hope,' said Miss Lily, 'that you will not ask questions like that in public. Ask a friend in private, or your maid. He is a friend,' she added more gently. 'Some men enjoy fox hunting. Lord Buckmaster prefers to chase what he calls "the perfect look". It is his hobby, if you like. Do you hunt, Miss Higgs?'

'Foxes? I've shot a few,' said Sophie.

Miss Lily laughed, another surprised and surprising peal of delight. 'That answer will infuriate every person in every drawing room in England, for several quite different reasons. I almost wish I could be there to see it. Good morning, Miss Higgs.'

'Good morning, Miss Lily,' said Sophie, still wondering how she might be of use to the cousin of an earl. As an amusement, like the monkeys on the brocade? She sat back to finish her kedgeree as Jones filled her teacup again.

Madame Theron was small, black-eyed, her back still straight as she bent over her embroidery. Her voice pecked, pausing between each word so her accent could be absorbed, her pupil's mistakes corrected.

Lord Buckmaster was in his forties, perhaps, but made to appear younger by his laughter. Madame Ellery, a tall black shadow, was elegant only when you realised she was in the room, wielding a tape measure while Lord Buckmaster laughed and sketched and smoked innumerable cigarettes, wafting the smoke through his fingers as he inspected Sophie's wardrobe, laid out for him in the library by Doris — minus all the embarrassing articles.

Sophie regarded Lord Buckmaster carefully. With the possible exception of Miss Lily, who was at least an honourable, he was the first English aristocrat she had met. But at first sight he could have been any of the men who worked in her father's office: he wore the same dark grey trousers and waistcoat, the same gold watch chain, the same white shirt. It was only when you looked more closely that his clothes seemed to fit him rather than the other way around, as though he dominated both fabric and colour, and had an air of easy familiarity with whatever room or garment he was in.

He lifted a pair of gold glasses from his pocket — this at least was different from the attire of all the other men she'd met — stared at her for less than a second, then nodded. As though I am an insect on a pin beneath a magnifying glass, thought Sophie; he had yet to even say 'Good day' — nor would he do so.

'So you are the latest lovely lady?'

'I'm sorry? Lord Buckmaster,' she added.

'Call me Bucky. I see you are the latest acquisition. A colonial this time.'

Miss Lily isn't even here to introduce him, she thought. In her world and, she suspected, in theirs, for a hostess not to present one guest to another was gross bad manners. But perhaps you didn't owe an acquisition good manners?

He pulled out his watch. 'Two hours and ten minutes till teatime. Lily has the most exquisite crumpets, don't you think? No one's crumpets are quite so butter-soaked as hers. And I am sure the source of her honey is England's deepest secret. So, let us get to work. Lily is correct,' he added, to her surprise. 'You are quite lovely. A small colonial arrow among the waving English debutantes. Your season will be ... interesting.'

Lily, not 'Miss Lily', thought Sophie, through her embarrassment. She had been told she was beautiful back home. She had not realised how she had assumed the compliment was as much due to her father's wealth as to her own appearance.

Lord Buckmaster glanced down at the draped clothes, pounced, plucked and rejected, leaving only the two jumpers knitted by Miss Thwaites ('Everyone, my dear, should have at least two garments made with love') and heaping the rest in a pile that made Doris blush with pleasure. 'For you, dear girl, or your sisters. Someone, I hope,' with an eyebrow raised at Sophie, 'who is long and slender and not made like an elf.'

'What do elves wear, then?' To her surprise Sophie was enjoying this. Buying clothes had merely filled in boredom.

Lord Buckmaster held up his glasses to inspect her again. 'Wine, not water. These,' he waved a hand at the discarded clothes, 'are water. You need a light champagne or ivory. Not white: your skin is far too brown. Riesling for parties on the river. Ellie, darling, do you have any of that divine soft purple tweed left?'

Madame Ellery nodded, her mouth full of pins as she tucked a paper pattern around Sophie's hips.

'Perfect. Now, put your hands on your hips, dear girl.' He nodded thoughtfully. 'I thought so. You have a waist. No chemise styles, no boleros, no draped coats. You have a shape, my dear, and you need to show it, otherwise you are so small it will be ignored. Pleats, darts, above all waists, high or low; it makes no matter as long as they are there. Velvets — no, you are too young for velvets, but remember them when you are twenty-five; you will look divine in a champagne velvet that looks as if it reflects the sky. No satin. Ever. We want the watchers to see you, not their chandeliers reflected in the fabric. When you are small, my dear, you need to make every glance count,' he added. 'Fabrics that cling but seem to flow. And hats.' He cocked his head. 'No, you are entirely too small for hats. A few feathers, a bandeau, a sunshade if possible rather than a hat.'

'Shoes?' asked Sophie hesitantly.

He looked at her reproachfully. 'Yes, you must wear shoes. Even elves wear shoes, at least in the best elf circles.'

'But what sort of shoes?'

He waved his hands again, puffing more smoke towards her face. 'Shoe type shoes. I am not interested in feet.'

'I can deliver by next Wednesday,' said Madame Ellery. They were the first words she had spoken.

'Perfect. Well ...' Lord Buckmaster looked Sophie up and down once more as Jones quietly opened the door. 'No doubt we shall meet again, if you are to be one of Miss Lily's lovely ladies. And no doubt when we do, you will look quite, quite different.' He bowed. 'Good afternoon, Miss Higgs.'

He followed Madame Ellery out of the library and Jones closed the door behind them. Off to crumpets, thought Sophie. And that cherry cake perhaps, and meringues, a private meal, as so many meals in large households were private. Lord Buckmaster's presence lingered in the library, though perhaps it was just the cigarette smoke. No man had ever smoked in front of Sophie before.

She felt again a breeze of loss that she was left out of what would no doubt be fascinating conversation in the drawing room. They'd talk of people she didn't know, she supposed, and matters like 'the Balkans', which she would begin to read about in the papers, starting today. But there was also a sense that all Lord Buckmaster had told her was right: she had been recreated, and she liked it.

She grinned at Doris. 'If you don't mind, I'd better borrow some of the clothes back, unless I'm going to be stark naked till next Wednesday.'

'Miss!' Doris blushed. Suddenly she didn't look like a rabbit at all, and not just because rabbits didn't blush. 'You've still got your knickers,' she added. 'We could dip them in champagne, and all.'

Silence filled the library for a moment. It was impudence from a maid. It could also, Sophie realised, be the first offering of real friendship.

'Does Miss Lily drink champagne?'

'Yes, miss.'

Sophie wrinkled her nose. 'Better not pinch any, then. Lord Buckmaster is right,' she added. 'You'll look far better in those clothes than I do. Your dark hair is glorious.'

Doris blushed again. 'Thank you, miss.' She touched a hobble skirt reverently. 'This is beautiful, if you don't mind my saying so, miss. Couldn't take my eyes off it when I saw you in it yesterday. I'll keep it for Sundays.' Another tentative smile. 'Can't step out to do my work other days, not in a tight skirt like that.' She began to gather the heaped clothes.

Sophie looked at her consideringly. 'Do you like kedgeree, Doris?'

Doris looked up, surprised. 'Yes, miss.'

So servants here gleaned leftover food as well as clothes.

'By the way,' she added casually, 'what is Miss Lily's surname?'

Doris's face grew carefully blank. 'She is Miss Lily, miss.'

Discretion was a servant's duty. It would be unkind to press Doris further, despite Sophie's growing curiosity. She pulled the bell. 'Tea,' she said to the footman who appeared promptly. 'In my room, please. Is there any cherry cake? And would you mind bringing two cups?'

Chapter 14

The days consume themselves as you get older. One needs to have a purpose or they vanish. Only our deeds and our children live on beyond the grave. And without children ... well then, one must rest on one's deeds.

Miss Lily, 1913

Autumn leaves blew yellow, orange and red onto the grass. They lay in a planned wild beauty, vanishing before they could turn brown, gardeners raking them away before any others except the housemaids were up. Bees hummed, audible through the open windows.

The house felt strangely isolated. There were no visitors, except for those presumably hired, or who had possibly volunteered, to refine the raw colonial ore into the gem of an upper-class debutante.

A middle-aged man who could either be a neighbour or a dancing master took Sophie through her paces like a horse while a phonograph scratched out waltzes, mazurkas, two-steps; he corrected her posture and the position of her hands. 'They are not bananas. You do not dance with feet alone; the positions of the back, the head, the hands, they are all as important as the feet.' He, too, then vanished to the small sitting room to take tea with Miss Lily.

French conversation continued each morning. Somehow by concentrating on speaking French with Madame's accent Sophie found her everyday accent changing too, her words sharper, clearer — not so much acquiring an English accent as losing the colonial slurring. This, it appeared, was all that Miss Lily desired, for she made no more references to Sophie's pronunciation. An Australian heiress would be expected to be Australian. A few words pronounced differently might be charming; to either ape an English accent or revel in the broad vowels of an Australian one would not.

Sophie rode around the estate, learning the neat rectangles of turnips, beets, the longer fields of far too white sheep against the grass that changed colour only to different shades of green.

The new clothes began to arrive as promised; not all at once, as Sophie had expected, but in parcels every few days. Most dangled on their hangers for use during her season. The pale purple tweed suit fitted so closely to her body that it might have been a single garment. The jumpers in champagne wool were dumped in the bathtub by Doris and stamped on in cold water, then carefully dried and ironed and hung up, so that when Sophie finally put them on they seemed to have been worn for years. Her money might be 'new', but slightly worn clothes implied that her 'class' was not.

The last of the leaves in the apple orchard turned brown; a few clung to bare branches. Letters arrived from Australia, from Miss Thwaites with a small note added in her writing from Dad, but unmistakably his tones. Three letters from Suitable Friends: one obviously hoping to make social capital and join her, another almost a schoolgirl's form letter about the weather — *I hope that you are well and enjoying England. How different it must be.* The third, though, almost sounded as if the writer missed her; Sophie had never considered that any of the Suitables might have wanted to be truly friends.

Weekly letters from Malcolm, full of news of Warildra, the trees, shorn sheep, the lack of rain, only once a romantic reference. *I went down the river after rabbits last night. The moon was so bright you could see every leaf and I thought of you.*

The words were sincere in a way longer protestations of love wouldn't be. They made her long to smell gum leaves after rain, see a sunset smudged with dust, the ducks skimming the river as they landed for the night. But she was all too aware they didn't make her long for Malcolm. She was even, she realised guiltily, glad he wasn't there to dilute her hours with Miss Lily.

Perhaps, as her father had implied, she simply hadn't known Malcolm enough to long for him — only the idea of him, of the life they might have had together. In this strange quiet house she had a life of her own, newer, more fascinating. She was like a snake shedding its skin and discovering what it was like to live starting everything afresh.

In one way, Shillings was the narrowest world she had ever been in, limited to her sessions with her instructors, and the nods from the tenants when she rode on the estate on a sweet mare she suspected was Miss Lily's. The only excursion away from the house was to church on Sundays, and even then she and Miss Lily sat in a closed pew above the rest of the congregation, arriving late and leaving early, to miss the greetings by the rector outside.

It should have been lonely. It wasn't. Sophie had been used to company that had been paid for, selected for her. Her life had contained little true intimacy and she felt no lack of it. Here, at least, she was learning something useful — intrinsically ridiculous, perhaps, like a 'good' accent, but useful if she was to wash away the stain of the corned beef.

She felt that not only had a door opened to her, but also that she was already across the threshold.

Miss Lily and Sophie shared breakfast and dinner, but never luncheon, nor tea, which it seemed Miss Lily reserved for the instructor-friends. Miss Lily's conversation was like none Sophie had ever known — not just the acerbic wit, but the evident vision of the world too. Mr Higgs knew only such politics as might have an impact on his business. Miss Thwaites knew every detail of the Battle of Thermopylae, but had never shown any interest in which party was in power in England.

This world was Sophie's to discover.

There were newspapers in the drawing room each day — not the one where Miss Lily had first greeted her, and where visitors were recieved, but another just off the hallway: a room of grey silk sofas and parchment-papered walls, a creation, Sophie supposed, of the earl's deceased mother. The fire was lit there each morning; the papers waited on the table — the morning papers delivered to Shillings from the first train, as well as the papers from the evening before — but as far as Sophie knew, she was the only person who used the room apart from the servants who dusted and raked the ashes and laid the fire and kept it glowing.

She had never really read the newspapers back home. Now she did.

She read of the arrest of suffragette Emmeline Pankhurst on her arrival back from the United States; about an Indian man called Gandhi, who wanted independence for his country and freedom of movement for Indians who had been imprisoned in South Africa (independence from the greatest empire in the world? why?); and about the banning of the importation of any weapons into Ulster. She read that the Kaiser had banned his troops and officers from dancing the tango or the two-step: such effete dances would harm their morale and fitness as proud members of the greatest fighting force the world had seen; even families who allowed the dances were to be shunned by officers on pain of dismissal.

It was ridiculous. It was funny. It was also disquieting, to realise how much of the world she knew nothing about.

She had just put that day's newspapers down, had reached for a cup of afternoon tea, complete with the cherry cake that Mrs Goodenough always made for her now, when she was aware of a shadow over her. It was Miss Lily.

Sophie stood, suddenly flustered. She had never known Miss Lily to deviate from her routine before.

'Sit down, Miss Higgs.' Miss Lily sat herself, at one with the brocade of the chair, with the air of one who has suddenly decided to enjoy herself. 'Tea in here this afternoon,' she added to Jones, who had appeared behind her. 'I have been dealing with rents for my cousin all day with his agent. Enough of duty.'

She nodded at the newspaper on the sofa. 'Have you become interested in politics?' Her mouth quirked. 'Or are you trying to make me interested in you?'

Jones has told her I read the newspapers each afternoon, thought Sophie. 'I don't know. At first it was because you implied I was ignorant. But now ...' she shook her head '... it's like a jigsaw I can't put together. Or maybe the pieces don't *go* together ...'

Miss Lily nodded. 'At least with a jigsaw you know the pieces will eventually fit. With politics and world affairs, you may never know the importance of one speech, one bullet.'

'Most of the time I don't even know the places. Montenegro, Gallipoli — if that's how you pronounce it.'

Miss Lily smiled faintly. 'But your memory is good enough to retain them.'

'What does it matter if the Greeks stop the Bulgarian army from landing there? Is it a town? I can't even find it on a map.'

'Most battles are fought in someone's fields; the Gallipoli Peninsula is probably just a convenient place from which to capture Constantinople.'

Of course Miss Lily would know exactly the event she had referred to. 'But what does the Bulgarian army matter to us?'

'Us?'

'I mean to England. To the Empire.'

'Wars are only interesting if they affect your own country?'

Sophie considered. 'Yes. There must be hundreds of wars happening. It would be impossible to be aware of them all.'

'Not impossible. Just perhaps not useful. One's heart can perhaps expand indefinitely with compassion, but the mind is finite. And I doubt there are hundreds of wars. Hundreds of trivial battles, perhaps. Family feuds. Of course when those families are at the head of empires, the feuds tend to get larger ...'

'But this Gallipoli?'

Miss Lily smiled. 'A place we shall undoubtedly never hear of again.'

'How do I know which are the events I can forget and which are the ones that matter, then? Why do the papers make the

Balkans sound important? Are they? Every week someone seems to be fighting with someone else there, or making a new alliance then breaking it the week after.'

'You would like me to explain the Balkan Conflict in three easy steps? If it were possible to explain it, possibly it wouldn't be happening. But at their heart the Balkans lack stability. The Turkish Empire is crumbling. Greece, Macedonia, Bulgaria, Serbia — perhaps they'll become independent. Or perhaps they will become part of someone else's empire — and that of course is the crux of the issue. Whose empire will claim them?

'The Treaty of London a few months ago was supposed to end it all. All Ottoman territory west of the Enez–Kıyıköy line was ceded to the Balkan League, and Albania was to be an independent state, but we have yet to see these things happen. Words on paper do not always change the fabric of the world, even when dictated by the leaders.' Miss Lily shrugged. It was a beautiful shrug. The silk of her dress rippled in the firelight. 'As you said, things change.'

'But why do the Balkans matter?'

'For those in the Balkans, they matter deeply. These are human lives, even if far removed from our own. Every life has significance, even if far away from yours. For England, well, we are officially a supporter of the Ottomans, but a strong Turkish Empire will also counterbalance the Russians. For Russia the current instability is a chance to pick up crumbs from the Austro-Hungarian Empire.

'But the Hapsburgs of Austria-Hungary are facing rebellious Serbs themselves, and they also hope that the collapse of the Ottoman Empire will give them access to the Mediterranean. Serbia wants Bosnia, which is held by Austria; Germany's Emperor Wilhelm promised to aid Austria but then drew back. Germany too hopes for crumbs if the Ottomans fall ... and in all this you have Christians against Muslims too.'

Miss Lily raised a perfect eyebrow. 'You have encouraged me to give you a history lesson before I have even had my tea. I had expected a diverting discussion about stainless steel.' Her tone made it clear that this was a joke. 'You are always unexpected, Miss Higgs. No, don't apologise. I should have said "delightfully unexpected". Thank you,' she added as Jones handed her a cup — milkless and pale green-brown, thought Sophie — then handed her the three-tiered stand: crumpets on the bottom, cherry cake on the next layer, small macaroons on top. Miss Lily took a crumpet and bit into it, the smallest mouse nibble of a piece.

'I do wish girls were taught history. Without history you are a blank piece of paper. If you have nothing written in your past, it is impossible to choose a future.'

Sophie flushed. 'Miss Thwaites taught me history. Much more than most girls, I think. But it was all about Henry VIII's wives and Hannibal crossing the Alps.'

'I don't suppose she mentioned that Henry VIII chose his wives for their religious and political alliances?'

Sophie stared. 'No.'

'Anne Boleyn was the exception, perhaps, though her family was powerful and saw the marriage as a way to become more powerful. But it's true: the old chant of "Divorced, beheaded, died, annulled, beheaded, survived" does have little relevance today, unless you are interested in why the Archbishop of Canterbury and other men in satin have so much political as well as spiritual power.'

Miss Lily smiled an almost complacent smile. Somehow the crumpet was gone, without Sophie's realising it had been eaten, without crumbs or drips of butter or honey on the smooth sheen of Miss Lily's grey silk. 'Boleyn was charming enough to catch her king when her sister became a cast-off mistress. But when she got him,' Miss Lily shrugged, 'she had no idea what to do with him. I like to think that if Boleyn had been skilled she might not just have survived but also have saved England the bloody business of Mary Tudor, even Oliver Cromwell. Women are rarely acknowledged in history, except as wives, but that doesn't mean they can't influence its course.'

'But someone like me can't change history.'

'It was you, was it not, who said stainless steel would change the world? Sometimes, my dear, the world changes and no one knows what was the lynch pin.'

'How do you know all this?'

Miss Lily smiled. 'I notice. I pull threads together. I cultivate friends.'

'Your lovely ladies?'

She stiffened. 'Where did you hear that phrase?'

'From Lord Buckmaster.'

'I shall have a word with that young man. Please never use the phrase again. I am most serious about this.'

Sophie frowned, then remembered not to. Why did it matter? She could see why discretion was necessary. But why such secrecy? 'Of course, Miss Lily.'

Miss Lily patted Sophie's knee. 'Never mind, my dear. You are lovely, and you are a lady. And yes, I know the world through letters from my friends.'

'Women friends?' Miss Thwaites had said that women friends were rarely stimulating. But in this world perhaps they might be.

'Women friends. Women have no overt power, which is why we are able to use it.'

'I don't understand.'

'A woman — a sensible woman, not a Mrs Pankhurst — never threatens. She charms. She can be pouring coffee when plans are talked of, can exchange news with like-minded friends. A woman can persuade where a man can only antagonise. A woman can convince kings and prime ministers, and never be noticed. It is the only power we have, my dear. We need to make the most of it.'

'By persuading our husbands?'

Miss Lily smiled. 'Did you enjoy your ride this morning, Miss Higgs? The last of the autumn leaves are always charming.'

Chapter 15

*A girl is supposed to 'come out into the world' during her season.
How curious that society speaks of only one world, as though there
were no others.*

Miss Lily, 1913

Winter sat upon the world as though it would never shift, like a
blanket of cold. Strange to be in a world with no green leaves,
except on the few dark, brooding evergreens down in the park,
all shadows now as though even they couldn't stay bright as the
warmth seeped away. Stranger still to be living in a house where
Sophie had to learn to please.

She wrote to Malcolm, to her father, to Miss Thwaites. She wrote
to some of the Suitable Friends, who might become real friends
when she returned one day, to become Mrs Malcolm Overhill.

Letters, rides in the park, the horse's breath a cloud of steam,
walks where the wind bit her nose and ears till she learned to
wrap a scarf above her chin: these filled the time between her
lessons.

She knew some of the farmers and their wives enough to chat
too now, as the women hung out the washing or carried back
their sacks of wheat gleanings from the harvest — the grain that
fell was free for all to gather. A good system, thought Sophie.
Though better wages would mean women and children did not
have to scrabble among the stubble even here, where the family
was kind.

The women proudly showed her their gleanings; the harvest
had been the richest anyone had known. The men explained the
finer points of drainage ditches, and if they were amused at a

young woman wanting to know about ditches — and a colonial who had never thought ditches might be necessary in a damp climate — they also seemed pleased to teach her.

But the focus and joy of each day were the meals she spent with Miss Lily. Each was still a lesson. But the lessons were more and more like a game now, one that both she and her hostess enjoyed.

Dinner was always at the long table, Sophie in ivory or riesling muslin, Miss Lily in one of her dark silks, delicately beaded in the gold that was echoed in her wisp of scarf. The earl's portrait stared at something in the distance above them. The earl wore grey, and a beard. He looked almost as young as Sophie.

'He looks ... lonely,' said Sophie, eyeing the painting. 'I'm sorry, that's silly. An earl can't be lonely.'

Miss Lily watched her without speaking. 'Perceptive,' she said at last. 'I believe my cousin was desperately lonely when that was painted, although even he perhaps didn't know it. It was just before he joined the army. He had not inherited the title then, of course.' She changed the subject abruptly. 'You look beautiful tonight, my dear.'

Sophie laughed. 'Miss Lily approves?'

'I do approve, but the remark was not a comment on your dress.'

'Dinner tonight isn't a lesson, then?'

Miss Lily's lips quirked. 'All of life is a lesson. We shall pretend that it is next year. You are a guest of, ah, let's see, General and Mrs Denison-Hughes. You are not, of course, sitting near your host, but in the middle of the table. Now, how do you open the conversation with your neighbouring diner?'

'"The weather is lovely for this time of year"?'

Miss Lily's lips twitched again. 'You have forgotten already. A girl in her first year out does not speak unless spoken to.'

'Not even to my maid?'

'Most servants do not exist. You neither hear nor see them, unless they do a special service for you. Every act of service by a butler is a special service; you thank him, quietly and politely.

Every service by your maid is also a special one; you thank her too in public. In private you may be as frank as you like. Now, let us try again. I am the Honourable Greston Gaulish. I am fifty-eight, and quite impoverished — no hostess is going to waste a wealthy man on a colonial. But I trust you will be kind to me, and only partly because someone you may find of more interest might see you across the table being kind. "Lovely weather we are having, Miss Higgs."'

'Yes, it is.'

'Yes, Mr Gaulish. You will have noted his name and it is polite to use it wherever possible. A brief answer — yes or no — is impolite. So you will add, "Superb hunting weather, I believe." Doris will have informed you before you go down that Mr Gaulish is Master of the Deepstele Hunt. He will then describe his adventures while you reply, "How interesting, Mr Gaulish" or "Oh, and what happened then?" Try it.'

Sophie swallowed a giggle. 'Oh, Mr Gaulish! And what happened then?'

'Now meet his eyes — no, your face remains bent down towards the table, your eyes glance up, both modest and fascinated. Always, always meet your companion's eyes, to show you speak to him, not to show yourself to the room. Yes, excellent. If eyes are a mirror to the soul, then yours is a good one, my dear.' Miss Lily smiled as Sophie flushed at the compliment. 'Wrists slightly higher, elbows closer to your waist. Press your wrists down before you speak — it adds to the sense of rapt attention.'

Jones removed the soup bowls.

'Mr Gaulish will now turn to the lady on his left. You will look at your ... ah, your pickled salmon, thank you, Jones ... but be ready for the slightest movement to your right. When the gentleman looks at you preparing to speak you must instantly turn your attention to him.'

'What if he doesn't turn?'

'He may, indeed, be so fascinated by his other companion that he breaks the rules and keeps talking to her. You keep on eating neatly, tiny bites so that you may appear intent on the food. Never let your plate sit there empty — you need something to focus on if conversation flags.'

'What if Mr Gaulish keeps talking to me during the next course?'

'You keep addressing him. But even Mr Gaulish must pause to take a mouthful, and your other dining companion may take that opportunity to speak to you. You can then turn to him, with a regretful but small smile at Mr Gaulish.'

'It sounds extremely boring,' said Sophie frankly.

'It is. You must keep to the convention that young ladies know nothing except drawing, music and a modicum of French.'

'How do people stand it?'

Miss Lily laughed. 'The men are flattered. The girls know that once they are married they can lead their own lives — dependent on their husband's, but if you have chosen your husband wisely, it can be a full life indeed.'

'You mean as a mother?'

'No. I am talking of political hostesses — women who have made or broken prime ministers just by the choice of guests at their table, the passing on of gossip at afternoon tea. I mean women who use their influence to campaign for whatever cause touches them most.'

'But women can't choose a husband. They can only say yes or no.'

'A woman of sufficient charm can attract the husband she prefers. A woman of sufficient sense can attract a husband who will give her the life she wants. Which I suspect is exactly what you did, my dear.' Miss Lily placed her knife and fork together. 'Of course it helps if a girl knows exactly what life she wants before she acquires that husband.'

Sophie stayed silent. Miss Lily smiled. 'You haven't thought what your life will be like beyond the clothes you will change into after your wedding breakfast?'

Sophie flushed. 'How did you know I'd thought about my wedding?'

'Every girl imagines herself a bride at some time. Do you like children, Miss Higgs?'

'I ... I suppose so.' She thought of the girls at the factory. 'I like them when they are older. Not very young children, I think.'

'Why?'

Sophie shrugged, then stopped as Miss Lily raised her eyebrow. Shrugs, it appeared, were ill bred, or at least not for debutantes. 'Babies are messy and they can't talk much.'

'Sufficient reason.'

'You mean I won't enjoy being a mother?'

Once again her hostess gazed at her, evaluating. 'No, I suspect you will.' At last Miss Lily gave a strange smile, almost as if it were made of regret and a dawning hope. 'Children do grow, and a nursemaid is employed for the more boring times. Often the choice of husband determines the degree of joy in your children. But to have only a life of motherhood, tennis parties, fashionable clothes ...'

Her hostess, if she was not mistaken, was goading her. 'What else is there? You said that my life will be ... limited ... when I go home.'

'Colonial life is always limited, Miss Higgs. Australia and your father's New Zealand are far from the centre of the world.' Miss Lily nodded to Jones to serve her more potatoes. 'Perhaps, after a little more time here, you will decide you wish to stay in England.'

Sophie stared at her. How could Miss Lily so carelessly dismiss Australia, New Zealand, the rest of the world? 'If there is a drought in Australia, England will not get her corned beef, or wheat — nor will your cousin receive his income from my father's factories.'

Her hostess looked puzzled. 'I don't quite understand your point.'

'Australia matters! You think England matters more because you are part of it. Australians invented refrigeration — could England even be fed without cool rooms on ships? Moonbeam Joe can tell you if it's going to rain next year, or if a bushfire will race over the hill. He'll never need to learn how to hold his soupspoon. But he matters.' She lifted her chin. 'My father matters more than some ... some duke who doesn't even manage his own estate.'

'I am glad you didn't say "earl",' said Miss Lily dryly.

Sophie flushed. She nearly had.

Miss Lily regarded her in silence. Finally she said, 'You have misunderstood me. Or, more likely, the fault is mine. I did not wish to imply that individuals in England matter more than those in Australia. Your father is indeed extraordinary, and Moonbeam Joe sounds as if he is too, in a different way. Both are possibly more interesting than all those you will find in English drawing rooms next year. But you have missed the point. Your father supplies meat to England. With no markets, your father's fortune would be small. And if the English government says, "Tomorrow we go to war", every country in the Empire will follow.'

Sophie said nothing. Miss Lily smiled. 'I had not expected these months to be an education for me too. Yes, refrigeration has changed the world, and stainless steel may too, and neither was previously part of the way I saw the world. But who is Moonbeam Joe?'

'A stockman.' Sophie considered. 'Theoretically. He doesn't give opinions much, but when he does, everyone listens, even Dad. He's Aboriginal,' she explained. 'He should be manager, but Dad says that the whites wouldn't take him seriously. Dad's probably correct.' She smiled. 'I've probably spent almost as much time with him as with Miss Thwaites or Dad. One of my treats when I was small was to be allowed to go to his place for Johnny cakes and golden syrup. His wife, Bill, made the best Johnny cakes ...'

Miss Lily choked slightly, and dabbed her lips with her napkin. 'Bill?'

Sophie laughed. 'Yes, really, "Bill". Not short for Wilhelmina. Bill used to be a drover's boy. Women can't go droving, of course, but Aboriginal women sometimes go as men. Everyone knows, and everyone carefully never notices. Bill didn't go droving once she married Joe and had children, of course, but she still wore trousers and boots, except when she went to church on Sundays.'

'She sounds ... extraordinary.'

'She was. She died while we were in Sydney, earlier this year. Some sort of fever.'

'You liked her.'

'I loved her,' said Sophie frankly. 'And Moonbeam Joe. He can whistle a lyrebird out to dance. They ... they loved me too. My father loves me, but I'm the only child he has to love. Miss Thwaites too. But Bill and Joe had six sons and two daughters, and loved me anyway.'

Miss Lily looked at her strangely. 'I think you are extremely easy to love, Miss Higgs. It is only the sheer size of your father's fortune that has made you feel insignificant beside it. Thank you, Jones, no more potatoes,' she added. She gazed at Sophie. 'I still believe a girl of your intelligence and energy will find more fulfilment in England. I am even beginning to suspect that the marriage you will find the most fulfilling is one far beyond what you expect. But perhaps one day I should visit Australia too.'

'You would love it,' said Sophie eagerly. 'Green is glorious, of course, but when you look at gold hills it's as if you can see the bones of the country, not just its clothes. You could stay at Thuringa ...' She stopped, suddenly wondering if the property of a corned-beef king was suitable accommodation for the cousin of an earl.

'I would like to visit,' said Miss Lily, her voice rich with unmistakable sincerity. 'Perhaps I even will.' She paused, carefully adjusting her knife and fork, then added slightly too casually, 'I forgot to tell you. I believe the earl has decided to come home for Christmas.'

Jones muffled an exclamation. Sophie glanced up at him, and then at Miss Lily. So Jones had not known that his master was returning. Surely he and Mrs Goodenough should have been told so the household could begin preparations?

How long had it been since the Earl of Shillings was home? And why come now?

Did the earl need her fortune? Was that the true reason why she had been invited here, to be made acceptable and encouraged to want a home in England?

Of course not. She was thinking herself the centre of the universe, just what she had attacked the entire English aristocracy for doing a few minutes ago. If the Earl of Shillings wished for a wealthy wife, there were a hundred eligible American heiresses he could have chosen before now.

'Do you have carol singers in Australia, Miss Higgs?' enquired Miss Lily.

Christmas began with the carol singers — children from the estate who sang in the hall for sixpences and hot spiced apple juice and mince pies and no apparent audience. Miss Lily listened from her drawing room, Sophie from upstairs, the servants presumably at doorways. The singers didn't seem to find it strange; they were happy with the punch, the mince pies and the fruitcake handed out by Jones and the footmen after the performance, and with a white banknote placed smoothly in the collection hat by Jones.

The earl was to arrive late on Christmas Eve — too late for dinner, or, Sophie expected, the usual line-up of the entire staff to welcome him. Possibly the man who had left his privileged position in England had no wish for such formalities.

Excitement sizzled. Three months ago it would have been for his title. Now she wondered if the earl was, just possibly, as fascinating as his cousin. He was old, of course, forty-six, but any man who had spent so long in the mysterious East must have had extraordinary experiences. The earl might also let slip exactly who the woman known as 'Miss Lily' was. But there was little Sophie could do to express her excitement, beyond wiring Miss Thwaites for another Christmas gift from Australia. Even her Christmas Day clothes and hairstyle would be chosen by Miss Lily, arranged by Doris, while Sophie sat and allowed herself to be prepared.

On Christmas Eve Miss Lily and Sophie delivered Christmas gifts to each cottage — or rather two footmen carried in the packages, while Sophie and Miss Lily waited in the carriage, dressed in fur-trimmed hooded cloaks and muffs to keep out the wind. Miss Lily was more silent than usual, almost nervous. Sophie wondered if she feared the earl might find fault with her care of his estate.

Every bundle had been carefully selected as appropriate for each family: beef and a ham for the labourers, with one of the puddings made at the Hall, so many that the scullery ceiling had been hidden by dangling brown cloth balls for the past month. Tenant farmers received a goose, port, a wooden box of crystallised fruit, and rhubarb from the earl's forcing houses, the greenhouses behind the Hall where fruit and flowers were grown out of season. Mr Manning, the earl's agent, received a more superior case of port, and one of claret too, and a box of cigars. Sophie assumed he had already been able to make free with whatever of the estate produce he wanted.

The cottages were all the same: all brick, with two windows each side of the front door, and a double chimney. Behind each were whitewashed mud buildings with thatched roofs that now housed pigs or lambing ewes, with hay stored up above. These had been the labourers' homes before the present earl had had the new brick cottages built.

'Thanks in part to your father's business acumen,' said Miss Lily as she gestured to Sophie to pull down the blinds to lessen the draught in the carriage. 'New cottages, proper drains; the estate employs almost twice the men it used to before the low-lying pastures were drained and we could run better stock.' She smiled. 'I told you there was an obligation to be met.' She hesitated, then added, 'It is also a deep pleasure to be able to discuss this with you. Few young ladies even know that cottages need drains.'

Sophie was silent.

'What are you thinking? Homesick?'

'A little. Remembering the workmen's cottages at Thuringa. My father had them rebuilt too.'

'Your father is a kind man. When someone reminds him to be, I suspect.'

'Samuel said that your family is a kind one too.'

Miss Lily raised a perfect eyebrow, though it was difficult to make out her face clearly within her fur-trimmed hood. 'What are you really thinking?'

'That the workers' houses on the Overhills' place are slab huts. With bark roofs.'

'A landowner is free to spend his income as he wishes.'

'You don't believe that any more than I do,' said Sophie.

'No,' said Miss Lily. 'Nor do I think that you would be happy married into a family that houses its workers in slab huts.' She met Sophie's eyes. 'Mr Malcolm Overhill may also find a wife who notices such things, and speaks of them, deeply disquieting.' She was silent for a while, then added, 'Your experiences in Australia have made you different from English girls. Your intelligence too, of course. More ... tolerant, perhaps, of those who are also different. You are unusual, Miss Higgs.'

'Thank you.' Sophie felt moved, as well as uncomfortable. Was Miss Lily's comment really a compliment? She tried to keep her tone light. 'It's strange, waiting for his lordship to arrive. I feel a bit like St Nicholas is going to visit, leaving an earl in my stocking.'

'A little too substantial for a stocking,' said Miss Lily dryly.

'If St Nicholas can drive his sleigh around the world in a night, he can fit an earl into my stocking.'

'You almost sound as if you still believe in St Nicholas?'

Sophie grinned. 'Of course I do! Or at least, I refuse *not* to believe in him.'

Miss Lily gazed at her from the shadowed corner of the carriage. 'Sometimes I forget how very young you are. Your father is correct. Eighteen is far too young for a woman to choose the man she will be joined to all her life.'

'Aren't you helping girls do just that in their season?' asked Sophie.

Miss Lily nodded. 'I can't change society's rules. The season is when girls of a certain class are expected to find a husband.

All I can do is help them to become more than inconsequential housekeepers or adornments. But as a colonial,' she gave a rueful smile, 'and with all that wonderfully valuable corned beef, you will have suitors for many years yet. Possibly I should not encourage you to make decisions now that will affect your entire life. You are in the unusual situation of being given time to choose. Despite that, ahem, "Understanding" with Mr Overhill ...'

It was the first time Sophie had heard Miss Lily sound uncertain. 'Did you have to make a choice so young?' She still wondered if the 'Miss' was assumed, whether Miss Lily had been married and widowed, or even deserted by her husband. But who could desert Miss Lily?

'Yes,' said Miss Lily softly. 'I had to choose.'

'Do you regret the choice?'

Miss Lily was silent so long that Sophie wondered if she had offended her by prying. At last Miss Lily said, 'I did not think so. But I have been wondering lately if perhaps my choice was wrong. If somehow I could erase ... the past ...' Her voice faded.

Sophie waited. Eventually she asked, 'Why might it have been wrong?'

'No,' said Miss Lily, her voice suddenly desperately sad. 'I had no choice. Not really. But perhaps there was another way. Another life ...'

The carriage stopped. Miss Lily put her hands back into her muff with what almost seemed like relief at the interruption. Evidently there were to be no details revealed of Miss Lily's youth. 'This is the Potters' farmhouse. Alfred Potter and his sister, Miss Amelia Potter. The Potters will expect to entertain us — they keep a drawing room. Miss Potter will serve us elderberry wine, which we shall drink, which is why this is the last of the calls for today, as tonight we shall both have a headache. A girl who is not yet out is expected to avoid wine, but Miss Potter refuses to believe that her innocent elderberries might produce anything so improper as alcohol. I advise eating two slices of her lardy cake, firstly because it is excellent, and secondly to buffer the wine.'

'Yes, Miss Lily,' said Sophie.

Dinner was ... strange. Miss Lily seemed distracted. So, too, was Jones, who even let a drop of red wine stain the tablecloth, a misdemeanour Miss Lily carefully did not see.

'Will you wait up for his lordship, Miss Lily?' When two women dined alone, even a young woman could ask questions.

'Yes. It is a long time since I have seen him.' The voice, the gesture, were as perfect as always, but Sophie sensed a strange tension.

'Shillings is so easy to love. His lordship must be fascinated by the East to spend so much time away.'

'I'm glad you have learned to love Shillings. It is deeply precious to me too. And all who live here.'

Miss Lily seemed to pay attention for the first time that night. Why was she so worried? Perhaps his lordship didn't know about her 'lovely ladies'. Though he must know about Sophie, for he had wired her father. Or had he? Anyone could sign a wire 'Shillings', especially a cousin who helped manage his estate.

'His lordship does know I am here?' she asked cautiously.

'Yes, my dear,' said Miss Lily quietly. 'He is very well aware indeed.'

Chapter 16

Men control the world. The less a man feels he controls in the world outside, the more stringently he will try to control his wife and daughters.

Miss Lily, 1913

Sophie woke early on Christmas morning, even before the maid had freshened the fire. She listened to the noises of the house. The faint clang of the char woman scrubbing the hall — reception floors must be scrubbed even on Christmas morning. Mooing from the dairy, the chatter of dairy maids — cows too must be milked no matter what the day.

At last Doris arrived with tea and biscuits, to conduct the morning ritual of washing, dressing, hairstyling. A white dress; discreet lace; pearls; hair looped in a slightly more complex way than usual.

'Have you seen the earl?' demanded Sophie.

Doris looked uncomfortable. 'No, miss.'

'But he has arrived?' Had he missed his train? Did earls take the train? Perhaps he had a yacht to bring him from France ...

'I can't say, miss.'

Sophie frowned. If the earl had arrived, his valet would have arrived too. No matter how late at night they had got here, his valet would be waiting in the servants' quarters for the bell to ring. Or perhaps an earl's valet slept in an adjoining room ...

Sophie carefully did not run downstairs, was hardly breathless at all when she entered the breakfast room.

Miss Lily sat alone, at her usual place, her face backlit by the winter sun from the window, her dress of blue silk deeply embroidered in an even richer blue, her scarf of cream chiffon shot with threads of silver, her hair, like Sophie's, dressed with an easy complexity to suit Christmas Day.

'Merry Christmas,' she said. Did Sophie imagine a lack of her usual warmth? 'I hope you slept well?'

'Yes, thank you. And merry Christmas! I hope his lordship has arrived safely.'

'His lordship sent a wire,' said Miss Lily, spreading a small section of her toast with strawberry jam. 'He is unable to come to England this year.'

It was a blow: both the news, and the blunt way it had been expressed. Sophie bit back questions, filled a bowl with porridge, then decided to ask them anyway. 'Why?' She deliberately didn't add the civilised extra words.

'You would need to ask him that.' Miss Lily pre-empted her next question. 'You would also need to ask him, not me, why he prefers to spend his time in the East, and not on his estate or taking his seat in the House of Lords.'

'You don't know why?'

'My cousin has discussed it with me, Miss Higgs. I was explaining how you might find the answers to your inelegant questions, rather than alluding to my own ignorance.' The voice was still the most beautifully measured Sophie had ever heard — but she had never heard it cold, till now.

Why the change of mood? Because Sophie was a colonial, and a colonial wasn't worthy of answers? Perhaps it was time that a colonial was not fobbed off. 'Who are you?' Sophie demanded bluntly, glad that breakfast meant that even Jones was not always in the room, hovering behind them.

'I beg your pardon?' The voice was even colder now.

'I can't find you in Debrett's or *Burke's Peerage*, or *Landed Gentry* either. There are people you might be — I mean who might be you. But they are all doing other things. Married, I mean, or living in other houses.'

It had occurred to her, briefly, that Miss Lily might be the earl's mistress, too unsuitable to wed. But one did not install a mistress in the ancestral home and allow her to invite guests, year after year. Nor could she imagine that Miss Lily would allow herself to ever be unsuitable.

Miss Lily's voice remained light, delicate, faintly amused. Too carefully amused? 'What conclusion have you come to?'

'That Miss Lily is a name you have chosen for yourself.'

The elegant eyebrow rose slightly. 'Perspicacious of you.'

Which meant that she was correct. 'And that you exist only here,' continued Sophie slowly.

Miss Lily looked at her without speaking for so long that Sophie put down her spoon.

'Very good,' said Miss Lily at last.

'You mean ... you really are someone else?' She hadn't really believed it — had thrown it into the orderliness of breakfast out of disappointment and anger.

'Of course not,' said Miss Lily calmly, nibbling and tucking toast and jam. 'I am myself. But it's true that I only use the name Miss Lily here, when I receive young girls.' The word turned to 'gels' as she pronounced it. 'The rest of my life is ... different.'

'Are you really the earl's cousin?'

'I am closely related to him, a member of his family. Cousin is not quite the accurate term. I would be grateful, however, if you would not tell the other girls. It is something each may possibly discover herself. Yes, I exist only here, and only from January to April.'

'But I came here in September ...'

'I made the decision to meet you.'

'Because of my father's wealth? The earl's investment?' Sophie was curiously disappointed. The last three months had been the first time she had felt like herself, and not a corned-beef heiress.

'Yes, because of your father, but not because of his wealth, though that has meant the possibility of a true season for Lady Alison.'

'What other reason could you have for making me one of your lovely ladies?'

'Please,' said Miss Lily, and this time there was iron in the quiet words, 'do not use that term.'

'I'm sorry. But where do you usually live? Who *are* you? I don't understand ...'

Miss Lily stood. Somehow Jones was back in the room, ready to usher her out. 'It is not necessary for you to understand. Miss Higgs, I know you will not like this, but I think it best that you attend a finishing school after all. Doris will go with you. You may spend a week with the other girls, to make their acquaintance, and then ...'

A slap on the face would have been less shocking. Sophie forced her voice not to tremble. 'Because I ask too many questions? Or because I have guessed the answers?'

'I might reply that it is because you begin your sentences with "because", and make demands of your hostess.'

Sophie stared at her. To be dismissed like this ... Surely Miss Lily didn't mean it. She didn't want to go to school! But the true devastation came from Miss Lily's desire to see her leave. Suddenly she realised how much Miss Lily meant to her — not just Miss Lily's insights, or her kindness to a colonial.

She had thought Miss Lily liked her. Truly liked her. She had been wrong.

'The true reason is that, on reflection, you will ... not fit ... with the company of the other girls, or not yet. Three months at the school will remedy that.'

It was as if the idyll of the last months had shattered, a toy made of sugar that she had played with, believing it to be real. Miss Lily couldn't really be telling her to leave! 'Miss Lily, please! I'm sorry. I'll stop asking questions. Please don't send me away!'

Miss Lily glanced out the window. 'It will be a wet walk to church,' she said. 'I think we should take the carriage.'

She cried, up in her room, as soon as they had returned from church. She had at least managed the Christmas ceremony dry-eyed. She cried not just for the loss of Shillings, which she realised she had come to love, but even more for the loss of her hostess's conversation, which had not just opened windows onto the world but washed the ones she had already known too, so that life looked clearer, different because it was more distinct.

She cried because Miss Lily did not want her to stay, and that was the hardest to bear of all.

And then she dried her eyes, washed her face, and lay for half an hour with a wet flannel upon it. Because if Miss Lily was not the friend and protector she had assumed, then Sophie refused to let her see her anguish.

She had been wrong. Miss Lily had enjoyed her mistakes because they *were* mistakes, the inelegancies of a colonial. Miss Lily did not dislike her, but neither did she like her enough to help smooth over any difficulties Sophie might have with three young aristocratic women. Sophie had been too used to having her father's money buy her whatever friendship she wished to have. Miss Lily had even warned her at their first meeting. Friendship cannot be bought.

At last she rose and rang the bell for Doris to dress her for luncheon.

She and Miss Lily opened gifts after luncheon: an almost silent meal, Miss Lily for once offering neither advice nor conversation. For the first time it was as if she, too, were hiding strong emotion. Sophie considered pleading to stay, apologising yet again for discourtesy. But if this was a punishment for defiance, the temerity to argue would not help her case.

The drawing-room fire snickered. Down in the servants' hall the servants, too, celebrated Christmas, leaving the two women more entirely alone than at any time during the past months. Even Jones was absent.

Sophie's first gift was a natural wool jumper, still rich in lanolin, and undyed, knitted by Miss Thwaites, the wool spun by old Mrs Amber, who was married to one of the Thuringa stockmen. Sophie breathed in its scent of sheep, of lanolin, smelled the shearing shed again, and home. Wool protected from the heaviest downpour, though it tended to stretch if you let it get too wet. She wondered how it would cope in

England's constant drizzle. The gift left her crying — just a little — for her home. She tilted her head, so Miss Lily would not see the tears. The cicadas would be singing, the bushfire smoke smudging the horizon. She hoped that Moonbeam Joe was exercising Timber.

The jumper's shearing-shed scent brought the memory of Malcolm too. She had sent him hand-hemmed and embroidered handkerchiefs, on the advice of Miss Lily. A purchased gift would be inappropriate on many levels. He had sent her a book of Robert Burns's poems.

'I expect his mother suggested it,' said Miss Lily dryly.

Sophie opened the flyleaf. *Ever yours, Malcolm.* The words were perfect, loving but not improper. They could have come from a textbook on what to write to a girl with whom one had an Understanding, not an engagement.

Her father had sent a sapphire brooch, large as a bauble on the Christmas tree. She looked hesitantly at Miss Lily, the open box in her hand.

'I expect he bought it himself,' said Miss Lily, and suddenly her voice was gentle again. 'Miss Thwaites would have chosen something a little ... smaller. He must love you very much, my dear. In my experience men rarely select gifts; usually they merely arrange for their purchase. Wear it sometimes with your friends. Gifts of love should never be rejected.'

Miss Thwaites had found and sent what Sophie had hoped were the perfect gifts for both Miss Lily and the earl: two small paintings of blue hills and drooping gum trees, simply framed.

'The painter is Australian, but he studied in Paris,' said Sophie hesitantly as Miss Lily opened hers. 'It's not of Thuringa, but it could be. Our trees have white trunks like that, though the soil isn't as red ...'

'It is beautiful,' said Miss Lily. 'I will treasure it.'

The words were perfect too. Sophie saved them to use again, when any gift was presented to her. But she doubted, now, that they were true. There was no reason for Miss Lily to treasure a gift from a colonial.

'This is for you, from me, my dear,' said Miss Lily, passing her a rectangle wrapped in parchment silk. Sophie opened it carefully, then gazed at the contents: two notebooks, covered in pale yellow silk.

'You will need to make detailed notes during the season,' said Miss Lily. 'Each person you meet, their background, their likes and dislikes, and later, when you are a hostess yourself, what meals you have served them, so you don't repeat the menus, unless they particularly like a certain dish. The smaller book will fit in a concealed pocket in your skirt, for easy reference.'

They were perfectly appropriate gifts, and deeply impersonal. Sophie forced herself to smile as warmly as her hostess. 'They are beautiful. Exactly what I need, as always, Miss Lily.'

She was the rich Miss Higgs: perfectly dressed, about to attend a select school, then meet the Queen, and celebrate a London season.

It was the emptiest Christmas of her life.

Chapter 17

Imagine a person with every right stripped away: no right to participate in the way their world is run, no right to live with whom they want or even to borrow money to buy a house or sign a lease for a safe place to live. That is the state of every woman in England now.

You would think that person lacked any power at all. This is why women's power has always been in some way secret. And some powers are among the most secret of all.

Miss Lily, 1914

The Prinzessin Hannelore ('You will call her Prinzessin,' instructed Miss Lily) and Miss Emily Carlyle arrived on the mid-morning train, either together or on friendly terms by the time the coachman opened the door for them — the prinzessin first of course — at the house.

Sophie watched them unseen from up on the balcony, ready to retreat into her room as they came upstairs. As she was not the hostess, it would not be appropriate for her to meet them till after they had been greeted by Miss Lily. She was still in her room, trying to memorise the rules of precedence and apply them to the names marked in pencil for her in Debrett's, when she heard the voices outside that told her that Lady Alison Venables had arrived also.

They were to all meet at tea, and so at five minutes to four exactly she walked downstairs in a soft, champagne-coloured wool skirt and fitted jacket, riesling silk blouse, her pearls, and high-buttoned boots a shade darker than her skirt, her hair plaited and tied in a loose knot behind, making her feel like a schoolgirl. But she appreciated the subtlety of Doris's suggestion. She was the social inferior of these girls. Best to suggest it with her hairstyle, she thought enviously, like a puppy crouching before a bigger dog before it joined the pack.

She counted to four before she opened the door. This entrance must be perfect, to show Miss Lily, the three girls, and herself, that she too could achieve perfection, if she chose.

Three girls' faces turned: the prinzessin's round and red-cheeked, the smile friendly, the eyes both amused and intelligent; Miss Carlyle both slightly porcine as well as clear-faced and lovely, as though a pig had learned its beauty secrets well; Lady Alison sitting slightly apart from the others, a blonde in pale blue cashmere, with a narrow head and long neck, totally still except for her fingers, which plucked at her cuticles.

Miss Lily gestured to Sophie to take the final seat as she made the introductions. She watched the four of them for a moment, then began to pour the tea, each gesture as fluid and direct as the liquid placing itself inside the cups.

Jones handed around crumpets, slices of fruitcake, and asparagus spears (forced in steaming manure pits on the estate) wrapped in bread and butter, then left. Sophie ate an asparagus roll; too much danger that a crumpet would drip or a cake crumble. Lady Alison's hands worked on a single crumpet, nibbled but never finished. The prinzessin and Miss Carlyle finished two each with dispatch, and neither dripped nor made crumbs.

'I hope the Channel crossing was smooth, Prinzessin.' Miss Lily ate a cherry from her piece of fruitcake with her silver cake fork.

'Lord George's yacht was most interesting.' The prinzessin reached for a third crumpet. 'The journey here was interesting also.'

'The park is looking beautiful.' Lady Alison's voice was tentative. Sophie glanced at her. She's as scared as I am, she thought. No, I'm nervous. She's scared.

What could make a girl from such an impeccable background scared?

'Do we have to make small talk?' Miss Carlyle dabbed at the butter on her lip with her napkin, then placed it precisely on the table beside her. 'We have less than four months here. I'd hoped for more than pleasantries.'

Sophie forced herself to take another asparagus roll, and not let her surprise show. What did Miss Carlyle mean by 'more than pleasantries'? The politics of which Sophie was supposed to be so ignorant? And was ignorant, she admitted to herself, although she at least now knew her ignorance existed.

'You've been in the house for less than two hours.' Miss Lily's voice was light. 'A few days to get to know each other, for you to know me, is not unreasonable. Besides, Miss Higgs will only be here a week. I hoped you would enjoy each other's company, so that she does not feel such a stranger when the season begins.'

'Then Miss Higgs won't be —' Miss Carlyle stopped.

The prinzessin glanced at Sophie, then at Miss Lily, with a final look that might have been one of warning at Miss Carlyle. She leaned forward. Her voice was light. 'Miss Higgs, you must excuse us. Miss Carlyle and I have discovered we share a most deep interest in politics with our hostess, but we mustn't bore everyone else with our preoccupations.'

She's used to making awkward situations go away, thought Sophie. She knows exactly why I'm here too: so that Lady Alison can have her season paid for. Miss Carlyle doesn't. Across the room Lady Alison lifted a hand to her lips, then forced it back into her lap.

Sophie felt she was trying to put together the jigsaw of European politics again. Something was happening in that room, but she didn't have enough pieces to work it out. She thought of the pieces she did have: a hostess who didn't quite exist; three girls of rank who most certainly did; her own three months of lessons.

Lessons, she thought. They are here for lessons too. Political lessons, the sort Miss Lily believed even young women needed. *Some* young women. Lessons that would make them part of Miss Lily's network of friends, helping each other understand and influence the male world.

It fitted. But it still did not explain the secrecy.

The silence had gone on too long. 'I'm interested in politics too,' said Sophie calmly. 'But entirely too ignorant. You would have a boring afternoon instructing me.'

Miss Lily met her glance. And no, thought Sophie, I'm not imagining approval there, or warmth. Miss Lily smiled. 'Shall we play a game, then, instead of discussing pleasantries or politics? A game for a cold afternoon by the fire.'

'Your English games are most interesting.' The prinzessin's tone was pleasant. 'I have played charades many times at home.' She turned to Miss Carlyle. 'I think I have told you that my governess was English?'

Miss Carlyle remained silent. Good attempt, Prinzessin, thought Sophie, but Miss Carlyle is annoyed. She'd hoped for something, and now for some reason she won't get it till I'm gone. But why not begin political discussions now? Why bother about boring a mere colonial? Was this, too, part of the secrecy, and those secrets could not begin until the temporary visitor had left?

Miss Lily laid her hands quietly on her knees. They were curiously ugly hands at rest, big-knuckled. Sophie realised she had rarely seen them bare of gloves, or unsoftened by the fall of long lace cuffs. Miss Lily's voice was low, amused. 'I hope you like this game as well, Prinzessin. I want each of you to shut your eyes. Imagine a swan, gliding through the water.'

Emily Carlyle again: 'A swan? Why should I —?'

Miss Lily held up a hand, so graceful you hardly noticed it was too large for beauty. 'Because I wish it. Because you are guests here at the request of my friends, who have asked that I share some of the skills that have made their own lives possible. You wish to comment further?'

Miss Carlyle was silent.

'Then imagine you are that swan. Gliding, gliding. Now, place your right foot exactly behind your left ... a little further, if you please, Prinzessin. That is correct. Place your hands to either side, level with your waist. Think of the swan again, gliding, gliding.

Now I want you to stand, in one slow gliding movement, your hands flowing down at the same time your body rises. Now ...'

Sophie blinked, then obediently shut her eyes again. It worked — or felt like it worked. Somehow she had risen to her feet as though she too floated on the water.

'Now sit. Arms rise as your body falls. Again. Again. Again. That is quite good.'

The voice was warm, approving. 'Open your eyes. Now smile. Not a grin, Miss Higgs. Just a smile. A smile for the world, because you are happy, because anyone who talks to you will be happy too. Not a smile that says, "You are a joke." A smile that gives, not takes. Imagine something you love — a puppy, perhaps. Imagine the puppy and smile.'

Sophie glanced at Miss Carlyle. Apparently she, at least, found a puppy worthy of a smile. Even Lady Alison was smiling for the first time since she had arrived. Was that why Miss Lily had asked them to play a game? To relax the tension in the room?

'Good. Now we will rise and smile and walk. But you are not walking across a room. You are a swan, a swan. One foot directly in front of the other, so that you sway, but your hands are floating on the water while your body moves ... again ... again ... again ...'

'Now sit. Let your body flow down. Now let each part of your body rest. Your hands are heavy. They fall, so. Your head is held up like a puppet's, held up by the sky. Now stand again ... and no, Miss Higgs, your hips should not sway. Your body sways. From now on this is how you will walk, and sit, each foot aligned with the other, your hands and body floating on the water ...'

An hour. Two hours. They sat. They walked. They talked like floating statues. I am a swan, thought Sophie vaguely ...

She was also hungry.

At last Miss Lily let them go. Sophie felt dazed; by the way the others blinked as they came into the hall she suspected they were dazed as well.

Was that what the others were here for? Lessons in grace? She walked, swan-like, along the hall and up the stairs. Was

Miss Lily creating perfect debutantes here? Girls who would live out the social life she eschewed? Sophie had a sudden vision of the four of them, swan-like in ball gowns, floating through a fairy palace.

'Doris, ring for tea, will you? And scones too, whatever Mrs Goodenough has. I'm too hungry to wait for dinner.'

'I'll bring it up myself, miss. They'll be busy down there.'

The tray had scones. It also bore four cups, not the usual two. Sophie glanced at Doris. Was this a hint to ask the other girls to share it, to make the most of her time with them instead of drinking tea with her maid?

Laughter came from the corridor, Miss Carlyle's and the prinzessin's. So they *had* known each other before. It would be an intrusion to ask them to join her.

She thought of Lady Alison, sitting in the armchair furthest from them all. She left the tray in her room, and knocked on the third door along from hers. 'It's Sophie Higgs.'

No answer. Servants just walked in, but servants weren't really supposed to be there, just their services. She knocked again.

'Come in.'

Sophie opened the door and stood in the doorway. Lady Alison sat by the window. Her hands were empty, nor was there any sign of her maid. 'I ... I just wondered if you were feeling sufficiently swan-like.'

'Quite.' Lady Alison gave the smile they had all perfected downstairs.

Sophie forced herself not to bite her lip, to keep the smile in place. 'I'm feeling more like a leg of lamb by now. You know, to be served up on a platter with mint sauce.'

'Or like a tin of corned beef on the shelf?'

Sophie froze, the smile still in place. 'I'm sorry, I'm interrupting you. I will see you at dinner.'

'Yes,' said Lady Alison.

Sophie closed the door.

Chapter 18

All things are ephemeral. A flower changes from one minute to another, from the bud's opening to the petals' fall. A woman's youth is more ephemeral than a man's. But grace, compassion and insight will last all your lives.

Miss Lily, 1914

Sophie had a bath before dinner. To wash away the scent of corned beef, to wrap herself in the perfume of gardenia and roses from the bath salts Doris scented the water with. She waited till the maids had lugged up the china bath with its faded rose pattern and placed it by the fire, and brought bucket after bucket of hot water up the stairs, poured them in and swished the water about till the salts were dissolved, checking the temperature. All before unbuttoning Sophie's dress, and stripping off the chemise, unlacing the corset and pulling down petticoat, stockings and then the final underwear, pale pink silk embroidered with roses.

'White,' insisted Miss Thwaites, but Sophie had laughed.

'Who'll see it?'

'The laundry woman. Your maid.'

'But the laundry woman won't know it's mine. She'll think it's yours,' and she had giggled at the look on Miss Thwaites's face.

She would write to Miss Thwaites tomorrow before breakfast. Dear Miss Thwaites.

She loved Miss Thwaites. She realised that she loved Miss Lily too, despite her rejection, in some way she couldn't define. She had never realised love could come in so many flavours.

In spite of Lady Alison's insult, she wanted to stay, even more deeply than before.

One of the downstairs maids entered, puffing and red-faced, with more hot water. Doris arranged the screen to keep out draughts, then placed small apple-wood twigs on the fire. It flared up, sending fresh heat through the room. Sophie took up the soap — Shillings had delicious soap — and the big round sponge and began to slowly wash her legs.

'Will I wash your back, miss?'

'I can manage, thank you, Doris.' Doris always asked, and Sophie always refused. Doris hovered anyway, folding today's clothes to be washed or sponged or laid in warm bran tonight to freshen and remove stains while Sophie was dining, checking that no hems needed stitching, the buttons were firm, there were no pulled threads in the stockings.

'Doris?'

'Yes, Miss Higgs?'

'Did your sister teach you all this?'

'Yes, miss.'

Sophie thought of Miss Lily's maid, black-garbed, eyes down, as swan-like as if she had been practising for twenty years. Which Sophie supposed she might have been.

'She's much older than you.'

'Twenty-four years, miss. There's fourteen of us, all girls.'

'Good heavens.'

'Grandpa worked on the estate till he went off to war in India with the earl. Never came back. It was long before I was born. But his lordship looked after Gran, let her keep our cottage. Mum married one of the Rowbottoms, but Miss Lily said she weren't having a Rowbottom in the house and told Enid to change it to Green when she came here. Miss Lily found positions for all of us girls as we became old enough to work. I was maid here afore — before — you came, to learn the gentry ways.' She ventured a smile. 'I was that glad to give up scrubbing, Miss Higgs.'

'Fourteen ladies' maids in one family?' She tried to think how fourteen children fitted into a cottage, two rooms up and two down. But of course the girls would have left home as they turned ten or twelve to start work.

'No — Mary's a nursemaid, miss. Gladys is cook–housekeeper to the rector. She married Mr Higgins, who does for the rector too. They have two children. The rector is ever so good: our Dorcas took over while Gladys was nursing, but the rector let the babies stay in the kitchen and everything. There's not many as would do that, miss. Nor be as kind as the earl and Miss Lily neither.'

This was a kind family.

'Did you want to be a lady's maid?'

'I like pretty things, miss. I always have. Soft things like silk and stockings. Miss Lily has a French lady come and teach us the latest styles. She subscribes to magazines too, miss. One of them's in French but it doesn't matter, because we just need to see the fashions. More hot water, miss?'

Sophie thought longingly of lying in scented hot water forever — or at least the next two hours. But the dressing gong would sound soon. Even as she thought it the boom sounded hollowly downstairs.

She stood, then let Doris dry her. Doris had laid out an evening dress — muslin, not silk, with a slightly higher neck than she had worn for the evening before, and in white. Lord Buckmaster was correct: white didn't suit her. She wanted to outshine every girl there. She had money, beauty.

But she was also their social inferior, and must not outshine them.

Stockings, clean underwear, fresh stays, silk evening slippers with a white rosette on each toe. Sophie raised her arms to allow the new clothes to be placed on her body, then sat and lifted one leg then the other for stockings to be slipped on and fastened, then evening slippers, then her opal necklace.

She moved to the dressing table so Doris could dress her hair, sweeping it back, brushing it over and over to bring out the shine, with drops of lavender oil on the brush, then pinning it behind her head in an artful sweep that looked elegant but was still 'down'. She was not to wear it fully 'up' till she had been presented.

Presented by the grandmother of that cold girl, presumably even colder than her granddaughter.

Sophie stared at her image in the mirror. Miss Lily had warned her that corned beef could not be forgotten. Why was she risking repeated humiliations? Would having a London season really make so much difference to her life with Malcolm?

Sophie hesitated. She had written dutifully to Malcolm every week. She loved him. Except now when she thought of him it was always at Thuringa ...

For the first time in her life she thought of what her life might be if she didn't marry at all. Not Miss Thwaites's life, forced to earn a living, but Miss Lily's. Whatever Miss Lily's life was like when she wasn't at Shillings, Sophie was sure it was full, and ... *lived* ... that was the word. Miss Lily lived her own life, not part of a husband's.

These had been the richest months of Sophie's life. And now they were ending, not just because she had to leave, but because she had been supplanted by three other 'lovely ladies'.

She rose, swan-like. 'Thank you, Doris. My hair looks perfect, as always.'

'Thank you, Miss Higgs.' Doris curtseyed, a flush of pleasure on her face. Sophie proceeded, swan-like, down the stairs.

It was strange to see so many places set along the table. The room had too much pale froth of dresses. It didn't suit the panelling, though the portraits of the earl and his ancestors on the walls remained impassive.

Turtle soup was served. Sophie had played with giant turtles at the zoo when she was small, ridden the cumbersome animals. They smelled. The soup didn't. Poor turtles, she thought. Reduced to a scentless soup.

Salmon replaced the soup, then chicken in a pale lobster sauce. Female food, thought Sophie. Men liked roasts they could carve.

Sophie let the talk flow over her. At first it was frothy like the food: gossip about mutual friends she had never heard of. Miss Carlyle had accepted the need for pleasantries, it seemed. She had been to a wedding since she had returned from school, and somehow the others all knew each person who'd been there;

they wanted details of the dresses, the groomsmen, the lace. The prinzessin had spent Christmas at a château on the Loire. Once again everyone but Sophie nodded at the names, knew about the mother of the hostess ... 'So sad to hear of her passing. She will be missed,' said Miss Lily.

Only Lady Alison contributed little. But even she, it was evident, knew the people, though she limited her remarks to 'Swansdown trimming, Prinzessin? How lovely. It must have looked so beautiful with her hair.'

The conversation changed with the meat course. Miss Carlyle especially seemed glad to see the gossip go. She sounded well informed about the defeat of Turkey at the hands of the Bulgarians, the declaration of Albania's independence at peace talks at Constantinople.

'My great-uncle is most pleased at this,' said the prinzessin, looking up placidly from her chicken.

'Who is your great-uncle, Prinzessin?' risked Sophie.

'His Majesty Kaiser Wilhelm,' put in Miss Lily quietly.

Oh.

'I am most interesting to hear what the English think,' said the prinzessin. 'My great-uncle too.'

Somehow Sophie doubted that the German Kaiser would care what Australians thought. But at least now she could take part in the conversation. 'Why is the Emperor pleased about Albania's independence? Prinzessin,' she added to make the blunt question more polite.

'Because it makes war less likely. If the Balkan states keep their quarrels among themselves, it lessens the threat of war between our countries.' Sophie had a sudden image of a baby German prinzessin being washed in a bath of Balkan states, then wrapped in a towel of flags. Corned-beef princesses were kept from the family business; this girl knew a great deal about hers.

'Our countries?'

'England and Germany, Miss Higgs. And Australien too, of course. I am sorry, I do not know the English word for your country ...'

'It is Australia, Prinzessin,' said Miss Lily. 'Almost the same.'

'Ah, thank you. I apologise, Miss Higgs. I have not come across the name in England before. But you must know how close the prospect of war is between the empires. Any lessening of tensions, or even deflecting of them, must please all people of sensitivity.'

'War between England and Germany?' Not only had it not occurred to her, but she was sure that even her father did not expect it, or he would never have let her come to England. 'But ... but proper countries, *big* countries, don't go to war against each other.' The newspapers hadn't even mentioned the possibility of war between England and Germany. Wars are fought in places like South Africa, thought Sophie, or the Crimea.

The prinzessin looked at her almost with amusement; there was the merest flicker of contempt from Miss Carlyle. Lady Alison pretended interest in her bread.

'Again I beg your pardon, Miss Higgs,' said the prinzessin. 'But I believe they can.'

'Why do you think England and Germany are increasing their armies, Miss Higgs, if not for war? And the Tsar too.' Miss Carlyle's tone was not as gentle as the prinzessin's.

'I ... I didn't realise they were. Nothing has been said in any of the newspapers I've read.' She wished at once that she hadn't said it. All the other diners glanced at her, then politely looked away.

'Newspapers never print what really matters,' remarked Miss Carlyle. The words 'to those who matter' echoed, even though unsaid.

'I think it must be comfortable,' said the prinzessin gently. 'To live so far away. If war comes, it may not touch your country or those you love.'

'If England goes to war, then Australia will fight too. We did in the Boer War.'

'Indeed you did.' Miss Lily smiled along the table. 'Miss Higgs has only a few evenings here. There will be plenty of other nights to discuss politics.'

Sophie flushed. Nights without the ignorant colonial? Suddenly she was all too aware of how little she had really learned from the papers, how much greater had been the depth of understanding in that one 'history lesson' from Miss Lily.

Maybe you needed to live in this world, as the others did, to understand it.

Her head ached. For the first time since she'd left Sydney she felt alone and very far from home, but too near to its shadows too. How dare that girl opposite taunt her about corned beef? Perhaps she even knew about her mother. At least my mother was beautiful, thought Sophie. People loved her. Who loves you, Lady Alison?

Someone was saying something. Sophie forced her mind back.

'Miss Higgs,' repeated Miss Lily. 'The prinzessin asked you about kangaroos.'

'I am most interesting in kangaroos,' said the prinzessin kindly. 'Also wildlife of all kinds, birds most especially. Do you have emus on your estate, Miss Higgs?'

'Yes.' She grasped at the change of subject. 'I saw an emu eat a pair of pliers once.'

'Pliers?' The smile was perfectly in place on Miss Carlyle's lips.

'They're tools, for fencing. The stockmen use them at Thuringa. That's my family's property.'

'I'm sorry. I thought ...' Miss Carlyle broke off.

That I lived above a corned-beef factory. But she didn't say the words.

'What is your Thuringa like?' The prinzessin sounded genuinely interested.

'About twenty square miles. It stretches along a river — there's no other water except what we pump up to the water troughs.' She smiled at the memory. 'There are as many windmills as trees in some places. But 'roos can live where it's too dry for cattle, and emus too. There used to be enormous mobs of emus when I was young — hundreds, maybe thousands, like a flood of feathers so you couldn't even see the ground. But that was in the drought;

they were travelling thousands of miles just to get to water. Now it's rained we just see one or two at a time.'

'How long did the drought last?' Miss Carlyle's voice had lost its contempt. She looked at Sophie with what Sophie was starting to recognise was her usual intensity.

'About twenty years. I was six when it finally rained. My governess says I demanded to know when the rain would stop; I'd never known more than a few minutes of rain at a time.'

The whole table was looking at her — at her, she realised, not at the daughter of corned beef. They seemed genuinely fascinated.

'It must have meant great hardship,' said the prinzessin.

'I suppose it must. I've never really thought about it before.' She knew cattle prices were lower now, and had a vague idea that her father had bought cheaply because property prices were low in the drought, and chosen Thuringa because its river frontage ensured a supply of beef for his factories. But had food prices been higher in the drought? She suddenly realised she had no idea of the cost of a loaf of bread, here or in Australia. Bread simply was, and rolls, and toast.

'Scarcity of supply is always hardest on the poor.' Miss Carlyle leaned forward in her eagerness. 'The Corn Laws created poverty where none need have existed.'

'The Corn Laws?'

'The tax on imported grains, on flour, from 1815 to 1846. The tax helped large landowners, but meant their farmworkers starved.' Miss Carlyle looked at her levelly. 'Your country was settled by starvation, Miss Higgs. The starving farmworkers during the height of the effects of the Corn Laws, the Scottish families turned out during the Highland Clearances, the starving Irish after the Potato Famine — did you know that even at its worst Ireland still exported food?' She shook her head. 'Politicians knowingly let people starve simply to make fortunes for themselves and others.'

Her father had joked once that childhood hunger had stunted him; he'd never had the food to grow tall. What had caused poverty in New Zealand? She had never even thought of wider causes of poverty before.

'You look solemn, Miss Higgs,' said the prinzessin.

'I was thinking of my father. He is so very proud of feeding people,' she added apologetically.

For a second she wished the words had remained unsaid. She had just put a can of corned beef on the table, symbolically at any rate. But the tension at the table seemed to relax a little, not increase.

'Feeding people is a most honourable industry,' said the prinzessin. 'My cousin married a Krupps heiress — not an honourable industry at all, making guns and armoured war machines. Of course one does not mention the connection ...'

'You just have,' murmured Lady Alison. They were the first words she had said for the past half-hour.

'Here we can speak freely,' said the prinzessin. 'Can we not, Miss Lily?'

'Of course.'

'Your father must be happy,' said the prinzessin kindly, 'with his useful factories and his Thuringa. It makes me all the more interesting to see this Australia some day.'

'But what about your home, Prinzessin? I'm sorry — when I think of Germany it's all snow and fairy castles. I know I am ignorant about Europe. As you say, we are very far away.'

'There is snow and there are castles. I am not believing in the fairies, though one of my cousins says she has seen a troll. But that was in Denmark. Perhaps it is different there.' It was hard to know if the prinzessin was making a joke or not.

'You live in a castle?'

'I live in an apartment in my brother's castle. My brother believes you must be cold to be strong, so it is a cold castle. You sit close to the stove and breathe the smoke, or you sit away from the stove and be cold. Either way you cough.' It was definitely a joke. 'So I go to Switzerland to the Ladies' Academy and I meet Miss Carlyle.'

So both of you were 'finished' before you came here, thought Sophie. Presumably that was the academy Miss Lily was sending her to. Was Lady Alison's family too poor to send her to school in Switzerland? But poverty was relative. Perhaps she was too timid to venture so far.

'Miss Carlyle also comes from a castle. But it is a warm castle and a very pretty one.'

'And very new. My grandfather built it. He made his money in soap.'

Their eyes met. The soap might be a generation away from her corned beef, but it was still trade, castle or not. And Miss Carlyle was admitting it at this table. It was almost a gesture of friendship.

'I am liking a new castle,' said the prinzessin. 'I am thinking only a new castle can be warm.' She pronounced it 'varm', but it was attractive.

And Miss Lily smiled, the firelight flickering behind her as Jones ushered a footman in with more apple wood for the fire.

It was late when they left the library, self-consciously walking like swans. The after-dinner coffee had almost tasted good. I could like it, thought Sophie sleepily as she trailed up the stairs with the other girls.

'Good night,' she called as the prinzessin opened her door along the hall.

'Gute Nacht. It was most interesting about the emus. I am hoping one day to see them, perhaps. It sounds warm, your country, too.'

'I would love to show you Thuringa.' To her surprise she meant it.

To her further surprise, the prinzessin's smile in response seemed real. 'That would be most interesting. And warm, I have no doubt.'

A talent for making commoners feel at ease, learned in her childhood or at finishing school? Yes, but there was something else there too. The prinzessin, like Sophie, had come there for a reason, and not just to escape the draughts in her castle.

'Good night.' Miss Carlyle, too, sounded friendly.

Sophie turned to Lady Alison, but she had already closed her door.

Chapter 19

Cooks study cooking. Politicians receive guidance on their way to prime ministership. But there are no schools for the most essential part of life.

I decided to remedy that.

Miss Lily, 1914

FLANDERS, 12 JULY 1917

The moon looked like a yellow rosette pinned to the sky above the crumbling farmhouse walls: a smudged rosette, dimmed by the smoke from the guns. The dog made a small noise in its sleep, half a whimper, breaking the night's silence.

No, not silence, thought Sophie. The front lines were never quiet. The guns' vibration came up through your shoes, through every surface you touched. Shellfire still hiccupped, but there had been no crossfire for half an hour perhaps, ever since it grew dark, too dark for her to look at her watch, an enamelled one on a gold chain from her father. 'Do you think they've gone?' she whispered.

'The Huns? Or our men?'

'Either. Both.'

'No. This is ground to be taken. Once they take it, it will be secured — which means searching it minutely for the enemy, for trip wires, for bombs.'

'How can taking a ruined farmhouse matter?'

'Ask the generals that. The bloodiest battles of this war have

152

been back and forth over a few hundred yards of mud and barbed wire. They'll be digging out bones for hundreds of years when all this is over. If it ever is.'

'So both sides are waiting for daylight?'

'Or moonlight, if the clouds clear.'

'Oh. When does the moon rise tonight?'

'In about three hours. Early morning. Sophie, keep on talking.'

'Why?'

'Because whatever happens I will only ever have this one night with you. If we get out of here, I will go one way and you another. If we don't ...'

'There will be other times. You have to believe that. Even an after-the-war-is-over time.'

He shrugged next to her in the sooty darkness. 'Four years ago I didn't believe in dying, at least I didn't believe dying was for me. I'd been in my first trench for seven minutes when I suddenly realised: That could be me.'

'What made you realise?'

'A chap put his head up to investigate a noise. Suddenly there was no head. Just red and white. Not even blood, just bits of brain and bone. And I thought, That will be me.'

'Could be. Not will.' She touched the dog's head gently, for the comfort of its fur. 'We should give it a name. Charlie.'

'Why Charlie? He's probably French.'

'You said he was Spanish.'

'Spain's a long way from here. They have sheepdogs like this in France and Flanders too. Well, dog, what do you think of Charlie as a name?'

The dog opened its eyes. It lifted its head hopefully, in case there was chicken.

'See? He knows it's his name now. Don't you, Charlie?'

'Ftth,' said the dog.

'The blood's dry,' said Sophie. 'Maybe he was hit by a cart, not shot at all.' She didn't add, 'Maybe he will live now.' If they died tonight, Charlie might too.

He scratched the dog's ears automatically. 'I've been thinking about what you said — that war is like a game of football. Would I kill the Kaiser?'

'Would you?'

He replied slowly, 'Would it make any difference? One kaiser is replaced by another. One general by another too.'

'So individuals don't have power?' asked Sophie flatly, still stroking Charlie. 'I don't believe it.'

'No, of course they do. But sometimes things grow too large to be contained or even changed by any one person.'

'The Kaiser could stop the war.'

'Not,' he said dryly, 'if he were dead.'

A mouse ran across the floor, hesitated as it smelled them, then darted back to its corner. Stupid mouse, thought Sophie. A war unlike any other is swooping across your world, and you are worried by the smell of two humans and a dog.

'If the Kaiser tried to stop the war … if he said, "No more. Put down your guns", it might mean even more killing. He might face a rebellion in his own country, like the rebellions in Russia. The Tsar lost his throne because of an army mutiny. Do you think the Kaiser's generals would obey?'

'They would have once,' Sophie said slowly. 'Now … I don't know. But it would be worth trying. Anything would be worth trying to stop all this.'

'You sound like a pacifist. Don't you think this war is worth fighting? Do you think that every man out there,' he nodded into the darkness, 'has died for nothing?'

She shivered at his bitterness. 'I have a friend who says that the Kaiser might have stopped the war, way back at the beginning.'

'The German friend who sends you letters in wartime, or the friend whose grandmother is a duchess?'

'Friendship is friendship, despite boundaries,' said Sophie. 'Miss Lily taught me that.'

Chapter 20

Practise delight in small things. It disarms those who might
otherwise worry that you may, indeed, understand what goes on
around you, in spite of being a woman. But it will also make you
happier. A woman's life, at every station in society, involves long
periods of boredom that we can rarely choose to temper. A delight in
small things will make this easier.

Miss Lily, 1914

SHILLINGS HALL, 1914

It snowed the night before Sophie was due to leave. She woke up
to silence.

No, not complete silence. Faintly she could hear the rustle
of a maid's apron in the hall, a voice from the kitchens. But all
sounds from outside had vanished.

Doris must have slipped in already. The fire glowed with fresh
apple wood. The room was warm. She ran to the window and
parted the curtains.

The world was white, with strange mounds of green and
brown.

Snow. Just like on a Christmas card. Real snow, the first she
had ever seen.

Shillings had given her a present for her last day there. Who
could have guessed white could be as bright as that?

'Miss, I'm so sorry, I didn't mean to be late.'

Doris placed a cup of tea on the bedside table along with a
plate of wheaten biscuits.

'You're not, I'm early. Doris, look, it's snowed!'

'Yes, miss. Horrid cold stuff it is too. Snow damp gets into everything, my mam says. I'll bring your hot water up, miss.'

'Not yet. Help me dress — something warm. I want to go out there. I'll bathe when I get back.'

'Into the snow, miss?' Sophie might have suggested dancing naked in the lane. She realised Doris might be worried about packing damp clothes. There wouldn't be time to dry anything before they had to leave for the midday train.

'If I get my skirt damp, just put it in front of the fire here.'

'Miss, I couldn't! Miss Green would skin me if she saw that!'

Strange to have to call your sister 'Miss', thought Sophie. But the servants' hall had rules as rigid as any above stairs. 'Why would she find out? Even if she does, you and I will be gone by tonight. She can't give you a rollicking till we get back. And I've never seen snow. I'm going to make a snowman. Except I never have. How do you make a snowman?'

'You roll up a big ball of snow,' said Doris doubtfully. 'Then roll a smaller one and put it on top of that, then another even smaller for the head. Me and my sisters used sticks for the arms, and a carrot for the nose.' She grinned. 'And me dad's hat once. We got a belting for that.'

'I need a carrot,' said Sophie. 'There must be one somewhere. Hurry, Doris! Just lay the clothes out and I'll dress myself. Snow!'

'Yes, miss,' said Doris.

The air outside smelled like cold tin. The snow crunched under her fur-trimmed boots. Who could have guessed that snow would crunch? Or that she owned fur-lined boots? She wondered briefly what other wonders her wardrobe had acquired.

Doris had put out mittens, not gloves, and Sophie soon realised why. The separated fingers of gloves would have let in the cold more than the snug leather mittens did. She tried to gather snow between her hands and was surprised as it easily compressed.

'What are you doing?' It was Miss Carlyle, speaking through a chink in the breakfast-room window.

'Making a snowman.'

'A snowman? But —'

'I've never seen snow before!' yelled Sophie happily. 'Real genuine snow!'

Another face appeared at the window. The prinzessin stared at her, bewildered. 'You are interesting in snow?'

The prinzessin must have been told that it should be 'interested', thought Sophie. It's an affectation. 'I've got a carrot for its nose and everything.'

'Ah.' The prinzessin looked thoughtful. 'A carrot. That is different. Who can resist a carrot?' The window closed.

Sophie concentrated on trying to cram more snow into a ball. It looked jagged and out of shape, not at all like the neat balls on Christmas cards. But children made snowmen. Surely it couldn't be too difficult.

'Not like that.' The prinzessin clumped towards her, immaculate in blue velvet, with what looked like chevrons on the sleeves, and a large and floppy blue velvet hat trimmed with white and black fur. Her boots left deep holes in the snow. 'You *roll* the snow. You see?' She bent and demonstrated.

'Hannelore, you are impossible! You hate snow!' Miss Carlyle appeared behind the prinzessin, dressed in boots and mittens now too. She carried an elderly top hat. Had it once graced Jones? Her look held a moment's calculation, as though she were weighing up the possible fun against the chances of getting cold and damp.

'This is English snow.' The prinzessin's face looked up innocently. 'I have never seen *English* snow before.'

'You've been to England a score of times!'

'But always in the summer. There is no snow in the summer. And I have never made an English snowman. We must give it a bowler hat.'

Fun won. Miss Carlyle tromped towards them, heaving her boots with each step.

'It's a top hat, I'm afraid,' apologised Sophie.

The prinzessin waved her blue-mittened hand, then went back to rolling up her ball. It was as high as Sophie's knees now. 'It is no matter. A top hat will do. And a pipe, Miss Lily!' she called to the face at the breakfast-room window. 'We need a pipe!'

'I will send Jones out with one.'

'No,' called Sophie hurriedly, thinking of the poor man wading through the snow. Jones's dignity would probably mean he wore his spats even out here. His toes would freeze — and remain frozen for most of the day. 'I'll come in and get it.'

'It will be a most magnificent snowman,' said the prinzessin. She grinned wickedly. 'We need another carrot. To place here.' She gestured lower down. Sophie blinked. Surely the prinzessin didn't mean ...

'Hannelore, you are wicked,' said Miss Carlyle, 'and impossible. Truly impossible.' But she was laughing too.

The snowman stared at them — still with a single carrot — through the breakfast-room window. He *is* magnificent, thought Sophie, from his top hat to the muffler Miss Carlyle had wrapped around his neck, and the eyes and 'buttons' made of lumps of coal. He even had a smile — a red rag provided by the housekeeper, slightly fragrant with lavender polish.

At least the snowman will stay for a little while when I am gone, thought Sophie. Miss Lily will have to remember me whenever she looks at him ...

She pulled herself up at the thought. Was she jealous of the others? Jealous that Miss Lily wanted them with her, and not Sophie? Of course I am, she thought. Anyone would be.

But at least there was the snowman.

She helped herself to grilled kidneys and a larger-than-usual helping of kedgeree at the sideboard, then sat at 'her' place at the table, opposite Miss Carlyle. The prinzessin sat at Miss Lily's right, with Lady Alison on Miss Lily's left.

'I'm sorry you missed the fun,' Sophie said to Lady Alison.

Lady Alison stared at the blackberry jam on her toast. 'I don't care for snowmen.'

Prig, thought Sophie.

'German manufacture is always superior,' said the prinzessin. A definite joke, Sophie decided.

'Nonsense. You said it was an English snowman. It is an English top hat.'

'The costume, it is English. The manufacture is German. Miss Carlyle and Miss Higgs merely helped.'

'Girls.' Miss Lily dabbed at her mouth with her napkin. 'If we could leave the subject of the snowman for the moment — delightful though I admit he is. I would like to go through the programme for today. As you know, Miss Higgs leaves on the twelve forty-two train.' She smiled at Sophie, her face showing genuine regret. 'I am so sad you have to go. At least the trains are still running, despite the snow.'

I don't have to leave, thought Sophie. You've *told* me to leave. The prinzessin and Miss Carlyle don't seem to mind me. And Lady Alison doesn't seem to like any of us, even you.

She wondered briefly whether it was the taint of money or the sense of unwanted obligation that Lady Alison resented. Perhaps she thought all the other girls knew her season depended on paid hospitality to a colonial.

'Miss Higgs, perhaps you would join me in the library after your breakfast?'

'Of course, Miss Lily.'

'Prinzessin, Lady Alison, Miss Carlyle, you will each find a book of woodcuts in your room. We will meet for tea at four o'clock, and discuss them.'

Chapter 21

Even when we take steps to create our own lives, so much is simply
luck. A dog walks in front of our carriage; the carriage stops;
a meeting happens or doesn't happen; a life is changed in a few
seconds that no one could predict.

Miss Lily, 1914

For the first time Miss Lily stood as Sophie entered the library.
She held out her hands and took Sophie's in hers. Strong hands,
for someone who lifted nothing heavier than a coffee cup.

'I am truly sorry you have to go, my dear. It's been ...' she
hesitated '... a good time.'

'You don't regret staying at Shillings longer than your usual
four months?'

'No.' The teacher's smile came back. 'Though if I did I would
never tell you. Kindness, my dear, is the most powerful of all
tools, no matter what your season of life.' Miss Lily pressed her
hands again, then sat, her skirts pooling around her. 'Will you
take a final cup of coffee with me before you leave?' She reached
for the bell.

'Miss Lily?'

Miss Lily drew her hand back from the brocade bell rope.
'You are going to ask me if you can stay.'

'Yes,' said Sophie.

'One word is too brief. I have told you before, abruptness is
not only bad manners, but also graceless.'

'Yes, Miss Lily. I am going to ask you if I may stay here.
I want,' she chose her words carefully, 'I want to learn about
power. That's what you really teach here, isn't it? How even a

woman can have more control over her life? It's not just etiquette or politics. It's how to charm men so they do what you want.'

'Very good, my dear. Not quite accurate, but good.' Miss Lily's hands rested in her lap now. 'I do not teach young women to be coquettes, though charm can be a weapon. Would it surprise you to know that one of the other girls has asked the same thing this morning?'

'Asked if I could stay? Which one?'

'Lady Alison asked me while you were making the snowman.'

'Lady Alison? But she dislikes me.'

'Perhaps. Perhaps she also dislikes the thought of being here alone with the prinzessin and Miss Carlyle. She would always be the odd one out.'

'And if I stay, *I'll* be the odd one out?'

'No,' said Miss Lily. 'I do not think you would.'

A clock boomed from the hall. A house such as this had many passages, so the booms echoed for a long time. Sophie counted the strikes. Nine ... ten ... eleven ... she would miss the train if she didn't leave soon. It was embarrassing enough to leave; worse to have to stay another day because she had missed a train. 'I've been bored so long. Boring lessons, boring piano. I didn't even know it had been so boring till I came here. You've made me realise that the rest of my life could be worse.'

'Mother and wife on a remote property in New South Wales, with visits to a colonial city as a treat? You no longer want that?'

'I don't know what I want,' said Sophie frankly. 'But whatever you have planned for the next four months here will be interesting.'

'Oh, yes. It will be interesting. Miss Higgs ... Sophie ...' For the first time Miss Lily looked unsure. 'I ... I am not convinced you need to go to Switzerland. I know you do not want to go. I must also admit that I ... I do not want to part with you. Lady Alison's wishes must be taken into account too. Her position is so different from those of the other girls.'

'You want me to stay?' Sophie gathered the words her hostess did not seem able to say.

'I have always wanted you to stay,' said Miss Lily softly. 'But now I am saying that if you wish, you may.'

'Of course I want to! More than anything!' To stay at Shillings, and learn the deeper recesses of the world she had taken for granted. To laugh with Hannelore.

To be liked.

'Very well.' Miss Lily smiled, deeply, genuinely, but her tone was serious. 'We must now have a ... necessary ... conversation. The other young women know that if they gossip about how they have spent their time here they will be tainted by it. But you can say what you like then vanish from any scandal back to Australia.'

Sophie blinked. What could be scandalous about their months at Shillings?

'I use the word "scandal" advisedly,' added Miss Lily dryly. 'The girls who come here are recommended by relatives who have also studied here. They are already part of a network of women, well connected, often influential. But you ...'

'I'm a cuckoo's egg,' said Sophie. 'I don't belong to any family in England. No mother to embarrass. I'm tainted anyway by corned beef, but my fortune will always secure me a reasonable life even if I'm scandalous.' She blinked, startled by a thought. 'My mother didn't come here, did she?'

'I have never met your mother,' said Miss Lily.

Sophie hesitated. The reply was ambiguous, but this wasn't the time to question further. 'You can trust me.'

'My dear, you say that without knowing what you are to be trusted with. Very well. There is no way I can put this without being blunt. The girls who come to me each year learn how to be women of influence, and not just by making marriages that suit their own interests rather than their fathers' pockets. They also learn how to manipulate other men, not only their husbands. Sometimes that charm need be nothing more than a smile. You will learn politics here. You will also learn ... arts ... that courtesans know, but that women of breeding are denied. Are you shocked?'

Yes, thought Sophie, so shocked I have to think to breathe. But she didn't say that to Miss Lily. 'No. I've seen the bulls brought to the cows.'

'The advantage of a country childhood,' said Miss Lily wryly. Her expression was impossible to read. 'Trust me, my dear, the ways of bulls and cows are not exactly the ones I mean.'

'Isn't it all simple?'

'No, my dear. It often isn't at all simple. But even when it is ...' Miss Lily laughed '... like good bread and sweet butter, the best of "simple" can be difficult to achieve. And as for why — because it will give you power.'

'Courtesans —' Sophie blushed, but said the word anyway '— do not have power. Women like us don't need to know those things, do we?'

'I do not teach my girls how to be courtesans. A courtesan charms only one client at a time, and receives only financial support for her pains. A respectable woman, choosing a perfect dinner, selecting exactly the right guests for a salon, hosting a discreet afternoon tea with an influential man, can be infinitely more effective than those who provide your, ahem, activities of bulls and cows. I show the girls who come here how they may charm an entire cabinet, or a king, and so wield the kind of power that will never be won by the vote alone.'

'And that could be scandalous?'

'A network of women, linked by their time here, affecting government policy across Europe? Of course. The concept of women who exert power would be terrifying to most men.' She smiled. 'Which of course is why I do this.'

'To terrify powerful men?'

'No, my dear.' Was Miss Lily trying not to laugh? 'Or perhaps I am ... What is the word that German psychoanalyst uses? Subconscious. Perhaps I am subconsciously slapping the faces of a few men who need it. But mostly, I do this because the power women wield can be discreet, and discretion can be a weapon too. A pro-peace speech in the House of Lords will be countered by an opposing one. But murmured suggestions over crumpets and tea, so subtle that the hearer thinks they are his own idea? That can have more effect than a hundred public speeches.' She looked down at her hands, then back at Sophie again. 'I accepted many years ago — for reasons I will not explain now, so please do not erupt into questions again — that this is the only way I can change the world for good.'

'By teaching women to be powerful through being charming and inconspicuous? I'd rather have the vote,' said Sophie.

'Women who haven't been taught to think will simply vote the way their husbands tell them to. True power is not wielded at the ballot box, but in back-room meetings. But you need not be inconspicuous, only wield your power inconspicuously, form friendships that are a network of useful contacts. I must also warn you, Miss Higgs, that far more than ... bulls and cows ... will be covered in the talks I have with the four of you. But too many young women go ignorant to their marriage beds, and their shock or even horror on that first night can harm not just their marriages but their whole lives.'

Power. Strangely, Sophie's first thought was that she might have the power to stay behind after dinner and talk business with her father and Cousin Oswald, not of having power in her marriage to Malcolm.

Her second thought was incredulity. Impossible to think of Lady Alison learning about ... bulls and cows. Not quite impossible the thought of the prinzessin ...

'Do the others know?'

'About the political aspects of their time here? Of course. About the bulls and cows?' Miss Lily's smile was wide now. 'The book they will have found in their rooms by now will make quite clear one aspect of their study. So, do you still wish to stay?'

'Yes.' She said it quickly, in case Miss Lily changed her mind again. 'I promise I won't tell anyone, ever, about what happens here.'

'I won't hold you quite to that. I know now that I can trust you — possibly more than any girl who has been here. What you promise me, you will keep. You might tell a friend, a lover, even another girl who might come here ... All I ask is that you refrain from talk that might hurt what I regard as my life's most important work. That you think — and preferably consult with me — before you do so. Is that acceptable?'

'Of ... of course. But I still don't understand why the others are here.' She thought of the penny broadsheets, the sort that didn't appear to come to Shillings — or at least not into the drawing room. The sort of papers that had delighted in retelling the story of her mother. 'The prinzessin must have enormous power. And she's charming already.'

'They will have to tell you that. You will need to trust each other. It is as good a way as any to start.'

'Miss Lily — can I ask you one more question? Who are you when you're not at Shillings?'

'I assure you,' Miss Lily's voice was dry, 'I don't vanish in a puff of smoke when I leave the Hall. I simply have other interests in my life. Which I hope you will have too. We owe a duty to the world, all of us with gifts of wealth or birth. But we need lives of our own too. You cannot understand the world enough to change it for the better if you live entirely out of it — and if you have no love.'

Sophie spoke before she thought. 'You have love?'

'Oh, yes,' said Miss Lily softly. 'There is love.'

Chapter 22

*Toast should always be served with butter. Butter has a way of
lubricating even the most difficult situations.*

Miss Lily, 1914

Sophie had almost reached her room when the door next to
hers opened. It was Miss Carlyle. She carried a book that she
immediately hid behind her back. 'Miss Higgs — you haven't left
yet.'

'No, Miss Carlyle. Miss Lily has invited me to stay on.'

'I'm so glad.' The answer was perfunctory.

'Is that the book Miss Lily asked you to read?'

'Yes. I ...' Miss Carlyle's face was half shocked, half
triumphant. 'It's in Japanese. But the pictures! Miss Higgs,
it is —'

'Interesting.' The prinzessin must have heard their voices and
come out of her room. She looked amused.

So the prinzessin had known that ... cows and bulls and even
more ... might be mentioned here. And Miss Carlyle hadn't,
quite.

The third door opened. 'Miss Higgs ... I ... I am glad you are
staying.'

It was Lady Alison. She scratched her hands nervously.

And Sophie saw why Lady Alison had been so nervous.
She had known about the cows and bulls. And hated it. Her
grandmother, Miss Lily's friend, must have warned her. But if
she found it so distasteful, why was she here?

Sophie stepped into her own room. She gazed at the book on
her bed, opened it, stared.

No, bulls and cows did not behave like that. Or that ... and certainly not that! But ... this looked like it might be fun.

Did men really look like that? And women when looked at from that angle? And, oh dear, could Mr and Mrs Overhill ever have done that?

She wanted to keep reading — or rather looking, for the words were foreign symbols, Japanese or Chinese, she thought. She stared at the next page, the figures twisting, smiling, contorting. How could she keep a straight face at lunch after seeing that?! But it would not do today, of all days, to be late. She shoved the book under her pillow and rang the bell for Doris to dress her in clothes suitable for luncheon, not travelling.

Tonight she must write to her father and Miss Thwaites too, to tell them of the change in plans, but not of this morning's conversation. Certainly she could never mention the book to them. Nor Malcolm. Somehow she realised that Malcolm might not expect the manner of bulls and cows, but could be shocked that his wife knew the variety, the sheer fun contained between those pages.

It was the first time she had deliberately hidden anything in her life from her father and Miss Thwaites, apart from that one ride to meet Malcolm. But she had Miss Lily to guide her now. She had discovered the first secret that must be kept too.

Chapter 23

Study small boys together; they may go for half an hour without a word, just making noises for their games. A girl will know the name of every person in the group within ten minutes and have made judgements regarding their dress and status. Which practice would prepare the better cabinet minister?

Miss Lily, 1914

Knowing that each of the others had seen the book too, Sophie watched them at luncheon: the prinzessin, spooning up chicken consommé, discreetly amused; Miss Carlyle, dissecting her cutlet from the bone, looking as if she had not quite hidden her glee at what surely must be secret knowledge, for if mothers told their daughters *that* to prepare them for marriage, then Miss Thwaites would have told Sophie too; and Lady Alison, automatically swallowing her chocolate mousse. She looked paler than usual, each mouthful a polite effort. Then Jones brought in the cheese.

Doris hadn't given the book a second glance. The servants knew about this too?

The talk flowed around Sophie: talk of the day's papers, more talk of the Balkans and their quarrels. Only Lady Alison was silent, except to thank Jones for the oatmeal biscuits with her cheese.

She needed to be part of conversations like these. She forced her mind away from the book. 'Prinzessin, if there was ever a war between England and Germany, who would win?' She knew the answer, of course — how could England's empire lose? But it was the only relevant question she could think of.

'Please, my friends call me Hannelore. I would be honoured if you would do the same.'

'I ... thank you. I'm Sophie.'

'And I am Emily.'

Lady Alison looked at her cheese.

'I thank you. Germany will win, of course.' The prinzessin — Hannelore — selected an almond from the dish on the table.

'But we're the largest empire in the world!' Sophie was too shocked to hide her true feelings.

'The sun never sets upon the British Empire? It is a most patriotic phrase. I am always wary of phrases that talk of greatness. If there is true greatness, why is there a need to tell the world?' Hannelore regarded the cheddar. 'Thank you, Jones. A small slice, if you please. But does the sun never set on your army, on troops who are trained and equipped? I think it does.'

'Germany has nearly five million troops. We have fewer than one million.' Emily looked in her element, prepared to memorise the name of every soldier and his battalion.

Five million! How many people were in the whole of Australia? She didn't know. One million? Two or three? 'So Germany has the largest army in the world?'

'Russia's is larger. Six million,' contributed Emily. She eyed Hannelore across the table. 'An alliance of England and Russia would defeat Germany.'

'The Russian army are serfs with pitchforks who will obey their masters. Or not, perhaps. Russia has had one revolution. It failed, but I think, next time, that it may not. I would not depend on Russia,' Hannelore gave a delicate shrug, 'for war or marriage.'

'Russia had a revolution?' Sophie shook her head. 'I'm sorry. I am so ignorant.'

Emily smiled. The pig resemblance vanished. 'Politics gives girls brain fever. Or makes them unable to bear children. No, don't laugh — our doctor warned my mother in just those words. The Russian Revolution was in 1905, by the way. But Hannelore is correct. Russia *is* deeply unstable, despite its wealth and size. The Tsar is not the ablest of men. But the United States is also mobilising half a million troops,' she added. 'The Americans have factories as good as Germany's. Better, perhaps.'

'The United States has never known a proper war, except against itself,' stated Hannelore. 'I do not think President Wilson would make a good commander. It is good commanders who win wars.'

'The Americans did win against the British when they fought for their independence,' murmured Miss Lily.

'Too long ago.' Hannelore's words were precise. 'Germany has the munitions factories. The men, the training, the culture of war that makes good officers. The English are schoolboys playing football.' Hannelore dabbed her lips. 'German sabres beat English footballs or Russian pitchforks every time.'

There was a silence at the table. If war comes, Hannelore and the rest of us will be on different sides, thought Sophie. 'So you really think war between our countries is possible?'

'Possible does not mean inevitable. War is never inevitable.' Miss Lily's calm voice made Sophie think of a swan again. 'Especially not if neither side is sure of winning. Germany may have more troops, but it does not have as many ships. It's called the balance of power. The Kaiser doesn't wish for war, nor does our King George. They are cousins, after all.'

It was as though a blanket had been lifted from the room. Even the candles burned more brightly. Of course England at war was impossible, thought Sophie.

Miss Lily smiled. 'The Kaiser keeps the Prussians, who are the holders of the military culture of Germany, in check. The English Liberals keep the Conservatives from mobilising more men. Every year that war doesn't break out means it is less likely. Peace becomes a habit, like war was a habit for Prussia for too long.'

'England worries about the Irish rebels in Ulster, and Germany worries about the Balkans. They have too much trouble on their own doorsteps to fight each other. They may compete in Africa, and in the Middle East, but not in Europe.' Emily looked at Miss Lily for approval.

Sophie looked out the window. The snowman had melted. The grass showed green under the lingering drifts of white.

Impossible that war could come to these gentle fields. Wars were from long ago, or in other places.

Chapter 24

*You can live your life for years making certain assumptions. Then
suddenly you look at them, and nothing is the same.*

Miss Lily, 1914

The silver coffee pot sat on the table by the fire. The cake trolley
sat next to it, laden with fruitcake, cherry cake, sponge cake
with jam and cream, and small madeleines with fluted tops.

It's to make this seem normal, thought Sophie. A chat around
the fireside, not a lesson in …

Miss Lily put down her plate. 'Very well. Let us begin. In
four months' time you will all be engaged in what is called "the
season". Girls your age, in your position, have less than a year
to acquire a husband and a mate who will provide them with the
life they wish to lead.

'Society likes to pretend that this season is a light-hearted
affair, not one with major consequences for the girls involved.
Girls are rarely trained to take best advantage of the months
ahead.

'So this is why you are all here. Each of you has decided you
should have the chance to manipulate your own futures. Women
have few weapons. Of these, the greatest is charm. Now I would
like each of you to say what has brought you here.'

'But it is private —' began Emily.

'Trust between us is, perhaps, the point.' It was Hannelore.
'Very well. I will tell you why *I* am here. The simple answer — that
is the correct phrase, is it not? — the too-simple answer is that my
mother's older sister suggested this visit. Suggested carefully, with
hints, since I was sixteen.' She smiled at Sophie briefly. 'You are

thinking that I am a fairy-tale princess. Perhaps that is true, if you have ever heard any of the fairy-tales of my country.'

Hannelore looked out the window at the vanished snowman. 'I was ten years old when a Serbian revolutionary blew up our carriage. We were driving out for a picnic by the lake. He rolled a bomb made from a wine bottle under the horses' feet. I saw him do it. I thought it was just a game, like English skittles. Have you ever seen horses explode, Miss Higgs? I remember that, although I know I could not really have seen it, except in one moment of clarity perhaps, before my life was shredded with them. Then I didn't think at all.' She looked down at her hands in her lap. 'When I woke I was in a peasant house. My mother, my father, my sister were laid out on the floor, very straight, very correct, with cushions under their heads as if they were alive. I think the peasants must have wiped off the blood too. I have scars —' Hannelore shrugged '— not where you see them easily, so they do not matter much. I was sent like a parcel to live with my aunt, till my older brother left school and took over our estates.

'One day, soon, I will be sent like a parcel again, into a marriage chosen by my great-uncle, agreed to by my brother. It will be a marriage that is good for Germany. I will have no choice.'

'Can't you refuse?' put in Sophie.

Hannelore smiled. 'Why should I do that, if it is good for my country? But I do not want my life to end with my marriage. When people speak of me at my funeral I want them to remember the woman who arranged alliances as well as dinners. The map of the world is changing. I can either sit with my embroidery and watch it happen, or I can be part of it.' Hannelore met their eyes. 'My ancestor was Catherine the Great. She created an empire, and she had lovers. One day, perhaps, I may do the same.'

The room was silent again. 'I ... I am so sorry about your family,' said Sophie at last. Lovers! she thought. A woman planning to have lovers! And an empire.

She would love an empire. The corned-beef empire. Or even to create her own. She almost smiled at her sudden longing. What empire could an ordinary woman create? An ice-cream empire?

She glanced at Hannelore. All thoughts of smiles vanished. Was this the first time the prinzessin had told anyone about her parents' death?

'It must have been terrible,' said Emily.

'Did you feel like a ghost — that perhaps you had died too, and no one had noticed?' asked Lady Alison softly.

For once Hannelore didn't smile. 'Will I tell you the truth in this too? I do not miss my parents. I did not even know them. My father was always at court, my mother at the Riviera with her lover. We knew about him but never mentioned it ... The revolutionary chose the one day of the year when we were all together.'

'And your sister?' asked Lady Alison, even more quietly.

'Yes. I miss my sister. Every day I miss my sister. But I will live enough for both of us.'

Miss Lily spoke. 'Thank you, Prinzessin. I know that was not easy for you. Miss Carlyle?'

Emily shrugged neatly. She put down her coffee cup. 'My father is not dead. That is the problem. Yes, I know that sounds heartless, but believe me, he wishes he were dead too.

'My father had a stroke two years ago. Since that time he has not been able to speak, has not been able to feed himself. He smells, despite the best of care, and he is conscious enough to know it. He used to be a cabinet minister. Every prime minister for twenty years has eaten at our table. As far back as I can remember, affairs of the nation were decided at our house parties. But his success was due to Mother too, and he knew it.' Emily glanced at Miss Lily. 'My mother studied here with you? She's never said she did, but she's implied it.'

Miss Lily nodded. 'One of my first. You might say we taught each other.'

'No one visits since my father's stroke. My mother stays at his side, her life as empty as his. But she will leave him to give me a season to find a husband who can offer me something of what I have lost.'

'Only one?' asked Sophie softly.

Emily shrugged. 'I might be invited to stay with family friends for a few days of the next season. But a girl who does not "take" in her first season is accounted not first-class marriage material.'

'And if you become a political hostess, then your mother may be part of that world again too.' Miss Lily's voice was soft.

Emily nodded. 'My mother said to me last year, "Sometimes I hear their voices in the dining room. But when I reach it they are never there." She asked me if I thought she was going mad. Sometimes ... sometimes I think she hopes she will. If she were mad, she couldn't do her duty, could be free. There is so much that needs doing in the world, and this may be the only way I can be involved.'

'At least you've been involved. I hardly knew your world existed.' Sophie looked at the others. 'I'm sorry. My being here is selfish. I have a father who loves me, a man who wants to marry me. I'm here because I thought it would make me more acceptable.' She stopped and grinned. 'Give me a way to crow over the unpleasant woman who will be my mother-in-law. That's not enough for me now. Miss Lily has shown me a richer world. I still don't know if I want to be part of it,' she added frankly. She glanced at Miss Lily. 'I'm trying to be honest.'

'And succeeding slightly too admirably,' murmured Miss Lily. 'Lady Alison?'

Lady Alison's hands were pressed down on her lap. 'I am here because my grandmother told me to come. I think she too is one of Miss Lily's "friends".' She made the word 'friends' sound like boiled lizards. Miss Lily merely nodded.

'My parents died when I was twelve. My cousin then became the present duke. The estate and all its income were of course entailed. My grandmother has no money, nor have I, although her expenses are paid for by the estate. The estate barely covers its expenses. My season will be paid for by Miss Higgs's father, a far more lavish one than my cousin would have provided for me. I ... I don't want a season. I hate parties and crowds. I don't want a husband either. But without one my life will be nothing when my grandmother dies, and she has said that my being here will

174

help me.' She met the eyes of the others. 'I think she is wrong. That book is disgusting. People should not be animals.'

Miss Lily bent towards her. 'Lady Alison, your grandmother the dowager duchess is very dear to me. If you dislike our discussions, you may read a book, or go for a walk — whatever you choose. But I hope you will stay for a few. Your grandmother feels your life has been too limited, too sheltered. It is just possible that she is correct, that you may find you enjoy the world once you are more comfortable with it. Not all marriages must be physical,' she added quietly.

Lady Alison's eyes blinked like a frightened sheep's.

Miss Lily sat back. 'So let us begin with the most important of all lessons. Charm.'

Sophie watched Lady Alison show faint relief. One of the Suitables had been to Charm School back in Sydney. It had involved flower decorations, and paper fans in the fireplace in summer. It had not involved bulls and cows.

Miss Lily was speaking again. 'They say you're born with charm. Anyone who says that, of course, isn't charming at all. Charm is learned. Sometimes it can even be taught. But there are two kinds of charm. The first is facile, like a bouquet that will be thrown away when no longer needed.

'True charm is based on care for other people. So often we are locked in the tiny box of ourselves. Caring is something that cannot be faked. Caring is when you ask about her ladyship's rheumatism, or about the major's gout, or little Billy's measles — and remember to ask the next day about his spots. Caring that your maid is tired after waiting up for you, and making sure that she sleeps too, when you have a nap the next afternoon before a ball.'

She smiled. 'Charm relies on pleasing others. But to please others you need to understand what they want. The word is "empathise". Think what it must be like to be the other person. What do they need to make them happy? Sometimes a word is enough — the right word, at the right time, even if the happiness it brings is fleeting.' Her lips parted in the deep Miss Lily smile.

'You may find that making others happy brings deep fulfilment to yourself as well. But a charming person also has power. And for a woman ...' She shrugged. 'Charm is the only power that lasts. Beauty fades. Money will be controlled by a husband or father or elderly uncles. But charm ... that is yours forever.

'So, I would like you to practise empathising with the servants.'

'The servants?' Emily gave a sharp laugh.

Miss Lily looked at Emily levelly. 'You use a servant to lace your dress, so you can use them to practise empathy. And one day you may find the loyalty it brings you — from your maid, your butler — will also bring you information, sympathy, discretion. Wages can pay for these, but you may not always have money. Loyalty lasts forever.'

'Do unto others,' said Lady Alison quietly. For the first time her hands rested calmly in her lap.

'Perhaps, my dear, you are closer to true charm than you realise,' said Miss Lily. She looked around at them, warm and welcoming within her perfect composure.

She likes us, thought Sophie. And then, But that's just the point. She cares about us. That is what she is trying to teach us.

'Once you learn to see and feel another's needs, to see them as a person as vulnerable as yourself, you will find that charm comes naturally. But until that time there are five steps, quite enough for a dinner party, for charming your hostess at a Friday-to-Monday, or even for willing the man you are interested in to your side. Yes, Prinzessin, you may take notes, but I think the steps are simple enough to remember when you have tried them once.

'Step one: make the other person smile. That is relatively simple: smile at them, with a delight at seeing them or meeting them, real or feigned, and they will smile back. Hannelore, if you would smile at Lady Alison?'

Hannelore gave a surprisingly impish grin. Lady Alison's face lightened automatically as she gave one of the few smiles Sophie had seen from her.

'You see?' said Miss Lily. 'So simple. Lady Alison smiles, and now, for a little while, she may even feel like smiling.'

Lady Alison's smile deepened. 'Perhaps,' she said.

'Now step two. Miss Higgs, could you say something one of us will agree with? Once someone has agreed with you, you have opened the door to their trust. The thought can be mundane and still be effective: "Lovely weather for this time of year", or "Don't the gardens look quite charming?" or it can be more profound — one inspired by true empathy: "No one can understand what it is like to lose a child, Mrs Smith." Miss Higgs?'

Emily, she thought, choosing the greatest challenge. Who is Emily? What does she feel? 'It is hard when men offer us nothing but trivialities, don't you find, Miss Carlyle?' she offered.

Emily stared at her, then nodded with reluctant admiration. 'If you came up to me at a garden party and said those words, I'd want to keep talking.'

'Then perhaps, Miss Carlyle, you will try this next step,' said Miss Lily. 'Say something that will interest your listener — and if possible make sure you have prepared beforehand something that will.'

Emily will try Hannelore, thought Sophie. She already knows what Hannelore is interested in. But instead, Emily turned to her. 'I imagine you have dogs on your property back home? You must miss them dreadfully. I don't suppose you would like one of the puppies?'

'I would *love* one —' She had almost forgotten it was an exercise.

Emily gazed at her, the triumph in her eyes not quite hidden.

'Was that true?' asked Sophie quietly. 'Are you really offering me a puppy?'

'Quite true. Would you like one?'

'The question is academic,' said Miss Lily. 'I will not have a puppy distracting you these next few months. I know my own limitations,' she added.

Suddenly they were all laughing. Just as Miss Lily intends, thought Sophie. Miss Lily met her eyes. Her own crinkled, even more amused.

'Step four: praise the person you are speaking to. But if you praise too effusively, you will appear to be currying favour. Casanova once said — I doubt your educations have covered Casanova; he was a man who spent his life attracting women, then evading the consequences — that if you want to attract an intelligent woman, you praise her beauty; if you want a beautiful woman to adore you, you praise her intelligence. Prinzessin, will you give us an example?'

Hannelore nodded slowly. She turned to Lady Alison. 'I think you have been unappreciated all your life, Lady Alison, by yourself most of all. You are beautiful, but have never seen it.'

'Oh.' Lady Alison stared at her, a flush beginning at her neck and rising into her face.

'That,' added Hannelore, 'was a most true statement too.'

'Good.' Miss Lily's smile reappeared. 'I happen to agree. You don't always need to praise with such insight, but the world will be a sweeter place if you can. But a simple "Oh, I was sure you'd know the answer, Lady William" will do.'

'Now for the last step. Praise another person. "Doesn't Miss Smith look lovely tonight!" Praising another person automatically makes the praise reflect on you. Criticism will rebound on you as well, so use it minimally, if at all. Better to say, "Oh, I am quite sure the rumour isn't true; she is such a lovely person." Lady Alison, would you care to try that one?'

Lady Alison nodded, the flush still on her cheeks. She turned to Sophie. 'The prinzessin is most kind, isn't she?'

'Always, I suspect,' said Sophie softly.

Hannelore shrugged. 'Kindness is all one has to give.'

'But you —' Sophie stopped. Hannelore must be wealthy. The diamond earrings she had worn the previous night had looked priceless. But one didn't speak of money, except in offices.

Hannelore smiled gently. 'I have much that is the prinzessin's, but little that is my own, to dispose of. The jewels must go to my children, or my brother's children. My bills are paid, my needs supplied from my brother's estate. But long ago my aunt taught me that kindness is still mine to give.'

'So,' said Miss Lily pronouncing it 'Zo', almost as though Hannelore's German accent were contagious. 'Have you charmed each other?'

Sophie looked at the girls in the room. It had worked. She no longer resented Lady Alison; a few minutes before she had wanted to protect her, as she would a lamb circled by crows. She respected Emily, and Hannelore she simply liked.

'Shall we run through the steps again? Miss Higgs?'

'Smile,' said Sophie. 'Make them agree. Ask a question they can answer. Praise them. Praise another.'

'Excellent. We will practise each of the steps again each night. Once you can do these without even thinking, whether to a colonel in the Guards or a dowager, a maiden aunt or an eligible young man, you will be noticed, approved of, and, more importantly, liked.'

Sophie knocked tentatively on Lady Alison's door. There was no answer. She knocked again, then said softly, 'May I come in?'

Still no reply. She opened the door and looked in. Lady Alison was huddled on the window seat, holding her legs, staring out the window. She glanced at Sophie, then looked back at whatever she had been gazing at. Sophie doubted it was the grass below.

'That book … it was a shock, wasn't it?' Sophie said.

'I knew it was coming.' Lady Alison still stared out the window.

'But not like that?'

'Exactly like that.' Lady Alison looked at her. Perhaps this is the first time she has really seen me, thought Sophie. Lady Alison took a breath. 'My grandmother made what is known as a good marriage.' There was the echo of a smile now. 'Grandmama was only the daughter of a country doctor, and in her forties too, when she met Miss Lily. They became close friends, despite the difference in their ages. Grandmama looked like a horse in a good light, all chin and nose, and about as wide too. But she had — has — charm. She told me that is what Miss Lily taught her: the charm and grace to catch a duke who sat in the House of Lords.

'I said I don't want to get married, but I know I need to. I don't want to have to work as some old lady's paid companion, as a telegraph operator, a nurse or a governess. What else is there? But it's not just for financial security.'

'I understand,' said Sophie.

Once again she had the feeling that Lady Alison was really looking at her. 'Perhaps you do. Women who don't marry are always standing outside the rest of the world. Allowed to visit, perhaps, to make an even number at table. Allowed to serve the ones who matter, as servants or governesses or companions or maiden aunts. I don't want that. I want my own life.' Her voice was fierce now. 'Not a big life, perhaps, but one of my own.'

'But you don't want ... a man,' said Sophie slowly.

Lady Alison stared out the window, her face red. 'Is it so obvious?'

'Maybe when you love someone it will be different.' Sophie thought of camellias and Malcolm.

'I don't like being touched. Or touching,' said Lady Alison flatly. 'Except babies, maybe. And dogs.' She looked at Sophie, then added suddenly, 'My parents' marriage was ... unspeakable. Literally. One does not speak of things like that. An alliance — a title on his side, money on hers. But the money vanished in the crash of the nineties. My father never forgave her, not just for that, but also for her inability to give him a male heir. She never forgave him for his contempt. Two people joined together for life, forced to smile together in public, can inflict extraordinary cruelty on each other in private. Neither of my parents forgave me either, for being a girl, for witnessing the humiliations they inflicted on each other.'

'I ... I am so very sorry. But all marriages aren't like that,' said Sophie.

'How do you know what happens behind the drapes? Once a woman is married she must endure in silence. There is no escape. If she tries to leave, legally she can be brought back. But if I want a baby — or a life — I know I have to learn to touch a man, and make him think I like it.'

'I'm sure it won't be so bad.' But what did she really know of marriage? She knew little of the Overhills' unhappy partnership, nor did she know enough of the Suitable Friends' parents' lives. 'Forgive me for being blunt,' she added, trying, somehow, to help. 'But you're not rich. Not titled. The man you marry must truly love you, value you. There are kind men in the world. My father is kind.'

But was Malcolm? She suddenly remembered the chains on the men at Warildra.

Lady Alison looked remote again. 'Would even a kind man accept a wife who hates to be touched?'

I haven't tried to understand her, thought Sophie. What must it feel like to be so afraid of touch? 'Alison —' suddenly the 'Lady' seemed irrelevant '— did you play lacrosse?'

The remote look vanished. 'At school. What has that to do with anything?'

'Did you, er, love your lacrosse stick?'

'What an extraordinary thing to ask. Of course not.'

'But you still played the game?'

'Yes. But —' Alison stopped. 'You mean that ... that being with a husband could just be a game too?'

Sophie shrugged. 'I don't see why not.'

'But a husband will expect ...?'

'It doesn't last long,' said Sophie, drawing on her bull and cow expertise. 'Just a few seconds, I think.' She wondered if men bellowed like bulls.

'Like being hit on the shins with a lacrosse stick?'

Sophie grinned. 'If you like.'

Alison watched her for a moment. 'Thank you.'

'There's no need to thank me.'

'There is, you know. For understanding. Though it's possible you've put me off lacrosse for life.' She gave an almost-grin. 'Don't worry. I never liked it much anyway. But I *do* want to thank you for the money ...' She paused. 'I'd have had a season anyway. Staying with my aunt, no ball of my own. But it will make a difference, not looking like a church mouse.' She tried to smile. 'My cousins call me Mouse. I suppose it fits.'

'I always thought a church mouse would live quite well. All those holy candles to eat. No cats.'

'There'll be cats in London,' said Alison dryly. 'All peering at us, hoping for evident flaws. There's nothing more savage than a mama on the hunt on behalf of her daughter.'

'Then we'll have to protect each other.'

'I suppose we will,' said Alison slowly. 'They'll want to gossip about ...' She stopped, as though unwilling to say the words.

'Corned beef,' supplied Sophie.

'Well, yes.' She bit her lip. 'Thank you. I ... I think, with a friend, I can get through a season. Maybe that is partly why Grandmama sent me here.' She managed a smile. 'And with a friend to confide in, I might even find the courage to ... play lacrosse.' She was speaking to herself as well. 'And, as you say, it won't be for long.'

'You just need a man who doesn't want, er, to play lacrosse very often.'

Sophie hesitated, then kissed Alison on the cheek. She was glad that Alison didn't flinch at the contact, either with her or the corned beef.

Alison looked curiously at Sophie. 'Miss Lily says you have an understanding with a young man in Australia.'

Sophie nodded. 'Malcolm Overhill. His father is MP for our district. His grandfather was too.'

'So your Malcolm is the next one?'

'I don't think he wants to be. It all seems such a long way from here.'

'Everything is a long way from here. That's how Miss Lily wants it.' She flushed. 'I wonder if you'd like to call me Mouse, like my cousins do. You know, I've never had a friend before. I ... I didn't like school. Grandmama brought me home after two months. And my cousins are so much older. Some of the other families we dine with have daughters, but somehow ... maybe I'm not good at friendship. Or at much else.'

'I've never had a real friend either. It's my own fault, I think. Friends, then?'

'Friends,' said Alison.

The days formed a pattern surprisingly quickly. Mornings meant breakfast at the long, dark table, discussing the previous day's newspapers, then political discussions and luncheon with Miss Lily. The footmen and Jones withdrew, leaving the food on hot chafing dishes on the sideboard. Then the afternoons were theirs, to do with as they wished.

'Do you think Miss Lily might be an ... an illegitimate sister of the earl's?' Sophie asked Alison one afternoon as they walked along one of the muddy lanes in the grounds. On one side of the lane, sheep nosed doubtfully at a rack of hay. On the other, the Shillings glasshouses gleamed, even the top panes dust-free and the autumn leaves cleaned from the roof. Hannelore and Emily were writing to their families, back at the house.

A few weeks earlier Sophie would never have used the word 'illegitimate'; she still wouldn't, except to very particular friends.

Mouse had become such a friend.

'Why do you think so?' Alison asked.

'No Miss Lily in Debrett's or *Landed Families*. Nor anyone who might be her.'

Alison nodded. 'It's possible. It may be why she's here when he's travelling in the East: so he doesn't have to publicly accept her.'

'But he admits her here ...'

Alison shrugged. 'If the tenants gossip, they'll be thrown off the estate. Lose their jobs, their homes, their families.'

'But Mouse ... that's terrible.'

Alison looked at her curiously. 'If one of your workers at Thuringa offends the family, doesn't your father send him or her packing?'

'He has sacked people, of course. Mostly for drunkenness,' she added. 'But I don't think Dad would ever kick a man's family out of their home; he'd let them live there till the man found another job.'

'Is that how it's done in Australia?'

'I don't think so,' said Sophie slowly. She looked at a man, puffing past them with a barrow of steaming manure. 'Mushrooms and asparagus,' she added.

'I beg your pardon?'

Sophie nodded at the glasshouse. 'They have great pits for manure to make the garden beds inside hot. I looked them over when I first came here. That's how we get the mushrooms, asparagus and rhubarb, even now in the cold. That's why they're called "succession houses". That one over there has pineapples and peaches.'

Alison laughed. 'You are impossible.'

'Because I'm interested in succession houses?'

'Because you investigate barrow-loads of manure.'

'A sign of my ignoble upbringing,' said Sophie lightly.

'No. Just you being Sophie. You could have been brought up in Windsor Castle and you'd still have poked your nose into succession houses.'

'Does your home have succession houses?'

'Wooten Abbey? Yes. But I've never been in one.' Alison grinned. 'Maybe we can explore them together after the season.'

Mr Jeremiah Higgs had bought Alison's companionship for the season. But not afterwards ...

Sophie smiled and nodded.

There were lessons in keeping skin white with rice flour and cucumber juice; on keeping it soft with lemon peel and jasmine oil; on mixing scents so each of the girls had a perfume all her own, Sophie's rose and lavender and lemon; on how to use a sugar toffee every month to make sure the face was free of tiny hairs, or a moustache as one grew older, and the legs and arms were hair-free as well.

Impossible to think they would one day be old enough to grow a moustache.

For Sophie, this was a time to learn more subtle things too, by watching the manners of the other girls, imitating them — Alison's accent, Emily's ease of conversation.

To her surprise, she found Hannelore studying Alison's and Emily's ways too.

'I am thinking I may marry an Englishman,' Hannelore explained one day at luncheon.

'What's his name?' Emily gazed at a dish of winter pears, selected one, placed it on her fruit plate and cut a slice with her silver fruit knife.

'I do not know,' said Hannelore calmly.

'Your family is arranging it?'

'My family will arrange a marriage to one of their allies. This year it might be an Englishman. I have no money.' Unless you count a fortune in jewels, thought Sophie. 'So I must sound as though I would be happy to have England as my home. It is a pity,' she added, 'that your princes are too young still to marry me. A German and English alliance is good for both nations now, I think.'

'You like England?' asked Emily.

Hannelore shrugged, and pulled her silk wrap higher on her shoulders. 'It is cold in England, also. Englishmen are not enough serious. They will be shooting and playing cricket. But when there is war I think it is better to live on an island like England. It is difficult for an army to cover ... what is the word I want?'

'Cross the Channel,' said Emily.

'Yes, that is it. It is difficult for an army to cross over so much water. So I will be better here, if my family can find a suitable alliance.'

'Do you think the wars in the Balkans will get worse?' asked Sophie.

Hannelore looked at her tolerantly. 'One country falls, the others go down, boom, boom, boom, like toy soldiers. You push one, then all the others fall.'

'Why not live in the south of France?' asked Alison lightly. 'It's warm there. And Frenchmen don't play cricket.'

Hannelore snipped off a cluster of grapes from the pile on the epergne in the centre of the table. 'France and Germany will fight. It is what they do, they fight each other. One day soon they will again. Your Lloyd George has called the build-up of arms "organised insanity". Every country in Europe I think is a little insane right now. No, I am good here ...'

'Better here,' corrected Emily.

'Thank you. Better here. Your royal family, they are German too.'

'The House of Saxe-Coburg and Gotha,' said Emily.

'And they are my cousins.'

'The royal family are your cousins!' Sophie had found it didn't matter showing shock at things like that now.

'King George is my cousin, I think, two times removed. There are more grapes, please?' She turned to Jones, silent behind them.

'Certainly, Your Highness.'

I'm sitting with a cousin of the King, thought Sophie. If Mrs Overhill could see me now.

Chapter 25

It is a sad fact of life that the more social power a man wields as he gets older, usually the less ... personal ... power remains to him. A successful man needs to seem successful in all areas. Remember this. A beautiful woman on his arm implies virility. And if he is not virile, then he is especially indebted to her, for adding that final polish to his success.

Miss Lily, 1914

A lesson. Miss Lily's drawing room, with its parchment silk walls. Miss Lily in grey silk, with grey lace at her wrists and neck. The silk crinkled as she moved. Three girls were arranged in chairs around her, the pastels of their dresses bird-like against Miss Lily's drab.

'I'm so sorry I'm late.' Sophie closed the door behind her and fell into a fourth chair. 'The earl has a mechanical ditch-digger. It's very efficient ...' Sophie broke off as the others looked at her, and laughed. 'Shall I count what I've done wrong? I'm late, I'm discourteous to my hostess and my friends, I forgot to be a swan, and mechanical ditch-diggers are not a proper topic for a debutante.'

'Unless your companion is fascinated by mechanical ditch-diggers too. My cousin would be enthralled.' Miss Lily inspected her. 'No leaf mould on your shoes. You have changed. Good. Now, shall I show you how all of those faults can be erased?' Miss Lily nodded at Sophie again. 'If you wouldn't mind going back into the hall. Now, when you come into the room again, pause for a count of four, then dip your chin towards your neck and lift your eyes to look straight into the eyes of each person here for a count of two, no more.

'If they are a friend, or a potential friend, smile. If they are a man, or someone to whom you owe deference — your hostess or any other older woman — drop your eyes and face, and give a smaller smile. If it is a child, smile too. But no matter how many are in the room, make that contact before you take a step.'

Sophie stood outside the door. Stupid, to be late; embarrassing to be caught being late; boring to learn yet another piece of meaningless etiquette, like placing your hands cupped and motionless on the dining table.

She opened the door. Caught Hannelore's eyes: a smile, immediately reciprocated. Caught Alison's, Emily's, Miss Lily's, gave a dip of deference. She began to step towards the chairs.

And felt ... different. 'It's not just manners, is it?' she said, sitting — swan-like this time.

'No. That meeting of the eyes is saying, "I like you. I am interested in you." Even the most formidable of matrons wishes to be found interesting, even by the most insignificant of debutantes. It is an opportunity and a beginning. It is the same when you are speaking to any other person, in company or not. Meet their eyes, smile.'

'No matter how boring they are,' said Emily.

'Especially if they are boring. Others will admire your poise or your charity. And if you must be bored, then you may as well make at least one other person happy by appearing to be fascinated.

'Miss Carlyle, if you would try it now. Enter, look, and sit ...'

The others were sitting now, swan-like, their backs only just touching their chairs, their hands in the 'sleeping crane' position Miss Lily had taught them, practised and practised until it was almost second nature to sit like that now.

In a year or two, thought Sophie, I will sit like this all the time. Unless I consciously decide I won't ...

Chapter 26

'Tea,' said Miss Lily, lifting the silver pot, 'is a meal that requires care. A man requires an excellent dinner, a perfect breakfast. Tea is a woman's meal — not that men don't enjoy it. But while you can make breakfast or dinner as elaborate as you like, too much display at tea, especially of sweet things, makes a man uneasy. It is as though the woman is laying claim to her own world, instead of fitting into his.

'Tea is a useful meal. At dinner the hostess decides where you'll be seated. You sit for the duration of the meal. At breakfast ... you can never be quite sure who will come down to breakfast, or when or even whether they might choose to be silent or read. But tea ... tea is the meal when you can in all propriety suggest a man sit beside you, so you can pour his tea. There is something innately innocent about taking tea. As long as there is a pot, a fruitcake and buttered muffins, no one can ever think that anything ... inappropriate ... has taken place.

'So ... a fruitcake.' Miss Lily indicated the slice of cake on her plate, dark with currants, topped with fondant and marzipan. 'Because no tea is complete without a fruitcake. Bread and butter of course, as well, although toast is preferable as long as it is freshly made. Gentleman's Relish — watch how he spreads it, thick or thin, then next time do it for him. But no sponge cakes, madeleines, éclairs, which are far too messy and distracting ... not unless you know that the man has a particular liking for them, and even then in moderation, only one such at a time. Instead ...'

Miss Lily lifted each of the silver lids in turn. 'Muffins, well buttered and kept hot.' Another lid. 'Crumpets, but with honey only, never jam. Jam clumps. So unattractive.' A third lid. 'Anchovies on toast. Men often prefer the savoury to the sweet, in food as well as women. Devilled mushrooms. Cheese savouries.' These were delicate small puffs. Sophie made a note to ask Mrs Goodenough how they were made. They looked like you'd need practice to get them absolutely right ...

'Now, to make the toast. Tea is a quiet time, my dears, a relaxing time — not a time for political discussions. And there is nothing as relaxing and companionable as making toast. Nor as intimate, whether it is a country party of twenty, or simply two of you, or three.

'So — one toasting fork, the bread, a bread knife, a kettle of hot water ... the bread browned to a shade of almost gold on one side, then the other, buttered straight away and eaten before it can get cold. But *dry* toast — which many gentlemen prefer ...' She took the knife and a piece of bread, dipped the knife into the kettle of hot water by the pot, then quickly cut the already thin slice exactly down its centre.

'Try it.'

They did. Only Emily managed to cut it from top to bottom without having the knife slip out the side, but even her cut wandered like a snake across the sand.

'Again,' said Miss Lily.

And again. And again. And again. And Miss Lily was right, thought Sophie, because by the fourth try they were all giggling, laughing by the fifth, and by the time each slice was on the fork, golden on each side, crisp then buttered with the lightest scrape of relish, salty but good ... there was no need to talk of anything except toast, and crumbs.

Four glowing faces. No, five, because Miss Lily was glowing too.

Chapter 27

What is the difference between a woman who marries suitably,
that is to a man of money, and a woman who takes money for her
services? Only respectability, of course, and certain protections in
law. If you can ensure you are respected, the possibilities of your
life will be enormous.

Miss Lily, 1914

'I hope I'm not disturbing you, Miss Lily,' said Sophie, seeking out Miss Lily some weeks after her reprieve from the afternoon train.

Miss Lily looked up from her desk in the library. 'No, of course not, my dear.' She gestured at the papers. 'Merely some accounts I said I'd look through for his lordship.' She smiled. 'His estate manager has it all in hand, of course, but it is good for one of the family to see to matters too. Do sit down.'

Sophie sat. 'I need advice.'

The smile stayed, but Miss Lily's eyes were watchful. 'Of course. How can I help you?'

'I need to write a letter. A ... a perfect letter. One that will hurt the person who reads it as little as it can.'

'Ah,' said Miss Lily. Impossible to miss the slight touch of pleasure and even relief in her voice. '*That* kind of letter. In that case a few small lies may be called for.'

'I don't understand.'

'It's very simple. The way to alleviate the hurt you must inflict on someone is to give them something in return. Shall we see what we can do?'

Dear Malcolm,

This is a difficult letter to write.

You are a man whom any woman would be honoured to marry, of enormous ability and integrity and charm. I will always think of you as one of the men I respect most in the world.

Since I have been in England, though, I have realised that my father is correct. I have seen too little of the world. I am not even sure how long I will stay here, much less sure I am able to make a commitment for the rest of my life. To do so, not knowing my own mind, would not be fair to you either, nor to my father, who has only ever wanted what he believes is best for me.

I hope we can continue to be friends. Please always know the sincere and deep admiration I feel for you.

Yours truly,

Sophie

The letter sat on her dressing table overnight. She gazed at it in the morning, as Doris drew on her stockings, arranged her hair. It was a most proper letter, even though almost none of it was true, apart from her wish to be free of the Understanding. She no longer admired Malcolm; she suspected his conversation would bore her after her months at Shillings.

Miss Lily had changed her. The old Sophie had fallen in love with a vision of a golden couple riding through the bush together. If I ever marry, she thought — and realised how far she had come in including the 'if' — it will be to a man who knows who I am.

At last she folded the letter and slipped it into its envelope, then picked up the other letter she had written, admitting to her father and Miss Thwaites that they had been right. 'Will you put these on the hall table to post, please, Doris?'

'Yes, Miss Higgs.'

But the memory lingered of a young man with the sunlight on his face, the gold filtering through the gum leaves. She touched her cheeks and found them wet. She would have to rest a damp cloth over her eyes before she went downstairs, to hide their redness.

Chapter 28

One does not dine to eat. Dinner on a tray in one's room is eating.
One dines to talk, and to listen. When you dine with others
you are, for a short time at least, part of their world. Good food
encourages both conversation and a certain lessening of reserve.

Miss Lily, 1914

The man who had just arrived was round. Sophie had never seen an entirely round man before, his waist a perfect circumference at the back and front, the tailoring of his coat exactly shaped to fit it. His eyes were surprisingly large and their blue colour looked faded, as he alighted from a motorcar of a darker shade. The chauffeur immediately put up the bonnet and began to rummage under it.

'It's Mr Porton,' whispered Emily. The four of them peered through the drawing-room curtains as Jones opened the front door.

'Porton,' said Mr Porton, handing his hat to Jones. 'An old friend of his lordship's. Is he at home? On my way to a meeting down in Portsmouth, but I'm afraid there has been a slight to-do with my car.' He waved a plump hand towards it as Jones ushered him in.

'Who is he?' asked Hannelore quietly.

'The Portons are a Sussex family,' whispered Emily. 'He's a cousin of Lord Declerk, married a Rivers, but you don't see his wife in society much. He was in the cabinet before the Upset.' The Upset, Sophie now knew, was when the unthinkable had happened, and the Liberal Mr Asquith had become Prime Minister.

'Mr Porton dined with us often before my father's illness. He has a post high up in the Admiralty now, I think.'

Sophie nodded. She didn't think that smooth face would willingly lose contact with power. 'Do you think his car really broke down?'

Hannelore glanced out the window again. 'I do not think so. See? It is proceeding quite efficiently behind the house, with Mr Porton's man and all his luggage.' She turned to the others. 'It is too convenient, I think, for his car to break down just before it becomes dark. Surely he would not have wanted to drive through the night? No, if he arrives now he must be asked to stay.'

'Good.' Emily checked her hair in the mirror above the fireplace. 'Two months in a household of women. But of course he can't dine just with us. Miss Lily must ask some other men to dine tonight.'

Sophie exchanged a glance with Alison. It had never occurred to her to regret the loss of male company. She suspected that Alison, and even Hannelore, felt the same. For the first time she realised how much freedom they'd had, over the past two months together. But it would still be fun to have a proper dinner, with men on whom she could try out her newly acquired charms.

The drawing-room door opened. Miss Lily stepped in, neither flustered nor surprised. 'Mr Porton will be staying the night. An old friend of his lordship's, I gather. I am afraid I haven't met him before. He seems amiable. I expect Miss Carlyle has told you his details.' She didn't wait for an answer. 'I have sent Samuel to ask the vicar and his curate, Mr Merryweather, to dine with us. It will still be an uneven table, I'm afraid, but one can't conjure male dining companions from nowhere. My dears, it is inevitable that Mr Porton will wonder why Shillings is inhabited by four young women and none of their older relatives. I have told him that he has sadly just missed Hannelore's aunt the baroness, and a cousin of Lady Alison's — a quite fictitious cousin, Lady Alison, so if he asks, you are free to portray her as you wish. She and the baroness are in London overnight, but will return on the four-ten train tomorrow, safely after Mr Porton leaves for his meeting. Emily, might I have a word with you before you dress for dinner?'

It was a dismissal. Emily smiled. The others wandered up the stairs. The house smells different, thought Sophie, noticing a lingering scent of tobacco and bay rum.

She let Doris place her best pearls around her neck: slight overdressing for a country dinner, perhaps, but tonight she wanted to put her wealth on the table, so to speak, along with the others' social positions.

The vicar and the curate were already in the library when she entered. So was Mr Porton, already talking happily to Emily, while the vicar and Hannelore compared English mid-winter myths. Mr Porton glanced at Sophie appreciatively as she paused in the doorway, but it was the look he might give a handsome horse, not a person he wished to know. It was evident he was aware who she was, and how little she mattered.

At any event, he would not be able to speak to her or Hannelore until his hostess introduced them, and darling Mouse was trying to be invisible, which left Sophie the curate to charm.

She ran through the next steps quickly in her head. 'Mr Merryweather, how lovely to see you again. Wasn't the vicar's sermon fine last Sunday?'

'Yes, indeed. A pleasure to see you again, Miss Higgs.' She had made him smile, and agree with her too. Now to show she was interested in him, and to praise him as well.

'Miss Lily has told me all about your sterling efforts with the village boys.' Which she hadn't, but what else would a curate do in so small a parish?

'The cricket club?' Mr Merryweather laughed. 'Truth to tell, Miss Higgs, I doubt if we shall see any of them play at Lords. But it is good healthy occupation.'

'I think it is wonderful of you,' said Sophie warmly. Step five to come: praising another. She looked across the room. 'Doesn't Miss Carlyle look beautiful tonight!'

The curate hardly glanced at Emily. 'She does indeed, Miss Higgs.' No, Mr Merryweather was not enchanted by Emily, although Mr Porton was, his nose just slightly too close to her bosom. As Sophie watched, he glanced around the room, with the contented smile of a sultan in his harem. He knew there was a household of women here before he came, thought Sophie. But how?

'I hear you are from Australia, Miss Higgs?' continued Mr Merryweather. 'I gather there are such interesting animals there.'

Mr Porton continued his flirtation with Emily.

Miss Lily entered, once more in blue, her evening scarf of blue and gold, and managed introductions a second before Jones announced dinner was served, so there was no time for more general conversation.

They entered the dining room — Hannelore on Mr Porton's arm, her royalty giving her precedence, the vicar with Alison, and the curate with Miss Lily, only an honourable even though she was hostess, which left Sophie and Emily together until Emily glided to the head of the table, to sit next to Mr Porton, on Miss Lily's right.

The vicar sat at the other end of the table, a long-faced, serious man, with Hannelore on his right, instead of in Emily's place, where she belonged. Alison sat on his left, then Mr Merryweather, then Sophie. With Emily on one side of her, she had only one other dinner companion to talk to, the curate, the least important man in the room. She suspected that Emily would focus on Mr Porton for the entire meal, not just alternate courses.

The table gleamed in the candlelight, Miss Lily's face in shadow from the sconce behind her. She looked younger in this light, her hair, softly gold as well as grey, piled on top of her head, her shoulders white under their soft draping of dusty rose lace, her fingers in their lace gloves lightly touching the small, plump hand of Mr Porton.

'Have you ever seen a kangaroo, Miss Higgs?' enquired the curate.

Sophie acquired a smile. 'Many times. There are great mobs of them on my family's property. One had the temerity to die in our rose garden. It took two men to haul it away.' The curate's gaze grew slightly, carefully blank. 'Die' was too direct a term for a dinner table, surmised Sophie, at least between a young lady and a curate. 'But tell me, Mr Merryweather, are you fond of animals?'

'Very much so, Miss Higgs.'

Consommé was served: an unfamiliar fish in an even less familiar sauce; lamb cutlets each with frills on its bone; then a roast of venison, sent down from the earl's hunting lodge in Scotland, served with Cumberland sauce and soufflé potatoes, and the asparagus that had been forced in the beds of hot manure.

The curate ate the potatoes and the asparagus, but although he allowed Jones to serve him the meat he left it untouched. Was he a vegetarian? She had read in *The Times* recently that Mr George Bernard Shaw claimed meat-eating made men slow and dull-witted. She thought of her father, with his hunks of beef and his beetle energy, and smiled. She'd have liked to ask the curate about the uneaten meat, but one did not talk about food at the dinner table.

Snatches of the conversation floated down the table; Hannelore and the vicar were comparing English and German snow storms now. Mr Porton described his last hunt while Emily gazed at him adoringly. The adoration couldn't possibly be genuine, not for that round marshmallow man. Is this what we have been trained for, wondered Sophie, to look like sheepdogs hoping for the master's notice? This was small talk about small things.

She had hoped for a male's insight into world affairs. Instead it was the most trivial evening she had spent in England.

Outside a wind blew — from the Arctic, thought Sophie, glad her seat was near the fire, for fashion dictated bare arms for formal dinners even in late winter. The wraps they had worn on other nights, women dining together, now hung in their dressing rooms.

At least dessert was a hot one: an orange soufflé, carefully ladled out with silver spoons by footmen in white gloves. She wished there were cocoa on the table, instead of wine. Only the savoury course to go ...

Emily laughed across the table, almost hidden by the epergne. Jones offered devils on horseback after the roast. The curate beamed at Sophie as she nibbled the bacon and left the prune on her plate.

'Go on,' he urged. 'Be a devil, Miss Higgs. Eat it all.'

Sophie wondered how many times he had made the joke. Probably every time devils on horseback were served. I should make him smile again, she thought. When conversation flags begin steps one to five again ...

... But I can't be bothered. Not for this man, with his silly joke, not for Mr Porton, with his soft hands and their rings. She looked up at the portrait of the earl, so slender and remote, gazing towards his duty, so unlike Mr Porton, the curate, or Malcolm ...

She stopped at the thought. Malcolm would fit in here. He'd be ...

... Unremarkable. A table-filler, Miss Lily said, was a good-looking, polite man, who would talk to dowagers and play a good hand of bridge, but not startle the company with his ideas, not take the centre stage away from the most important guests, the ones you needed to flatter, who needed to star. The curate was a table-filler too.

'And koalas ...' said the curate. 'Tell me, Miss Higgs, have you ever held one?'

'No, I'm afraid not. They can be savage, you see, especially in the mating season. My aunt was gored by one. A terrible tragedy.'

The curate hesitated, then forced a smile. 'They look so cuddly, like a furry cushion. I had a toy rabbit I loved when I was small, Miss Higgs.' He bent towards her, confidingly. 'I took it everywhere.'

Sophie shut her eyes briefly.

She was sitting at the same table as a senior officer in the Admiralty, and talking about toy rabbits. At least at the Overhills' table there'd be gossip about people she knew.

Miss Lily's light laugh floated across the table. Mr Porton was telling her about the pheasants he had shot: forty-eight on one beat, whatever that meant.

'... had my loader since I was a lad. Fourteen I was, my first shoot. He was the same age, one of the estate lads. We out-shot half the men there that day, and he's been my loader ever since. Why, three years ago ...'

How could Miss Lily be interested? Or the vicar in Hannelore's story about her great-aunt? We talked about Albanian independence last night, thought Sophie. How can they babble like this now? Was this what she faced in English society?

She turned to the curate. 'Tell me, Mr Merryweather, what do you think of Home Rule for Ireland?'

He blinked. 'Well, Miss Higgs, that is a complex question —'

'Hurrumph.' She had never heard anyone hurrumph before, except a bull. Mr Porton glanced down the table at her, then spoke to Miss Lily. One did not, of course, speak across a table. 'What we need are more troops in Ulster. Keep the lid firmly on, and we'll hear no more talk about Home Rule ... What was I saying? Ah, yes, three years ago ...'

Miss Lily's expression hadn't changed. Nor had Hannelore's or Emily's. Alison bit her lip and looked down at her plate. The vicar took a sip of wine, though Sophie noticed that the level in his glass was the same when he put it down.

She smiled at Mr Merryweather. 'Well?'

'As I said, the answer depends.' His voice was soft enough to reach only her ears.

'On what?'

'On who is listening, Miss Higgs.' His voice was still soft and affable, but there was a hint of something else in his eyes.

'You mean the topic isn't suitable for a woman? You don't believe that women should know about such things? Or vote on them? We have the vote in Australia.'

Again, the whole table had heard her words. Mr Porton dabbed at his lips with his napkin, his face as red as the Cumberland sauce. 'Just what I was talking about. Rabble! Can an Irish oaf govern himself? Suffragettes are the reason we can't give votes to women either. No respect for law or for position.'

'My great-aunt,' said Hannelore clearly, 'since she was five years, I think, always had those terriers ...'

'One is always happy to talk politics with a woman,' said Mr Merryweather, even more quietly. 'But not with a Hereford bull.'

The conversation had risen around her. She met the curate's eyes: he was no table-filler. This man had a brain, his own ideas, for all that he was trying to herd her back to trivial conversation.

'Shall we talk about your native bears again, Miss Higgs? The savage ones that gored your aunt?'

'I knew a curate back home,' said Sophie. 'His name was Mr Stevenson. He had a plan for fallen women.'

The curate smiled.

'No,' said Sophie, 'not *that* sort of a plan.'

He was trying not to laugh. Sophie clenched her napkin.

'None of this is real,' she said quietly.

Mr Merryweather looked at her, amused. 'It seems real enough. Or do you refer to the insubstantiveness of matter? We can discuss that if you prefer.' Again he spoke too quietly for others to hear.

'My father's factories make corned beef,' said Sophie. 'People eat corned beef. Back home I made my father start a dinner programme for my father's workers.'

'And then there was your curate,' murmured Mr Merryweather. 'I can see why your father sent you here.'

The meaning was like cold water on her face. The fact that it was possibly true made it worse. Her father had not just been worried about her marriage to Malcolm, she realised. Jeremiah Higgs was no fool. He had also almost certainly been worried about Sophie's growing and unsuitable interest in his business, and in even more unsuitable charities like helping fallen women.

She had to get out of there. Not just the dining room. Not even just the house. She had to get back to what was real. At least in Australia she could —

'Miss Higgs.' Mr Merryweather's voice was firm now as well as quiet. 'I think, later tonight, our hostess will want to talk to you.'

'To tell me to mind my manners.'

'No. To tell you that it is possible to have a real life, even if at times one must play by the rules of small talk.' His eyes met hers again. 'Small talk is a good word for it, don't you think? Talk about small things that matter to no one. But that is why they are useful. Small talk brings people together.'

'We're playing games,' said Sophie.

'Yes. But trust me, you have no idea what games they are.' There was no playfulness in his voice now. 'I admire your hostess and her ideals very much indeed.'

He had known she was going to bolt. Was he simply trying to lessen the embarrassment for his hostess? And his employer too, she realised, for the vicar and the curate must be appointed by the earl. Could the earl sack them? Could the vicar sack Mr Merryweather, if he failed to do his social duty to the hostess of Shillings? Was that what Mr Merryweather meant by 'it depends who is listening'?

Was she endangering the man's job?

She looked at Mr Merryweather, then at the vicar. Somehow she had the feeling the vicar knew exactly what had been said, even if he hadn't heard it. He was a man who was good at watching.

And neither he nor Mr Merryweather, she realised, looked like those who would live a life made up of nothing but foolish games.

She glanced at Miss Lily. Miss Lily met her eyes for one sharp second. Her smile changed, almost imperceptibly, before it was bestowed again on the man at her side.

Miss Lily rose, her silk dress reflecting the flames. Sophie and the other girls rose at her signal. It was time for the women to leave the room. Emily bent down so that she almost whispered in Mr Porton's ear. 'I do so hope you won't be long.'

'One glass of port only, little lady.' The man was obviously entranced.

Sophie caught Emily's glance. Mr Porton was married ...

Jones brought in a salver of nuts and raisins.

Chapter 29

*The book of life has many pages. You only see how each connects
to make a story as you read.*

Miss Lily, 1914

The men were still with their port and cigars in the dining room.
Miss Lily bent her head to her coffee cup.

'The dear vicar,' she said. 'He will keep Mr Porton there for at
least an hour more.'

'So you have time to reprimand me? Your cousin pays the
vicar, so the vicar does what you want?'

'Not quite like that,' said Miss Lily. 'Nor does one discuss that
in the drawing room.' She sipped her coffee. 'But if we decide
that this is a schoolroom, then if you like, we may discuss the
prerogatives of vicars.'

Sophie looked at the others. Hannelore looked amused, Emily
strangely excited.

How could anyone be excited about Mr Porton? Emily must
have met dozens of men as important.

'Sophie ...' said Alison softly. It was as much a warning as a
plea.

If I walk out of here along with my father's money, Mouse
won't get her season, thought Sophie. If I disgrace myself, her
season won't happen either.

The thought troubled her. She caught Alison's eye, smiled,
shook her head: Don't worry, Mouse. I'll behave.

'If the vicar were really being helpful, he'd bring Mr Porton in
to tea instead of filling him with port.' Emily put her cup down
restlessly, then moved over to the window and parted the curtains.

'Mr Porton is a bore,' said Sophie. 'Let the port entertain him.'

'Mr Porton is an important man.' Emily shut the curtains again. 'If you are too ignorant to understand, then you can at least be quiet.'

'If he's so important, why did you let him go on and on about shooting pheasants?'

'Because that is the way things are done.' Emily looked at Miss Lily. 'Hasn't she learned anything about the correct way to behave?'

'She knows,' said Miss Lily. 'It appears that she did not feel it was worth her while.'

'Then stop spoiling it for me!' snapped Emily, a small silk-clad tiger.

'It is always enjoyable,' said Hannelore smoothly, 'to renew acquaintances. Alison, will you play for us?'

Alison went to the piano and lifted the lid. She played well, but mechanically. Emily paced to the next window. The last two months' camaraderie had gone.

There is something happening here, thought Sophie. Emily wants something. Miss Lily knows more than she's told me, and so does Hannelore. Alison doesn't, I think. The urge to get up, go to her room, vanished.

A voice rose in the corridor. 'Admiral von Tirpitz may gloat over his fourteen new warships all he likes. I tell you, sir, the Germans won't stand a chance. Can't tell you any more — under the rose, eh? But we're onto something that will beat any Prussian airship or Krupps machine gun. Something that could change warfare forever.' Mr Porton came into the room, the vicar behind him, the curate trailing. Mr Porton looked like a beetroot tied into evening dress: his face was red and his shirt was white. He rubbed his hands as he gazed at the female faces.

Sophie made a sudden decision. She smiled up at the curate. 'Mr Merryweather, do please sit here. I'm afraid I am terribly ignorant about cricket. It comes of not having brothers. I shall be sadly at a loss when summer comes.'

The vicar and Mr Merryweather glanced at Miss Lily. She nodded slightly. Mr Merryweather smiled back at Sophie. 'It would be a pleasure, Miss Higgs.'

Emily ran the tip of her tongue across her lips. 'May I show Mr Porton the conservatory, Miss Lily?' Her eyes met Mr Porton's, not Miss Lily's.

'I am sure he will find the blooms enchanting.' Miss Lily put down her cup. 'Do make sure he sees the camellias. Fresh coffee, if you please, Jones.'

Sophie's bedroom fire had sunk almost to black coals. Down in the hall the clock struck two. She could ring for more wood to be added to the fire, or for another eiderdown, but she didn't want to wake Doris. Her maid had been up late, waiting for her to come to bed, and would be up at six as usual.

She slipped out of bed, arranged the wood as she'd seen it done a thousand times but never done herself, and felt satisfaction as it dutifully flared.

She was just about to slide back into bed when she heard a stair creak. She moved silently to her door and opened it just as Emily, standing in the corridor, reached for her own doorhandle next door.

Emily was still in evening dress, impeccable in the palest pink silk, the ribbons in her hair and her silken slippers the exact same shade. One hand held a candlestick. The other hand was empty.

Their eyes met. Emily flushed, nodded, then slipped into her room.

Sophie went back to bed and waited till the warmth of the bed seeped into her skin again. But it was still impossible to sleep.

What had been happening? Surely not ... the obvious.

A telephone rang, in the depths of the house below, a single note before it was answered. Someone had rung the exchange, then, and this must be the exchange ringing back with their call. Even Mr Porton wouldn't have business to conduct at this time of night. It had to be Miss Lily ...

Chapter 30

*Secrets? Of course I have secrets. You think because I am frank
about some matters that I am completely open about everything?
I don't lie, my dear. But neither do I always tell all.*

Miss Lily, 1914

Doris brought Sophie breakfast in her room. The sounds of
maids carrying trays came from the rooms on either side —
Emily's and Alison's.

She suspected that only Hannelore, the most imperturbable,
the most dutiful, had shared breakfast with Mr Porton below.
Poor Mr Porton, denied a final meal with the other lovely ladies.
But at least he had enjoyed the company of one last night.

It was nearly noon before Jones announced that Miss Lily
was downstairs, and free. He announced Sophie at the door of
Miss Lily's private drawing room. Miss Lily smiled — an almost
normal smile — as she entered.

'Sherry?'

'Thank you.'

Miss Lily handed her a fragile glass of straw-coloured
liquid, the lip so fine it might have been worn thin by time.
Sophie held it to her lips. She hated sherry. But it was a ritual,
like dressing for dinner and waiting for the gong before going
down, part of the skeleton of their days, the structure that
supported society.

Miss Lily sat back on her sofa, the fire behind her casting its
usual shadows. 'I presume you saw yesterday's newspapers.'

She had expected to be reprimanded, even warned that she
risked losing her season. Not this. 'Yes.'

'Mr Churchill's new navy budget is the largest in our history. *It is our intention to put eight squadrons into service in the time it takes Germany to build five*, he says. And that on top of his demand for two and a half million pounds to build up the battleship and air-force programmes.'

'I'd hoped we'd talk about it last night. I ... I apologise for my behaviour. Mr Porton must work closely with Mr Churchill at the Admiralty.'

'He does.' Miss Lily bent and picked up a letter from a side table. 'Hannelore's aunt has written to me to say that the Tsar has given orders to quadruple the size of his army, to wipe out pan-Germanism forever. Her estates are close to the Russian border,' she added. 'If there is war, they will be among the first occupied. Children starve as Europe's wealth is spent on fripperies.' Miss Lily might have been talking about hats instead of warships.

She's trying to make me agree with her, thought Sophie, remembering the five steps. Emily has mentioned that I saw her coming to bed. Miss Lily will praise me next.

'You looked quite beautiful last night, Sophie. I am sorry you were bored. I did warn you that a young lady in her first year is expected to smile, know little, and say less. Dinner tables do grow more interesting later.'

'It was ... informative,' Sophie said carefully.

'It was meant to be.' Miss Lily sipped her own sherry. Unlike Sophie, she actually seemed to drink it. 'So what information did you gather?'

'I learned there is a telephone here.'

The glass halted on the way to Miss Lily's lips again. Whatever she had been expecting, it wasn't this. 'It's no secret.'

Had a telephone been mentioned before? She couldn't remember.

'Did you wish to call someone? As I recall, there is no submarine telephone line to Australia yet, or I'd have suggested you call your father at Christmas.'

'No, thank you.' She felt as though she were about to plunge into the swimming hole at Thuringa, not knowing how cold the water might be once she had left the sunlight. 'But *you* called someone last night.'

'Perhaps I called my cousin. They do have telephones in the East, you know. And a time difference. Perhaps, Miss Higgs, I might tell you that this is my business, not yours.'

'But you carefully haven't told me either.'

A small smile lifted Miss Lily's lips — coloured, Sophie knew now, with the smallest amount of strawberry juice mixed with cold cream to make them look pinker but not painted, fuller and shinier, just as her invariable scarf was to hide the slightest crepe of her throat. I still can't even guess how old she is, thought Sophie. So much about Miss Lily is hidden. 'I am quite pleased with you, my dear. How do you know?'

'Because you said "perhaps". You don't lie,' said Sophie. 'You just select the truth. Just like you selected me.'

'No. I hoped you might be suitable, when your father first enquired about sending you to England for a year. Not because of your father's money, although that will give you a kind of freedom that few women enjoy. I hoped you had inherited your father's will to succeed, and his intelligence too. And his integrity, perhaps. But it was impossible to tell until I knew more of you.'

'We're here for a purpose,' said Sophie slowly. 'It's not just to amuse you, or for our own sakes either.'

'And what do you think my purpose is?'

'I think you are a spy. Like Napoleon had spies in England.'

She had expected Miss Lily to protest. Instead she appeared unsurprised. 'Your Miss Thwaites must have taught you some history, I see, even if she didn't teach you much about the world today. History is a useful subject if you wish to decode the present.'

'You mean you really *are* a spy?'

Miss Lily laughed. 'You don't quite believe it, do you? So who am I spying for?'

Once again she had failed to answer the question. 'I don't know,' said Sophie frankly. 'It's either for Germany or England. I've learned enough of politics while I've been here to know it all boils down to those two.'

'"All boils down to" ...' Miss Lily waved the distressing phrase away. 'My dear, if you must use clichés, please, not the ones from the abattoir ...'

'*Are* you a spy? I don't want to charm the answers from you over the next few weeks. You wouldn't tell me anyway, if you didn't want to, no matter how much charm I used. Did you telephone Hannelore's aunt last night? Does the vicar know what you're doing here? Please don't answer me with more questions.'

'If you promise me most faithfully you will try subtlety in the future ... then yes to all three questions. But I do not spy for England. Nor for Germany.'

'I don't understand. France? The Tsar?'

'For myself. For close friends with similar views; one day, I hope, *you* will be such a friend.' Miss Lily put her sherry down, then folded her hands in her lap. She gazed at Sophie without speaking. The fire crackled behind her. A log fell, scattering sparks. 'What do you think Miss Carlyle was doing last night?'

'Not ... not what it seemed. Not ... flirting or even ... the things in that book ... with Mr Porton. Looking for plans, perhaps. He said he was going to a meeting down at Portsmouth. He works for the Admiralty ...'

'Oh, dear. You think Miss Carlyle searched Mr Porton's pockets to find the plans for a new submarine while he was trying to kiss her? Was she carrying anything when you saw her?'

'Only a candle.'

'Miss Carlyle needs to learn more discretion, to charm without having others notice. But she did achieve what she set out to do. The prinzessin, who understands these things, helped her do it, by letting her focus on our guest.' Miss Lily folded her hands like a steeple. A ring glinted in the firelight. 'Miss Carlyle acquired Mr Porton.'

'As his mistress?' She couldn't believe that.

'My dear, you're far too dramatic. A mistress is too often discarded. But a girl who admires you, who makes you think that you are still young, still desirable enough for a wealthy, beautiful girl to want you ... that is precious to the Mr Portons.

Miss Carlyle and Mr Porton were in the conservatory, talking. Miss Carlyle was confiding her dearest hopes and dreams ... or a version of them, at any rate. I was in the library, only a few yards away, with the window open into the conservatory. I am not such a lax chaperone as you imagine.'

'But why did you allow them to be alone at all?'

'Relatively alone. I did not "allow" it. I engineered it, both for Miss Carlyle and to see if you have absorbed your lessons here. Which you have not.' She placed her sherry glass on the table. 'Men such as Mr Porton influence the way others think. Girls such as Miss Carlyle can influence the Mr Portons. After last night Mr Porton will listen to anything Emily says. Mr Porton is an investment, just as my cousin invested with your father. Mr Porton may not change his views or actions easily, or for rational reasons, but when Emily invites him to her dinner table, with carefully chosen companions, he will be there.

'All this fighting for women's suffrage.' Miss Lily waved her hand. 'How much power will the vote bring? Are there any female politicians in Australia? I thought not. Women have stood for parliament there and failed. Australia, like England, is still governed by the Mr Portons.

'Here is another cliché for you: the power behind the throne. The throne matters far less these days, although Their Majesties do still have considerable influence. But it is the Mr Portons who have real power.'

'And you and your friends ... and girls like us ... are supposed to be the power behind the Mr Portons? Why not influence good men, not fools? And he is a fool,' said Sophie.

'For many causes. Primarily, just now, for peace,' said Miss Lily.

Chapter 31

A smile can be more effective than a thousand placards.

Miss Lily, 1914

The sherry decanter glowed in the firelight. There was always a plate of oatmeal biscuits next to the decanter, smelling freshly baked, though Sophie had never seen anyone eat one. Perhaps the earl liked oatmeal biscuits with his sherry, or the earl's father or great-grandfather, and they had become a household tradition ...

I am thinking about small things, thought Sophie, because I can't take the big ones in.

She tried to focus. 'Peace?'

'My friends work for the many things that women care about more than men. Proper education for girls — and for poor boys, for that matter. Free health clinics. Birth control for those who are too weak or tired for childbearing, or cannot afford more mouths to feed. An end to bear-baiting — one of my friends is passionate about that,' said Miss Lily. 'But last night, today, tomorrow, peace between England and Germany, or France and Germany, is our most pressing concern. What use is anything we might achieve if we don't have peace?'

'You think England and Germany might really go to war?'

'Inevitably they will, should relationships continue on their current course. But that course can change, if enough people of good faith act. Because of Emily's charm, Mr Porton will now dine with those who don't accept the urgings of, say, young Mr Churchill, who wants us to keep matching Germany's munitions factories and armies. He will at least listen to those who urge Irish Home Rule, might even accept that free clinics need to be funded for those who can't afford medical help. I can't see Mr Porton ever *championing* either Home Rule or free clinics. But I can see his unthinking opposition perhaps changing over a period of years.'

'I'm sorry. About suspecting that Emily did anything wrong … about secret plans.' She tried a smile. 'Too many romance novels.'

Miss Lily looked at her with a curious smile. 'If there had been secret plans, I wouldn't have told Miss Carlyle about them. Emily is, as you have seen, not entirely subtle either yet, nor are her views entirely her own. She is still at the stage where she can be swayed by whoever she is with — or by her self-satisfaction when she makes a conquest. Perhaps she always will be, although I hope not. Should there have been secret plans, it would have been Jones searching Mr Porton's rooms while Emily entertained him and his valet dined below stairs. But of course I am speaking entirely hypothetically.'

Excitement almost stopped Sophie's breath. Was this a test, to see if she could be discreet? 'So you — hypothetically — might have manoeuvred Emily into charming Mr Porton so Jones could search his room? And hypothetically made his car break down?'

Miss Lily gazed at her. 'Hypothetically — I knew Mr Porton would pass near here on his way to Portsmouth, and if I knew that the meeting in fact involved trials for a new weapon — a weapon that is rumoured to be so dangerous it might change warfare forever — I might have asked a friend to let him know that Shillings had a most charming set of guests just now. Few men can resist being the only stag among the deer.'

'Mr Porton arranged his own breakdown,' said Sophie slowly. 'So what — hypothetically — might the plans be for? What — hypothetically — will happen to them?'

'I might, entirely hypothetically, pass them to Hannelore's aunt in Germany, just as the baroness might, again hypothetically, pass documents to me for my cousin to pass on to his contacts in the Admiralty. Thus do we keep the balance.'

'No one is even supposed to see us walking in the village. But Mr Porton is going to be talking about his dinner here for months, a houseful of "lovely ladies". What was worth risking your secret for?'

'A new weapon,' said Miss Lily slowly. 'One that doesn't kill at once but keeps on killing. Soldiers can ignore dead bodies, but not their comrades screaming in agony for days around them as they die, or linger neither alive nor dead for months or even years. No nation can afford the burden of ten thousand screaming veterans.'

Sophie stared at her. 'What weapon could do that?'

'I can't tell you.' She held up a hand. 'No, I do trust you, Miss Higgs. You must know that I do, or I wouldn't be telling you even this much. But I can't tell you what this weapon is. Only a ... a strange mind could have thought of something as horrendous as that man carried last night. But once the idea is known, perhaps it wouldn't be impossible to recreate it. The fewer people who know just what it is, the better.'

'But if the Germans make it —'

'If the inventor knows that we have it, and believes that the Germans have it too, then perhaps both sides will not develop it further. A weapon one side holds can start a war ... a weapon both sides hold may stop one, especially if it would cause extreme destruction. But in this case,' she shrugged, 'the plans will vanish, embarrassing Mr Porton and those who believe this weapon should be developed. War is played by rules, Miss Higgs, at least here in Europe. After last night perhaps the men in power may stick to their machine guns and warships.'

'But Mr Porton will know his plans disappeared here.'

'Mr Porton's valet will vanish at Portsmouth. To an extremely good job, incidentally, in South Africa, where his brother already lives. He will inevitably be blamed for the loss of the plans.'

Sophie was silent for a moment. 'This matters to you, doesn't it?' she said eventually. 'It's not just moving pieces on a chessboard to make life more interesting. But I don't understand. War ... it's men's business, not women's. Women can't be soldiers.'

Miss Lily stared at her for a moment. 'My dear, you speak like a colonial, from a country that has never known a major battle on its shores. Soldiers have wives, sisters, mothers whose lives can be destroyed along with the lives of the men they love. War takes over the land where it is fought. Women, children, everyone is caught in it. Battlefields are not set aside, like cricket pitches. They are highways, farms, villages full of civilians.'

'You speak as though you've seen it.'

'I have,' said Miss Lily. She stood and walked to the window. 'War is unthinkable till you have experienced it. The Mr Portons, even the Miss Carlyles, cannot believe war could ever come to England's "green and pleasant land". But it has, in the past, and it can again. Hannelore understands, I think, but that is because she has seen violent death at first hand.'

'What war did you see?' asked Sophie, trying to juggle dates. The Franco-Prussian War ...?

'You make it sound like a painting to be viewed at the Tate. I experienced war on the North West Frontier,' said Miss Lily.

'But that's where my father served! And your cousin, yes?'

'I would appreciate it if you would not mention this to your father. I am sure he doesn't connect me with ... with what happened then.'

'What did happen?' asked Sophie slowly.

Miss Lily turned. For the first time the colour of her lips and cheeks looked artificial. 'I had gone there for adventure. So many girls go to India — they call them "the Fishing Fleet". Shiploads of husband-hunters. But for me ...'

'You were visiting your cousin?'

'Yes. Exactly that. I hoped it would be a fascinating place, exotic, if not comfortable. And it *was* fascinating, for a while. The bazaar with its piles of rugs, the spitting camels, women draped like lampshades and others wearing a hundred bangles and necklaces that caught the sun. The heat, the smells ...'

Miss Lily looked down at her hands. 'To this day I don't know if the local Pathans broke the truce. Later they claimed it had been strangers from the hills.

'They took the fort, then broke into the compound at night, slit the guards' throats, then killed every soldier, every woman and child. But first ...' She sat back against the sofa, for once graceless, as if charm had slipped off her like a shawl. 'They raped. I heard the screaming, ran into the corridor. Two men held a child, a little girl, three years old. I had bought her a bracelet in the bazaar for her birthday the week before. I ran to her.'

'Miss Lily —'

Miss Lily held up a hand. 'I managed to grasp her for perhaps a second before they tore her from me. Her mother was already dead, her nightdress up over her face. Then they raped me. I struggled. At first they thought that was funny, and then one hit me across the head. When I awoke it was hard to move. I was sick, over and over again. The house was so quiet. They were always quiet houses, with those thick mud walls, but now there was no sound at all.'

'The little girl?'

'I crawled over to her. Dead. Her body was quite cold. Her blood was all over me. I think that saved me: the men thought I had been stabbed too. I checked the other bodies, still crawling. I was the only one alive in a house of death. Flies feasted on the blood, and at night the rats came out of the walls to eat the flesh. I tried to keep them away, but I grew sick and lost consciousness again.'

'Miss Lily, I'm so sorry. So sorry. I should never have asked.'

'It is a long time ago,' said Miss Lily gently. 'Strange: talking about it hurts less than I thought it would ... A party of British soldiers arrived the next day, or maybe a few days after that.' Another shrug. 'Your father was one of them. He wrapped me in a rug. He even tried to convince my cousin when he returned that it had not been my cousin's fault. They struck up a true if unconventional friendship. I think that incident was why both men left the army; why, perhaps, my cousin lent your father the money to found his first factory and helped him gain his first major army supply contract.' For the first time her voice broke. She looked out the window. 'I should not have said this,' she whispered. 'Not to a young girl.'

'Perhaps girls like me need to know what the world beyond our drawing rooms can be like,' said Sophie quietly. 'What did you do then?'

'I stayed in India, up in the hills. I couldn't come home — couldn't face finding life here going on as normal when for me so much had changed. After that I travelled — families like mine have friends and relatives across the world. My people became used to my absence. The place I might have occupied in English life just ... closed over. I have been forgotten, I think. Travel, however, is a diversion, not a cure.

'Unhappy people draw others to them who are unhappy too. It was at that time that I met Alison's grandmother; she was a drudge, with no hope of anything more. Hannelore's aunt too; the baroness had lived through a Russian invasion. I have never heard her story, but suspect it is no less horrifying than my own.

'I began to see other people, Miss Higgs. I had lived in a cocoon of my own needs and desires until then. Slowly, my friends and I began to realise we might use our needs and desires to try to gain some control over the life others' expectations had forced on us. Lady Alison's grandmother learned enough not just to escape her drudgery but even to become a duchess. The baroness hosts hunting parties that even Kaiser Wilhelm attends. Hers is the sort of life Hannelore will have too, if she learns her lessons here.' Miss Lily tried to smile. 'Have you any more secrets you wish to prise from me, Miss Higgs? I seem to be vulnerable in telling secrets today.'

'Only one,' said Sophie slowly. 'While ... while you are in a mood to tell secrets. You said you'd never met my mother. But you do know more about her, don't you?'

Miss Lily smiled tiredly, and Sophie years later would remember that, and realise it was the smile of an elder, resigned to the self-absorption of youth. 'My knowledge of your mother is simply one of life's coincidences. She was the daughter of a Captain Dodds. Your maternal grandmother died of fever, I believe, and her husband lost his life on the Frontier a few years later. Your mother was perhaps seventeen when she was orphaned. She became a governess in the household of the colonel of the regiment and his wife. I knew the colonel and his wife slightly.'

'My father never speaks of her.'

Miss Lily inclined her head. 'That is all I can tell you, I'm afraid. Well, Miss Higgs, may I repair to my room now? I think, perhaps, I will forgo luncheon in the dining room today.'

Sophie stood. The cascade of information and emotion deserved words far beyond those Miss Sophie Higgs could fashion. At last she said, 'Thank you, Miss Lily. I'm ... so very, very sorry. Thank you for trusting me.'

Miss Lily stood too, and took Sophie's hands in hers, the large-knuckled fingers in their lace mittens that still seemed the most graceful Sophie had ever known. 'Thank you, my dear, for being someone I can so deeply trust.'

And that, thought Sophie, is a truth.

216

Chapter 32

*Make plans for whatever disaster might befall you, then once you
have planned, look forward to good things too. Take joy in small
things while you can. The taste of tea, the butter on the muffins.
It will break your heart otherwise.*

Miss Lily, 1914

Muffins steaming on the salver. Emily and Alison sitting on the
hearth, each holding one on a toasting fork in front of the flames;
Sophie spreading them with butter and honey; and Hannelore
and Miss Lily with sticky fingers, crumbs on their laps.

Their last teatime together at Shillings.

'Not the last,' said Miss Lily. 'I hope you'll visit again. All of
you. Whenever I am here.'

The others have homes to go to, thought Sophie. The only
home I have in England is here. She would be staying with Alison
at the duke's London residence, but that was not a home. One of
Hannelore's many uncles had taken a house in Grosvenor Square
for the season too, only a short distance from Alison's cousin's
town house. But Sophie had no one this side of several oceans.

Not true, she corrected herself. I have Alison, and Hannelore
would convince her uncle to let me stay. Emily? No, she
thought. Emily will see me as a competitor, at least until she
is safely engaged. Hannelore will have her husband chosen for
her; and despite the last four months of training, Alison will
never aggressively seek out a man to marry. But each year there
is only a certain number of eligible men for the new market of
debutantes. If there is a prize catch this year, Emily will want
him for herself.

To Sophie's surprise, she felt amused by the thought of Emily peering across ballrooms, evaluating each available man. She had told Malcolm the truth about feeling too young to make a decision about marriage.

She was just beginning to understand what Miss Thwaites had for so long tried to show her: her father's money would mean there would always be suitors. She could wait ten years for marriage, if she wanted to. Hard to imagine life more than ten years from now ...

Alison turned her muffin over to toast the other side, then blew on her fingertips. 'I wish you'd come up to town with us, Miss Lily, just for a few days.'

'You won't,' said Miss Lily gently. 'Not when you are there. You'll have other things to think of, and your own life to create. But I hope you will write to me — not just about political and social matters where shared information will be useful, but also about the dinners, the afternoon teas, the hunting parties, where I hope all of you will delicately urge your companions towards viewing the Empire as one of peace and prosperity, not war.'

She met their eyes, one by one. 'I hope that in the years to come we will not be students and teacher, but friends. I hope you will stay friends with *each other* too.' She glanced at Emily. 'But do not feel betrayed if you do not. People change, and you will as well.'

She accepted another muffin from Sophie, then licked a drop of the honey from its edge with the tip of her tongue. She is perfect, thought Sophie. Everything she does is perfectly judged.

She says that she has love. How can she stay here, then, for so many months, alone except for the girls who come here?

'So,' said Miss Lily. 'This is the last lesson.'

'What is it?'

'Dear Sophie, always so direct. No, that wasn't a criticism. Your questions have a softness now that they didn't when you first arrived. You no longer seem to challenge the world. So, the lesson ...

'Enjoy yourselves, my dears. I wish I could give each of you the promise of a life of happiness to come. But I can remind you that even when things are harshest there are good things too. There are friends, there is the opening of a flower, and somewhere there is laughter, for others if not for you. Think of that and be happy for those who can laugh. Take pleasure in doing your duty, because you are going to have to do it anyway, so you may as well make the most of what you can.' She hesitated. 'Be there for each other, if you can. If I have given each of you anything at all, I hope it is a taste for friendship.'

'Thank you, Miss Lily.' Hannelore rose in a swan-like sweep. She bent and kissed their mentor on both cheeks.

Miss Lily was crying. Sophie found she was too.

I don't want this to end, she realised. I want the five of us to stay like this, sheltered from the world, forever.

But even as she thought it, part of her was excited about London, and balls, and new experiences.

I am a swan, thought Sophie. I radiate the wonder of the world.

There was a final and private goodbye for each of them in Miss Lily's small, grey, silk-covered drawing room. Sophie wondered if the room was ever used when the earl was in residence.

Miss Lily stood as Sophie entered the room. A greeting of equals, these days, or at least of those who gave each other respect. 'My dear Sophie.' She held out her hands. They felt chilly under the lace gloves when Sophie grasped them. Miss Lily sat on her brocade sofa, with Sophie, as so often before, on the chair in front of her.

'Well, my dear, do you regret your visit?'

'No. I ... I think this has been the most wonderful time of my life.'

Miss Lily laughed. 'Then make sure it doesn't stay that way. Life should be better year by year, or you are seriously at fault.'

'Do you regret accepting me?'

'If a lone woman can give herself the airs of a university, I think that you and Hannelore are my only true graduates this year. I had hopes of Emily, but she focuses on her own advancement.' Miss Lily smiled. 'Just now Lady Alison is still a hedgehog, curled around herself for her own protection. If she ever uncurls, well, we'll see. But you will be ... interesting, in the next few years. You're not nervous about meeting Her Grace?'

'No. I almost feel I know her already, from everything Alison has said.'

'She won't be grandmotherly to you, but she will be kind. She is glad her granddaughter has found a friend. And young Mr Overhill? I gather his letters have stopped?'

'I think he has accepted I won't marry him. Truthfully ... I don't know if I want to marry an Englishman either. Not if it means never living in Australia again.'

'You may change your mind when you have seen more of England, and English life.' Miss Lily spoke with the certainty of one who, despite her travels, considered England to be the still centre around which the world revolved.

'Perhaps I'll be like you, and never marry at all.'

'My dear, your mother may have vanished, but that doesn't mean the person you are now must disappear with *your* marriage. That is what you fear, isn't it?'

'I ... yes, a little.'

'As you know yourself better, there will be less chance that marriage will subsume you into the identity of your husband.' She paused. 'Why do you assume I never married?'

'We call you "Miss".'

'Yet you know I use a pseudonym.'

'What is your real name, then? You have told me so much already. Are you married — or were you once?' she added, thinking of widows. A soldier husband, killed in India. Of course, that would fit. Her husband, not Miss Lily, might be the relative of the earl ...

'If you ask me the next time we meet, I may tell you. In the meantime, you have your father's drive and intelligence, as well as what I imagine was your mother's beauty. And money — even from corned beef — gives immense opportunities, if you are prepared to take them.'

'So I should find a suitable husband?'

'That is what the season is for. But for you? Wait a little, my dear, until you are deeply sure not just that you have found a man to share your life with, but that the life will be fulfilling for you too.'

'If I do, will you come to my wedding?'

Once again, Miss Lily looked startled. 'You are the only girl who has ever asked me that.' A strange smile lurked as she added, 'No, my dear, no matter who you marry, there can be no Miss Lily at your wedding.'

'I still don't understand. Why do you have to vanish?'

'Think about it. A certain Miss Lily gives sometimes quite shocking lessons to young girls, receives information and passes it to others. There can be gossip, no matter how discreet everyone is. Lord Buckmaster and his talk of my "lovely ladies". Others may talk too, with more malice or carelessness. But, you see, there is no Miss Lily. None in Debrett's. They ask the Earl of Shillings about his cousin. He replies, quite genuinely, that he has no relative called Lily. I don't exist, so that I cannot hurt you, or my other young women. So that we can continue with our work.'

'I ... I hope I can be of use, then.'

'Probably not, in your first season. It will be filled with the trivialities you so despise. But remember that you will be making useful connections, useful friends. Starting, possibly,' said Miss Lily lightly, 'with Hannelore's uncle, who has access to the German Foreign Office.'

Sophie stared at her. 'But surely Hannelore ...'

'Is German. She may pass on information she believes will help keep the balance of power, will certainly cajole the Kaiser into keeping England's friendship, but never doubt her loyalty to her country. It is also likely,' added Miss Lily, 'that her uncle will speak more freely of his work to a charming colonial than to his niece.'

'What kind of information?'

'That is impossible to say. A private meeting with the Tsar, for example, might mean a treaty or simply dinner. Small matters, like agreeing to stand godfather to someone in Luxembourg, may be part of a jigsaw that others can put together. But mostly, this year you are a cygnet, still to find what kind of swan you truly are.'

Sophie sat silent.

'Of all the girls who have been here,' said Miss Lily at last, 'I think you have been closest to my heart.'

Sophie felt her throat close up with tears. Surely Miss Lily couldn't mean it? 'The ever-charming Miss Lily, knowing just what to say?'

'I told you once I would never lie to you. If I ever had a daughter, I would wish her to be like you. Nor was that calculated charm, to a girl who I know is motherless. It is nothing less than the truth.' She added — probably to let me compose my face so I don't cry, thought Sophie — 'I don't expect you to reply, "You are exactly what I would have wanted for a mother." I am quite unsuitable as a mother, and I hope you know it.'

Sophie hoped her nose wouldn't run. Tears could be ignored, but not a runny nose. 'I wish this weren't really goodbye.'

'It doesn't have to be. My dear, next Christmas, if you are not engaged by then, not committed to another's family nor back in Australia, will you spend it here? I have decided I need another Christmas at Shillings. I think I can guarantee, too, that this time the earl will be here also. I would very much like you to meet him — something else I have not said to any of my girls before.'

'I ... thank you, Miss Lily.'

'Thank you, my dear. My nanny told me once — she was in her nineties then — to make sure that as I grew older I had young friends too.'

'Why did she say that?'

'Because the old ones just go and die on you.'

Sophie laughed. 'I won't go and die on you. I promise.'

'I'm grateful,' said Miss Lily dryly. 'I would hate to have wasted these last months' work.'

Sophie and Alison left first, with their maids, driven to the station in the earl's carriage. Miss Lily felt it inadvisable for all four girls to travel up to London together in the same train. Their trunks, hatboxes, travelling rugs and luncheon hamper ('Never trust that you will find anything resembling food on any but French trains,' advised Miss Lily) had already been taken to the station.

They all hugged. Emily's grace already almost rivalled Miss Lily's, and she displayed no hint of regret at leaving.

To Sophie's surprise there were tears on Hannelore's face. The prinzessin stood back, fumbling for her handkerchief — which was even more shocking, for Sophie hadn't seen Hannelore fumble with anything before.

'It has been a good time here,' she said abruptly, aware of how much she had revealed. 'At home I am the prinzessin; at the school in Switzerland too. Here I have been Hannelore.'

'You will be Hannelore to us, always.' Alison hesitated, then kissed her on the cheek. 'We will see you soon, you goose. Come to tea, tomorrow.' They looked at each other and laughed. Tea would always be a special word for them, thought Sophie: full of memories of crumbs and laughter.

'And if London gets too cold, there is Thuringa,' said Sophie lightly. 'If you ever need a warm retreat from the world, I can promise you one there.'

'One day. Perhaps.'

Sophie thought she meant it too, though she realised how little escape was possible for a prinzessin.

She glanced at Emily. A smiling Emily, but preoccupied, as though her mind were already on the world she planned to conquer. She hasn't asked us to tea next week, thought Sophie, or even said she'll come to visit us with Hannelore.

The staff lined up to bid Alison and Sophie farewell — the maids, the footmen, even Mrs Goodenough, and Jones immaculate in his tails, opening the door of the carriage for them himself, rather than the coachman: a singular honour.

Doris already sat inside, clutching Sophie's jewel case. She seemed elated, not tearful, at leaving the only home she'd known. Alison's maid, with perfect discretion, looked almost invisible against the leather seats.

The staff waved as the carriage crunched across the gravel to the gates. Sophie craned to get a final look at Miss Lily. She wore a hat, wide-brimmed and heavy with silk roses, her scarf draped delicately about her neck even for this brief excursion. Careful of her skin, thought Sophie. If I'm not more careful, I'll be leather by forty.

But forty seemed a very long way away.

The driveway flickered on either side, the trees in leaf, the shadows soft and deep.

Goodbye, Shillings, she thought. To her surprise, she was nearly as sad to leave the place as she was to farewell the woman still standing on the stairs.

Chapter 33

Do not be afraid to think you have taken the wrong road. Someone who never feels that has never considered what she wants from life.

Miss Lily, 1914

2 May 1914

Dear Dad and Miss Thwaites,

I have met the Queen!

Her Grace took Alison and I — sorry, Alison and me, Miss Thwaites (but it still doesn't sound right!) — to Windsor Castle for tea. We didn't go in the front, with all the guards, but through an ancient gate called King Henry VIII's Gate, then up through something called the Lower Ward. It has ancient stone walls and still has a portcullis (I think that is how it's spelled) that can be raised and lowered to keep out attackers. Or maybe colonials, if they aren't accompanied by the King's second cousin by marriage and the Queen's goddaughter!

I'd expected something all grand and ancient. It WAS ancient, but not nearly as grand as the Sydney Town Hall. Alison says that is because the Sydney Town Hall wasn't built to keep out invading armies, and that is what castles are really about.

All Windsor Castle feels damp because it is so near the river. Somehow we acquired a footman. He was quite old; I think the old ones get the honour of escorting Her Majesty's goddaughter and a duchess. The footmen really do still wear powdered wigs and they smell of sweat and mildew, which I think must be from their coats, as they do not look like they are cleaned very often!

Our footman didn't even look at us, or not directly, and we were really looking very pretty, but I suppose it is his duty.

Her Grace is what people here call 'distinguished', which means she is large but solid, and as tall as a man. But she moves and dresses beautifully, mostly in grey or mauve lace that drapes at her neck and wrists and skirt. It was grey lace today, and Alison and I trailed after her like cygnets after a swan.

We went through a narrow stone passage — damp and smelling like the bat cave at Thuringa — into the castle itself. It really does look just like a proper castle: wonderful stone ceilings, vaulted I think they are called, and oak panelling, which I know about now.

We kept passing lots of other footmen and pages, and they bowed low as soon as they saw us and didn't look up till we had passed. They must know the shoes of everyone in the palace.

MY shoes were ivory kid, very plain, without even buckles. I wore my new ivory silk with narrow sleeves and large cuffs, and ivory stockings and gloves and hat, and Alison wore white in the same style so we matched, which I think was deliberate on Her Grace's part to make me seem one of the family.

The footman opened the door to a, well, quite plain-looking room, and there was Her Majesty Queen Mary just sitting by herself KNITTING, and I realised that of course this is their home as well as being a fortress. She didn't stand up when Her Grace went over and gave a tiny curtsey and kissed her cheek all at the same time, which must take a lot of practice, especially when there is so much of you to curtsey. I didn't think ANYONE kissed the Queen — though of course her own family must, or at least the King.

Alison and I curtseyed and I did it PERFECTLY. Alison only had to give a little bob, as she had met Her Majesty previously, but I had to go right down to the floor with my head lowered, then up again. Next time it won't have to be so low — if there IS a next time, of course.

Then the Queen invited Alison and I — me — to sit down and asked me about koalas and kangaroos, and I gave her the answers I've given two thousand people in England so far. Then another three footmen brought in 'tea': Earl Grey in a silver pot, with a samovar for more hot water, which is most efficient, and toasted crumpets and fruitcake and sponge cake and bread and

*butter and tarts called ladies-in-waiting. I'd been too nervous and
excited to eat lunch and was starving, but you can only eat if Her
Majesty does, so I just sipped my tea and FINALLY she took a
piece of bread and butter, so I could too, but only the bread and
butter, because she never touched anything else. While this was
going on Alison and I listened to Her Majesty talk to Her Grace
about people I'd never heard of.*

*I was starving by then and so was Alison. I think Her Majesty
guessed, because she gave a sudden twinkling smile and said, 'Run
along now, Alison, and show Miss Higgs the kitchens.'*

*We left Her Majesty and Her Grace talking about what
His Majesty's cousins in Germany think about the rebellion in
Albania. I also think Her Majesty didn't consider the subject
suitable for young ears.*

*Alison and I went down several dim stone passages with tiny
windows set into walls fourteen feet thick, and finally got to a
HUGE kitchen containing hundreds and hundreds of shining
copper frying pans and saucepans. It had electric stoves and
electric heating tables as well as the old wood stoves, and a giant
fireplace — big enough to roast an ox in, just like in the stories,
though there wasn't an ox in it — and there were people running
everywhere and girls doing the washing up. It seemed an awful lot
of food for just the royal family, but of course everyone else in the
castle must be fed too.*

*One of the cooks was called Dorothy and she knew Alison;
she had worked for Her Grace when she was younger — the cook
I mean, not Her Grace, though come to think of it both would
have been younger then. She'd known we were coming and had
made ginger nut biscuits specially because Alison loves them, and
a sponge cake with Devonshire cream and strawberry jam, and
fresh bread rolls with cheese. We ate at the staff dining table;
it's enormous and full of ridges from all the scrubbing it gets. We
weren't allowed to sit up near the top: the head butler is meant to
sit at one end and the housekeeper at the other. In the Windsor
Castle kitchen even the Queen's goddaughter isn't as important as
a butler.*

*Alison told Dorothy about the plans for our coming-out ball,
and our new dresses and hats and who is making them and what
they are made of and how everyone back at the Abbey is. Then
Dorothy wrapped up some of the special ginger nuts in a napkin
and we took them out into the park.*

*Alison showed me Queen Anne's Garden (Queen Anne was so
fat that she had to be carried around it on a sling carried by heaps of
footmen). Then we went down to the river and just sat there nibbling
ginger nuts and talking, and I kept thinking, This is me, Sophie
Higgs, eating the Queen's ginger nuts and sitting by her river.*

*Tomorrow night is Alison's and my ball. It is funny, though: it
is WONDERFUL about my ball and I can't thank you and Her
Grace enough, but somehow it feels like that moment by the river
was the happiest in my life.*

*Love from your very excited,
Sophie*

The river curved with a grace that seemed as old and practised
as every ritual in the castle. The high grey walls and towers of
Windsor Castle gleamed in the low rays of the afternoon sun.

Such different light here from Thuringa's, where the river was
curling and shallow, and the black swans honked.

A swan — a white one — paddled towards them, as though
England itself were trying to be nice to Sophie. Three cygnets
followed it, not quite as serenely.

'Mouse, look, there's a swan!'

'Belongs to the King,' said Alison idly. 'All swans belong to the
King.'

'I was too scared to be swan-like except for my curtsey,'
Sophie confessed. 'But Her Majesty seems nice.'

Alison glanced at her. 'You sound surprised.'

'One doesn't think of queens as being nice.'

Alison laughed too. 'Queens are just like other people.'

'No, they're not.'

'Well, all right, they're not. I meant that every queen is
different. Her mother-in-law Queen Alexandra isn't like Queen

Mary at all. Even before King Edward died she was much more informal; she loves charades and word games and practical jokes. She'll turn up unannounced and stay to dinner like an ordinary person.'

'An ordinary person wouldn't just turn up and expect to stay to dinner.'

Alison didn't answer. Sophie looked over at her. 'What are you thinking, Mouse?'

'I'm thinking I wish it could always be like this.' She paused. 'Miss Lily told me she has found a husband for me,' she said abruptly.

Sophie turned and stared at her. '*Found* you one?'

'Sort of found. She has written to him, and he says he will see if we might suit each other.'

'Who is he? What's he like?'

Alison watched the clouds again, swimming across the mist-damp sky. 'Miss Lily wouldn't tell me his name. She said it would look more natural if he courted me in the ordinary way. Maybe we'll dislike each other on first sight.'

'No one could ever dislike you, Mouse. Not unless you wanted them to.'

'Miss Lily says he's "well bred, well read and well situated". And that he would like children, or at least a child, but otherwise would be happy with a companionate marriage.'

'Companionate?'

Alison shrugged. 'I suppose it means, well, companions. No lacrosse.'

'You don't mind it being sort of arranged?'

'No. Really and truly. It would be a relief to have it settled. If he likes me, he'll let me know he knows Miss Lily, so I'll know he's the right one. When I'm besieged with suitors.'

'Hundreds of them, lined up down the carriage drive.'

'Thousands. All adoring me and laying their fortunes at my feet. She understands,' added Alison.

Sophie squeezed her hand. 'It'll be all right. I'll be with you. And if it doesn't work out ... if you don't like him or something ...

you can come back to Australia with me. I've enough money for both of us. You'd love Thuringa.'

'What would your father think of that?'

'You're the daughter of a duke,' said Sophie dryly. 'He'd dance a jig all around his office. You might even get him invited to Government House. In fact I'm sure you would.'

Alison grinned. 'Then I'll visit. Married or not. Just to make sure your father dines there at least once.' She looked up at the sky again. 'When we are old and grey we will still be friends.'

'As long as the river flows,' said Sophie. She passed Alison another ginger nut and took one herself. They bit into them together, as though to seal the contract.

The Duke of Wooten's London ballroom floor shone like wood fused with glass. The footmen had been dragging bags of sand around on top of candle shavings until it was so smooth you'd slip unless you were in dancing slippers. Now the orchestra tuned their instruments while Ffoulkes the butler checked their list of dances.

Each crystal in the chandelier had been taken down, washed, polished and then delicately rehung by a man like a monkey who had dedicated his life to light. The duke's section of the cellar, locked to his tenants, had been opened. Champagne had been purchased by Mr Slithersole, manager of the London branch of Higgs's Corned Beef, but certain dusty bottles were carried reverently up the stairs to be decanted for the fraternity who knew about such things: not the young dancing partners but the older men who would head for the bridge tables in the library, or conversations in the conservatory. A young man might be dazzled by a debutante, but in most cases it was his father and hers — and their men of business — who would negotiate the marriage contract.

Jellies cooled in the pantry; meringues filled the housekeeper's sitting room, away from the kitchen steam so they didn't soften. An oozing jelly, a watery ice, a cake in which the cream had curdled would be a disaster. The tale of the cockroach in the syllabub at the Honourable Miss Alice Farham's coming-out was still whispered around society's kitchens, as well as the story of the lopsided crab puffs at a ball the season before. A sitting room festooned with meringues was a small price to pay for perfection.

The police were already stationed at the end of the street to stop all other traffic so that guests could come and go with ease, or at least the ease allowed by the crush of another two hundred and nineteen guests and their carriages or cars. Two parlour maids stood guard over every great pedestal of flowers to wipe up fallen pollen and petals.

All this for one night, thought Sophie, staring into the mirror in her bedroom upstairs, as Madame Lynette, the hairdresser hired for this night, lowered a ringlet onto her neck. But of course it was only one night for her, and for Alison. For everyone else it was part of centuries of alliances out of which the cloth of society was formed. We are a thread of embroidery, nothing more, she thought. And then: I hope at least I'm a charming one.

She took a deep breath, trying not to show her terror or excitement, or, even worse, a hint of victory at being there, at the London house of a duke. Smile, she thought; make them agree with you; ask them a question; praise them; praise another. My eyes will linger on each gentleman's face for just a second too long; I will glance up at him through my lashes as we dance. I will listen reverently to every dowager, with my eyes downcast. I am a swan ...

Madame Lynette coiled another ringlet, fresh from the hot iron, around her finger. It glowed in the gaslight. Madame had sprinkled rose oil on the hairbrush to give a glow and enrich the colour of Sophie's hair, as well as to help it stay in place during the dancing later. Tonight was too important to leave the dressing and hairdressing to Doris, who was standing beside them, intent on every artistic manoeuvre.

Long white gloves, the correct debutante colour, buttoned tightly at the wrists. The ivory silk dress, its neckline drooping low over Sophie's breasts, with shawl sleeves arranged in a delicate gather of pleats on each shoulder, the smallest train —

she had practised looping it about her fingers to dance — white kid slippers, an ivory fan, quite plain, and a dance card with ivory ribbons.

I look ... the same, thought Sophie. She had expected to be transformed, to see a society debutante gazing back at her from the mirror. But she was still Sophie Higgs, even if her skin was less tanned than it had been when she arrived in England, her bosom plumper, held up in the whalebone cups of a French corset.

Two corsages rested on the dresser, one of white roses with a gold-edged card from Alison's cousin, the duke. The other had ribbons of a slightly creamier shade. Its three carnations sent out a scent of spice and sunlight missing from the hothouse roses. The card said simply, *To Sophie, from the Shillings conservatory, with love.*

Politeness dictated she should choose the duke's flowers, but she suspected he wouldn't even know which blooms his secretary had sent. She would carry the ones sent to her with the word *love.*

The door opened. Doris stood back as Her Grace stepped into the room.

Her shoulders were as wide as a draught horse's, her face so plump it was entirely unwrinkled. Her arms emerging from the sleeveless evening gown were round too — not flabby, like those of working women, but fat as mushroom tops.

A corset like a battleship kept the lines of her body smooth, and on top she wore an acre of antique Chinese silk patterned in blue and gold, the hem line and train trimmed with dark brown mink, with a froth of white crepe on one side of her waist and tall white feathers behind the sapphires in her hair, fetched from the bank that morning just like the jewels at her neck and wrists. Sophie wondered how many others at the ball that night would know that none of the stones was real, as all the family's precious gems had been sold on the death of her husband. But even high-quality replicas such as these were valuable.

Her Grace assessed Sophie in six careful seconds. 'You look charming, my dear.'

'But not too charming?'

'Not too charming, nor too rich.' It was easy to see that Her Grace was Miss Lily's friend. 'But there is one addition I think will be permissible.' She held out a flat blue velvet box.

Sophie opened it. The pearls inside shone quietly. 'They are beautiful!'

Were they her mother's? Her mother had left her jewels behind when she disappeared, hadn't she? But these looked new ...

'A present from your father,' said Her Grace. 'Although he allowed me to choose them. Not too large but perfectly matched.'

And much more valuable than mismatched pearls of a larger size. The world grew steady again. The pearls were a way of saying, 'This girl has money, but knows not to flaunt it, and has superb taste.' Her Grace nodded again, as though she'd caught the thought.

'I am glad you are here, my dear. Alison has needed a friend. I will see you both dance tonight with pride.' She bent and kissed Sophie quickly on the cheek.

Four hours later Sophie's back ached from the twist of her corset — her bottom pushed out one way and her bosom the other — her feet hurt, and even her teeth felt exposed from so much smiling. She had given her hand to all of society's top six hundred families, at least, and possibly their third and fourth cousins too, standing in the receiving line next to Alison, smiling, greeting, smiling again and looking demure.

Tomorrow she knew she would remember this night with wonder. Just now she wished she could stretch it out somehow, so she could absorb each moment slowly enough to taste it individually, or maybe post a few minutes home.

No one had sniggered, or even given her a sideways look, except perhaps of admiration.

Alison's cousin, the duke, her host, had led her in for the first dance. He was a rabbit-like man, but a dutiful rabbit. Sophie's dance card was full: not a tribute to her, but to the dowager's organisational skills. And not just full of the names of younger sons, or of 'the usuals' swept into any invitation list to dance with wallflowers. Nor was her dance card filled with the names of potential husbands.

This night was to show that Miss Sophronia Higgs was accepted and acceptable, dancing with a duke, a viscount (old enough to be her grandfather), three venerable honourables, a general whose knees creaked, and a former home secretary.

This was a night not to laugh too loudly, a night when society's hostesses would inspect her and hopefully decide, 'A nice little thing, no airs. How much did you say her father was worth?' and remember that the corned beef — and the potentially embarrassing progenitor — were safely two oceans away. This was the night that would — or would not — lead to years, or a lifetime, of invitations.

The ballroom smelled of fresh wax, French powder and ironed silk, of roses and gardenias and very faintly of sweat. The other rooms echoed with the peacock-high chatter of the girls, the owl booms of the dowagers, the pigeon coos of mothers, the deeper but still too-sharp voices of the men. Even the laughter seemed at a higher pitch than that of any crowd Sophie had known.

Every member of society with eligible daughters, sons, granddaughters, grandsons, nieces or nephews was there tonight, as well as unattached bachelors, to cast an eye over the 'runners' for this year's marriage stakes, or even put a wager on which would do well. Others were there for the conversations and cigars in the card room, or more intimate meetings in the library, to discuss the King's extraordinary veto of parliament's decision to give Home Rule to Ulster.

Was it fun? Yes, but not in the way that Sophie had expected; there was too much crammed into too few hours, less gaiety than the New Year's Eve dance at Thuringa, when she danced with the stockmen and the gardener's boy. This was fun in the way Miss Lily had described: knowing why her partners mattered, seeing circles twist into other circles and beyond, understanding the connections and networks and underlying agendas.

Every girl, every corseted, jewel-encrusted mama, was evaluating each man she saw. It was like attending the yearling sales back home and trying to guess which of the sleek, skittish young thoroughbreds might fulfil their potential and which might break down or just disappoint.

A taste, a tiny taste, of what Miss Lily offered. Power and the knowledge of how power worked; being aware of who pulled which strings, and why.

Sophie glanced across the room at Alison, who was between dances like her. Alison's posture was perfect, just like Miss Lily's, the shoulders relaxed. She wore the smile of someone who was enchanted by her partner. But even from where she stood, Sophie could see Alison's fingers pleating her dancing card.

No, this was not fun for Mouse.

Emily was there, surrounded by three young men and four far more interesting older ones. Even as Sophie looked, she glanced up at one of the older men, her lips moving in what Sophie was sure was step number two, *say something you know he will agree with*. She and Emily had only exchanged brief greetings at the receiving line, nor had Emily's mother called or left a visiting card since the girls had arrived in London. *I've been discarded*, surmised Sophie. And Alison too — so it was not corned beef alone that had done it. Emily had no wish to be in the company of those who were skilled in the same charms she had been taught, Sophie realised. Emily's next months would decide who she would be for the rest of her life.

'Sophie, may I present my uncle? Uncle Dolphie, this is my friend, Miss Sophie Higgs.' Hannelore was as composed as ever, in pale yellow instead of white, perhaps to indicate that she had no need of this society's approval, just as she'd had no need to be presented to a queen who had held her as a baby at the recent ceremony at the palace.

Ah, so this was the uncle with 'connections'. The young man clicked his heels and bowed. Blond hair, small waxed moustache, brown eyes. 'Count Adolphus von Hoffenhausen at your service, Miss Higgs.'

Sophie smiled to make him smile too. He grinned down at her, clearly liking what he saw.

'You are very young to be an uncle, Count von Hoffenhausen. I'm so sorry, but is that the correct way to address you?' She leaned forward, looking up at him confidingly. 'I have never met a German count before.'

His grin widened. He was perhaps only ten years older than Hannelore, her mother's much younger brother. Despite the precision of his heels he looked like he had a sense of humour too.

'My title is really "Graf". But that sounds like gruff, and I am never gruff. You must call me Dolphie. My niece has ordered it, so we must obey.'

Say something he'll agree with, say something that will interest him, praise him, praise others. The next four steps were almost automatic now. 'Surely I must obey the wishes of a count too. Though Hannelore's views are always wise.' And Hannelore knows exactly what I'm doing, she thought, refusing to catch her friend's eye as she finished off step five.

'I would ask you to dance, Miss Higgs, but I am sure your card is full. Perhaps you would be so kind as to accompany me to supper instead?' Dolphie offered his arm.

'But supper isn't served yet. There is another dance ...' She glanced at her card.

Dolphie grinned again. It made him look even younger. 'Supper will be served when we go to the supper room. If we wait, we might miss the meringues.'

A demure young lady must wait for her hostess — Her Grace — to lead the way to supper. Sophie paused for perhaps three seconds.

'It would not be good,' she said, 'to miss the meringues. But,' she glanced down at her dance card, 'the Honourable Peter Jamieson —'

'He is not a count,' said Dolphie, 'so he doesn't count.' It was obviously a pun he had made before.

'Mr Jamieson,' said Hannelore as the elderly man approached.

'How very lovely to see you again! Have you come to take pity on a wallflower?' She gazed up at him ... What had Miss Lily said? A woman can look up at any man, even if he is only four foot three.

'My dear, yes, but no, I, really, you see ...'

'Miss Higgs releases you, don't you, Sophie?' said Hannelore demurely, defanging all possible affront the man might feel that a German whippersnapper had removed his dancing partner. 'It is so long since I have seen Mr Jamieson.'

'Of course,' said Sophie. She touched Mr Jamieson's wrist with two gloved fingers, briefly, made sure her smile met his eyes, to show she did indeed regret the loss of this dance, then took Dolphie's proffered arm. Her left foot stepped precisely in front of her right, creating the perfect amount of sway as they walked into the supper room.

She was not surprised to find Her Grace almost at the supper-room door too. Her Grace, it seemed, knew that her duty was to stay a step ahead of Sophie Higgs tonight. Sophie stood back to let the dowager duchess pass, then followed, her gloved fingers lightly touching Count von Hoffenhausen's arm.

The supper room was empty, of course, apart from the white-coated waiters, and table after table clothed in damask, with white roses in silver ribbons tied to each corner, and centrepiece epergnes decorated with more roses. The jellies shimmered — big quivering ones with raspberries and cream, the pale aspic coating the cold salmon, the chunks of gelée around the galantines of venison and chicken, the cranberry jelly around the hams. Blackly glistening caviar edged with chopped hard-boiled eggs stood in jelly-like mounds. Cut glass and gold-edged china gleamed, as did the silver cutlery, ancient and heavy, the silver dishes for the hot foods ...

The voices followed Sophie and the count in, now that Her Grace was seated and accepting a glass of champagne. Sophie sat at the table just below her, smiled a brief apology and got a raised but complacent eyebrow in return.

Dolphie fetched meringues; somehow she was calling him Dolphie as he had asked. He had guessed — from experience, she supposed — that she wouldn't eat; even a debutante without Miss Lily's training would know there was no way to look elegant while putting food into your mouth. Eating was permissible at a dinner party — small bites between the demands of conversation, with the lighting dim — but not here, where someone's first glimpse of you might be with your mouth open for the approaching forkful of chicken in mayonnaise.

Instead she played with her food, lifting the meringue towards her mouth then dropping her hand back towards the plate.

Ten minutes later Alison joined them, with another young man, who stammered, but seemed kind. Somehow he had found out already that Alison liked ginger: the plate he fetched was crowned with ginger truffles.

Was he the one Miss Lily had chosen?

Mr Jamieson held out a chair for Hannelore. She sat in a froth of butter skirts, her back slightly too rigid for swan-like beauty. Dolphie stood and bowed. 'Mr Jamieson, I regret to inform you that I have already won Miss Higgs's hand.'

'Uncle Dolphie!' rebuked Hannelore, tapping the table with her fan. 'Behave!'

'But I am being so good.' He pronounced it 'gut'. 'And I meant I'd won her hand when she accompanied me to the supper room. I am sorry,' he added to Mr Jamieson. 'We foreigners and our poor English, you know.'

Somehow, the candlelight, the rising bubbles in the champagne, the music and the laughter made Dolphie seem unbearably funny, the wittiest man she'd met. I am sitting with a princess, and a lady, thought Sophie, who are my friends. I am staying in the house of a duke. I am practically impregnable, thanks to Miss Lily.

'I say.' Mr Jamieson peered at Sophie and Alison as though conscious of duties not yet performed. 'An ice?' he suggested.

'An ice would be lovely. You are so kind, Mr Jamieson.'

He returned with a waiter who bore a tray with six ices, each in long frosted glasses, touched with dew. Sophie thought back to the ice-cream outings with Miss Thwaites, impossibly far away. She waited for the ice to be set before her: always wait, said Miss Lily. You never know what else might fit into a moment.

Alison reached for hers without waiting.

'Oh!' The damp glass slipped from her fingers. The table was silent as Alison gazed at the ice cream that oozed down her dress. She seemed more frozen than the ice.

Sophie reached over quickly, scooping it up with her napkin. But it was too late: a wet smear slid from her breasts to her stomach.

She can get changed, thought Sophie. She has to get changed and come back down; it would be a scandal if a girl left her own ball. But to get to the stairway, or even through the kitchens to the back stairway, Alison would have to pass a hundred guests, looking at her wet dress out of the corner of their eyes, laughing at it later. 'Funny little slip of a thing,' they'd say. 'So embarrassing for her. Never thought she'd amount to much. No money either, is there?'

Alison's partner was as frozen as she was.

'Lady Alison?' It was a man she hadn't seen in the crush of dancers, or perhaps he had arrived too late for the receiving line. Thirty-five perhaps, with a scar like a burn on his neck; an intelligent face. He bowed to Alison, then to Hannelore then Sophie. He knows who we are, she thought. The bows were in exactly the right order of precedence. He turned back to Alison. 'We have been introduced, but so long ago I'm afraid you'll have forgotten me.'

'I ... I'm afraid ...' Alison's voice trembled.

'Major Philip Standish.'

'Of course, Major Standish.'

Major Standish caught the eye of the waiter who had brought the ices. 'Could you ask Lady Alison's maid to bring down her wrap? It's chilly outside.' He smiled down at them all. 'A friend of mine told me that the roses in this garden are the most beautiful in London. And roses are always sweetest at night.' He glanced at Sophie. 'Will you join us, Miss Higgs? Miss Higgs's wrap too, if you don't mind.'

'And mine too. I am most interesting in roses,' said Hannelore. She tapped Dolphie on the hand with her fan. 'You will come too, Uncle. It will be educational for you to see roses.'

'I am always most happy to see beauty,' said Dolphie, smiling at Sophie.

Sophie let out as deep a breath as her stays would let her. The stain would be covered by the shawl. And what could be more proper after supper than a tour of the rose gardens? For somehow she was sure Major Standish would gather others to come too, to wander the gravel paths, the French doors open, the breeze whispering between the curtains. Many other women, though hot from dancing and the chandeliers, would want their wraps too, would take the air out on the balcony ...

He had managed it in thirty seconds.

Alison's hands were still in her lap.

He's the one, thought Sophie as Major Standish smiled down at Alison. He is the one Miss Lily has picked. Now Mouse is safe.

Chapter 34

A true friend is honest, and that of course is why I have so few true friends. I am so lucky in those I have, like you.

Miss Lily to Isobel, Dowager Duchess of Wooten, 1914

5 June 1914

Dear Dad and Miss Thwaites,

Alison is engaged to be married!

The wedding will be at the beginning of August, because after the 12th everyone goes back to the country to shoot grouse — they call it the Glorious Twelfth, but I don't imagine that is how the grouse feel about it. The bridegroom's name is Major Philip Standish. He is very nice, a bit older than Alison. He is an officer in the Guards but is going to resign his commission, as when he is married he will inherit money from his great-uncle and do what he really loves, which is painting. His uncle left the money to him 'on the condition he marry a suitable girl', and Alison is very, very suitable.

I will be one of her bridesmaids and THE KING AND QUEEN WILL ATTEND. Imagine, Their Majesties sitting down at the front, watching Sophie Higgs walk behind Alison down the aisle!

I am still enjoying myself, though being a debutante is a lot of work. I can see why women in society all have secretaries to sort out their invitations and arrange fittings for dresses and hair appointments. Her Grace has her own secretary for the season and an assistant each for Alison and me. I have been fitted for new dresses every second day; it is not 'done' to appear in the same dress twice and some days I need to wear five different outfits,

though usually only two or three. They are very lovely, of course,
but somehow it is easier to be excited over ONE beautiful ball
dress than fifteen, especially when you have to stand still for so
long during the fittings, in case the pins stick into you. Her Grace
has a 'shape' made to her size so she doesn't have to put up with
the pinning. But as we are just 'gels', our shape will change, so we
can't escape the pinning.

I'm sorry: I sound like I'm complaining! It is all very, very
wonderful and I can't thank you enough for arranging all this for
me (and Alison), but I don't think I'd want to do 'the season'
again. There are so many people to meet that there isn't even time
to have a proper conversation with any of them.

Maybe I am just a little homesick. But don't book my
passage home quite yet. I want to see snow again and more of the
English countryside. Her Grace has kindly asked me to stay at
Wooten Abbey after Alison's wedding, and I would like to very
much. There are also other invitations to stay at house parties for
MONTHS after that, and she will chaperone me to them.

Love,
Sophie

As John the coachman handed Sophie and Alison down from
the carriage the Grosvenor Square gaslights were sheathed in
fog — four am fog, wispy like chiffon scarves, as though trying
to work out whether it wanted to join the coal smoke to make a
pea souper. Ffoulkes held the front door open for them. He looks
more tired than I do, thought Sophie.

In fact she was more bored than tired. She had so little in
common with the young men she danced with, having to endure
endless conversations about horses and other parties, endless
repetitions of 'I say, do you know ...?' Could any one of these
men have run a property, or forged a corned-beef empire?

She kissed Alison good night at the top of the stairs, still
thinking about it. Yes, of course they could ... or some of them
could; they were probably already learning how to manage their
estates. But balls were parrot chatter, nothing more.

She opened the door quietly, then stood, staring.

Doris sat with her back to the door, waiting up for her mistress, as a good maid did every night — catching a few minutes' sleep sitting in a chair perhaps, but never going to bed until her mistress was settled.

Doris wasn't dozing that night. Instead she held one of Sophie's white kid gloves. Each one had been tailored to cling to Sophie's fingers, made from the thinnest, most blemish-free leather. As Sophie watched, Doris rubbed the glove delicately across her cheek, then looked at it and smiled. She reached down to the powder bowl at her feet, lifted the puff and then shook a tiny amount of powder into the glove.

It was curiously intimate — the girl, the glove.

Sophie spoke softly from the doorway, trying not to startle her maid. 'I wish you'd have a nap in the dressing room on these late nights.'

It didn't work. Doris jerked up. The powder spilled onto the carpet.

'Oh, blimey', and then, with even more mortification, 'Oh, I'm sorry, Miss Sophie, I shouldn't of said that!'

'I shouldn't have startled you. Here, let me help clean it up.'

'You'll do no such thing. I mean, I'm sorry, I can manage it, Miss Sophie.'

'I'll mention at breakfast that I spilled some powder when I got up. They'll never know it was left all night. Please, Doris.'

'Yes, miss. Thank you, miss.'

'Good night, Doris,' said Sophie, as Doris turned down the gaslight and stepped quietly out.

She was too tired to sleep. There was a silver flask of cocoa wrapped in a wool cloth by her bed, and a plate of Bath biscuits in case she felt hungry in the night. She took a biscuit and nibbled it.

More dress fittings in the morning. A demure ride along Rotten Row in Hyde Park; a dinner at night; the Ascot races next week, which would be interesting, especially as she would be admitted to the Royal Enclosure.

For some reason the scene with Doris had upset her, the intentness on the girl's face over something as trivial as gloves. This season mattered far more to Doris than it did to Sophie

Yet this was what she had travelled across the world to do.

'I don't want to marry any of them,' she said softly into the darkness. 'This is the season to be married, and I'm not in season yet.' Then she giggled, and wished Alison or Hannelore were there to share the joke.

Marriage to Malcolm had seemed like her only escape from the world of corned beef. But now even as a single woman back in Australia she would be invited to Government House. She was no longer limited to Suitable Friends, but could visit dukes' estates in England or castles on the Rhine.

She was hungry for a conversation beyond pins and polo. No man had even mentioned Irish Home Rule, universal suffrage or the military budget, not to a debutante; nor had she been able to coax even Dolphie into talking about more than German Wildschweine and Australian kangaroos.

Miss Lily had let her glimpse a world that might be hers if she married the right man: a world that a debutante could only trust existed after the life-changing procession down the aisle.

But how could you find the right man among the peacock posturing?

She met him at a Friday-to-Monday.

It was at Fenthorpe Hall, Emily's home: an invitation Sophie suspected was a duty, left until it could no longer be denied that Sophie was accepted by society, and thus any excuse to leave her out of invitations had vanished. It was a large house party, one where one debutante more or less wasn't likely to matter. Alison, indeed, had made her excuses, but the dowager had insisted for some reason that Sophie accept.

Dappled greens flashed by on either side of the duke's motorcar, zipping along at a daring thirty miles an hour, until the dowager duchess tapped on the glass between them and the chauffeur. Even the shadows here were green, not purple. England in June was ... magic: every stretch of grass printed with flowers, as if an eager housewife had covered half the countryside with chintz; flowers even in the hedges; a sky as soft as a silk scarf; days that lingered into impossibly long dusks, the light slowly seeping from the world, as though in summer England only needed a brief nap before the new day.

Two flat tyres later, the gates of Fenthorpe Hall appeared: tall wrought iron, open, with half a house on either side. A man in a cap appeared from one side, his hand to his forelock.

She had expected something sharp and modern, like Emily herself. But this house was beautiful: mellow stone, one pure tall length unadorned by anything other than steps and a portico and three lines of windows, growing smaller with each storey.

By the time they had parked on the gravel out the front, a butler had already descended the stairs, accompanied by three footmen for their luggage: six trunks and eighteen hatboxes for a two-day stay, all packed into the back of the car with the three maids.

Mrs Carlyle swept the duchess straight to her own sitting room, leaving Sophie with the butler. 'Miss Carlyle is still out, Miss Higgs. There is tea in the library, or shall I show you to your room?'

Sophie noticed there was no mention of the master of this house, confined to his bed and small world upstairs.

'She wants tea, don't you, darling?' Hannelore emerged from a doorway further down the hall, her dashing uncle behind her. She looked deeply weary, as did Dolphie, but smiled as she pressed her lips to Sophie's cheek. 'Lots of English teacakes too, and buttered crumpets.'

Dolphie bowed over her hand. She was glad to see him. The season was too hectic ever to know if there would be someone you were acqainted with — or, better still, liked — at any of the places you were invited to. Dolphie had been at most of the London affairs she had attended, but they had been too crowded for her ever to have a long conversation with him, or any other man. A Friday-to-Monday might give them time to talk about things that mattered. Even things worth writing about to Miss Lily ...

'The other guests are out walking up hills,' said the count. 'If I had wanted to go on a march up hills, I could have stayed at home and joined the army.'

'I am sure you march divinely, Dolphie.'

'I waltz divinely. I march reluctantly. Do you know German officers are forbidden to waltz? It might corrupt them.' Dolphie waggled his eyebrows at her. 'Will you waltz with me one evening, Miss Higgs?'

'I would adore to waltz with you.' She gazed at him through her lashes. 'I would adore to talk to you properly too.'

Dolphie bowed over her hand again. 'Conversation with you is almost as good as a waltz. Come, I will beat away the English hordes to find you an egg and lettuce sandwich. Do you know the English feel that egg is naked with no lettuce? I assure you, I have noticed this is true.'

She glanced at him more closely. There was something behind the frivolity. His eyes were shadowed.

Had this tea with Dolphie and Hannelore been contrived?

There was a fire in the small room to which he and Hannelore led her, which was not a library. Why had Hannelore drawn her in there, and not to the library where the other guests might join them? And why was tea set here too, when the butler had said tea has been served in the more public room? The table was laden: a samovar steaming gently over its burner, a silver teapot and a coffee pot, and, yes, the buttered crumpets and the teacakes, a Dundee cake, scones and sandwiches.

She sat on the elegantly uncomfortable sofa next to Hannelore, bit into an egg and watercress sandwich and leaned back lightly, elegantly. Elegance was too deeply ingrained in her to be abandoned now. 'You promised me lettuce,' she complained.

'It is green. Possibly for the English that is enough.' Dolphie raised his eyebrows at her. 'Alone at last!' It was a line from a melodrama they had seen the month before. 'I never see you alone,' he added plaintively — and yet there was something else in his flirtatious tone, something she had never heard before. 'How can I ask you to marry me unless we are alone?'

'We're not alone. Hannelore is here,' Sophie pointed out. Nor did she think a proposal was why Hannelore had brought her to this room.

'Nieces do not count. Besides, Hannelore wishes you to marry me, don't you, my dutiful niece?'

Hannelore reached for a teacake. 'I would rather you married Sophie than a Krupps heiress. My cousin's wife has a moustache,' she added.

'No wife should have a moustache larger than her husband's. If I married a Krupps heiress, I would have to grow a much larger one, and that would be a nuisance.'

Sophie laughed. 'Dear Dolphie. If I accepted you, you'd probably faint.'

'Only with joy.' He lifted her hand and kissed it. But once again she felt his playfulness was forced.

Hannelore frowned at him. 'Stop that. You are not to kiss her hand until she is married.'

'But this is Sophie! She is our friend! And I am just a dear old uncle. Besides, she might marry me and then I may kiss any part of her I like.' He raised his eyebrows again suggestively.

Sophie took a smoked salmon and cream cheese sandwich — they really looked very good — bit it, and glanced up at him through her eyelashes, an automatic semi-flirtatious gesture. 'Dolphie — joking apart — you don't really want to marry me, do you?'

For the first time the laughter left his eyes. 'I think it would be good for me. You have money and charm and intelligence and much beauty. But for you — no, I do not think you should marry me.'

'Since you only want me because I don't have a moustache?'

'No.' He gazed at her over his coffee cup, the laughter gone. 'I would like to show you how the leaves herald the sunlight in spring, in the woods at home. England has no old forests left, the ones where the trees have stood for thousands of years, and you can feel each century as you walk through them. I have seen paintings of Australia, its bare plains and thin trees and forests with blue leaves and strange dapples. I would love to show Miss Sophie Higgs a true European forest. You do not truly know Germany until you know our forests. That is where you will find the heart of every true German.'

She had never heard Dolphie sound poetic. Or serious.

Dolphie smiled at her, the brown eyes sad. 'If we were living in a different time, I would ask you to marry me, even if you had no money, and perhaps we would be happy. I think perhaps there is a forest in your heart too, even if it is an Australian one. I wish you could show me your forests too. But in a few weeks there will be war between your country and mine. I must go back to Germany tomorrow, and I will take my niece with me.'

The season's fashionable skin slid away, leaving only shock. Hannelore couldn't go! To have so recently found a friend, and now to lose her so soon? Sophie was strangely bereft at the thought of not being able to have a true and deep conversation with Dolphie either.

What had created this urgency?

Sophie glanced at Hannelore. Only a friend would notice the extra tension in her body. Sophie looked back at Dolphie. 'Why? What's happened?'

'Our cousin has been shot,' said Dolphie flatly. 'The news will be in all the newspapers tomorrow. Our so-kind English hosts have given us this small drawing room to ourselves to honour our grief. And because we will be enemies soon too, of course they do not wish their guests to see us in their house. The Carlyles will be glad when Hannelore and I are gone tomorrow morning.'

'I'm so sorry about your cousin. But I don't understand.'

'There is no real grief for either of us, which is sad, perhaps, for I think he deserves grief ... I have met him six, perhaps seven times, Hannelore not at all since she was small. But there are many others who will grieve for him, and millions more for what will come after. His name was Franz Ferdinand. He is ... was ... an archduke, and the nephew of the Emperor of Austria-

Hungary, and his heir. That in itself is bad enough. But he was shot in Bosnia, where the police did not even guard him as he was driven through the streets. The man who shot him was a Serb, one of the secret Black Hand society, taking revenge for what they call the oppression of the Serbian people.'

'They shot him in the neck,' said Hannelore softly, and Sophie knew she was remembering another attack, many years before. 'But he did not die at once. His wife saw the man raise his pistol again. She flung herself in front of her husband, trying to save his life. The Serb shot her in the stomach. She died too, many minutes later. I wonder,' she added quietly, 'when people talk about this in years to come, whether they will remember her, as well as him.'

'I don't understand. I really am sorry.' She glanced at Hannelore, wishing she could put her arms around her. But you didn't do that in someone else's house where anyone, guest or servant, might come in. 'But there have been terrible things happening in the Balkans for so long, and none of them have led to war with England. Why should this bring war now?'

'Because Germany and England have been heading towards war all year,' said Dolphie. 'Ambassadors and even kings, exchanging letters, making treaties, tearing them up and making new ones, and all the time the German and English armies growing, steel being hammered for the German and English navies. Do you know why you have never thought of marrying me, dear Sophie? Because deep in your heart you have known we will be enemies.'

'But ... we are on the same side, not wanting war ...'

'Before war comes, we can be on the same side. Once war overtakes us, we become enemies.'

'I could never think of you and Hannelore as enemies.'

'Trust me, one day you will.' He smiled. 'Of course I accept I may not have ever won your heart. But I am a ... little sad ... that you have not even considered it.'

Sophie was silent. For all his joking Dolphie was no fool. She had suddenly glimpsed the real Dolphie, and liked him. 'Dolphie,

I'm sorry. I think perhaps I haven't wanted to fall in love with anyone this season.'

'A little comfort,' said Dolphie. Once again it was hard to tell if he was serious.

'It is best that I go home,' said Hannelore. 'There will be unrest on our estate, perhaps. My family will need me there. Also,' she tried to smile at Sophie, 'England would be a good place to be if the war were only between Germany and France. But this will be a war on English soil, once France falls. You have, what ...? A million men in the armies of your empire? We have more than seven million in ours.'

Seven million, thought Sophie. It was five million only a few months ago. Has Germany been so seriously preparing for war? And Hannelore has known this?

'Germany will win,' said Hannelore matter-of-factly. 'I do not want war, Sophie. You know how much I do not want it. But it is better to be in a country that wins a war than loses it.'

'If I were your father,' said Dolphie, 'I would order you on the next ship to Australia. As a man who might, perhaps, have been a friend, if never more, I would ask you most earnestly to book your passage home, now.'

'Australia will fight with Britain.'

'But it is far away. Those in Australia will not suffer. Not like the English will when their country is invaded.' He hesitated. 'I have been home since I last saw you. The plans for the invasion have been drawn up. They are very, very detailed, including a war of terror on civilians to hasten the surrender.'

Sophie glanced at Hannelore. Hannelore nodded. 'Miss Lily knows. She will tell her friends.' She met Sophie's eyes. 'You should go home, Sophie. The plans intend rape as a tool of war. Babies on bayonets carried through the streets.'

'You ... you can't be serious!' Impossible, with the bees buzzing outside the window, the far-off voices of men forking hay. 'They wouldn't ...'

Suddenly she noticed the door was open. A man stood there: nondescript at first till you noticed the intelligence in his thin face. How much had he heard? 'Ah, Prinzessin, Count von Hoffenhausen, I hope I am not intruding.'

This man had known exactly who was in this room before he opened the door.

Dolphie stood politely, a mask of polite superficiality gliding over his face. 'Of course not, dear chap. Have some tea, do. Though I do not recommend the coffee. Hannelore, you remember Mr Lorrimer. Miss Higgs, may I introduce Mr James Lorrimer. Mr Lorrimer, this is Miss Sophie Higgs.'

Mr Lorrimer bowed to Hannelore, then to Sophie, and stepped towards the fire. He was in his thirties, with brown hair and brown eyes. Nothing special, yet in those seconds she was able to use all the skills she had learned at Shillings.

This man was important. The way he carried his shoulders, the way he evaluated each one of them in a brief moment. And he had come to evaluate how two highly connected Germans felt about the day's news. 'You seem to be having such an intent conversation.'

Sophie turned, showing her length of neck. It was partly instinctive now, to charm a man; it was also partly a way of drawing attention from Hannelore. She looked up at him from under her lashes and met his eyes, allowing her smile to ripen. He smiled back.

Step one achieved, she thought. She made her voice light, as though it carried to his ears alone. 'Count von Hoffenhausen was explaining that while he wants to marry me, it would not make me happy, because his country will soon be at war with ours, and they will win. But I'm sure you don't think so.'

She felt slight guilt at seeming to trivialise Hannelore's very real worry. But there must be nothing that could brand her or Dolphie as spies for either Germany or England.

The newcomer's eyes widened in surprise, and then with interest. Vaguely she was aware of Hannelore's recognition of exactly what Sophie was doing.

But this was personal too. James Lorrimer was ... intriguing.

The man in question turned to Dolphie briefly. 'Ah, an interesting way to phrase a proposal, Count. I wish I had heard more. Yes, I will have tea, thank you.' Sophie poured and handed him a cup. He took it, sipped. 'So you believe war is inevitable, Count von Hoffenhausen?'

'Don't you, sir?'

Cleverly done, Dolphie, thought Sophie. James Lorrimer sipped again. 'I do, though possibly not for the same reasons as you.'

Sophie forced her voice lower. (A high voice is a sign of nervousness, Miss Lily had told them. A husky one speaks both of passion and self-assurance.) 'Why is that, Mr Lorrimer?' This man must seem to be the centre of my world, she reminded herself. Do not look at Hannelore. Do not look at Dolphie or at the teacakes. Look at *him*. Keep your feet facing the table but incline your body ...

'Why do I think there will be war? Or why do I assume my reasons are different from the count's?'

'Both, please.' She could have been a child asking for a treat, or an empress asking for a colony. Make him feel important, she heard Miss Lily whisper.

Mr Lorrimer looked at her thoughtfully. And he smiled, a different smile.

No, there was no need to make James Lorrimer feel important. If anything, she felt he might keep himself unnoticed, so that his true importance would not be recognised except by those who needed to know.

He knows what I am doing, she thought. Knows I am being deliberately charming, and that I have the skills to turn a conversation from areas that might be ... unwise. He approves of that. But how much did he hear earlier?

'I think that you,' James Lorrimer inclined his head towards Dolphie, 'believe that there will be war because both countries have prepared for it for so long — though Germany, I admit, has done so far more thoroughly — and that only the timing of the war is in doubt. That diplomacy has become a game of chess, and soon someone in a high enough position will say, "Checkmate" and the real game will begin.'

So *this* was how politics joined with flirtation. Had Sophie ever felt quite so alive?

James Lorrimer's smile was for Sophie now. 'But I believe that war will come because too many people want it. Not just the politicians or industrialists who think they move the chess pieces. I believe that when war is declared — and I say when, not if — there will be cheering in the streets.'

Suddenly Sophie forgot to flirt. 'But that is terrible!'

'Yes. But it is also true.' James Lorrimer sipped again.

'So people of good faith can do nothing?' asked Hannelore.

'If I thought that, I wouldn't be in the job I'm in, Prinzessin,' he said gently. 'Foreign Office,' he added to Sophie. 'One of His Majesty's humbler servants.'

Somehow Sophie doubted the 'humbler' part.

'How can anyone want war?' Her eagerness to hear his view wasn't performed now. This was a man who knew the hidden crevices of politics, and might explain them.

'Boredom? Even villagers are getting glimpses of a wider world. War gives them a chance to see it, to be part of it. But mostly,' James Lorrimer took another sip of his tea, 'it is fun to hate an enemy.'

'My cousin has just been killed, Mr Lorrimer,' said Hannelore. 'I do not think that is fun.'

Sophie reached over and took her hand.

'My dear Prinzessin,' his voice sounded truly regretful, 'you have my deepest apologies. I should have remembered how personally you are enmeshed in this before I spoke. But too many enjoy playing enemies. If there is not a real war, they manufacture one.'

A good man, working for his country, not personal prestige. Suddenly Sophie was sure that if their earlier conversation had been overheard — and she was fairly sure it had been, and deliberately — there would be no mention of Hannelore's or Dolphie's name in James Lorrimer's report to Whitehall.

The door opened again. 'Sophie, darling,' said Emily, with no particular welcome in her voice. Sophie stood. They kissed the air beside the other's cheek. 'So lovely to see you,' said Emily, not looking at her, but at the man at her side, 'Mr Lorrimer.' It was as though Sophie had vanished from the room, and Hannelore and Dolphie too. 'I am so glad you could come. But you should be in the library! You know Mr Churchill is due here tomorrow?'

He nodded, his eyes amused. Mr Lorrimer knows Emily is deliberately charming him too, thought Sophie. I suppose she will charm Mr Churchill as well. But Mr Lorrimer prefers my charm to hers.

Emily leaned in close to him. 'I have placed you next to me at dinner. Mama would have had you on her right, of course, but I couldn't resist. We can resume our conversation from luncheon.'

So, thought Sophie, watching the intentness as Emily met James Lorrimer's eyes, this is a man Emily would like to acquire as a husband, not a Mr Porton.

'Enchanted, Miss Carlyle.' Once again James Lorrimer was amused, though Emily didn't appear to notice.

Neither Hannelore nor Dolphie was at dinner. Sophie supposed it had been tactfully suggested that they might like to dine in their rooms because of their early departure the next morning. She'd need to leave the drawing room early, to see Hannelore before she went to sleep, to try to reassure her, or offer the consolation of friendship and understanding at least.

Surely Hannelore and Dolphie are wrong, she thought. The assassination of Hannelore's parents hadn't led to war. And that part of Europe had fought other wars on and off for years, without the English or German empires getting involved. Miss Lily said war could be prevented. Mr Lorrimer had too.

Sophie took her place at the table, well below the salt. The dinner table was the longest she had ever seen: at least fifty guests, far too many for general conversation even if etiquette hadn't demanded she speak only to the men on either side. One of whom, to her delighted surprise, was Mr Lorrimer.

She spread her napkin over the silk of her lap and hoped it wouldn't slide off, glad that the pale rose-coloured silk showed off the slope of her bare shoulders. 'I didn't expect you at this end of the table, Mr Lorrimer.' (If you are delighted, show it, Miss Lily had said. She didn't try to hide it now.)

He smiled at her. 'I arranged for the name places to be changed.' He didn't seem worried that he might have offended his hostess or her daughter. Which means, thought Sophie, that *they* are eager for his favour, not the other way around. There was something ... formidable about Mr Lorrimer.

Soup was served. Turtle, garnished with croutons and caviar. She took the silver spoon in her hand, almost caressing it, then smiled up at him. 'Do we continue our conversation about war?'

'I'd prefer to talk about peace. War is simply war. But there are different kinds of peace.'

Once again flirtation vanished in fascination. 'You've seen war first hand?'

'South Africa.'

'You were in the Boer War?'

'For a time. Territorials, not the regular army. I came home when my wife became ill.'

She flushed. 'I'm sorry. I hope she recovered quickly.'

'It was just the beginning, I'm afraid. She died two years ago.' He spooned his soup.

'I'm so sorry,' she said again. She shook her head. 'There has to be something more to say to news like that, but I can't think of it. It must have been so hard for you.'

You have told me you are now unmarried, she thought, as well as that you loved your wife enough to leave the army for her.

'It's the hardest thing on earth to see someone you love suffer. So, let's not talk of war, or death. How about the life of Miss Sophie Higgs?'

She spooned up a little soup before replying. 'Is there anything about me you don't know already, Mr Lorrimer?'

He laughed out loud, so that other guests turned to stare. 'You are wonderful. No wonder the count asked you to marry him. You'd be running the country in a week.'

'I don't want to run Germany.'

'And yet you are close friends with two most important Germans.' The tone was light. The meaning was not.

She flushed. 'So is His Majesty. I may be a colonial, Mr Lorrimer, but my father fought for the Empire, and then helped make it prosperous. I wish I had the power to do the same.'

She had said too much. How many times had Miss Lily impressed upon her that a lady's influence should be inconspicuous? But he was looking at her with even more interest, and a gleam of admiration.

'Why did you come to England?'

She looked at him frankly. 'You know my background?'

'The Corned-Beef Princess.'

She was hot again. 'Is that what they call me?'

'Some do. Are you surprised?'

'No. Although I'm glad it's only some.' She wondered if Emily was one of them. 'I'm here because having a season, being accepted, gives me greater choices, either here or at home.'

'You have been more than accepted. You are a success.' He smiled at her faintly. 'Only Miss Carlyle's odds of a prize marriage are better than yours at White's.'

White's was a gentlemen's club, infamous for the miscellaneous bets inscribed in a particular book. Gentlemen did not tell women about White's or the betting book. This man had offered her a nugget of reality in the middle of society's games.

He looked at her speculatively. 'Miss Higgs, I am now going to make what is undoubtedly a social blunder, and possibly a personal one. But it is important.'

She looked at him, intrigued.

'I ... not quite accidentally ... heard part of your conversation this afternoon. If your friend has seen the plans he referred to, it would be a great service to our country to discover the route as well.'

She forced herself not to stare at him, eating a small mouthful to cover her shock. The query had been so obliquely phrased that a casual listener would never have guessed that a guest at this table had just asked another to spy on another.

'It is an interesting question, isn't it?' he added lightly. 'Does friendship matter more than thousands of lives?'

'It is one Hannelore — the prinzessin — answered earlier,' she said quietly. 'If war cannot be avoided, it is best if one's country wins.' She could not tell him that Hannelore, and possibly Dolphie too, had already told Miss Lily about the planned attacks on civilians, and that Miss Lily would undoubtedly make sure that the information reached the Foreign Office.

But warning of terrorising civilians was a long way from giving the enemy vital information about which country would be first attacked.

Should she do this? *Could* she do this? What would Miss Lily advise? But she at least knew what her next move should be. She looked up at James Lorrimer, met his eyes, smiled, saw his smile answer her. 'I will see Hannelore tonight, to say goodbye,' she said. It was neither acceptance nor denial. She saw him not just realise that, but also approve.

'I ... I should perhaps tell you this,' she added. 'I heard a few months ago that Germany had five million men in uniform. Today Hannelore spoke of seven million. I don't know if this is accurate ...'

'I suspect it is, Miss Higgs. An interesting increase, is it not? I am grateful that you trusted me with it.'

A footman took their plates. It was time to turn to her other side for conversation during the next course. 'I admire you, Miss Higgs,' he said quietly. 'There are few people who decide their own futures. Fewer still are women.'

She did not think the compliment was to manipulate her. 'Thank you, Mr Lorrimer.'

He smiled. 'Until after the fish, Miss Higgs.' Then turned to the lady on his left.

It was nearly eleven when Mrs Carlyle rose, signalling that the women were to leave the men to port, cigars and discussion. Sophie followed the herd with their trains and plumes of feathers into the drawing room, then glanced at the miniatures on one wall till Emily had served most of the women their tea while her mother poured the coffee. She made her way past the gossiping groups slowly.

'Tea?' Emily asked Sophie.

'Please.'

'You and Mr Lorrimer had a lot to talk about.'

'War, mostly,' said Sophie, although it wasn't true.

Emily concentrated on the teapot. 'It is inevitable.'

'You've changed your views?'

'No. I simply did not mention them to our hostess.'

So you took what Miss Lily could teach you, thought Sophie, including acquiring Mr Porton of the Admiralty, with no intention of working for her cause. She felt chilly, despite the fire's heat. How much had Miss Lily said in Emily's hearing that might brand her a traitor?

Miss Lily must be told of this too.

Emily looked at Sophie directly for the first time. 'This country needs war. Striking miners, all the unrest among the unemployed — war will stop all this Bolshie nonsense.'

'What do you mean?' asked Sophie quietly.

'War would end unemployment, end the ridiculous pretensions of the Labour Party too. The important thing is that we win. We have to make these months count, build up our army, equip our navy properly.'

I don't know you, thought Sophie. Did I ever know you? Did Miss Lily ever know you?

'Ask your father what he believes,' said Emily. 'As a businessman, and a successful one, he'll know how Germany is limiting our expansion into Africa, the Pacific, the Middle East.'

'You think my father wants war so he can make more money?'

Emily shrugged. 'That is what men like your father do, isn't it? Make money?' She met Sophie's eyes. What she is really saying, thought Sophie, is, 'Leave James Lorrimer to me.'

'It is the most delightful house party,' said Sophie. 'You and your mother are so kind to have invited me. I do hope your father is resting comfortably.' She meant it as a slap; saw Emily flush in momentary shame. At least some of these visitors might have been taken to visit their invalid host, to give him the illusion he still mattered in the world. But that would temper the carefully planned gaiety of these days with illness.

Sophie picked up her teacup and went to the piano, to listen to another of the season's debutantes play, and wait for the men to join them.

Chapter 35

Dear Dad,

Excuse this short note — I'll write properly to you and
Miss Thwaites tomorrow. But tonight I need to ask a question.
TWO questions. DO you think war is coming soon, and

She looked at the paper, then tore it up. There was no need to ask a man who had lost his leg on the North West Frontier if he wanted war to come. She knew her father too well. Stubborn, sentimental, ruthless at times, he loved the challenge of making money and the sense of superiority it gave him, as well as the money itself. But he would not want war.

And Miss Lily? Did she realise that Emily had been in the pro-war camp all along? And what would she say about Mr Lorrimer's request?

Sophie rang the bell. 'Doris, I need to call Shillings. Could you ask the butler to call for the exchange for me? I'll tell them the number myself.' A small breach of etiquette, but she did not want Emily to know about this call.

Half an hour later the voice on the other end of the telephone line said, 'The Earl of Shillings's residence.'

'Samuel? This is Sophie Higgs. I am so sorry to call so late, but may I speak to Miss Lily?'

'Miss Lily is not in residence, Miss Higgs.'

Why was Samuel answering the telephone? Where was Jones? 'Would you know how I could contact Miss Lily?'

'I believe she is travelling, Miss Higgs. But if you care to send a letter, I will forward it.'

A letter could be read by others. Implicate her, as well as Miss Lily. And surely Miss Lily's contacts had already told her about Emily's true opinions. The inevitable march to war might even be why she was discreetly unavailable.

'Thank you, Samuel,' she said slowly. 'I ... I will do that.' Though the letter would contain only the most veiled reference to Emily. 'Please give my regards to all at Shillings.'

'Of course, Miss Higgs. Thank you, Miss Higgs.'

She put the receiver down.

It was late when she knocked at Hannelore's door, but there were faint sounds from within. Hannelore's maid opened it, a froth of tissue paper on the bed behind her. She curtseyed as Sophie stepped past her. 'So you are really leaving?'

'I must.' Hannelore looked like she had been crying. For the past, wondered Sophie, or for what might come?

Sophie put out her hand. Hannelore grasped it in both of hers, then said something to the maid in German. The woman bobbed another curtsey, swept the tissue paper and a pile of silk underwear from the bed, and left with them cradled in her arms.

'No one downstairs said the war was likely to happen so soon.'

'I think they do not know what this will lead to in Austria, in Germany. But my aunt does, and Dolphie.' She tried to smile at Sophie. 'And your Mr Lorrimer as well.'

'He isn't *my* Mr Lorrimer,' said Sophie.

'He could be. I think he could be good for you, Sophie, darling.' Hannelore still pronounced it 'gut'. 'You feel so too. Better than Dolphie would be.'

Dolphie had been *serious*? Perhaps, if the hours that rushed about them now had not been war-shadowed, he *would* have asked her to walk through the time-hushed forests; would have asked her to be his wife. But he and Hannelore were correct. If war came, Dolphie would be an enemy.

Suddenly she knew exactly what she should do. 'I ... I have been thinking about what Dolphie said, using terror as a weapon against Belgian civilians. Is there no way to stop it?'

Hannelore sat back on the bed. 'Liebe Sophie. You are so very new at this.'

'I ... I don't understand.'

'But I do,' said Hannelore softly. 'I have been living with court intrigues all my life. Quite long enough to know when someone is trying to find out information. Dolphie did not mention Belgium, or any country that borders Germany.'

'I'm sorry. So very, very sorry.'

'Do not be. I would have done the same. Some things should not be secret, and those I share with Miss Lily, and with you. But others ...' She shrugged.

'Hannelore, will I see you again?'

Hannelore hesitated. 'I do not know,' she said at last. 'You have lived far away from all these intrigues. I live on the edge of the volcano. One day's march and Russian soldiers will be on our estate. The Black Hand will find more targets, I am thinking too.'

'Then don't go back,' said Sophie urgently. 'Come to Australia. Say you are "most interesting" in kangaroos and need to see them in person.'

'Liebe Sophie, do you think a German would be welcome in Australia when there is war? No,' said Hannelore lightly, 'it is my duty to go home. Emily and Alison were at Miss Lily's to learn to find a husband. You were there for amusement, mostly, perhaps. But I was there for duty, no matter what I might pretend. If in any small way I can help stop this war by going back to Germany, then I must go. If I must marry to help my country win a war, then I must obey in that too.'

Hannelore looked at Sophie seriously. 'But at Miss Lily's I learned that friendship goes beyond borders or duty. Whatever happens, I hope we will be friends.'

'Always,' said Sophie fiercely. 'No matter what.'

Chapter 36

When you are young, life is like a dance. It is fun to change partners, to see what the music will bring. But slowly one longs for the familiar.

Miss Lily, 1914

It was hard to see Hannelore leave in Dolphie's long Rolls-Royce the next morning; it was strangely difficult to say goodbye to Dolphie too, as the chauffeur, Dolphie's valet and Hannelore's maid tried not to too obviously watch the personal lives of their employers. Neither Emily nor Mrs Carlyle joined her on the stairs to wave them goodbye. Friendship could be discarded — or disregarded — as easily as a man lying lonely and helpless above could be ignored.

James Lorrimer sat next to Sophie at breakfast with his neat bowl of porridge, topped with sugar and milk. 'You look beautiful, Miss Higgs. Your friends left safely?'

At least a dozen pairs of ears were listening; nor as a debutante could she talk to him privately without scandal.

'It was hard to say goodbye to the prinzessin. I asked about her travel plans on the continent, but I think everything is too uncertain for her to plan ahead.'

He understood. 'Will you write to her?'

'Of course. But if I do, I don't think she will be able to tell me more.'

He nodded, as if it were of little consequence. 'Our hostess suggested a walk to the old abbey this morning ...'

It could have been any country party conversation.

She met James Lorrimer six times over the next ten days. Once at a party; he danced well, though in a businesslike manner that suggested that he was dancing for a purpose, not for enjoyment. He did not mention Hannelore. In his quiet way he made it quite clear that his interest was in Sophie, not information. Twice he called at the duke's town house — both times towards the end of teatime — Sophie assumed with Her Grace's permission.

The first time he found her pensive: she had just refused her first offer of marriage, if you didn't count Dolphie's. It had hurt to do so. She liked the young man, and if he must be intent on gaining her fortune, she suspected that was not her only attraction for him.

But as he had sat beside her — Her Grace tactfully out of the way (the young man had certainly explained the situation to the dowager first) — she had found herself remembering how the sunlight kissed Malcolm's hair, the way the light shone red through the dusty afternoon. Her longing hadn't been for Malcolm, but for home. An English husband might agree to live in Australia. But if he didn't like it, he could return and his wife would be legally bound to follow him. It would need a different man — or a different life — to tempt her into staying in England.

Should she do what Dolphie had suggested? Book a passage for Australia now, in case war broke out? But ships still sailed in wartime. Navies might fire on each other's ships, but passenger liners would be safe. In six weeks she could be under the gum-tree shadows, hearing the sharp bark of ducks calling their young on the river at night.

'I'm interrupting your thoughts, Miss Higgs.'

She looked up as James Lorrimer came in, secure, amused, intent. He was good at paying attention; she wondered what it would be like to have such close attention paid to a kiss. She let her lips linger in a smile. 'Oh, I'm so sorry. Yes, I was far away.'

'May I ask where?'

'Australia. My family property. Thuringa.'

'A lovely name. Where does it come from?'

'You know, I've never thought to ask. Can you imagine the

beauty of a gold world, Mr Lorrimer, not a green one? Grass like kangaroo fur in the afternoon light? I'm so sorry — please do sit down. It is very good to see you. I'll ring for fresh tea.'

'Thank you. It would be welcome. Yes, I saw golden plains in Africa. I can see how the love of wide horizons might seep into your soul. But I'm a man of quiet hedges and the slightly less quiet chatterings of parliament, though I must admit at times I suspect they sound like your colonial cockatoos. My aunt has a cockatoo. He sounds alarmingly like Lloyd George. The same insistent way of saying a phrase over and over, as though everyone else must feel it as important as he does.' He sat down on the chair opposite Sophie. 'I met young Graveshead on the stairs.'

'He was here a moment ago,' said Sophie.

James Lorrimer raised an eyebrow. 'He looked like a young man who just had his proposal of marriage turned down.' He laughed. 'You are too young to have learned to disguise your feelings. And you are too intelligent,' he added with even more amusement, 'to stay ignorant of that skill for very much longer. Poor Graveshead,' he continued. 'He looked shattered.'

'I suspect he would be more shattered at the loss of my fortune than of my person. *If* he asked me, which of course is only your supposition.'

James Lorrimer looked at her speculatively. 'Is that what you think?'

'Of course. Why else would a young man with no fortune make an offer to an Australian with no background?'

'Love?'

'I think,' she said slowly, 'that love takes time to grow. Or maybe it comes in a shower of petals and you know you are bound forever. But either way, neither of those was the case for Mr Graveshead and me.'

'You underestimate him, you know,' James Lorrimer said gently. 'He has no money now except an allowance from his great-uncle. But the great-uncle is bedridden, and likely to last another season at the most. And the estate is entailed. It will all come to Mr Graveshead.'

'Then he will be rich?'

'Quite rich. Would that have made a difference to your answer?'

So *that* was why the dowager had agreed to allow him to propose. 'No. But I ... I might have thought of him more charitably.'

'Thank you for that, my dear Miss Higgs.' For once his smile lost its slightly mocking edge.

Somehow she had forgotten to deliberately charm James Lorrimer. 'I think ... though I'm not sure ... that this is a subject that men don't ask about, and women don't speak of.'

'I suspect you are correct. Shall we change the subject? Her Grace's tea is always excellent.'

'I think she buys it directly from Ceylon. Alison has a cousin on a plantation there.'

'So you *did* refuse Mr Graveshead?'

'Yes.'

'I'm glad.'

She wasn't. The season was a game, with a game's rules, and it had only just occurred to her that young men could be hurt by it too. 'And I shouldn't have told you. Not about his offer, nor my refusal.'

'That depends,' said Mr Lorrimer, 'on how you see me. A serene old codger, available to chat and advise young girls? You could tell a man like that anything.'

She smiled properly for the first time since the disappointed young man had left. 'Not that.'

'Or a man you think that one day you might care about. Someone you enjoy speaking to freely. I mean a friend,' he added. 'Though it might well become something else. So are we friends?'

This moment was important. Moisten your lips, whispered Miss Lily. The tongue is the most intimate part of you that can be exposed if you still want to appear to be discreet and proper. 'I do hope so, Mr Lorrimer.'

'That will do. For now.'

The door opened. The maid had intuited that Sophie would require more tea and was wheeling in a fresh trolley with a silver teapot (How many does the house have? wondered Sophie), fresh scones to go with the cherry cake, and fresh muffins with a pot of honey.

Mr Lorrimer looked at the muffins with pleasure. 'Muffins and honey. Her Grace remembered how much I love them. The Wooten Abbey honey is always superb.'

The maid bobbed a curtsey. 'Her Grace said to give you her apologies. She will be here shortly, sir, Miss Higgs.'

'I expected she would be,' said Mr Lorrimer. 'Leaving her charge with one eligible man per afternoon is acceptable. Leaving her with two hints at negligence.'

The maid bobbed another curtsey and retreated. Mr Lorrimer took a plate and spread a muffin, already buttered, thickly with honey. 'Muffins, honey and Miss Higgs,' he said. 'I can think of no better way to end a working day.'

James Lorrimer was at each ball after that, although Sophie was sure he hadn't been to the ones earlier in the season. He must have found a way to know in advance which ones she would attend, for he didn't seem like a man who enjoyed parties.

He would arrive in time to dance with her twice before escorting her to supper: an efficient way to make a claim without wasting time on unnecessary social pleasantries. By the end of a fortnight she knew that they were being spoken of as a couple.

'Rosie in the kitchen said that Lady Charles's maid told her they are offering short odds on his offering for you by the end of the season,' said Alison.

'What are the odds on my accepting?'

'You've let him take you in to supper five times in a row.'

'Because he's interesting. And balls aren't. Not many of them, anyway.'

Alison laughed. 'It's not for much longer. Neither of us has to do it again until we have daughters of our own. But you do like him, don't you?'

'Yes.'

Sophie liked being held by him when they danced; liked the way he didn't smile when someone at the table said something foolish. She liked the fact that he was interested in corned beef, or at least its ability to feed many people far from where the cattle that produced it had lived. She even liked the way he had asked her to do something that crossed the bounds of both friendship and etiquette. There would be nothing she'd need to hide from James Lorrimer, possibly little that she could even try to hide.

'I don't quite understand why he should want to marry me, though. His family is wealthy.' Her Grace's secretary checked potential fortunes carefully.

Alison looked at her oddly. 'It's as though you think your money is the most important thing about you.'

Sophie shrugged. 'Usually it is.'

'Not to Mr Lorrimer. You interest him. He finds me boring,' added Alison, seeming to accept Lorrimer's evaluation with no regret. 'Although he's too polite to show it. He never really listens when I talk. He listens to you. And you are very beautiful, you know.'

'You think he's ... in love with me?'

Alison hesitated. 'I think he's watching you to see if you fit into his world, before he lets himself fall in love.'

'That's perceptive, Mouse. You always underestimate yourself. Emily already fits into his world. But he doesn't dance with her.' Sophie had watched carefully for any sign that Mr Lorrimer was interested in Emily.

'I don't think Mr Lorrimer was looking for a wife at first. He didn't go to any of the events of the season; Grandmama was surprised he was at the Carlyles' Friday-to-Monday. But then he met you.'

If I loved him, she thought, I might be hurt that he is testing me for suitability. Instead she found herself intrigued. What did a James Lorrimer need in a wife? And might it dovetail with what Sophie Higgs wanted in a husband?

Chapter 37

Most people accept the existence the world offers them. A few —
a very few — have both the insight and the courage to change it.
Miss Higgs was a delightful shock: a girl who knew what the world
thought of her, but never conceded that she should accept the world's
view as fixed.

Miss Lily, 1914

Sophie found out three days later.

There had been a choice of invitations: an evening on the river in barges hung with silk, with Handel's *Water Music* played by a floating orchestra; or a dinner with a hostess whose name was unfamiliar. As usual, Sophie let Her Grace decide, then discovered that Alison was to go on the water with her fiancé and his aunt, while Her Grace accompanied Sophie to the dinner.

The address was just two blocks away, but the carriage took them anyway, cloaks donned for the five minutes it took to get there and be escorted down by footmen in white wigs.

Sophie let her cloak and muff be taken, lifted her skirts as she followed the silken width of Her Grace down a wide hallway and waited while they were announced.

The room was already full: men in dinner jackets instead of tails; women in silk of claret or peacock blue, or grey with hints of gold. For the first time this season, Sophie's was the only pale dress in the room. I am the only debutante, she realised. Tonight is real.

A few guests glanced up as they came in, then bent again to their conversations. The voices in this room sounded different: lower pitched, not so much the chattering of monkeys but more a merging of many murmurs, like rivers meeting at the sea.

'Your Grace, Miss Higgs.' James Lorrimer stepped towards them, ignoring Sophie, as was proper, to exchange greetings with Her Grace first before the older woman turned to speak to an old acquaintance.

Which left them by the fire together.

'Everyone looks so serious.'

He looked at her curiously. 'You don't believe the situation is serious?'

'Between Austria and Serbia? I've been trying to follow it in the papers. No one else seems interested, though.'

'By "no one else" you mean your dancing partners?'

'I'm sorry.' She could hear phrases from around the room. These people weren't discussing fashion or the field. 'I only know enough about politics to know how little I do know.'

'That is probably the most intelligent observation any debutante has ever made. Austria has demanded Serbia allow it full control of the investigation into the assassination of the archduke. By the end of the week I expect the Austro-Hungarian Empire and Serbia will be at war.'

'And will that mean Germany will be at war with Serbia too?' She thought of Hannelore, back in her cold castle, so close to the Russian border. She had already received a letter from the prinzessin since Hannelore had returned home, and another from Dolphie, a silly letter, full of charm, giving no hint of the political tensions they had gone back to. Hannelore's letter had been coloured with regret at their parting, but also contained reference to neither politics nor Miss Lily.

'This is more than the usual hostility between Teuton and Slav. Russia will protect Serbia; Germany and Italy are bound to Austria.'

'The Triple Alliance.'

'Exactly. France and England are connected by the Triple Entente, though no one can be sure quite how cordial it is. But,' he shrugged, 'if we wish to have a reason to join the forthcoming celebration of the warrior, we now have it.'

'But surely if enough people of good heart are against a

war …?' She was parroting Miss Lily. She stopped, knowing that she had nothing of any more substance to offer.

'Germany is mobilising. The Austro-Serbian conflict is a smoke screen. One way or another, Germany is going to provoke England.'

'But how can they do that if England doesn't want to fight? Can't we just say no?'

'There comes a time, Miss Higgs, when peace is no longer possible, no matter how much one may prefer it. Germany is going to invade Luxembourg, Belgium or France. My instinct says Luxembourg or Belgium. A direct attack on France would not create the instant sympathy in England that an attack on the smaller countries would evoke. An attack on Luxembourg or Belgium would have the English public clamouring for war — as long as the attack is savage enough.'

Sophie thought of Hannelore's description of the German military's plans to terrorise civilians. Was that not just to get the country they invaded to surrender, but to bring England into the conflict too?

'Does Germany need to provoke England into war? Why not just invade?'

'This is a scene played on a large stage, Miss Higgs.' To her surprise, he didn't seem to be bored explaining what must be all too familiar and obvious to him. 'Invading England might bring America onto England's side. Nor perhaps is the pro-war party in Germany strong enough to allow an unprovoked attack of England.'

'Our royal family is German,' said Sophie.

'That helps. But they are from Saxe-Coburg and Gotha, not Prussia, and it is the Prussians who are in control now. And the most vicious quarrels of all are family quarrels. Haven't you found it so?'

'I don't know. I'm an only child.'

'As I am also. Perhaps outsiders understand families best.' He shrugged again. 'For what it's worth neither His Majesty nor the Kaiser wishes for war. Even fifty years ago kings warred with kings, but now they are expected to obey their parliaments.' He raised an eyebrow. 'Our own king might refuse to sign the bill that allows Ulster independence. But he will not refuse parliament on this. The parliament wants war.'

'So the Mr Churchills have won?'

'Not yet. But soon.'

'Do the people in this room want war?' A few faces were turned their way now, assessing her, she thought. Wondering if she would be one of their social group by the season's end.

'Not if it can be avoided.' He offered her his arm to go in to dinner.

She watched her hostess, Lady Williams, during dinner: sloping shoulders above a low-cut gown of burgundy silk and lace, making the guest on each side of her feel the sole object of her attention, but aware, nonetheless, of every dish served, every conversation being conducted at the table.

Lady Williams would have chosen this menu — the consommé, the turbot in sorrel sauce, the venison sent down from the estates in Scotland. She would have known that her kitchen could cope with turning out sufficient orange soufflés to place one before each guest, that her butler had measured the distance between each knife and fork and the edge of the table. This was her choice of flowers, her balance of guests. Sophie wondered if there were children upstairs, or at boarding school.

Sophie's father managed fourteen factories and nearly thirteen thousand acres. Was her hostess's work as complex or as far-reaching? What decisions or plans would be made at her table tonight, conjured from a conjunction of the right people mellowed by good food, well-matched wines and fine cigars?

Was this what James Lorrimer would expect from her if they were married? I could do it, she thought. It would take time to get to know the connections, but she was sure her wit and her memory were up to it. Her Grace would help find housekeepers, butlers, to take charge at the London and country houses Her Grace had already ascertained that he owned. Probably he had competent servants already; he would tell her, at least at first, whom he wished to have at his table and why. Her luncheons would captivate the wives who would accompany their husbands to the dinners. She could captivate the husbands too, gather her own following of Mr Portons.

And there would be children, of course.

'Do you shoot, Miss Higgs?'

She had been neglecting the man on her left, smiling automatically and, she hoped, sufficiently. Now she lowered her chin and gave him her most enchanting under-the-eyelashes smile. 'I'm terribly uneducated about English shoots, Mr Porter-Smythe. Will you forgive me? I've shot rabbits back home, but never pheasants or grouse. Not proper shooting.'

'No forgiveness necessary, dear girl. You need taking in hand.' He patted hers with his own be-ringed fingers as if to demonstrate. 'A few weeks up at Quigley and we'll make a sportswoman of you yet.'

'It sounds wonderful. Your wife is a noted shot, I believe?' She was grateful for the notes Her Grace's secretary had prepared, guessing who would be her likely partners, with useful points on each.

Her companion glanced across the table at his wife and exchanged a fleeting look. A good marriage, thought Sophie. He could flirt with a debutante, but his wife still responded with a smile. 'She is indeed, Miss Higgs. I know she has been planning to call on Her Grace before the end of the season.' He shook his head. 'Of course by the end of the week we may be thinking of shooting in quite another way.'

'Unless England remains neutral.' She offered it tentatively and was grateful when he didn't take it amiss, or try to take the conversation back to chit-chat. Instead he showed the faintest sign that he was glad of a debutante for whom he need not tame his conversation.

'Yes, but can we? That is the real question. Is Germany's target simply France, or will France be a springboard to take on England too? It is we who are their real competitors, not France.'

273

'But France is Germany's traditional enemy. We are their natural allies. General Blücher fought with us at Waterloo ...'

'Your father is a businessman in Australia, Miss Higgs?' He made it neither patronising nor an insult. 'Germany and England compete economically in Africa and the Pacific, for instance in your New Guinea, and even in the Middle East and Asia. There is money to be made in war, and not just in providing armaments.'

'But there is so much to be lost too.'

'Indeed.'

She saw him glance at his wife again, and understood. 'You have sons, Mr Porter-Smythe?'

He cleared his throat. 'Four, Miss Higgs. Two in the Territorials. The other two would join up, of course, if we are forced to mobilise.'

'And you were in one of the Boer wars?'

'No, Miss Higgs. But my father was at Crimea, and its tragedies were the ghost throughout my childhood. I don't want to see the same ghosts haunt my sons. But perhaps we will have no choice.'

Sophie nodded, then looked back at her plate.

Miss Lily had promised her choices. But here was a man ... many men ... who were finding that they too had no choice at all.

Who wants war so badly, she thought, that they have brought us to this?

Lady Williams rose from the table later than was usual; at this dinner the men were not expected to delay the 'real' conversation until they were left with the port. She led the way to a drawing room, which all the ladies entered exactly as the tea trolley was wheeled in.

Sophie fetched the duchess tea from the tray, then sat next to her on the sofa. Several of the women in the room looked familiar, but there were none with whom she had ever had a conversation. A girl in her first season didn't strike up a conversation with her elders.

'Isobel, it has been too long since we've seen you.' The newcomer was Her Grace's age perhaps, sixty at least. She wore a velvet tippet over her shoulders, as though she cared more about keeping off the chill than fashion.

'Far too long. The season is as boring as it ever was, but I have missed my London friends. Mary, may I present my granddaughter's friend from Australia, Miss Sophie Higgs. Sophie, this is Lady Mary Eldershaw.'

Sophie stood and gave a half-curtsey, a conservative compromise between the previous century's deeper curtsey and the modern convention of a debutante's polite head bob. 'Lady Mary.'

Lady Mary seated herself opposite them and sipped her tea. 'How do you find us, Miss Higgs?'

'It has been a fascinating time, Lady Mary. Everyone has been most kind.'

'How many times have you had to say that in the past months, eh?' Lady Mary sipped again, then handed the thin china cup to a footman. 'What are you doing tomorrow evening, Miss Higgs?'

'I believe it is a Venetian dinner.'

'The world mutters about war and children starve, and you wish to go to a Venetian dinner?'

'No,' said Sophie frankly. 'But offending my hostess would be poor thanks to Her Grace for all her kindness.'

'Send your apologies.'

Sophie looked questioningly at Her Grace, who seemed amused, either by the invitation, or by the fact that it was addressed to Sophie alone, not herself and Alison. 'Shall we compromise? Miss Higgs will be free from five until nine o'clock tomorrow. That will give her time to bathe and change before the dinner at ten.'

'Till nine o'clock will be sufficient.' Lady Mary looked at Sophie. 'Wear something warm.' She stood as the men began to trickle into the drawing room. 'Until tomorrow night, Miss Higgs.' Then she departed, leaving Sophie — no doubt deliberately — to wonder what was planned.

The carriage was old-fashioned: a faded crest, good horses, but not a matched pair. A driver, no footman, till Joe, one of Her Grace's footmen — or rather *His* Grace's, borrowed for the season — helped Sophie and Doris into the carriage then joined the driver up on top. Doris sat with her back to the driver and ran her fingers over the seat dismissively. 'Needs re-covering, miss. And a good scrub.'

Sophie nodded, preoccupied. Her Grace had refused to tell her where she and Doris were going, simply advised her to wear her blue serge. Sophie wished Alison were there, but Alison was having dinner with a great-aunt of Major Standish.

Was this part of Miss Lily's mysterious world of power?

The drive seemed long; she was used to travelling the few blocks of fashionable London. She pulled aside the curtains at the window. She saw shabby shops, not houses, what could only be a pub, and men in caps gathered around a gas streetlight, as though waiting for it to add its glow to the twilight.

She sat back.

Doris shivered. 'I don't like it, miss.'

'Nonsense. Lady Mary is a friend of Her Grace's.'

'Whom she hasn't seen for years. You said so, miss. What if Lady Mary's a white slaver?'

Sophie blinked.

'You know, miss. They lure white women onto ships and take them to sell to sheiks of Arabia or to South America. They say the men in South America go wild for white women, miss.'

'I think a lot of the women in South America are white anyway.'

Doris considered. 'Well, they would be, miss, if the white slaves had babies. They might 'ave been doin' it for years ...'

'White slavers don't send carriages, and they don't choose girls with families who love them.'

How long ago had that conversation about white slavers with her father been? She'd thought far less of her mother during this time of balls and visits than she'd expected to.

'I suppose not, miss.' Doris seemed slightly disappointed. She looked out her own window and sniffed. 'I can smell something sour, miss, an' I don't think it's the beer.'

The carriage stopped. Sophie waited for the footman to hand her out, then looked around.

A sour stink, as Doris had said. It took her a few seconds to realise it was the Thames, mixed with sewage and rubbish and the mud flats exposed at low tide. The carriage stood at the end of a lane; small houses crouched along each side, black with old smoke or just dark brick, and yellow fog licked their roofs. The building in front of Sophie might once have been a factory. Now it bore a roughly painted sign: *The Workmen's Friendship Club. All Welcome*. Sophie hesitated, then stepped inside.

The room was big; it had a concrete floor, stained despite evident recent scrubbing, and rough walls with wooden benches around the sides, except at the far end, where trestle tables had been erected. An urn steamed on one gas ring; giant black pots sat on two others. Three women in white aprons sliced bread at one trestle; two others seemed to be chopping vegetables at another.

She realised it was a soup kitchen where she was expected to volunteer. She felt vaguely disappointed — then guilty at the disappointment.

'You must be Miss Higgs.' The young woman who approached was perhaps a few years older than Sophie, her dark hair pulled back in a no-nonsense bun, wearing a blue serge skirt and jacket much like Sophie's, under a wide white apron. Sophie knew enough about English accents now to hear that this young woman was middle rather than upper class. 'Lady Mary said you'd be coming. I'm sorry she's not here to meet you — a crisis with the Mothers' Committee: an outbreak of scarlet fever I think. Anyway, they're all in quarantine ... I'm Leticia Blessington, but call me Dodders — everyone does.' Dodders grabbed Sophie's hand and shook it.

Sophie tried to hide her shock. She had never had her hand shaken by a female before.

Dodders turned to Doris.

'I'm sorry,' said Sophie. 'This is ...' she was going to say 'my maid' but something stopped her '... Doris Green.'

'Wonderful to meet you, Miss Green. May I call you Doris? And you Sophie, Miss Higgs? We're all on first-name terms here. Come and I'll get you aprons.'

'I saw the Workmen's Friendship Club sign as we came in.'

'I know, it's a bit wobbly. None of us is an artist.'

Sophie stared at the simmering pots. 'You provide meals for workers here?'

Dodders looked at her speculatively. 'And their families. And ... other things too. It's stew and bread and scrape at night, bread and cocoa for breakfast. It's the only food some of the children around here see. Oh, thank you,' to an older woman who handed her the required aprons. Sophie fumbled as she put hers on, she had never worn an apron. She saw Doris resist the instinct to help her with the bow.

'This is Mrs Henry Fordyce, but call her Lizbeth. Lizbeth, two more recruits —' (Are we? thought Sophie) '— Miss Higgs and Miss Green, Sophie and Doris. Doris, could you help peel the vegetables? Sophie, would you mind going on the bread table?'

She's wondering if I've ever sliced bread, thought Sophie. She smiled at the memory of Miss Lily's teatime lessons.

'Stir the cocoa too, or it catches. The mugs are over there ... Mrs Gibbs, how good to see you.' Dodders darted towards the door again. At first Sophie thought Mrs Gibbs must be another volunteer — or someone else who had been shanghaied into helping like them, as dexterously as any white slaver would. But one look at the woman's face, her darned hem, the two children clinging to her skirt, told a different story.

'Sophie, this is Mrs Gibbs, and these are Billie and Jenny. Sophie is going to give you some nice cocoa and bread and dripping till the stew is ready. Thank you,' she added to Sophie, who somehow managed to fill three mugs without spilling more than a few dribbles, and passed them over.

An hour later the room was full. It smelled of damp and river mud; of sweat and desperation. Children with dribbling noses and grimy faces; men with swollen red 'gin noses', who looked at the floor, not even muttering thank you for the swede and turnip stew, the slabs of bread and dripping. The women rarely spoke, even to each other — they came, they accepted what was offered, they ate and then they left.

Sophie looked at the knot of children in front of her trestle. Five of them, from knee high to twelve years old, perhaps. Had that hair ever been combed? Faces the brown of grime, clothes the grey of repeated washings or years of fading, stringy colourless hair; the only colour in the whole room seemed to be the dresses of the servers and the yellow light, now that the gas lamps had been turned on.

She hated it. Hated the smells, the hopeless faces, the children who grabbed and never gave their thanks. The children in her father's factory had been hungry, but they'd never had the quietness, the hopelessness of these. At least her father's employees had food and sunlight. These people knew nothing but this stretch of laneway and the river. Even their accents were almost impenetrable.

She had talked to the labourers at Thuringa and Shillings. But these shrunken, slum-twisted people ...

... were people. What would Miss Lily say? Try to think like them, be like them, feel what they are feeling.

She looked at the child in front of her again. A girl with a wizened monkey face and already rotting teeth, the too-long skirt rucked up with a piece of rope. How many adults had worn that dress, for how many years, before this child was given it? The girl stretched out both hands, red and scarred from chilblains, to take the mug.

What did she feel? Hunger, thought Sophie, and I'm giving her food. Hopelessness, but I don't have any hope to give her. Drabness.

The girl seized the cocoa, then rubbed her sleeve across her running nose.

'Here.' Sophie pulled her handkerchief out of the almost invisible pocket Madame had sewn into her skirt.

The girl looked at the scrap of lace and linen with a look of disbelief. She touched it with one shining finger, then grabbed it and ran for the door.

'It'll be in a pawnshop by breakfast time,' said Doris. She looked shocked, and wary too. She laundered and ironed that handkerchief, thought Sophie, and keeps count of the numbers and state of all my linen.

'Have you any more?'

'Handkerchiefs, miss?'

'Yes. Please, Doris.'

Doris looked briefly mutinous, then reached into her larger pocket and brought out three: two obviously spares in case Sophie needed them, and one without lace and less neatly hemmed, with a D embroidered in one corner.

Sophie handed it back to her. Doris put it away. 'My sister Dorcas gave me that for Christmas. But them, those others, miss, that's Belgian lace at four guineas a length.'

Sophie wished she had brought money with her. Ladies did not carry money. Even the 'pin money' she had for tipping servants would be a fortune here.

She met Dodders's eyes. Dodders nodded, satisfied. 'Lady Mary said you'd be a good 'un.' She shrugged. 'We can give them food, but what they need is real change: housing projects, health clinics, schools. Decent jobs with decent wages.'

'Don't you worry none about jobs, miss.' The man was tall, thin, and had only three teeth. 'We'll have jobs soon enough when we attack the Kaiser.'

War, thought Sophie. It's not a matter of if now. It's when.

She kept cutting bread. At least there was no need for thin slices here. The thicker the slices the better. Doris stood by her side, now the swedes and turnips had been chopped, slathering on dripping, which smelled of rosemary.

Sophie wondered which kitchen it had been collected in. Would Her Grace's kitchen supply dripping if she asked? Or was that something a guest might not ask her hostess? Alison would know.

But on Saturday her Mouse would be married. For the first time, she realised how Alison's marriage might affect her too. No more after-dance confidences; so many house parties Alison simply wouldn't attend.

It's not fair, thought Sophie. I've only just found a friend. I don't want to lose her already.

Nor could she see herself coming back here, to cut bread and butter. Yes, these people deserved her help. But her money could do that far more efficiently than her hands. She should be feeling happy to be of use, especially when her life consisted of the dinners and parties of the season. But if Miss Lily was correct, this season might lead to another life, with far more purpose. Her hands were worth, what, a shilling a week?

'Sophie?' Dodders was at her side again. 'There are some people I'd like you to meet.' She smiled. 'We won't be long, Doris.'

Doris looked uncertain, clearly knowing her place was at Sophie's side, but just as clearly too used to obeying orders to object. Sophie followed Dodders curiously.

The room at the back of the hall was smaller, containing twenty or so chairs arranged in a circle. Only two were vacant. The women in the others were well dressed, though only two others as fashionably as Sophie. This group was not part of the 'six hundred first families' of England.

'Sophie Higgs,' said Dodders shortly, waving Sophie to a chair. 'Lady Mary vouches for her.'

The others scarcely looked at her. She and Dodders had evidently interrupted a heated discussion.

'But the workers *want* war.' The woman who had spoken wore a white shirt and tie under her cloth coat. 'Giving working men the vote will make things worse. Only the educated should have a voice. Men *and* women.'

'You mean rich women. If men are to fight a war, they have the right to vote as to whether there should be one.' This speaker's accent pronounced her as upper class, as did her shearling coat.

'Palmerston said it best,' argued the first speaker. '"What every man and woman too have a right to is to be well governed and under just laws."'

'Every man?' said Dodders disgustedly. 'I bet those women out there don't want their sons going off to war.'

'Just starving here?' The third speaker wore pantaloons and a jacket just long enough to hide the way her nether garments divided below her hips. 'That's what I was saying before. We need to educate the workers *before* they get the vote ...'

Sophie sat, fascinated. Words flashed past her ... an even more passionate discussion about whether the group should stay with the Women's Freedom League, or participate in direct action with Emmeline Pankhurst's 'Deeds not Words' Women's Social and Political Union; whether they should focus on women's rights, or on votes for all.

'Don't you see?' said Dodders passionately. 'The Labour and Liberal Parties will never agree to female suffrage if it just means getting more Conservative voters.'

'Karl Marx says —'

'Don't bring that man into it,' said Dodders heatedly. 'There'll never be a workers' revolution in England.' She turned to Sophie. 'Miss Higgs, is it true that all men and women in Australia have the vote, even those who don't own land?'

'Yes,' said Sophie, then stopped as Doris appeared at the door, looking both determined and terrified.

'Miss, it's time to go. The carriage is here.'

Sophie shook her head. For the first time since she had left Shillings, she was with a group of women with whom she felt a true bond. Women who were doing something with other women, not waiting for a man to shape their lives.

'Her Grace will be waiting for you, miss.' Doris's voice was urgent.

Doris might get into trouble if she were late. And it would be discourteous and ungrateful to prevent Her Grace from honouring an invitation she'd accepted, to an event she might even be looking forward to, for she certainly wouldn't go before Sophie returned.

Dodders stood. 'Lady Mary said you'd need to leave early. I'll see you out.'

Which decided the matter. They slipped out a back door, into the full stench of the river again. 'We're not usually as scatty as tonight,' said Dodders. 'The talk of war's got everyone on edge. There's some decent work going on here. Night classes for everyone, men, women and kids — most of the youngsters work around here. The bloated capitalists don't have to pay them much.'

What are 'bloated capitalists'? thought Sophie as she stepped towards the opened carriage door.

'And there's the lending library, and the Support for Mothers, and the Marie Stopes Clinic. Contraception for the working class is so important ...'

'Miss,' said Doris, pleading. Sophie stepped into the carriage.

Dodders peered up at her. 'You'll come again?'

It had been fascinating to see the world from such a different perspective, although it was impossible not to feel that James Lorrimer's insights were far deeper than those of the women she had left. But this evening had also shown the possibilities of friendship beyond Mouse, Hannelore and Miss Lily.

Suddenly she liked Dodders enormously. Trusted her enough to say, 'You need decent organisation. All that arguing. Why not just break into groups to do what you are best at, instead of everyone having to agree? And why waste educated women's abilities on slicing bread?'

'To feel solidarity with the workers,' said Dodders.

'Which is more important — privileged women like us learning "solidarity" or actually getting the most done for the most people?'

Dodders stared at Sophie, her smile growing. 'Is that what you'll tell us, next time?'

Yes, there would be a next time. Sophie nodded. 'It may take a few weeks, or even more than that before I'm free to come again.' She grinned. 'In the meantime I'll send a cheque so some of the women who come here for bread can be paid to slice it instead.'

Dodders held out her hand. Sophie took it, suddenly no longer finding it strange to shake another woman's hand. 'You're on,' said Dodders.

Chapter 38

*I am against the new fashion for brides to wear white. It implies
the girl is a blank canvas, to be designed and painted on by
her husband after the 'one crowning hour' that is her wedding.
Too often the symbol mirrors the reality.*

Miss Lily, 1914

1 AUGUST 1914

The Times lay on the table at breakfast. Sophie refused to look
at it, even at the headlines. Today was Alison's, not the Empire's.

'No regrets, Mouse?' she whispered, so Ffoulkes didn't hear
as he brought in fresh toast.

'No. Thank you, Ffoulkes. Could I have a kipper, do you
think?'

'Of course, Lady Alison.' Ffoulkes left the room.

'I'll miss you,' said Alison abruptly.

'I'll still be here when you get back from your honeymoon.'
Sophie didn't say she had been feeling the same thing.

'I just have a feeling that things are ending. Good things.
I wish Hannelore could be here. I wish ...' Alison's voice trailed
off.

'Darling Mouse, you don't have to go through with it.'

'I'm not scared of marriage to Philip. I'm scared I'm going to
trip over my train, or get the hiccups when I'm supposed to say
"I do".'

'I'll take care of the train. That's what bridesmaids are for.
And if you get the hiccups, I'll put a cold key down your back.'

'Where will you get a cold key?'

'I'll tie one especially under my shoe for emergencies.'

'Your kipper, Lady Alison,' said Ffoulkes. 'And may I say on behalf of all the staff, how happy we are that ...'

The bride wore lace and an expression that was half terror and half happiness as she rested her hand on the arm of her cousin, the Duke of Wooten. Above them, royalty gazed down with practised smiles and eyes that only those who looked closely would find preoccupied. The groom also looked preoccupied at times, as well as happy. Alison had told Sophie that under the circumstances he had withdrawn his resignation from the Guards. He had been given only five days' leave for a honeymoon.

One of the bridesmaids floated down the aisle like a swan, in pale blue deeply embroidered with crystal; the other four, Alison's young nieces, walked with the happy anticipation of those who know they are on display, with their seasons yet to come.

This is it, thought Sophie. A season almost over; everything she had ever hoped for almost achieved.

She caught Emily's eye from one of the pews, gave her a fraction of a smile and swam on. Emily too had succeeded. Her engagement had been announced the week before, to the Honourable Colonel Gilbert Sevenoaks. Not the most brilliant match of the year — had Emily wasted too many of her few months trying for James Lorrimer? Colonel Sevenoaks had wealth and breeding, but no political connections.

But I will have, thought Sophie, if I marry James Lorrimer. She had already asked him, carefully casual, what he felt about extending votes to all men, as well as women. He had both seen through her casualness, and given the answer she had hoped. 'Universal suffrage may not be politically expedient. But it is just. And in the end, justice should prevail.'

She had a brief vision of Emily, sitting well below the salt at her dinner table, hoping for a glimpse of the world she hadn't quite been able to enter. But perhaps this was just the first step in Emily's campaign to raise her husband to prominence. Emily had been right about the need for England to mobilise; Sophie would need to acknowledge that somehow — at the reception later, maybe.

I will not think about the war right now, she thought. Just about today, and Mouse. Just happiness, for today.

She looked for James Lorrimer in the crowd, but he wasn't there.

Chapter 39

When an animal comes into season it means mating, short and to the point. The London season is much the same, the girls briefly the subject of an enormous amount of attention. Few realise quite how brief their season is.

Miss Lily, 1914

The marquee was white, the champagne bubbly. Sophie sipped it cautiously. Her Grace had decreed that she could drink champagne now the season was almost over, a half-glass, no more, without risking censure.

It was three days after Alison's wedding, and her host's birthday — a second cousin of Alison's. She wasn't sure she even knew his full name. Nor, perhaps, did many of those here. His wife had organised the luncheon, or rather his wife's secretary had, using the list of acceptables edited during the season, a list Miss Sophie Higgs was securely now on.

'A beautiful hat, Miss Higgs.'

'Mr Lorrimer! How lovely to see you.' She carefully didn't mention how many days it had been since she'd seen him last. He looked preoccupied, as though 'Attend garden party, meet Miss Higgs' had simply been on his list for the day, among many other duties. Even she could see England sliding into war: Sir Edward Grey, the Foreign Secretary, had tried to conciliate between Austria and Serbia and received a stern rebuke from Kaiser Wilhelm for his impudence in interfering with Austrian and German affairs.

Belgium had refused to allow German troops across its territory to invade France. If Belgium were invaded, England was bound by treaty to assist. Even attempts at peace were taking Europe closer to war. Yet Mr Lorrimer had still found time to be here.

'I have a table under the trees.' James Lorrimer was already moving her away from the crowd as neatly and quickly as a sheepdog might.

He held out a chair for her until she sat, fleetingly aware that her skirts had fallen perfectly. She could see hats, trimmed hedges beyond and the high bulk of the house.

'I'd like you to see Halburton. My home.' He spoke quickly and efficiently, not in the relaxed tones of a garden-party guest.

'I would love to.'

James Lorrimer didn't mean his London house. No Englishman she had met meant that when he said 'my home'.

'Next week, perhaps.' He hesitated. 'It depends on how things develop. I have checked with Her Grace. She says you are both free.'

She was fairly sure they hadn't been free until James Lorrimer asked.

'What is Halburton like?' She didn't say Doris had given her a copy of *Town and Country* with a feature on the estate. The magazine had been more than a decade old, but she suspected little had changed since.

'The original hall is fifteenth century. Two wings added by my great-grandfather. My mother planted the rose gardens. They're modelled on the Empress Josephine's at Malmaison.'

She didn't say she knew that too.

'I'm not going to ask if you like roses, Miss Higgs,' he added.

'Because both the question and the answer would be too predictable? I look forward to it enormously, Mr Lorrimer.'

'Good.' He smiled down at her. For the first time that afternoon, he seemed to look at her alone.

So, she thought, he is going to propose, if not this afternoon then at Halburton. And she would probably accept. No, not even probably. She *would* accept. She'd clung to 'probably' because, well, love was supposed to feel more fluttery than this. *Had* felt fluttery, when it had been Malcolm.

But she liked this man. Respected him. Admitted, finally, that she had never respected Malcolm. And she liked the fact that James Lorrimer admired her.

Even for the corned-beef princess there came a time of choices. She could stay in England one more year, perhaps, without encouraging people to talk. She had friends she could stay with now, and work she could do wholeheartedly and with comradeship from Dodders and her friends, or perhaps she might even start a group herself, once she had a household and husband to give her the freedom of social approval. But a third year here, without marriage ...

And home? She longed for Australian sunlight; the drab kiss of khaki trees on deep blue sky; the song of rain or of cicadas. But Australian empires were those of the squatters, where Sophie Higgs could have no power, or those of men like her father, where she too was shut off from rule.

She would visit, take the children back every Christmas perhaps. But she could find no life of fulfilment there.

She wished that an English luncheon gave the same opportunities as a Thuringa party, that somehow if she felt James Lorrimer kiss her she would feel more confident that accepting his proposal was the best path for her life to take. She caught his eye, full of an intentness it had never had before. Had he been thinking about kissing her? But James Lorrimer's cheeks did not flush like hers.

'A penny for your thoughts, Miss Higgs.'

He knew exactly what she had been thinking, and liked it. 'I was just thinking —' She broke off as a man in a chauffeur's uniform approached. He bent and whispered in Mr Lorrimer's ear.

And suddenly it was as though she weren't there. As though the marquee had vanished, and the top hats and feathers. He stood, lifted her hand, kissed the air above it. 'Miss Higgs, I'm sorry. I have to go.'

Suddenly she knew exactly why he was leaving. 'Of course, Mr Lorrimer. I hope it isn't bad news.'

He seemed to see her again. 'Germany has invaded Belgium; there will be more news in about an hour.'

'Is it war?'

'Yes. By tonight, Miss Higgs, we will be at war.'

Chapter 40

People speak of war as though it is all one country. But every war is a separate land.

Miss Lily, 1914

The night was filled with cheering, their street crammed with a parade of men with brooms and shovels on their shoulders instead of rifles, marching from all across London till they finally paraded around and around Grosvenor Square. By midnight the marchers had gone, but not the drunks, singing and yelling insults aimed at the Kaiser.

'It's like a bank holiday, miss,' said Doris, putting a screen against the window to muffle the noise. She unhooked Sophie's dinner dress; they had dined at home, the dinner they had been meant to go to cancelled because their host was leaving for his regiment. Doris helped Sophie into a robe, then kneeled to take off Sophie's stockings. 'Don't think I ever heard so many people so happy before.'

'How do *you* feel, Doris?'

'Me, miss?'

'Your father died in a war.'

Doris looked at her sideways, as though considering what it was safe to say. 'I'm glad I haven't brothers, miss,' she said at last.

'Me too.' Would James Lorrimer join the army? Surely he would be needed at home. Malcolm, the young men she had danced with ...

Was far-off Dolphie in the Kaiser's uniform now?

'What do women do when there's a war?'

'We wait, I reckon, miss. That's what Mam did.'

There was no visit to Halburton.

Men evaporated. Not just the men she knew, but footmen, chauffeurs; even the milkman's horse and cart were driven by an older man, hunched and grey.

There was little war news yet, apart from the German boots and bayonets in Belgium, the ghost faces of refugees caught in photographs, moments perhaps before death or escape: old women carrying bloody children or cherished pigs; bodies curled like kittens on the road.

The atrocities Dolphie had prophesied were all there, not the blood rage of battle, but carefully planned. Sophie wondered if the photographs were also planned, by Englishmen urging working men to rage and to enlist.

She wished, deeply, that she could talk of this to Miss Lily. Her Grace would also understand. But Her Grace had worry enough: almost every male in her extended family and social group was either in the army or an officer on the Reserve list, called now to lead his men.

It seemed that the exact timing of this war, expected for so long, had taken the leaders by surprise. The Kaiser had been on his annual holiday on his yacht; the German General von Moltke, Chief of the General Staff, taking the cure at a French spa; the French President on a state visit to Russia; the Serbian Prime Minister in the middle of an election campaign; and the Russian Ambassador, who had taken such a big part in previous negotiations in Vienna, on leave.

War had been anticipated for decades. Now, it must be organised at short notice.

Some hostesses clung to the world of parties. Most accepted that this was a new world, the world of war. Suddenly it was possible to send regrets, which the duchess did, on Sophie's behalf. Instead Sophie spent that week with Dodders and the women at the Workmen's Friendship Club, serving stew not just to their regulars, but to white-faced Belgian refugees too.

This was not the time to reorganise operations here. Many of the women were already talking of directing their energy to war work; to convincing politicians — who probably needed little convincing — that women could do men's factory jobs while the men surrendered themselves to war.

Her Grace, Dodders and her friends assumed Sophie worked from charity and comradeship. Perhaps she would have done so. But she had also received a note from James Lorrimer: an apology for withdrawing the invitation to Halburton, and a veiled request. 'I hear you are working with the refugees. I know you will listen to their stories with your usual sympathy and understanding.' He had signed it 'Yours always, James Lorrimer'.

She understood. If the trembling and terrified, driven from their homes, said anything of military significance, James Lorrimer would be told.

Sophie arrived there each afternoon, with Doris, thin-lipped, in tow, and John the coachman to keep an eye on them, and to lug the coal to keep the fires going. By the end of that week she had a nickname — Soapy — but had heard nothing except tales of terror, or worse, blank faces that saw nothing, unable to move beyond the horror they had known.

How can Dolphie support a country that does this? thought Sophie as she and Dodders bore away the pads from a child still haemorrhaging from rape, followed by bayonets.

'I'm glad we're going to fight,' said Dodders abruptly as she thrust the dressings into the copper to be boiled, then reused. 'I was afraid that our wretched government would declare neutrality, let France go under.'

Sophie said nothing. It had seemed so clear back at Shillings that any war was bad. Yet you couldn't see this child and do nothing. Which was exactly what Dolphie had predicted England would feel ...

What *would* Miss Lily say now? Would she somehow produce an argument that showed how fourteen million men could stay in their homes, forget the song of war? Emily had seen what was happening, she thought. And Hannelore had known too. She longed to place a call to Shillings, to give comfort or to receive comfort, she wasn't sure. But there would be no Miss Lily there.

Alison returned to the house she had been married from, not her husband's estate in Derbyshire. Major Standish had been recalled to his regiment. Both his house and their London residence would be shut up for the duration.

Sophie sat on Alison's bed — a more sumptuous one than her own, with a dressing room between her room and her husband's — and watched Alison unswathe the tulle and remove her hat. It was crimson with purple feathers, so different from the whites and pastels she had worn before.

'Do you like it?'

'No,' said Sophie.

'Neither do I now. But one has to shop in Paris, so I did. And we saw the Louvre — Philip explained the paintings to me. Well, not all: my feet hurt, so we went on the Seine and he told me about the Ile de France and all the history too.' She sat on her chaise longue, her hands strangely useless in her lap. 'It's odd being back here, when I thought I'd be at Philip's. He's worried about my being alone. He says there might be food riots.'

Sophie nodded. Already it was difficult to get bread for the Workmen's Friendship Club. Food wasn't rationed, though rumours said it soon would be, and it seemed everyone was buying what they could, just in case. England's imported wheat, corned beef, chilled lamb, citrus and so much else came in ships that would be needed now for war — or might be sunk by enemy ships.

Ships with passengers, as well as food, thought Sophie. But she wasn't leaving anyway.

She looked at the strain on Alison's face. 'What's wrong? Are you worried about him?'

'No. The Guards won't be sent to fight. It's just,' she shook her head, 'the refugees from Belgium and Luxembourg. We drove past columns of them for hours after we left Paris.'

'I've been working with them,' said Sophie quietly.

Alison shivered. 'Thousands of people, all bundles and bags. One old woman carried three children, despite a bayonet wound in her back. We offered her a lift, but she shook her head and said, "Where can we go?" I gave her what money I had. But it was so little. War is so big, Sophie, and this is just the beginning. No one even cried. They just looked ... blank. Madame at the hotel had her niece there, from Belgium, and ...' she looked down at her hands '... I tried to talk to her but she just sat looking at the wall. Wouldn't speak. Madame had to spoon food into her. They'd just buried her sister. The soldiers had raped them both. She was four years old, Sophie!' Alison shut her eyes. 'How can men do that?'

Sophie thought of Miss Lily, and shook her head.

'I was against war. But we can't not fight now. Not after what I saw there.'

'Not a good way to end your honeymoon.'

'I think I'm glad I saw it. I've been in a dream the last few years, just thinking of myself. But now I'm Mrs Major Philip Standish, I'm ... stronger. At last I'm really someone.' She flushed. 'I like him, Sophie.'

'So I should hope,' said Sophie lightly.

'No, I mean I really like him. He ... he doesn't expect things from me. He's the only person who never has, except you. Grandmama expected me to marry well and so did Cousin Frederick. Miss Lily wanted me to be like you and Hannelore and Emily, able to talk about politics and Home Rule for Ireland. Philip's just happy for me to be me, because now he can be who he is too. And, Sophie ... it wasn't as bad as I thought. And over quickly.'

It took a moment for Sophie to realise what Alison was talking about.

'I'd like a baby to cuddle,' said Alison softly. 'They are so soft, aren't they?'

Sophie tried to smile for her. 'If I end up in Australia after all, will you ever come out to visit me, do you think?'

'Of course. Philip will let me visit anyone I like. He's so kind.'

A kind master, thought Sophie, thinking of Samuel's words about the Earl of Shillings. But still a master.

'The war can't last long,' said Alison. 'The generals say it'll be over by Christmas, at the latest.'

Sophie nodded. Like Waterloo, she thought. One major battle and it will be over.

Chapter 41

Business carried on as usual during alterations on the map of Europe.

Winston Churchill

2 September 1914

Dear Dad and Miss Thwaites,

You'll see by the address above that I'm staying with Alison and Her Grace at Wooten Abbey. The duke has joined his regiment, with most of the men from the estate. The town house has been lent to a charity to house Belgian refugees, and the duke has offered it to the Admiralty for the duration of the war after the refugees move to more permanent homes.

It is so beautiful here in the country that it is hard to think of the war beyond these shores. The harvest is being taken in, and the fields are all golden wheat or yellow stubble. The workers are shorthanded because so many men have joined up, so the women are helping, with their skirts tied up with rope, and big straw hats. They say it will be the best harvest ever. The men and women sing as they work, old songs about the king of the grain.

All one talks about here apart from the harvest is what is happening in Belgium. Such a tiny country to be so brave. They could have declared neutrality and let the Germans march through to France. But instead they stood up to them, and are paying for it now. Everyone, I think, wants to do their bit to help, but there are so few 'bits' to go round.

A friend of mine from the Workmen's Friendship Club has begun work as a VAD (Voluntary Aid Detachment), a sort of nurse's assistant, at Bedford, where the Territorial Highland

Division and other units have been stationed before they go abroad. She says that more than a hundred men have died already of measles — epidemics of one disease after another just sweep through the camps. Many of the young men have never gone past the next village, and the city diseases are strange to them. But again, do not worry: there are no army camps near here, nor are there likely to be any, as we are so far out of the way.

Her Grace is the chairman of the local Red Cross. She doesn't actually do anything, of course, except accept a bouquet of flowers at the Red Cross fête that is held in the grounds here every year. But now even she is attending the first-aid classes held in the church hall every Wednesday night. I am practising my bandaging and studying my first-aid book too. My knitting is improving, you will be glad to hear, Miss Thwaites. I have knitted seven balaclavas already. Alison has knitted ten and Her Grace fourteen, which is remarkable, as Alison says she has never seen her knit before, but she must have learned when she was young.

Five of the footmen from the Abbey have joined up; Her Grace has hired more maids to take their places. It is strange to sit down to dinner with only Blaise the butler and women in caps and aprons, not footmen in their striped shirts and ties. Her Grace has decided there will be only one hot dish at breakfast too, while the war lasts, though of course there is still ham and cold game pies and toast — Her Grace's idea of 'austerity' is like most people's idea of a feast, so do not think I am starving.

PLEASE do not worry about me. I am really safer here than I would be sailing home, especially as there may be fighting in South Africa by the time a ship to Australia reaches home. My love to everyone at Thuringa, and my special love to both of you.

Yours,
Sophie

Blaise's silver tray was laden with letters each morning at breakfast. Women across England, it seemed, were writing to each other. Even Sophie had letters, from Dodders and Lady Mary, still at work at the club, as well as two notes from Emily, one announcing a jumble sale with proceeds to go to the Red Cross, and the other asking for volunteers to collect comforts for Belgian refugees, establishing her own small empire.

James Lorrimer wrote twice a week: brief, almost businesslike letters. Keeping me connected, she thought approvingly, while he is needed elsewhere. She was glad that among the bumblings of politicians and generals there were men like James Lorrimer, and she wished she had heard something of value to offer him. Perhaps all she could give him now was understanding and patience.

Seventy thousand men of the British Expeditionary Fleet had sailed for Belgium in secret, landing before the Germans knew they had even left, the French forming a line along the south of Belgium to repel the invasion of their own country. But the Germans had centred their attack on the north. Yesterday had brought news of the English retreat from Mons and the French retreat to the Somme, the last defence post before Paris. If I had managed to get Dolphie or Hannelore to confide in me, she thought, the war might already have been won.

If Paris fell, France herself was as good as lost. The Russian army too had lost to Germany at the Battle of Tannenberg, white-horsed Russian cavalry facing grey-uniformed men with Krupps machine guns. Exactly as Hannelore had predicted, what already seemed a lifetime ago.

Hannelore's estates were between Tannenberg and the Russian border. Was Hannelore safe? Were any of them? Suddenly it seemed that if the war were over by Christmas it would be because Germany had won it.

But none of that could be put into a letter to her father.

Sophie looked up at the dowager, her thick fingers holding *The Times*. Only one copy was delivered now that the duke was not in residence; she and Alison had to wait for the news. The dowager ate slowly but steadily, even as she read.

Sophie looked at her face as she laid the paper on the table. 'More bad news, Your Grace?'

'It is difficult to tell. The Allies have retreated again. Field Marshal Sir John French says simply to a better position, but then he would say that. A supremely silly man. The sort of man who'll exhaust six horses on the hunting field and then strike the seventh when it stumbles.' The dowager stood, her flesh wobbling slightly. She must have left her corsets off. 'But now he is destroying men's lives, not just horses. The losses have been enormous. Tens of thousands. Stupid, stupid man. Alison, how many wounded do you think we could take here? It seems there is not enough hospital space for the wounded coming over from Belgium and France.'

Sophie stared at the old woman. She had spoken as casually as if she had suggested an afternoon tea.

'I don't know,' said Alison more calmly than she might have if she'd had to organise a luncheon for twenty, six months ago. 'Twenty-three bedrooms, and then there are the servants' quarters. Eighty beds, perhaps?'

'I think perhaps more than eighty beds are needed,' said Her Grace quietly. 'One must do one's bit.' She turned to the butler, who was setting the porringer straight behind her. 'Blaise, would you be so good as to ask Mrs Bettersley to come and see me?'

'Certainly, Your Grace.' Blaise gestured to the footman to take the message to the housekeeper.

'Mrs Bettersley will know what to do,' said Her Grace.

Mrs Bettersley asked, 'Turn Wooten into a hospital, Your Grace? But His Grace would never —'

'His Grace is doing his duty. He would expect us to do no less here.' The dowager sat rigid-backed in her silk-covered chair.

'I can have the rest of the beds made up, Your Grace. If the maids share rooms, we can find near seventy beds. But wounded men will need nursing, Your Grace. We're short-staffed as it is.'

'Two hundred beds,' said Her Grace calmly. 'See to it, Mrs Bettersley.'

'But Your Grace ...' The woman seemed near tears. 'How, Your Grace?'

The old woman stared at her. She has been used to saying 'See it done' for the past twenty-five years, thought Sophie. Has she any idea what she is asking this woman to do? Sophie glanced at

Alison. But she, too, seemed simply to expect the servants to fulfil orders.

And they couldn't.

Sophie stood. 'Your Grace, may I have a word in private?'

Her Grace looked surprised. 'Of course, Miss Higgs. Mrs Bettersley, if you will see to making up what beds we have.'

The woman bobbed a curtsey and escaped.

'Yes, Sophie?'

'She's never had to face anything like this before,' said Sophie quietly.

'Has any of us?' For the first time the old woman's lips trembled. How many of her friends' sons are in France, thought Sophie, or grandsons or great-nephews? How many are dying for lack of a bed and nursing?

How could a country spend decades preparing for war, but not preparing to treat the wounded?

What would her father do, faced with the old woman and the young one, bewildered but desperate to do their duty?

'Your Grace, Alison, will you forgive me if I am blunt? We need to make a list.' The dowager pulled the bell. Blaise appeared, miraculously with pen and paper, ink and blotting paper, and a small escritoire on which to rest it all. 'Thank you, Blaise. Beds ... the army should be able to help us there, even if they are camp beds. Your Grace, do you have contacts in the forces?'

A smile was growing on the lined old face. 'The lieutenant colonel of the county should be sufficient.'

'Tell him we need two hundred camp beds. It will be more efficient to have wards of many beds, especially if we don't have many nurses. Possibly the great hall and the main drawing room could be used as the main ward, with more critically ill men in the smaller reception rooms on the ground floor. Camp beds are smaller than regular beds too, so we can fit more in. But we need to designate where the nurses and doctors will sleep as well — upper bedrooms might be best kept for them.'

'And for the more senior officers,' added the dowager. Her face held only relief, not resentment.

It was as if her old life had peeled off like corsets, allowing her mind to breathe, to organise. Was this what Dad had felt when he began his empire? All she had absorbed, watching his business, planning for the Workmen's Friendship Club, came together with a power and an energy she had never let free before.

'Yes, Your Grace. Supplies ... I'll call Mr Slithersole, my father's London agent. Flour, potatoes — I'll see what Cook recommends for feeding lots, fast.' She grinned. 'At least we know we can get corned beef.' Sophie scribbled as she spoke. 'Bedpans, bandages, of course, buckets ... Do you have any other suggestions? I suppose the kitchen has big cooking pots? Iodine, aspirin ... Do we need a pharmacist to prescribe that?' She wished her knowledge of nursing needs were better. Perhaps Dodders knew some more VADs, trained ones. No, the Red Cross, of course. 'What Mr Slithersole can't supply he'll get.'

'How can you be so sure?' asked Alison.

'My father wouldn't employ him if he weren't efficient. Thank goodness he's too old to enlist. Alison, would you mind going around the estate? We can't take more men from the farmwork but ask if any daughters could be spared to work up here as nurses or maids, or in the kitchen — there's going to be far more cooking and cleaning needed. My father will cover the wages,' she added, then flushed. 'I apologise, Your Grace.'

'There is nothing to apologise for,' murmured the duchess. She heaved herself to her feet. 'I had better begin my task, had I not?'

'Your Grace ... have I been unforgivable?'

'No. Merely your father's daughter, for which I am profoundly grateful.' The smile was warm. 'Miss Lily did warn me what I was taking on. I said it would be a pleasure, and it still is. Alison, dress warmly before you go out. The wind has a bite to it. The telephone and the household are at your disposal, Miss Higgs.'

'Thank you, Your Grace,' said Sophie.

The camp beds were delivered two mornings later, the army truck bumping and burping up the drive. A voice on the telephone, its owner describing himself as an aide de camp, suggested that isolated Wooten would be more suitable as a convalescent hospital than for urgent surgery cases. The first of Mr Slithersole's supplies reached them that afternoon, in a more efficient truck, with *Higgs's Corned Beef* on the side. Sophie immediately telephoned Mr Slithersole again: a truck of their own would be useful, and a driver too. 'Could you have it repainted, Mr Slithersole? White, I think, with *Wooten Hospital* on the side.'

'Yes, Miss Higgs.'

'Mr Slithersole, you are wonderful. How do you manage it?'

A pleased cough on the other end of the line. 'It is my job, Miss Higgs.'

'My father has a treasure in you, Mr Slithersole. And please remember me to your wife, and when you know, tell me how young Albert is doing in France.'

She had just replaced the telephone, thinking that Miss Lily's six steps worked on the Mr Slithersoles of the world too, when Blaise quietly entered the room. 'Her Grace's compliments, Lady Alison, Miss Higgs, but the men have reached the station.'

'The men?'

'The wounded men, miss. Her Grace believes that the household may be of assistance down there. She has ordered the carriage.'

But we're not ready, Sophie thought. The beds hadn't even been made up, no soup had been cooked. But then, who in France or Belgium had been ready? 'Thank you, Blaise.' She hurried upstairs to change into whatever outfit Doris had deemed suitable for the occasion.

The station was small, serving a branch line, with one platform; the train passed and then returned. The stationmaster raised Buff Orpington chickens, which ran about the lines between trains.

The station courtyard had seemed small a few weeks ago. Now it seemed to have been magnified a hundred times.

How many men could fit into such a space? Her Grace had said two hundred. How many more had the army crammed onto the train? Men on stretchers, men on blankets, others lying on the muddy gravel. Bloody bandages around men who seemed unconscious, not asleep, others muttering wildly. And these were 'convalescent'?

No, not convalescent. These were men who had been judged not worthy of surgery, either because they could survive without it, or because it had already been done, or because, surgery or not, they would die.

How could they possibly get them to the Abbey?

The driver helped Her Grace from the carriage. The old woman stood silent for a moment, then spoke to the driver. 'Finchley? Please return at once. Tell Blaise to send to the Home Farm. I want every cart and every car in the district here, and every man. Haycarts — whatever they have. Bring blankets. Do you understand?'

'Yes, Your Grace.' Finchley's face was white. He flicked the reins. The carriage turned back and disappeared up the muddy lane.

Sophie gazed at the men: I must think of each one. Feel what they are feeling, like Miss Lily said.

No. If she did that, she'd be overwhelmed. She turned instead to the dowager and Alison, to find them looking at her. They want me to tell them what to do, she realised. Where to start …?

She turned to the men. 'Who is in charge here?'

No one answered. She stepped between the bodies, through the waiting room onto the platform, trying to meet men's eyes, to nod apologies, to see them still as human, not just 'the wounded'. The stench was incredible: not just blood but also urine and faeces.

No nurses. No one who looked remotely like a doctor, nor an officer in charge. No Red Cross, for this must be happening all across southern England. Men who might have been orderlies or the less badly wounded, their uniforms too crusted with blood to tell, held water bottles to men who reached out weakly.

Sophie looked down at a man in front of her. He wore the purple uniform of a wounded man — someone had given him that, at least — but the wound on his leg was seeping blood. As she looked, something white crawled around in the blood.

She had seen fly-blown sheep before. Never a fly-blown man. For a second she thought she was going to be sick, then glimpsed Alison sway behind her ...

'Your Grace, would you mind asking the stationmaster to send a telegram to your friend the lieutenant colonel? We need nurses, or at least one so she can tell the rest of us what to do. Alison, do you think you could go to the ladies' washroom and rip up your petticoats?' And be sick where none of the men can see you, she thought.

'For bandages?'

'No, to wrap strips around their arms to show which men must go to Wooten first.'

'Of course,' said Her Grace. 'The most seriously wounded.'

No, thought Sophie. The ones who look like they might live will go first. But she wasn't going to say that in front of the men.

And at last she caught the eye of one of them, saw an individual. They were all individuals, loved ones, lost ones, and she couldn't bear it. But she would. She must. 'Water,' she said quietly. 'I'll get the stationmaster's bucket and whatever cups he has. At least we can give them water till the carts arrive.'

A few months earlier at Windsor Castle she had seen that a palace was a fort. Now she realised an abbey could play the role of a gentleman's home for generations, but then revert to its true essence: a place of refuge for the needy.

They came from the station in trucks, in haycarts, in army vans. There weren't enough stretchers or even blankets to lift the wounded onto. The ten-minute drive between the station and the Abbey became a two-hour nightmare. By the evening of the first day Sophie no longer tried to talk.

For two days the road between the Abbey and the station held a solid procession, then it thinned, but kept on coming.

Two nurses arrived on the next train, in starched white aprons despite the journey, with a note from Mr Slithersole: he had recruited them from a small maternity hospital. His apologies, but it was the best he could do. He had found one doctor, elderly and harried, who seemed to doze on every chair he passed, snatching a brief nap before he continued around the wards that only two days earlier had been drawing room, library, dining room, great hall.

In the first forty-eight hours, Sophie managed perhaps four hours' sleep. Then she let herself sleep for eight hours in the old tower she had chosen as her room: small and inconvenient and cold, but romantic. Less so when the steps seemed long and the way down all too steep and the world was spinning with her weariness.

The newspapers had spoken of two thousand casualties, but at last count four hundred men had been delivered here — and this was only one of many temporary hospitals around the country. What was really happening over the Channel?

Ours is not to reason why, she thought, misquoting Tennyson, from her lessons with Miss Thwaites. Ours is just to watch them die.

Her Grace had ordered Sophie, Alison and herself special uniforms, nurse-like, from Worth the society dressmaker, neatly tailored to their figures, white with a high neck, a looser skirt than usual, and a veil. Now Her Grace stood in this uniform, pearls at her throat and ears, in the entrance hall directing new arrivals, with Blaise standing beside her softly countermanding her orders when necessary. Just as the Abbey seemed to have found its true form again, Her Grace seemed to fit her title: not with grace of form, perhaps — the bulk was undiminished — but with grace to give and keep on giving, as though there were nothing on her mind but to do her duty as long as she was able.

One of the real nurses bent to a man on a stretcher, or rather to a head of bandages and bandaged hands too. Doris and the other personal maids had been set to scrubbing floors and lockers, to washing bandages and swabs. Sophie had a sudden vision of Doris's hands reddened by soapsuds, and experienced a guilty sense of relief that scrubbing was not required of her.

What *am* I supposed to do? she wondered. Pretending in a fake nurse's dress. I can put the curate's arm into a sling, or bandage a cut knee. It took months to train even as a VAD — nor could she abandon Wooten to do so. What in heaven's name am I supposed to do here?

A row of tidy beds and tidier patients, their sheets and bandages blinding white, along each side of the room. It would have been less frightening if they cried out, or thrashed around. Anything but the stillness and the silence.

Sophie had thought blood was red. Most of the stains on these men were black.

'What can I do to help?' She tried to keep her voice calm. The memory of a paddock of lambs with their tails freshly docked came to her. She had almost fainted. Malcolm had laughed.

The nurse avoided her eye, embarrassed at giving orders to a social superior. 'Would you mind delivering meals?'

'No, of course not.'

She did mind. Anyone could deliver meals. But meals must be delivered.

Strange to be pushing a trolley of meals. All her life food had just appeared. She had never realised how many corridors and steps lay between dining or breakfast room and the kitchens. Suddenly she felt the sense of wrongness ... no, the deep inefficiency ... she had felt at the Workmen's Friendship Club. Others could do this far better than she could — women trained as nurses, or even as maids. Am I an unnatural woman? she thought. Women are supposed to naturally know how to tend the sick, to smooth men's fevered brows, to serve their food, but it bores me witless. Yet what else can I do?

'Good evening,' she said brightly. Too brightly, she thought. The sound of her voice seemed to crack the ward's silence. 'I'm Miss Higgs. Supper is served.'

Two of the men looked at her blankly; two others seemed to be sleeping. Sophie hoped neither was dead. The face of one was bandaged, all except his mouth and a single, slightly purple ear.

A fifth man murmured, 'Good evening, Miss Higgs.' A cage above his legs kept the bedclothes off whatever wounds he had there.

Sophie took the cover off one of the dishes. The man reached for it. At least he seemed able to feed himself.

Sophie approached one of the sleeping men. She touched his arm gently.

He woke with a small shout. 'What is it? What is it?'

'Shh. It's all right. I have your dinner here.'

Both of his hands were bandaged. He lay back, obviously trying not to sob.

'It's lovely, er ...' She peered down. 'Actually it's rather horrible-looking prunes, custard and rice pudding. How could anyone put all three together?'

'A Hunnish trick.' That was the man with the bandaged face. Sophie looked at him gratefully and smiled, then realised he couldn't see her expression.

'Exactly.' She gently touched the man with the bandaged hands again. 'Do you think you could manage a few spoonfuls, though? Here comes the first one.'

The man opened his mouth obediently, swallowed, opened again.

The plates were cold by the time she got to the last man, the one with the bandaged face. She touched him softly on his hand to show him she was there. 'Sorry it's taken so long.'

'No matter. Nothing better to do.'

'Cold rice pudding is even worse than warm rice pudding.' She hesitated. 'It won't hurt you to eat?'

He began to shake his head, then gave a gasp of pain. 'No.' It was obviously a lie. 'Better than lying here in a black night,' he added.

She hadn't thought what it must be like, lying with nothing to see, nothing to hear but the mutters and cries of the injured. She made a sudden decision.

'I'll be back in a minute.'

She wondered if there was a smile under the bandages. 'I'm not going anywhere.'

Did she imagine a slight lightening of the room as she came back in? Better to wonder where I dashed off to than just lie here, she thought. She held up a bottle. 'Whisky. It's good whisky,' she added.

'How do you know?' The bandaged man below her sounded genuinely curious.

'Because it's His Grace's, and he likes whisky. I don't know a good one from a poor one.'

'Nothing but the best for the dying, then.'

She gazed at him, startled. 'I'm sorry, I didn't know —'

'Nay, I'm not dying yet.' His voice had the trace of an accent again. 'Not until these bandages come off and they send me back to France.'

'I … see.'

'Unless I'm blind, of course,' he added conversationally. 'They can't send back a blind man. Though, come to think of it, it would make precious little difference. Nothing but smoke and dark when you go over the top. And mud. Don't need eyes for that.'

She sat, unable to find words.

The man across the room said, 'Be kind to her, man. Pay no attention to him, miss.'

'I …' She took a breath. 'No, he's correct. You've faced all that for people like me. The least I can do is hear what it's like.'

Silence stretched through the room. She had said the wrong thing, though she had no idea why it had been wrong.

At last the bandaged-face man said, 'Don't worry yourself, girl. We volunteered, each man in this room. If it's not the war we thought it would be, it's no fault of yours. And we fight it so you don't have to see what it's like.' He reached out, searching for her hand. She gave it to him. 'Feed me my rice pudding, and I'll behave myself.'

She held a spoonful up to the gap in his bandages, relieved when she saw he could open his mouth wider within them. The door opened and Alison came in carrying a tray with six glasses and the whisky decanter. Blaise sees everything, thought Sophie.

'Ah, that's the stuff to give the troops,' said the man opposite admiringly.

'Didn't seem fair,' said Alison. 'Whisky for one and not for all.'

'Whisky now, or after the pudding?' Sophie asked the man with the bandaged face.

He was silent.

'What is it?'

'I really need the bedpan,' he said reluctantly. 'I don't suppose you could ring for a VAD?'

'We don't have any VADs yet. I think the War Office is going to send some. I can handle a bedpan.'

It wasn't true. She had no idea how to hold a bedpan, how a wounded man would manage it. But somehow bedpans seemed … realer than spooning prunes and custard.

'Just the bottle this time, not the pan.'

She looked at the table by the bed and saw what he meant, a wide-mouthed pottery jar.

What next? Just as she thought it, he pushed aside the bedclothes and rolled onto his side. Even without the lessons of Miss Lily's book — and books at home — it was obvious where to hold the bottle. She waited till the trickling finished, was glad to see no wiping was necessary, then put the bottle back on the table for a maid to collect, covering it with its starched cloth.

She stayed with him while he sipped the whisky.

'More tomorrow,' she promised.

'For breakfast?'

'Don't push it, my lad.' She tried to sound like Miss Thwaites. He chuckled. 'How old are you?'

'As old as my tongue and a little older than my teeth.'

At least when she pushed the trolley from the room two of them were laughing.

Chapter 42

Now I lay me down to sleep.
I pray the Lord my soul to keep.

Sophie stared at the man in front of her. Lucky Doris, to only have to scrub.

The man had no face.

She had faced blood and wounds in the past month, but this man was beginning to heal.

To what?

His eyes were gone; they were a sheet of shiny tissue. Most of his nose had vanished too, though somehow his nostrils had been kept open. His scalp was a skull, hairless. No hair would ever grow there again.

But he had a mouth, twisted, almost lipless. How had he survived? And then: Dear Lord, how will he live now?

The man turned his stump of head towards her. One ear, she thought. At least he has an ear.

I can't do this, she thought. And then: *He* has to. Every day of every year, if he survives. He has no choice.

She looked at the slate bearing his name and rank at the end of the bed.

'Good morning, Sergeant Brandon.' Her voice, she was glad to hear, wasn't just steady. She had never worked so hard to make it even slightly flirtatious. My smile has to be in my voice, she thought. 'I'm Miss Higgs.'

She touched his hand lightly to let him know she had sat down by the bed. A fingertip stroke, reminding herself as well as him that he was still a man. His hands were scar-free: recent calluses, but not a manual labourer's hands. 'I know it's most improper,' she lowered her voice, 'but call me Sophie.'

'Yes, miss.'

She had made him say 'yes', at least. She touched his hand lightly again. 'Perhaps when we know each other better. Is there anything you'd like me to read to you? I brought a book. *Three Men in a Boat*. It's very funny.'

He hesitated. 'If you don't mind, miss, I'm not one for laughing at the moment.'

'I ... I'm sorry, I thought ...'

'Seeing as I'll never see a boat again. Won't see nothing, ever, will I?'

'No, Sergeant Brandon.' But he hadn't drawn his hand away from hers.

Try to be the other person.

She asked desperately, 'What did you do before the war?'

'I did the accounts, miss, in my uncle's factory.'

'Really? My father has a factory.' She didn't mention that there was more than one. 'He cans corned beef. What does your uncle make?'

'Corsets, miss.'

Was there the smallest hint of a smile in the twisted mouth?

'Really?'

'Really.'

'Well, Sergeant, you may never see a corset again, but thank God you'll still be able to feel what's inside them.'

She had shocked him, as she hoped. 'Miss!' His stumpy fingers touched the scar on his face. 'Not like this, I won't.'

'No, not like that.' Would the truth help every man? She doubted it. Yet she thought it was what this one needed. 'But the scarring will fade in the end. And if you wear a cap pulled right down, it will be hidden.'

'You think any woman would want a husband hidden in a cap? One who has no eyes?'

'Yes,' said Sophie steadily. 'If that's the worst you can offer them. I've known women to stand by men who beat them, who starved their children to pay for drink. You think your face is worse than that?'

'You're supposed to be cheering me up,' said Sergeant Brandon.

'Well, aren't you smiling?'

'Am I?'

'You know damn well you are. Pardon my French,' she added.

'That ain't French. I been there.'

'I know you have.' She tightened her hold on his fingers. 'Sergeant Brandon ... forgive me ... I've no idea how I'm supposed to talk to you. Thank you for telling me I was making a hash of it. I might have made an even worse hash if you hadn't been honest with me now. Chattering away while —'

'While we screamed inside and tried to smile?'

'Yes. Sergeant, you said you did accounts. My governess once showed me a thing called an abacus.'

'I seen an abacus once. Don't know how they use it, but.'

'I don't either. But there must be books. Maybe if there's one in the library here I could read it to you. It would be better than *Three Men in a Boat*.'

'You think I could use an abacus?' he asked. 'Do the accounts, even if I can't see?'

'I don't know. Someone would have to read out numbers to you, but anyone can do that. It takes experience to do a factory's accounts. I know that much. Do you think it might work? Every factory in the land is crying out for help,' she added. 'Your uncle would be glad to have you back.' Please, God, let that be right, she prayed. Don't let me give this man hope then take it away.

There was a moment's silence, then: 'Won't know if I don't try, will I, miss?'

'No.' She paused. 'We'll need to get you an abacus first. Some of the men are doing carpentry down in the ballroom. The rector is teaching them. Maybe they could make one if I can find a book about them.'

'What does a rector know about woodwork?'

'About as much as I do about an abacus.'

'Or them generals know about how to run a war.'

20 November 1914

Dear Dad and Miss Thwaites,

I received your two cables. Please understand: I can't come home right now. For the first time in my life I am truly needed.

Her Grace is wonderful, but she is nearly seventy, and caring for hundreds of wounded men is so far beyond anything she has known. She has aged dreadfully in the last month, or maybe is so tired one sees how old she really is. Alison's husband is overseas, as is His Grace.

The army is supposed to have taken charge of the medical side, but the lord lieutenant has only managed to procure one medical officer, Major Tindal, and Lieutenant Gladders and Sergeant Morris, who do the paperwork. The doctor Mr Slithersole found is needed back at his own hospital — he is now the only doctor there. Lieutenant Gladders is recovering from a hit he took at Mons, and may be transferred back to the front when he is recovered. I think that without the intervention of the lieutenant colonel of the county we wouldn't even have them.

Mr Slithersole's nurses are training four of the farmers' daughters from the estate in how to dress wounds. I have persuaded Major Tindal not to sign off some of the men who have recovered and who are willing to help as orderlies, lifting patients and doing other heavy work. Any who wish to go back to the front of course we allow to return there.

The family — I am included in the family now — has moved into the pensioners' wing, along with the servants who are too old to help on the wards. Blaise the butler is most upset, as we have now far less sumptuous quarters than he and the cook and housekeeper do. But we have what they don't have: privacy.

The patients wear a sort of uniform now: ghastly blue suits with red ties that make them look like shoe salesmen. The enlisted men are in wards in the ballroom and hall and reception areas, and the officers are two to six per room in the upstairs bedrooms.

Dad, thank you for your help. I know this costs a lot, and you know that I don't just mean money. But please don't ask me to come home again. The army seems to regard the wounded as just a nuisance, which I suppose they are to those who direct the battles. They ship them away from the front and then leave it to the Red Cross or volunteers to get them to where they need to go. We had a telegram two days ago, saying that two hundred and forty more men would arrive on the quarter past two train. Just that, no nurses or stretchers. Anyway, we were there to meet the train, but no men, two hundred and forty or otherwise. It was a good thing we waited, though, as a special came an hour later; I am sure the poor men it held would have simply been unloaded onto the last platform and left there until the stationmaster telephoned us, had we left.

Please give my love to all at Thuringa, and my very best indeed to those who have enlisted. When you send them comfort parcels from home, which I'm sure Miss Thwaites has organised, could you say they are from me too? And truthfully, they are better with socks or balaclavas knitted by someone else. Her Grace knits whenever she has a spare moment, but the only sock I tried to knit had enough holes to put five feet into. Forgive me for staying here, but please understand.

Your loving,
Sophie

Two letters for Sophie lay beside her place at breakfast: porridge and crumbly toast these days, with oats, bran or even potato added to the bread.

The first letter had a Swiss postmark. She opened it, blinking back tears so the maid didn't see. At least Hannelore was alive. The letter was brief, a paragraph talking about the autumn weather, and sending her love. There was no return address. Please let her be away from the Russians, Sophie thought. She almost certainly was not in neutral Switzerland, but had somehow managed to get a letter out from there. But please let her stay safe.

The other letter was from James Lorrimer.

4 December 1914

My dear Miss Higgs,

I hope you will forgive my tardiness in replying to your last letter.
Please also forgive the brevity of this note — in truth I have been
fifty-two hours without sleep already and there is another meeting
before I might, with luck, find something resembling dinner.

I am really writing to say that despite all, you have been in my
thoughts. If it is at all possible, and if Her Grace has no objections,
I would very much like to see you. (You will realise, I know, that I
may not find the time to come.) I have heard of your sterling work
at Wooten. I pray God that we have better news from France soon.

Yours always,

James Lorrimer

Not a declaration of love, but one of respect, perhaps. *You will*
realise.

Yes, she thought. I realise.

No letter from Miss Lily. She did not expect one: there had
been none since war was declared, but even so every morning
she felt a slight devastation to find that none had arrived.

She wrote to her, nonetheless, at Shillings — day-by-day
accounts of life at Wooten — hoping that wherever Miss Lily was
the letters would still reach her. None said what she desperately
needed to say ...

Dear Miss Lily, a few months ago I felt at the heart of
everything. Now I don't think there is any woman in England
who has any power at all. Even the Queen is helpless, except to
make speeches at munitions factories ...

Dear Miss Lily, I was a success, wasn't I? And it was wonderful,
for a time. Will there ever be a time as carefree as that again?

Dear Miss Lily, we lost. War has come and sometimes I think
it may never go away.

But there would be Christmas at Shillings. She clung to that.

She put the letter at Her Grace's place for her to read — as
Sophie's chaperone, nominally at least, it was still her duty to read
all Sophie's letters except those from her father — and took a last

317

gulp of tea before going back to work, but just then Alison came in, her face pale. Sophie looked at her. 'Mouse, are you all right?'

Alison glanced around to check they were alone. 'I'm breeding.'

For a second Sophie thought she meant dogs, and wondered at the waste of time. No! 'You're going to have a baby? Why didn't you tell us before?! Oh, dear Mouse. I'm so very glad.'

Alison was smiling. 'I wanted to be sure. There was so much death and horror I felt as if a baby couldn't be born. But I don't feel like that now. It's as though the child is meant to be, don't you think? It means that Philip will be all right, that one day we will have a home and a normal life ...'

It meant none of those things; it meant nothing at all just yet, except that Sophie would have to make sure Alison rested, and was kept away from infection. She would need to find another woman to help too. One of the farmers' daughters? But they were doing men's jobs already.

'I wrote to Philip this morning. I wish he hadn't chosen to go to France, but I'm proud of him too. It's so good that I can make him happy with this.'

Sophie stood and hugged her. 'I'm glad as well. Have you told your grandmother?'

'Not yet.'

'It will be good news for her too,' said Sophie softly. 'Good news at last.'

Her seventh week on the wards. Sergeant Brandon was pushing the beads on his abacus, his lips moving as he counted.

'How is it going?'

He knew her voice by now. 'I think I'm getting it. Miss, I've had a letter. From my uncle, I think. Would you mind reading it to me?'

'Of course not.'

She shut her eyes briefly. Please let it be good news. She read through it quickly before she spoke.

'What is it? Come on, I know you've read it by now.'

'He ... he says if you think you can still do the job, he'll give you a go.'

Silence. 'Can't say fairer than that, can he?'

'You can do it,' said Sophie. 'He says there's a girl who'll read the figures out to you.'

'As long as she don't run screaming at the sight of me.'

'She won't if she wants to keep her job,' said Sophie. She wondered if one of His Grace's silk smoking caps would fit Sergeant Brandon.

He snorted. 'You don't spare a man, do you?'

'When she sees you the first time she'll only see the scarring. When she sees you the second, you'll be nice Mr Brandon with the scar. But the third time, if you play your cards right, you'll just be nice Mr Brandon.' Who had said something like that to her? Miss Lily, of course. Just over a year ago ...

Where was Miss Lily now? Her Grace might know.

Christmas, remembered Sophie. I am going to Shillings for Christmas. They said the war would be over by then.

She doubted it. You didn't go through all this for a war that only lasted a few months.

'I'll read you the whole letter now,' she said. '*Dear Bertie ...*'

Chapter 43

Letters are always an adventure.

Miss Lily, 1914

Christmas: carol singers to organise for the men; the children would sing only outside the doors, in case a child looked at a soldier in horror, or even screamed. Puddings that were half carrot and parsnip, boiled in the same copper they used for cleaning bandages. Somehow they would give these men Christmas.

Sophie sent a Christmas card to James Lorrimer and received a brief note within a card in return, signed *Yours always* by a man who obviously wasn't, or not entirely, at least not just now. She also posted a cake to Dodders, and a letter to her father and Miss Thwaites, with a sketch that one of the patients had done of her, roughly framed. Her father sent hampers, via Mr Slithersole, of Harrods luxuries taken for granted before the war, and equally taken for granted as unnecessary now: crystallised fruit; giant hams; Gentleman's Relish; marmalade — how had Mr Slithersole managed that, with both sugar and oranges no longer imported?; marzipan fancies ... enough not just for the household, but also to share with the men.

And then, a week before Christmas, a small parcel and two letters — one hand familiar, one not, the second with the Shillings seal on it.

The earl. She picked his up, not Miss Lily's, hands trembling. She could think of only two reasons why the earl might write to her: if Miss Lily had died after writing the letter that now lay in front of her; or if, just possibly, Miss Lily had been imprisoned as a spy, after Emily and Mr Porton between them had worked out that it was Miss Lily, not the missing valet, who had taken the plans for that unknown weapon.

Had she truly destroyed them? Of course, thought Sophie fiercely, angry even at her momentary doubt.

She turned her mind to the earl's letter:

> *My dear Miss Higgs,*
>
> *Please accept my profound apologies for my absence during your stay at Shillings. I assumed, like most of the world, that we had endless time to play with. We did not. I cannot tell you where I am at present, as it would be scrubbed out by the censor, but that in itself will tell you why I cannot be at Shillings to greet you this Christmas.*
>
> *I hope there will be a time soon when we can meet — not just because you are my cousin's friend, and the daughter of a man I deeply admire, but also because your own efforts in the past couple of months at Wooten have been extraordinary, far beyond the organisational brilliance one might expect even from your father's daughter.*
>
> *One of the men from my brigade wrote to me* [a section blackened by the censor] *that you smile at the wounded as if they are men, not* [censored again].
>
> *My profound thanks and admiration,*
> *Nigel Vaile*

Where was he? In France? Flanders? The Middle East? They would have made him shave his beard off, she thought vaguely, unless he was in the navy.

She opened the other letter.

> *My dearest Sophie,*
>
> *I promised you peace, or at least implied it, when I encouraged you to stay in England, rather than sail for home. I am deeply sorry you are in this land of war, but also deeply glad, for an England with Sophie Higgs just now is a richer one. I am not referring to your father's money, a blessing though it is.*

There is also another matter about which I believe I should have been more frank with you. It concerns your mother. I told you the truth when I said I knew nothing about what might have happened to her, but, as you have so bluntly pointed out, I do, at times, tell less than the entire truth.

I have heard of a Mrs Higgs who lives in Paris. Whether she is your mother I do not know, nor how she came to be there. She may be no relation, but it is a slightly unusual name, at least for a resident of Paris. When you were at Shillings I was reluctant to distract you from your season with what might be a vain or distressing meeting. I now regret that, but alas none of us realised that things in France would become so chaotic so soon.

I will give you Mrs Higgs's address, as well as tell you the little more I do know about your mother, when we meet again. I very much hope that this will be soon — though I very much doubt it will be, nor can I encourage you to come to Paris when it may be occupied any day by the enemy.

I gather from Her Grace that you have Wooten thoroughly organised, and its home farm too. I am proud of you, my dear, and look forward to our next meeting, and to introducing you, at last, to my cousin.

Yours, with love,
Lily

The letter was postmarked Paris. Was Miss Lily working at one of the volunteer hospitals? Organising supplies for refugees? Or did the 'chaotic' mean she felt it safer to be out of England, in case she was accused of helping the enemy, before the war? Perhaps Paris was simply where she lived, when not at Shillings.

She opened the parcel, almost in a dream. It was a box covered in old faded leather. Even before she opened it she could smell the scent that had lingered in the parchment silk sitting room of Shillings. She looked at the card inside: *To Sophie, with love.*

There was no signature. Somehow she was glad of that. Miss Lily had not signed her false name this time, even if she would not give her real one.

Sophie lifted the cloth. Beneath it was a piece of jewellery, small, gold, with an emerald heart. It had the beauty of age; it was not just old-fashioned but almost ancient, the pattern that was etched into the metal softened by time. It might have at one time been a man's cravat pin or a fob, but now it was a brooch, and hers.

She sat with it in her hand, ignoring the tears that slid unwiped — tears not just for the lost Christmas at Shillings, nor for the men in their wards, and for the whole mad world of war. These tears were full of joy too.

I am so lucky, she thought, to have so much love.

Chapter 44

Why does no one write about the beauty of men? Even artists rarely celebrate it. Would it be different, my dear, if women were allowed their own voices?

Miss Lily to the Duchess of Wooten, 1899

JANUARY TO APRIL 1915

Winter sat heavy on Wooten: the cook harried from trying to feed the patients as well as the staff; the dowager confined to her bed with arthritis in the cold weather; Blaise affronted by an orderly who seemed to think the army's orders outranked a butler's; Doris crying in the linen closet, her hands red and swollen from scrubbing, not the lady's maid's soft hands she had been so proud of; the Home Farm ploughman enlisted and the farmer was desperate to find someone who could handle a plough before the spring planting.

Sophie changed the staff mealtimes to an hour earlier and arranged with two of the tenants' wives to bring big pots of potato and corned-beef stew to the big house twice a day, placated Blaise with charm and the orderly with offers of tea with a genuine duchess, moved the dowager's bedroom to one where she could share old Nanny's sitting room and fireplace, and convinced a father his daughter could learn to handle a team and plough as well as she could horses and a carriage.

Doris was reprieved from scrubbing: she and Alison served the meals now. As Alison said, once you'd taken the trolleys around three wings and three floors it was time to begin the next round.

Doris was immediately happier — happy, even — in one of the 'nurse's' uniforms.

Most of Sophie's time was spent on administration now, with Her Grace confined to bed: ordering supplies, checking their arrival, receiving calls from the tenants and solving more of their problems, deciding which of the woods were to be cut for timber for the army, making sure that while the hunters might be taken as war horses enough plough horses were left.

One day she was at what now passed for family luncheon — just Alison and her — when Blaise entered the room, a silver salver holding a yellow telegram in his hand.

Blaise's face was white. 'Lady Alison.'

Alison stood. 'Thank you, Blaise.' Her voice was calm, her step unhurried as she took the telegram. She stood without opening it. 'You may go, Blaise.'

'Lady Alison, I know it's not my place, but —'

Alison touched his arm briefly. 'That will be all, Blaise.'

'Yes, my lady.'

Alison waited till the door was shut, then moved over to the window.

'Mouse, darling — do you want me to leave?'

'Stay.' She ripped open the envelope, then stood staring at it, her face expressionless.

'Mouse?'

'Dead.' The voice was flat. 'He could have sat the war out behind a desk back here ...'

She was crying, Sophie realised, even though her voice was steady, the tears dripping down onto her pearls.

'You know what the joke is? I loved him. Not like a husband maybe, not yet. We hadn't known each other long enough. But as a good man, a kind man. I wanted him to see his child. I could have done that one thing for him, at least. Who am I now, Sophie? I was someone because I was his wife. Who am I now?' Her face crumpled. She sank into a crouch by the wall, rocking back and forth.

Sophie kneeled beside her, holding her, trying to muffle the wails. 'Shh, darling. Shhh. It will be all right.'

Stupid words, she thought. But what could she say? It wasn't all right. Alison had no husband now, never would have one again, perhaps, as more thousands of men died each day. The world had accepted that war could happen on a scale never known before. It would never be all right again.

They held the funeral in the chapel: family, servants, a few convalescents who'd got attached to the quiet Lady Alison. Later, a small man with a smaller beard read the will. It was a simple one. *Everything I own to my wife, Lady Alison Standish.* Irregular, said the little man, but signed and witnessed. It would stand.

Sophie stared at her friend, her face hidden by the small black veil on her hat. She was rich. Not as wealthy as the Higgses, but rich. It made no difference now, of course. There were still the chamber pots to empty, the letters to be read aloud, lint to scrape for bandages, used bandages that had been boiled to roll again, suppers to spoon into a hundred helpless mouths.

Later, perhaps, the money might mean freedom, choices that could be made if Alison had the courage or even the power to imagine what they might be. But that would be in another land, one harder and harder to imagine. The land of peace.

Whitehall, London
20 April 1915
My dear Sophie,

Please do pass on my most heartfelt sympathy to Lady Alison. I have sent a card, but it will be one of so many. I would like to think a more personal message might be added too. I met Major Standish only briefly, but he seemed a good man and one who knew his duty. It would be trite to say he was a hero who died for his country, and yet it would be true. No matter how many times one writes it, it is still true.

Forgive me for writing like this. I am tired, and I confess I am weary too, which is not, I find, the same as being tired.

Tomorrow I leave for the United States, for reasons you can probably guess. One cannot say, of course, that without assistance we cannot win the war, and so I shall not say it. I CAN say, however, that if negotiations go as planned I shall return to England in about three months, but my absence may, sadly, be far longer. By then I hope to have earned at least an afternoon to call my own, or at least the right to assert that a weary tool will be of more use to his country after rest.

May I make a request of you, and of Her Grace? I shall of course write to her separately. An American, Mr Thomas G Kranowski, is in this country briefly. Like your father's, his empire is based on exporting food. His is based on rice, and I hope very much to persuade him, despite the risk to his ships, to continue to send his rice to England. It is possible that seeing your work at Wooten would encourage him in that, and also, perhaps, make him a stronger advocate of England's need for help.

Please give my regards to Her Grace, and again, my sincerest condolences to Lady Alison.

Yours always,
James

Once she would have shivered at the thought of James Lorrimer's trying to get yet another nation into the war. Now she only thought of how Mr Thomas G Kranowski could be charmed, not just by her, but also by a 'genuine English' duchess, as well as by seeing England's need embodied in its wounded.

When had James Lorrimer begun to call her Sophie in his letters, and sign himself simply James? She put the letter into the box where she kept all her letters now. It was easier to keep them all than think, Who is important to me? Whose letters should I keep?

It seemed as if her life had expanded then contracted, like a balloon a child kept blowing up and letting down. The small life back home had become the larger life of English society; the war's initial challenges had now shrunk again into days of ordering stores and checking bandage supplies, gobbling down hurried meals and the blessed blank each night as she fell over the cliff of sleep.

And now Mr Thomas G Kranowski to persuade. She did not even realise how far she had come in this last year, when neither the logistics of his tour, nor the charm needed to persuade him, seemed more challenging than simply ensuring that Wooten had food for the coming month.

Chapter 45

*I keep thinking, I can't do this. But then I find I can do it, after
all. That's all we can do, isn't it, Soapy, old girl?*

'Dodders' to 'Soapy', 1915

20 May 1915

Dear Dad and Miss Thwaites,

   You will see from the address that I am in London for a few
days. Alison and I have come down to select which of Major
Standish's paintings and other valuables and sentimental objects
should be sent to Wooten. The house will then be sold. Alison
never lived there with Philip, so it has few memories for her, nor
does she enjoy London society. Going through his things is hard for
her especially in her condition but necessary, and also in a strange
way seems to have made her happier, linking her again to the father
of her unborn.

   Alison has also seen a medical specialist to make sure there
are no problems. I accompanied her. Dr Hilson says she is in the
best of health, despite her loss and hard work, and the baby can be
safely delivered at home, as she wishes, with no need to stay in a
London clinic.

   We are staying at the duke's London residence. The Belgian
refugees have left for more permanent homes, and the Admiralty
refused the offer of the house, as it needs too many repairs to be
suitable. The furniture is mostly under holland covers, but the
housekeeper is still here and Mr Ffoulkes the butler, who is too old to
enlist, and the boot boy and a couple of maids-of-all-work, so we are
well cared for. I am glad that by the time you get this I will be back
up north, as you probably already know about the London air raids.

Alison and I went up onto the roof and watched the searchlights and the big shells fired at the enemy planes — they looked just like fireworks, and went woof, woof, woof like massive dogs, and the whole house shook. People ran through the streets as soon as the 'take cover' siren sounded, but there isn't really anywhere safe to shelter except in the cellars, and I would hate to be trapped by rubble underground. Many people go and shelter by the big guns, thinking the guns will protect them, but I think the Germans are more likely to try to hit the cannons.

We stayed up there till part of a shell broke one of the nearby lime trees and Mr Ffoulkes came up himself to ask us to come down to the kitchen to reassure the scullery maids, which was a tactful way of telling us to behave ourselves and get inside.

The next night Mr James Lorrimer and a friend of Alison's husband, Major the Honourable David Threasington-Blythe, came to dine, and stayed with us during the raid. Alison is still in mourning, of course, but these days widows seem to be allowed company, though it was a very informal affair. Major Threasington-Blythe told us how to tell the German planes from ours by the sound of their engines. He is on leave from France. He would not tell us anything about the war. He doesn't realise how much we have learned already from the patients at the Abbey.

Alison and I have been invited to visit Windsor Castle. It is a royal command, so we have to go. We had Mr and Mrs Slithersole to luncheon. I know it was a waste of Mr Slithersole's time just now, but it pleased Mrs Slithersole no end to lunch at a duke's residence. Mr Slithersole has been a rock, and he was pleased at her happiness.

I can't thank you enough for funding Wooten. His Grace has given his agent orders to sell the woods if necessary, but the army has requisitioned the timber so I doubt anyone would buy them at the moment.

Lady Alison and I will be safely on the train to the Abbey tomorrow, with twelve newly qualified VADs. I considered training to be a VAD too, but Her Grace pointed out that I don't take orders well and might have to spend the war scrubbing floors.

Don't worry, there are no more London trips planned — Her
Grace doesn't want us near the air raids again, especially with
Alison in her condition. Her Grace and I had hoped Alison might
stay in London for the next month, where there are experienced
obstetricians, but that was before the air raids.

Alison is well and sends her best regards.

Love from me,

Sophie

It still seemed strange to get a taxicab to Victoria Station, instead of a private carriage with footmen to guard them. But the carriages, the footmen, even the horses, were needed for the war now.

Sophie stared out the window. London had changed even in a few months: not many people on the streets, and most of those women; *Call to arms* posters and the Union Jacks. The world of the debutantes' season seemed far more remote than it was.

The porter at Victoria Station wheeled away their luggage: one trunk for the two of them for the whole week they had been away, instead of the multitude of hatboxes and luggage they had previously needed even for a Friday-to-Monday.

'Sophie? It *is* you, isn't it?'

'*Malcolm!*'

The chuff of a train turned into the buzz of cicadas. He looked exactly the same, despite his uniform, and totally different too. His face was almost as brown as it had been at home.

'What are you doing here?'

'I thought you would have gone home.'

They spoke together, broke off together too, laughed. And suddenly it was simple.

'Alison, this is my old friend Malcolm Overhill. Malcolm, this is Lady Alison Standish, wife of the late Major Philip Standish. I'm staying with her family up north.'

'Doing a sterling job too.' Alison glanced down at his kit bag, then at the insignia on his arm. 'You're about to catch a train, Lieutenant Overhill?'

'No, just got in. Forty-eight hours of leave before we head off over there. I'm sorry, Lady Alison, my sincere condolences.' He turned back to Sophie, ignoring deeply pregnant Alison in her crepe veil. 'I took the first ship over here when war was declared — I want to be where the real action is, not stuck in some colonial regiment. Sophie, how long are you in London?'

Another sixteen minutes, thought Sophie.

'Another night,' said Alison. She took her calling card from her handbag and offered it to him. 'Won't you join us for dinner, Lieutenant Overhill? Sophie, darling, I will see you after lunch. I need to make sure the porter has put that package on the train.' And get our luggage back, thought Sophie, and inform Their Majesties we will be a day late. She wished she could tell Malcolm all that. She looked back at him as Alison made her way through the crowd. She suspected Alison would also be heading for the loo; the baby was pressing on her bladder.

'There are buns,' she said, pointing to the canteen for soldiers along the platform. Her head filled with memories of Thuringa, of rides under the trees. A world before bandages. 'Or we could find lunch somewhere. Where are you staying?'

'The parents of a chap I trained with are putting me up. Out Hampstead way. I say, would Lady Alison mind frightfully if he came to dinner too? He's a good egg, I promise you.'

Hampstead. Not a good address, Sophie thought automatically, while saying, 'Of course.'

'Do you know somewhere we could lunch? Sophie, it's good to see you.'

'And you.' She meant it.

'You look ... different. Beautiful.'

'I'm still the same.' She led the way automatically to the taxi rank; thought, equally automatically, that if James or poor Philip or Dolphie were there she would be following instead.

It was an old-fashioned restaurant: booths instead of tables, plush red bench seats. James had taken Alison and her there, a world ago. She hoped James wouldn't enter and find her here lunching with another man, even innocently. He was probably far too busy for restaurant lunches, in any case.

They sat opposite each other, studying the menu. I need to speak, she thought. They both knew there were rocks to clamber over before they could talk normally.

She took a breath. 'Malcolm, I'm sorry. I know what you must think of me.'

'I thought you had found another chap,' he said with honesty. He gestured to her left hand. 'But you're not engaged.'

'I was too young, that's all — just as I told you.'

Malcolm looked up at the waiter. 'Clear soup and lamb chops, I think.' The man had moved off before Sophie realised Malcolm had ordered for them both.

'Funny to be here unchaperoned,' she said lightly. 'It would have been unthinkable a year ago.'

'Yes.' He grinned. 'And in a few days I'll be taking pot shots at the Hun.'

She was about to say he didn't have to pretend at heroics, not with her. And then she saw his excitement was real. Perhaps he *would* be a hero, accepting the front lines as calmly as he might a broken arm after a game of football. Or perhaps, in weeks, this young man would be gone — irrevocably changed, if still alive.

'I was afraid it would be all over before I got through training.'

He knew less than she did. Saw it still through a thrill of excitement, was aware of only what the papers published.

I know the Kaiser's cousin, she thought. I've met the men who make decisions. I've helped nurse those who carried them out.

Before Miss Lily, even before Sergeant Brandon, she might have dismissed him as an ignorant colonial, a boy who still believed that heroics were enough to win a war. Now she smiled at the waiter who placed the soup in front of her, then smiled at Malcolm too. 'We'll have to make the most of twenty-four hours.'

The pre-dinner sherry was awkward: four strangers worlds apart. Malcolm and his friend Bunty Armitage admired Philip's French Impressionist paintings with some reserve. Sophie could see they really considered even the graceful Monet mere daubs of paint. They spoke of their just-completed basic training with the army as a lark, learning to make out the shapes of men in sand hills in the dark, as though war came with toast and honey and perhaps charades afterwards.

The dinner gong was a relief. Lieutenant Armitage took Alison in to dinner; Sophie placed her hand on Malcolm's arm.

Ffoulkes served; he wouldn't demean the house by letting a maid do so. Soup first: a mutton broth. The silence was becoming increasingly uncomfortable. Sophie hunted for conversation. 'At least we're not talking about kangaroos.'

Malcolm grinned in relief. 'Have you been asked about kangaroos too?'

'Endlessly. I even told the truth about them at first, but then it got too much. I told one man I had a pet kangaroo in Sydney.'

'You mean you don't?' asked Lieutenant Armitage too innocently. 'Malcolm, you rotter, you told me you had one too.'

'That was a pet emu. Well, a pair of emus. They pull our carriage when the horses need a break.'

'You have never mentioned emus.'

'It's true, isn't it, Sophie?'

'Of course. Kangaroos have more endurance than emus, but they're far too jerky to pull a carriage.'

Alison laughed. It was so good to hear her laugh. 'Sophie, behave yourself.'

Sophie smiled at her, then at the men. This has to be a good night, she thought. It may be the last good night they have. A night of laughter for Mouse too. She leaned across the table to Alison. 'Shh,' she whispered. 'If you give me away about kangaroos, I'll tell them about your giraffe.'

Lieutenant Armitage grinned. He had a scatter of pimples on his chin. 'What giraffe?'

'Alison had a pet giraffe when she was small. Well, no one could see him, but he was there.'

'Of course he was there. His name was Wuffles,' said Alison with dignity. 'And he was pink.'

'A pink giraffe?'

'He was my giraffe, so he was pink.' This was a different Alison, a relaxed and happy hostess, despite her uncomfortable bulk. Miss Lily might have given her the skills to charm these young men, but her marriage had given her the confidence to use them.

'Quite right, Lady Alison. It's far better to have a pink giraffe than kangaroos.'

Ffoulkes removed the soup.

'What did you do before the war, Lieutenant Armitage?' asked Alison, shifting uncomfortably in her seat. Sophie mentally prepared a tactful way to remove a woman in labour from a dinner party.

'I was at Oxford, studying chemistry.'

'One doesn't study chemistry,' said Malcolm. 'You simply do it and it smells. Or blows up in your face.'

'I say, old chap, that's a bit rich. Sheep smell too, you know.'

'But they smell of sheep,' said Sophie. 'Now, kangaroos smell of roses. Except in spring, of course.'

Turbot was served next, and they were still laughing, at ease with each other now; venison from Wooten — last night's leftovers heated up; she noticed that Alison was given a single thin slice, and herself too, while the men had larger portions. Alison's instructions, she was sure. This was followed by a potted shrimp savoury — probably pre-war — and an apple meringue, the fruit and eggs sent down with them from Wooten.

She and Alison withdrew to the drawing room. She doubted the men would be long over their port.

Alison settled herself awkwardly on the sofa — grey silk, like Miss Lily's. Where is Miss Lily? thought Sophie. There had been no more letters, from her or the earl, though Sophie had written to them both.

'So that's your Malcolm. I like him.'

'I like him too. But not enough.'

'He's very young.'

'Older than me.'

'You know exactly what I mean.'

335

'Yes. I do. He won't be young when he gets back, though.'

Alison watched her. 'Were you hoping Mr Lorrimer would propose?'

'I don't know,' said Sophie slowly. 'I don't think this is a time for marriage.'

Alison nodded. 'Not to acquire a young wife who's never managed a household before, especially not for a man in his position.'

'You make me sound like a dog he doesn't have time to train. A fox terrier, perhaps. But I don't want to leave Wooten just now anyway.'

'I'm glad,' said Alison simply. 'I don't think we could do without you.'

'You'd manage.'

'Oh, yes, we'd manage. But you do more than manage. Grandmama heard from the lieutenant colonel that he's recommended your system of sorting the wounded into categories for use at other army hospitals.'

'Really?' She felt absurdly pleased.

Male voices sounded in the hall. Alison added fresh hot water to the teapot.

Sophie saw them to the door, Ffoulkes tactfully absent, Lieutenant Armitage even more tactfully just popping outside 'to check the cab, old thing'.

'May I kiss you?'

The kiss was gentle. Then he kissed her harder, and that was different too. It tasted of desperation, neither sex nor love. She wondered what she should have felt, suspected that whatever it was, he had failed to find it too, wondered also if she should have felt she was betraying James. But then James had neither kissed her nor proposed. And at least Malcolm had given her a kiss goodbye. He stood back. 'I'd better go.'

'We'll come to the station to see you off.' Suddenly she realised that they would be leaving the next morning. But before she could speak, he shook his head.

'It's too early. No, truly, I'd rather say goodbye here than with a hundred chaps watching.' He grinned at her suddenly. 'Don't look like that.'

'Like what?'

'Like I'm a poor doomed soldier off to unknown horrors.'

She made herself smile. 'I'm sorry. Too much nursing.'

'Nursing?'

She'd never told him, she realised. Had laughed about giraffes, but not told him anything of real importance about her life over the past nine months. 'The Abbey has been turned into a hospital. I'm not really a nurse, though I'm doing my first-aid exams. We just help where we can.'

'Sophie, I had no idea. I thought you were,' he shook his head, 'partying. Having dinners with the gentry.'

She laughed, determined to lift the cloud. 'I *am* having dinners with the gentry. It's just that those dinners are usually vegetable soup and Irish stew. Or bread and cheese if we're too tired to eat a proper meal.'

'Can we meet again? On my next leave?'

'Of course.'

'There's no of course about it. Do you realise we don't know each other? I don't think we ever did. I'd like to get to know you now. Like to know I've a friend from home in England.'

He kissed her cheek, a gentle kiss. 'I'm not going to die over there, Sophie. I'm not even going to be one of your wounded. They breed us tough at Warildra.'

She believed him.

Even Windsor looked different as Sophie helped Alison off the train, the Guards' band playing 'Auld Lang Syne' and 'God Save the King' as a trainload of cheering soldiers left for the front. They looked so young, so much younger than the patients at the Abbey.

The trees were leafless, the lower Home Park and Eton's playing fields beyond were a grey mirror of floodwater, as though it couldn't be bothered flowing down to the river.

The castle was even colder than in summer, with white-faced women in heavy mourning imploding along the corridors: Guards' wives — now widows — lodged at Windsor and on its outskirts. The Guards had been hit hard. So many widows in so short a time.

Alison and Sophie stayed in adjoining rooms in Henry VIII's tower. Queen Mary's physician gave Alison a fresh examination — presumably on Her Majesty's orders — and then they dined with the royal family and their guests. The old rule about not publicly receiving anyone in trade had gone with the outbreak of war. Even actresses could be admitted now.

The food was simple: like the War Secretary, Lord Kitchener, the King had forbidden the household alcohol, hoping to set an abstemious example to the factory workers. They ate mulligatawny soup, followed by turbot and vegetable cutlets with green peas.

'The chef threatened to resign,' said Queen Mary as a footman in white wig and brocade — which seemed still unwashed since their last visit — served cold custard in little cups, and rice pudding. 'He says there is no call for his art now.'

Admiral Campbell looked up from his rice pudding. 'Then let him. He can cook for the men in the trenches.'

Queen Mary smiled, but didn't answer. She had shadows under her eyes, and her skin looked like tracing paper. She had spent the morning at one munitions factory, the afternoon at another, giving small speeches of encouragement, then had visited the local hospital.

After dinner the women knitted. Her Majesty knitted perfectly, Sophie noted, as she tried to hide the holes in the soldier's belly band she was working on — she had given up any attempt at socks. She felt a moment's incredulity that Sophie Higgs was sitting with the Queen, knitting, while the King and his advisors discussed affairs of state only a corridor away.

Such a womanly occupation, knitting. And such a treat to have a whole evening of doing it, of being attended, not attending.

Chapter 46

Every spy is a patriot — to the other side. Every patriot is an enemy to those who prefer peace.

Miss Lily, 1915

MAY 1915

Alison did not go into labour from the rigour of the journey, as Sophie had feared. She was still determined to have her baby born at Wooten, as her father and ancestors had been.

Now, back at work, it seemed that new days were no longer being created, just part of already lived days patched up and returned to them. Routine had become drudgery. Wooten ran as though it had always been a convalescent hospital. Each day differed only in its petty crises and its tragedies: men crippled, blinded, or muttering in madness and kept isolated till they had healed enough to be moved to an asylum. Graves stretched across part of the church's hay paddock.

Newspapers arrived but were rarely read, except the casualty lists, which all obsessively checked for names they knew.

Malcolm's friend Lieutenant Armitage had been wounded after only two days' active service, and sent to Cambridge again, still in uniform, missing half a finger but already working in research. Sophie had no idea what one researched in wartime, but at least he was safe. Lord Buckmaster was map-making, of all things. Safe. The Duke of Wooten was now in Mesopotamia. Safe when last heard of. The Earl of Shillings, promoted to a colonel, was not yet on the casualty lists as wounded, dead, a prisoner or missing. Malcolm had been mentioned in dispatches for gallantry in the same skirmish that had wounded his friend. Safe when last heard of too.

The Wooten postboy, Ernest: dead. The butcher's son, Eric: dead. The Honourable David Threasington-Blythe: dead. Eight sons from the Wooten estate, two of whom were husbands and fathers: dead. Another legless; yet another with a head wound, unmoving, unseeing, back in his small room under the cottage eaves. So many of the young men Sophie had danced with: dead, missing, wounded. Time consumed lives in greedy gulps, turning what should have been lifetimes into hours or days.

And yet time passed. The war had become bogged down in mud. France, at last, was no longer being nibbled into by the German armies. Both sides had dug a continuous line of trenches from the North Sea to Switzerland. Small parties made brief sorties to capture a few yards of hill or opposite trench, but even more time was spent playing cards in sodden dugouts, or football around the tangles of barbed wire.

All ships in English waters, neutral or not, were targeted by German guns and submarines now. Germany intended to starve Britain if it couldn't conquer it. The price of bread soared, but Mr Slithersole still came through for Wooten. Sophie saw each bowl of corned-beef stew with pride.

Women worked in fields that had known only men before — hoeing, mattocking, digging drainage channels. Women drove the farm carts. Women volunteers drove other carts carrying the wounded or the convalescent to the hospitals or rest homes that were mostly private homes, requisitioned by the military or offered, but still run partly or even mostly by volunteers. Where had this vast array of skills come from, these women so suddenly knowing and capable? No one, thought Sophie, had time or energy to enquire.

No changing for dinner these days, but one did, at least, change one's apron and remove one's veil. Alison, once again quiet as the mouse for which she had been nicknamed, growing even larger, refused to rest in the afternoons, even for her coming baby's sake.

'It's all I can do to repay Philip,' she said, when Sophie once more urged her to lie down. 'I ... I miss being hugged, Sophie. Philip hugged me every morning at breakfast. It's funny, but that's what I miss most.'

'You are very huggable, dear Mouse,' said Sophie, suiting the action to the words. 'By me. By your grandmother. I'll hug you every day from now on. I promise.'

'Grandmama doesn't believe in hugs, I think. But soon I'll have my baby. They are so huggable, aren't they?' She looked at her belly. 'Soon,' she said. 'Soon.'

More days. The baby did not come. More vanloads of men did. Mr Slithersole's corned-beef truck was outfitted with rows of sliding stretchers now, so it could carry thirty men, as long as they could bear another layer just above them for the ten minutes it took to drive from the railway to the Abbey. Life went on, and so did pain and death.

Sophie had just finished the new staff rosters — they still tried to give each servant a half-day off a week, and time for church every third Sunday — when Alison found her in the corridor.

'Sophie? My waters broke.' Alison smiled faintly, seemingly matter-of-fact. 'Thank goodness for petticoats. I don't think the men noticed.'

Sophie hid her relief. Alison was more than a week overdue, the duchess about to wire a physician to come from London. 'I'll take you up to your room and get the doctor.'

'I don't want a man now. Sister Martens has delivered hundreds of babies.'

Sophie silently thanked Mr Slithersole for finding them nurses from a maternity hospital.

'Don't worry, darling,' said Alison. 'It will be fine.'

Thirty-six hours later Alison was screaming. Labour had been slow, stopping and starting till the last six hours of constant pain. The dowager duchess sat beside her, alternatively knitting and holding Alison's hands while she strained and pushed.

Sister Martens checked under the sheet again. 'I'm going to fetch the doctor,' she said quietly.

'But Alison didn't want —' began Sophie.

'The baby needs forceps if we're going to get it out,' said Sister Martens, more bluntly than she'd ever have spoken in the days of the maternity clinic. 'I don't have any.'

Has he ever done a forceps delivery? wondered Sophie, but Sister Martens added, 'Don't worry. I'll tell him what to do.'

Sophie sat by Alison's side. 'It'll be over soon. Soon.'

'Sophie ... don't tell Philip I screamed, will you?'

Philip is dead, thought Sophie, just as Alison shook her head, said, 'I forgot', then screamed again.

The doctor arrived smelling of port. He washed his hands briefly in the water bowl, then pulled the forceps from his bag.

'Try to time pulling with a contraction ...' began Sister Martens.

He silenced her with a look. 'Now, then,' he said, in a gust of false cheer and port fumes. 'Let's be doing with this, shall we?'

It took another hour. An hour of screams, of blood running into the sheets, and down Alison's chin when she bit her lips. At times Sophie wondered if the duchess was going to faint. But she stayed where she was, a rock no one dared try to move.

At last, the baby cried.

Sister Martens took it, gazed without comment at the bruised head, then quickly and efficiently wiped it with warmed wet cloth she'd had waiting, swaddled it, and placed it in Alison's arms then, as the doctor left, bent down again to deal with the afterbirth.

Sophie held Alison's hands more firmly around the baby. Alison had no strength, but wasn't going to let it go. The duchess sat, her face unmoving, tears streaming down the leathered skin.

'A girl,' said Sophie softly. 'Clever Mouse.' She exchanged a look with the duchess. A girl couldn't be swallowed up by war. And she's going to have all her mother never had, thought Sophie fiercely. Money enough to do what she likes. We will tell her she is beautiful and intelligent and hug her every day.

'I'm going to call her Sophie,' Alison whispered through white lips. 'Philip agreed.'

'But not Sophronia. Please.'

A shadow of a smile. 'Not Sophronia.' Her eyes closed.

Sophie took the duchess's hand to help her up. 'Happiness is a baby,' the old woman whispered. 'Even in these days. So very happy.' Her eyes closed, as if to stop the tears she would not acknowledge.

By evening Alison was drinking broth made from a rooster the housekeeper had been saving specially, the baby with her now-swollen head nuzzling at her mother's breast. 'I know nursing spoils the figure. But it doesn't matter in my case, does it?' She gazed down at the baby. The bruises were purple, but the child sucked strongly and waved her tiny fists. 'It's funny; I woke earlier and thought, The war will end now my baby has been born. There has to be a safe world for my baby.'

'She will be safe,' said Sophie. 'Always.'

Alison nodded. 'Mine,' she whispered. 'Somebody of my very own, at last.'

Sleep came like a blow from an axe that night; it had been impossible to do more than doze every now and then in a chair by Alison's bed the last two nights.

Sophie was woken by urgent knocking. She sat up, dazed. A servant would enter without knocking, otherwise only Alison ever came to her room.

'Come in,' she said.

Sister Martens appeared at the door. 'Miss Higgs, I think you should come. It's Lady Alison.'

'Is something wrong? She was doing so splendidly.' Sophie grabbed her dressing gown and slippers, and followed Sister Martens and her candle down the corridor.

The dowager duchess was already there. Alison sat up from her pillows as they came in, red-faced and sweating, shadows almost green about her eyes.

'Lie back,' instructed Sister Martens, and then to Sophie, 'Sponge her face. Keep her cool, if you can.'

'What is it?' asked Sophie urgently.

'Puerperal fever,' said Sister Martens. 'Childbirth fever, if you like.'

'Have you called the doctor?'

'He's already seen her. He's given her something for the pain.'

'There must be something else he can do!'

Sister Martens frowned, then drew her out into the corridor again. 'Miss Higgs, I'm sorry.'

'What is it, Sister?'

'Puerperal fever is an infection, Miss Higgs.'

'Infections can be cured.'

'Not this one. Miss Higgs, no mother survives puerperal fever.'

It took another day. By midday Alison knew no one, though in between her mutterings she called for Sophie, unaware that Sophie sat there, holding her hand, sponging the flushed face, trying to hope it was something else. Measles, or influenza ...

Some time that afternoon Doris was there too, sitting side by side with the dowager duchess, neither seeming to think the conjunction strange.

At ten past three in the morning Alison died.

It was a small funeral. They always were these days. Grief must be compressed by war too: not the depth of sadness, but the moments spared to show it. No horses to pull the hearse; no hands to tend the flowers to make the wreaths — just small bunches from the gardens of the estate, daffodils and bluebells from the woods. The mourners were all women. Doris carried the baby, had tended her since Alison's death, had somehow found a farmwoman to wet-nurse little Sophie that first night when Alison grew ill.

'It's all I can do for Lady Alison now,' she said to Sophie. 'Please, Miss Higgs, can I be her nurse? Then her maid maybe, as she grows older?'

'Of course,' said Sophie. The dowager would have no objection; she would be glad someone suitable had offered. Someone who had known Alison, and who would love her child.

Sophie walked back to Wooten behind the dog-cart that had carried the duchess. The old woman had borne it all without tears; she had simply stood there, leaning on her stick, watching as the earth was scattered on the coffin, watching as though to gather the last second of her granddaughter's existence.

Alison, gone forever. Hannelore vanished among the enemy, and Miss Lily. Sophie wondered what Emily was doing. Still creating an empire of jumble sales and collections for refugees? She didn't care.

She had never truly hated the war till now. She had seen what it had done to men, to the women and children left behind. But this was the first loss that had struck at her personally. For the war had killed Alison too — she knew enough of nursing and infection to realise that.

She should have insisted on that London clinic; overruled physicians and Alison's wishes. Alison should have been kept from a place where infected wounds were commonplace; where a tired doctor simply rinsed his hands before attending her.

I failed you, Mouse, she thought. My first true friend, who needed me, who trusted me. And I let you die.

Chapter 47

If I had one wish, today, it would be to be able to say the things that cannot be said.

Miss Lily, 1915

Wooten Abbey
20 November 1915
Dear Dad and Miss Thwaites,

It was so good to get your letter. I miss home dreadfully. The days here at Wooten all seem to run together. Every morning I expect to see Alison at breakfast, and yet it seems decades since she died. So many deaths since then that sometimes I feel guilty for mourning one so much, but the men have mourners too. It is hard to remember that they have homes as well, as so few families are given permission to visit.

Sometimes I dream that I'm going to open my eyes and I'll be at Thuringa, and the lyrebird will be singing out the window, imitating the sheepdogs. Do you remember when I was small and tried to find the dog up in a tree, but it was a lyrebird?

I could almost have booked my passage home but I can't abandon Her Grace now, nor Alison's baby. She is the dearest little thing, sitting up already and eating mashed carrots, the same colour as her hair — at least by the time she has finished with them. Since the Germans sank the Lusitania no passenger ship is safe anyway, even if it has a neutral flag. Truly, I am better to stay here.

I was sorry to hear the horses have gone from Thuringa. It is hard to think of Moonbeam Joe without his charges, but I realise the Australian army must need mounts. All of the riding and most

of the carriage and farm horses have been taken here, but somehow
I never thought of Australian ones going to war too.

We have different burns cases here now. A nurse came down
from London to show us how to care for them. They are from the
chlorine gas the Germans are using at Ypres. It floats in a green
cloud, the men say, then attacks their eyes and lungs when they
breathe it in. At first men ran when they saw the cloud coming
but now the orders are to stay in place, as more of it is breathed in
when you run, and to stand up on the parapet and not lie down
in the trench, as the gas sinks to the ground. The men soak their
handkerchiefs in water and put them over their mouths and noses,
but gas pads are more effective, as they hold more water, which
stops the gas. They are just rolled linen with straps on each end so
they can be tied around the head. They are easy to make. I usually
make two or three while I have my cup of tea after dinner — and
am very glad not to have to knit instead.

Your loving,
Sophie

The war, which had seemed to eat time in the first months of
transforming Wooten into a hospital, now stretched it so every
minute was a struggle to complete, weariness competing with
boredom.

Horror could be boring. A corporal, dying of gangrene, had
told Sophie that the boredom was the worst illness of the trenches,
how at the end even a severed hand could not elicit shock.

The work she did now was necessary. It also confined body
and mind. At night she dreamed she was the eagle at Thuringa,
playing with the wind. Free.

The patients changed; lived, died, recovered. Supplies arrived,
were delayed, had to be pleaded for. But real change happened
only in the world beyond Wooten.

The papers they got at Wooten were a day late now, with
fewer trains running.

The war had yet another battlefront now: Gallipoli. It had
been strange to see the Australians' fighting so prominently

mentioned, after more than a year when the word *Australia* was only in the shipping news and sometimes the cricket. The whole world was ringing with the Australians' heroism, it seemed. Australian soldiers had a new name now: Anzacs, sharing it with the New Zealanders, who were at Gallipoli too.

Gallipoli was in Turkey, an ally of Germany, so Sophie supposed they were trying to capture Constantinople — wasn't that what Miss Lily had said it would be good for the first time she had read about the place?

Meanwhile she visited baby Sophie and Doris in the nursery, where sunlight and the smell of baby hair almost banished Wooten's scent of disinfectant. In these few moments of poignant joy each day, holding Mouse's baby, Sophie wondered if the war would eat her entire life. By the time it left her free she might be old. Perhaps she was already old, in spirit if not in body.

The dressings were an endless job now that even she had to make time for: the burns from the chlorine gas festered, requiring constant cleaning and fresh coverings. Often the dressings had to be soaked off, which meant returning, hours later, more prodding, poking and tearing of newly granulated skin.

She had just finished the last of her wards that day when Blaise appeared, grey-haired, grey-faced. 'Miss Higgs? Telephone for you: Mr Slithersole.'

For a moment she panicked, imagining bad news from Australia — her father with a heart attack, or news of Malcolm ... But no, Miss Thwaites would have sent a wire to the dowager duchess if there had been any hard news to break, not delivered it via Mr Slithersole.

'Miss Higgs speaking.'

'Miss Higgs, I have some good news. Higgs's Corned Beef has been able to do, shall we say, a *favour* for the Medical Corps.' Which meant cheaper corned beef, she supposed, or supplies of the new line of dried beef tea: just add hot water for a nourishing beverage in the trenches — assuming hot water, or even clean water, could be found.

'That's wonderful, Mr Slithersole. Er, what is the good news?'

'VADs, Miss Higgs!' She could almost see his smile. 'Twenty of them will be down at Wooten on the eight-ten train tomorrow.'

'Twenty! Mr Slithersole, that's not just good, it's miraculous! Twenty!'

No more dressings, she thought. Trained hands to pull off the bloody linen, not hers ...

Where should she put these new VADs? Four in her old room. Four in Alison's? No, she couldn't ask the dowager for that. Move the officers from the far end of the east wing and make that a sort of VAD headquarters, with the red room as a sitting room — they could make toast and cocoa at the fireplace ...

I shouldn't feel so glad, she thought. But for the first time since Alison's death she felt a smile — a real smile, not a 'duty' smile — spread across her face. 'Mr Slithersole, you are an angel and a joy to the heart. Please tell Mrs Slithersole I told you so. She is well? And Albert?'

'Both in the pink, thank you, Miss Higgs. I reckon my boy is as safe as anywhere in the Catering Corps.'

'I'll warrant he does sterling service there too, Mr Slithersole. An army marches on its stomach.'

'A remarkable observation, Miss Higgs.'

Except Napoleon observed it first, she thought, and Miss Thwaites observed it to me. She ended the call with more profuse thanks and good wishes, then went to tell the dowager duchess the news.

It was warm in Her Grace and Nanny's sitting room. Gloriously warm, the wood fire glowing in the hearth. Nanny Hawkins sat in her chintz-covered chair, knitting. It had been years since she had been able to conduct a conversation, but she could still spoon her food for herself, still knitted sock after sock, still smiled when any young person came in. The room was furnished now with the grander furniture from upstairs, but still small enough to heat through and through so even your bones felt warm.

'Good afternoon, Nanny.'

A smile. The old woman held up the sock, and then her cheek to be kissed. Her eyes went down to her knitting again. Sophie wondered who Nanny mistook her for — which of the many children Nanny had loved and cared for. She let her body fall into a chair, the twin of Nanny's.

'Sophie?'

'Your Grace? I have the most wonderful news.' Sophie stood up again as the dowager shuffled in from her bedroom, leaning on her stick. She looked a decade older than she had last year, her body bent by grief as much as the arthritis. But she greeted every new arrival, farewelled every man who left, attended the funerals of strangers who now lay in the family plot in the churchyard. 'Twenty VADs arrive tomorrow!'

Suddenly she realised she should have asked the old lady's permission. This was still her house, or at least her nephew's. She of all people was due the courtesy, even if the VADs were officially a gift of the War Office, not Sophie Higgs.

But the dowager simply smiled. 'So you can rest a little at last, my dear. Can you spare the time to sit with me now?'

Guilt struck her. It had never occurred to her that, despite the invasion of so many, the dowager might be lonely. 'I'm so sorry. I thought you and Nanny might want to be alone.'

The duchess picked up her knitting: another balaclava. 'Why does one need to be alone at my age? One will have plenty of that soon enough. Or reunion with all whom I have loved and lost, perhaps, but you will not be among them for a long time.' The leathered eyes crinkled. 'So I treasure our conversation now. And Nanny likes company too, don't you, Nanny?' Nanny beamed vaguely at the sound of her name. 'Sit down again, my dear.'

Sophie waited till the old lady had made herself comfortable first, then sat as well, leaning back into the softness of the chair. She closed her eyes; opened them perhaps ten minutes later to find the duchess watching her.

'You're exhausted. It must be hard for you, away from your family.'

As you have lost most of yours, she thought. 'I miss them. I miss Australia too. Well, my small corner of it.'

'Do James Lorrimer and that young Australian still write to you?' Now Sophie was officially 'out', Her Grace no longer felt it her duty to read Sophie's correspondence. In this new world of war, such things hardly mattered.

'Yes. James is back in the United States. I never know if I will get one letter from him, or three at once. Malcolm just had a week's leave in Paris. But my heart doesn't go all a-flutter when I get their letters.'

'All a-flutter?'

'That's what Cook says Elsie feels when her young man writes to her. Her heart goes all of a flutter.'

'Elsie?'

'One of the kitchen maids.'

'I think you know my staff better than I do.'

'Maybe I just like kitchens, like my father.' She tried to smile. 'It's in the blood.'

'Not yours alone, my dear. I spent a good part of my youth in the kitchen. I don't know if Alison told you my father was a vicar?'

'Yes, Your Grace.' It hurt to hear Alison's name. It helped too.

'We had a maid-of-all-work, of course — Mattie, a darling woman. I don't think I ever saw her hands at rest. Even when she sat down she'd be stirring, or darning a sock.' The old woman smiled again. 'Maybe that is why at the end of my life I find I am happy in somewhat more intimate circumstances than alone in the rooms upstairs.'

'You're not at the end of your life at all, Your Grace.'

The wrinkled eyes were shrewd. 'I have another decade left, perhaps. Which may seem a long time to you, but is all too short to me. It is good to have my own hands occupied with real work again. I never did enjoy petit point or embroidery, and as for tapestry ... This house is full of the handiwork of ten generations of bored women, and a nice job it is protecting it from the mice and moths too. The Abbey doesn't need my contributions.'

'I wish my knitting were as good as yours.'

'I had three younger brothers. There were many socks to knit when I was young.'

'What are they doing now, Your Grace?'

She expected to hear that they were vicars too, or in some form of public service. But the neat grey head bent down to the sock growing between her fingers. 'Thomas and Henry died of the diphtheria when I was ten years old, Clarence of typhoid a little later. It was typhoid that took my parents too. Bad drains, my dear — the privy was only two yards from the well, but one never thought of those things back then.'

How much loss had this woman borne? 'I'm so sorry. I can't imagine how terrible that must have been. Where did you go when your parents died?'

'I was in my forties, far beyond an age when I might hope for marriage. I became a governess — more a nursery maid, really. Quite nice children, four and six. I was lucky, though I didn't think it then. But that was how I met Lily, of course.'

'Miss Lily?' Sophie had grown so used to not saying the name. But of course there was no one now except Nanny to hear.

The duchess laughed. 'She does make such a fuss, insisting we don't talk about her. Sensible, but quite unnecessary between ourselves. She and I write to each other, of course. She asks after you in all her letters. I had one from her last week.'

Sophie tried to quell the jealousy. 'Of course, you are old friends.'

'Old, old friends.'

'How did you meet?'

The duchess laughed. She seemed to be enjoying herself. 'Oh, it was scandalous. Wonderfully, terribly scandalous. We met on the ferry from Brindisi to Greece. The family I worked for were prostrate with seasickness down below. I had come up to empty the chamber pot; the stewardess was rushed off her feet. And Lily was in the lounge, so glamorous. Make-up, of course, so shocking, except you would never have guessed it, and every gesture so graceful. Every man on the ship watched her. She saw me looking at her too, and beckoned me over, chamber pot and all — thank goodness it was at least empty by then — and we began to talk.'

'Go on.' Sophie felt breathless.

'By the time the ferry docked she had invited me to Shillings. Lily took on the challenge of making me beautiful. I was a carthorse then, just as I am the size of a battleship now, and middle-aged to boot. But Lily insisted. She had known an elderly Japanese woman, bent and grey-haired, who still held the attention of every man when she walked into a room. Lily said beauty was as much grace and belief as body. We had nothing in common, Lily and I, and at the same time everything, including a desire to free women from what are often intolerable situations, although, of course, they must continue to be tolerated.'

'You were the first of the "lovely ladies"?'

Her Grace laughed. 'Scarcely lovely, and much older than Lily. His lordship held a house party for me, a year after I came to Shillings, and that was where I met and attracted the man who would be my husband.' She smiled at the memory. 'Not, I think, because I had acquired much of Lily's ability to charm, but because Horace needed someone to take charge of his life. He was a widower, with a young son. Who more appropriate to acquire as stepmother than an ex-governess? I met a young woman that year whom I thought Lily might enjoy transforming, though she needed far less than I had. And she met others, and so the tradition began.' Her gaze was far away. 'It was a happy marriage, till Arthur — that was my stepson, Alison's father — died. But I was lucky. Darling Arthur was not. He married against my advice. But a stepmother is perhaps the worst person to advise her stepson on love.'

'Alison told me her parents weren't ... happy.'

The duchess nodded. 'A tragedy. Many tragedies, and then their deaths. It shouldn't be more tragic when a son dies than a daughter, but of course it is, when it means the succession moves from the direct line. You never recover from the loss of a child, or grandchild. You pretend to, of course, but the pain is always there. I loved him as my own, right from the first, as Horace had known I would, and Lily. Alison was such a comfort ...' She gazed into the fire, then back at Sophie. 'I should have done a better job of caring for her. And for you.'

'You gave Alison happiness. And you've been a fairy godmother to me.'

'Fairy godmothers do not get arthritis. I believe,' she added, 'that you need a change.'

'What kind of change, Your Grace?'

'Sea air. A friend of mine wishes to turn her house into a convalescent home, much as we have here. She is rather at a loss just now. Her husband and both sons were killed at the Somme with Allenby last year, so she is alone and her life empty. I think you would be good for her. She can wait awhile, though, for you to organise the new gels here into the correct routines.'

The dowager raised an eyebrow, startlingly like Miss Lily for a second despite the horse face and the wrinkled jowls. 'I think the challenge will be good for you. Other gels would enjoy promenading on the sea walk, but you, I suspect, will do better getting something done.'

'My lack of breeding, Your Grace?' Sophie said lightly.

'Shall we say your *extremely good* breeding, Miss Higgs. Racehorses are bred to race, and do it well. Some women are bred to do their duty, and you and I are two of them. Sometimes I think that if one's duty evaporated there would be nothing left. I ... I do not think I could have survived Alison's death if it were not for my duty here. Duty dulls the pain, Miss Higgs, even when you tire of it. It even at times leaves a little happiness in its wake. But you,' the old woman shook her head, 'you, my dear, have been bred to manage empires, not tend the sick. Why don't men like your father see that their daughters can inherit their genius, as much as their sons?' She stood, her hands trembling on her stick. 'If you would be so kind as to see me back to bed? I hesitate to ring — the staff are so busy these days.'

'Of course, Your Grace.' The dowager seemed too light for her large frame.

'Good night, Nanny,' said Her Grace.

Nanny nodded and gazed peacefully at the fire.

Chapter 48

You think you have achieved exactly what you need in life,
and then life catches you and throws you elsewhere. Duty, of course,
is the greatest snare of all.

Miss Lily, 1916

APRIL 1916

Sophie had expected an ancient stone mansion, mellowed by
sea winds. Instead she found red brick, as though a bungalow
had blown up to fifty times its normal size and a crazed cook
had added turrets and crenellations like icing on a cake. Only
the view was beautiful: white-tipped waves and white cliffs,
sparkling in the spring air.

In a few months the war would be two years old. Only two
years, though it felt like two centuries.

A maid answered the door, showing her into a room with
bright green-papered walls, covered with paintings of wet
animals: a wet deer under sodden trees, a basket of sodden
kittens, a sodden dog retrieving a duck from a lake with a hunter
in a rainproof cloak. Sophie was wondering at the desire to have
extra moisture depicted on the walls, given the English climate,
when a black-clad woman who must be her hostess hurried
down the stairs.

'Miss Higgs? Hideous paintings, aren't they? But my husband
was stationed in the Kalahari for ten years — I met him in
Africa; my parents were missionaries — and he said it gave him
a longing for good English damp, though the drains here, thank

goodness, are excellent. Tea, Mavis, in the morning room. I hope you will forgive the morning room, Miss Higgs. I haven't been able to face the drawing room or dining room since ... since it happened. It is one of the reasons I wish to change the house completely. My men's place is in my heart, Miss Higgs, not as ghosts on their chairs. But the morning room was really my room.' She opened the door. 'Please do sit down.'

'I'm sorry, Mrs Fitzhubert, I don't understand.'

'I shall take a flat, and Mavis, and the paintings, and my memories, and know that I am doing my bit as they would want me to ...' The flow of words stopped, like a rock had dammed a creek. The silence grew.

What would a ghost woman need? Sophie thought. Miss Lily's step two: boost Mrs Fitzhubert's confidence with something she could agree with, a question that would bring her at least partly back to this sitting room, away from the long-imagined gunfire of the Somme.

'Do you know how many beds you have, Mrs Fitzhubert?'

Mrs Fitzhubert looked bewildered. 'Yes, of course, Miss Higgs. Eighteen in the house, if you count the servants' quarters.'

'How many do you think the house can accommodate?'

Mrs Fitzhubert's voice was already stronger. 'I thought about seventy, if the men don't mind sharing their rooms.'

'They are used to it. I do so admire you, Mrs Fitzhubert. You have obviously given this so much thought. Not one woman in ten thousand would have the courage to do what you are doing, after you have lost so much.'

The too-white face flushed slightly pink. Mavis entered with the tea.

'Tea, lovely, I'm parched. And teacake — I haven't seen that in an age. You have a treasure in Mavis, Mrs Fitzhubert.'

'She has been with me since my marriage, Miss Higgs. I ... I'm not sure what I would have done without Mavis.'

And this is the first time you've told her that, thought Sophie.

Tears stood in Mavis's eyes. 'It's been my pleasure, ma'am. I know how hard it's been for you.'

Some of the house's depth of silence — which had not been broken by her hostess's rushes of words — lightened.

Sophie smiled. 'Shall we have tea and begin? And Mrs Fitzhubert, would you mind if Mavis joined us? I am sure she will have valuable insights.'

It took three weeks to arrange what would have taken a year, perhaps, before the war and Sophie's newfound confidence in organising and giving the kind of orders that had been the prerogative of men, and without the assistance of Mr Slithersole. Sophie suspected Mr Slithersole now had a small office dedicated to the instructions of his employer's daughter. She also suspected that he had long since stopped checking her requests with her father — that both men were according her a respect now that perhaps neither was even aware of, but which was real, nonetheless.

Mrs Fitzhubert was installed in a serviced apartment in a red-brick, centrally heated building overlooking the bay. Mavis would be her personal maid and companion, and they would fill their days with bandage-rolling and Comforts for Soldiers committees in this strange new society where maid and mistress could sit and knit side by side as long as it was for The Cause.

Sophie's job was done. Her Grace had been correct. She had enjoyed it deeply, had liked helping Mrs Fitzhubert arrange her new life too.

'We must celebrate,' said Mrs Fitzhubert, the night before the first convalescents were due to arrive.

'Champagne?'

'I thought we might go to an enlistment rally at the pier tonight.' Mrs Fitzhubert made it sound like a night at the music hall, with a lobster and caviar supper thrown in. But at least she was back from the imagined mud and anguish of the Somme now. 'The speaker will be Captain Angus McIntyre. You must have heard of him, Miss Higgs? He won the Victoria Cross at Ypres. When they took the hill he crawled out under heavy fire to bring back his lieutenant, and then returned twice to get more of his men.'

Insane, brave or innocent? thought Sophie, thinking of Malcolm. His letters still spoke of *giving the Hun what-for* …

'What fun,' she said, wondering if she could slip off and walk along the cliffs instead. But Mrs Fitzhubert might stay at home without the excuse of 'May I introduce dear Miss Higgs from Australia?'

The dusk was faintly orange from the smoke across the Channel, and the crowd was thick when they arrived. The amusement arcade was closed for the war, the painted walls of clowns' faces already battered by windblown sand. But tonight the gaslights were lit against the growing shadows; bunting hung from every possible surface, with posters plastered over what had once been a dance room — *Your country needs You!*

'Mrs Colonel Sevenoaks organises everything so perfectly,' said Mrs Fitzhubert, just as Sophie said, 'Emily!'

Emily approached, two older men and one young man trailing behind her. She wore dark green, a feather in her hat.

The young man was another feather. He looked insubstantial, as though his body were there but his reality elsewhere, his good manners tethering him to them as he answered Emily's remarks obediently and politely. His eyes were shadowed in the way Sophie had seen in patients with blood loss. He had a mostly healed scar on his forehead that she suspected went deep into his hairline. He walked with hesitation, as though he had recently stopped limping. Youngish, thirty perhaps, sun-browned skin, a touch of blond in the brown hair.

How had Emily acquired him? Charmed him like Mr Porton?

'Miss Higgs, how lovely to see you,' said Emily.

Ah, thought Sophie. I am 'Miss Higgs' now.

'Captain McIntyre, may I present Miss Sophie Higgs, from Australia.'

'The place with the kangaroos,' said Sophie, and was glad to see a flicker of amusement light up Captain McIntyre's tired eyes for a brief second. 'Mrs Fitzhubert, I believe you know Mrs Colonel Sevenoaks? She and I were presented in the season before the war.'

And I married at the end of it, and you did not, said Emily's smug smile. I have a war hero at my side and a husband waiting for me on the podium, while you are a spinster, with a father in trade.

'We must go,' said Emily, ushering Captain McIntyre towards the stage. 'Do stay for tea afterwards, Mrs Fitzhubert, Miss Higgs. I believe there will be buns.'

'Buns. Delightful,' said Sophie.

They sat. Colonel Sevenoaks gave the introduction. He spoke well, his voice reaching even to the end of the pier, and clearly enjoyed it. Definitely a political candidate if the war ever ends, thought Sophie. If he hadn't considered it before, she was sure he had now. And his wife was evidently charming his way to future power.

'And I say this to every boy and man here today, to every mother of every son, to every wife and sweetheart. Our boys are dying for each and every one of us over there, and without more men to back them up they will continue to die. If there is a man here with iron in his backbone, if there is a woman here with the courage to tell her men to do their duty by their nation, then England's green and pleasant land can never be conquered. Not while Englishmen live and breathe and serve her!'

He waited while Emily began the applause. A well-dressed man in the bowler hat of a butler in mufti — clearly a plant — yelled 'Hear hear!', promoting more cheers from the audience.

The colonel beamed. 'And now I have the honour of presenting one of England's finest, the hero of Ypres, winner of no less than the Victoria Cross. I had the privilege of being there when His Majesty himself pinned the medal to this great man.'

Though I bet you weren't there to receive a medal, thought Sophie. Colonel Sevenoaks had the easy look of a man who had never faced an enemy, except perhaps those armed with spears in North Africa two decades before. Despite his rank, he had clearly not elected to join a regiment overseas.

'Let me tell you what His Majesty said. "Give me ten Englishmen like Captain McIntyre and the war will be over by Christmas."'

Which Christmas? thought Sophie as the colonel at last sat down.

The cheering didn't have to be prompted this time.

Captain McInytre faced the audience. He looked so tired; it was a curiously dead look. Sophie had seen it too often at Wooten — men who had given up, who would die of wounds where another man might live.

The silence grew. Emily made a restive gesture towards her husband on the platform.

And then the young man spoke. 'Actually, I'm a Scot.'

The crowd's laughter was as much relief as amusement. Someone yelled, 'Show us yer kilt, then!', but it was good-humoured.

'I'm afraid it got a bit muddy at Ypres.' He pronounced it correctly, not 'Wipers', as most of the troops had renamed the Flemish hill. Nor did he have a Scottish accent. English boarding school, thought Sophie.

'Had to leave my kilt behind. But I did bring what I am going to tell you home with me.' He shut his eyes for a second. He is going to tell the truth, thought Sophie, not say what Emily wants him to. 'I left good men behind me too. Men who need help, if we are to win this war. I'll tell you who the real heroes of this war are. The men who are there, because, by heaven, it is so very easy not to be there.' The words seemed to have stopped. He looked almost confused for a moment, nodded abruptly and said, 'Thank you', then sat down.

Emily stood, smiling as though she had expected this ten-second speech, instead of a ten-minute one, charming the entire audience, as Miss Lily had taught them to charm a dinner table, meeting the eyes of every person on the pier briefly, intimately. 'Thank you, Captain McIntyre, for that wonderful lesson in why every man and boy here is needed at the front, why every single woman here tonight must urge the men of her family, her neighbours, even on the street if she must, to support our heroes overseas. And now tea will be served by the St Anne's Ladies' Guild and War Widows' Society, new members always welcome. And if there is any man here who has heard the call of his country ...' Emily's eyes swept the audience '... Sergeant Harrow here will take his details and give him his shilling, and Captain McIntyre will shake his hand.'

'Three cheers for the captain!' It was the butler in disguise again. But once more the cheers were real. The young man sat awkwardly, then followed Emily obediently down onto the pier, like a dog, thought Sophie, not a lover. This man was in the shadow world, neither back in the trenches nor quite here.

Back on the stage, a choir, not quite in tune, broke into 'Land of Hope and Glory', their singing almost overwhelmed by the clink of teacups.

Sophie fetched Mrs Fitzhubert a cup of tea and left her with the St Anne's Ladies' Guild, to offer her services, find yet another place of fellowship for the days and years to come. Sophie took her own tea to the edge of the group around Emily, her husband, the local vicar, and the captain.

Suddenly the captain put down his tea. He muttered a brief excuse and made his way through the crowd, stopping only to shake the hands of men who pressed theirs into his.

Sophie waited till he had reached the edge of the pier, then strolled after him. Steps one and two — from compassion, not because she wanted anything from this shadowed man. Smile then make him say 'Yes'. 'Captain McIntyre? If you are looking for the facilities, they have been closed for the duration.'

'Er, yes, that's what I was looking for.' He smiled back at her automatically, seized on the excuse with edgy eagerness. 'Miss ... Higgs, isn't it?'

'You are good with names, Captain McIntyre.' And you really need to get away from that crowd.

'Thank you, Miss Higgs.' He was still answering on automatic.

All at once she could almost feel his desperation. 'I suspect that men who, ahem, need a washroom use that dark area behind the ice-cream parlour. No one can see what goes over the rail there.'

He looked at her then.

'It's dark and quiet, Captain McIntyre.'

361

'Thank you.' He slipped into the narrow space between the parlour walls and the railings. Sophie stood, guarding the passageway, her skirt and hat blocking what little light might shine there.

An aproned servant, or volunteer — these days it was hard to tell — took her teacup. A seagull shrieked above her, awakened by the pier lights, hoping for scraps. She couldn't remember the Sydney seagulls' cry, just that it was different from this one.

Mrs Fitzhubert made her way through the crowd. 'There you are, Miss Higgs. I hope you don't mind, but Mrs Arnold has asked us back to supper. Her late husband was in the same regiment ...'

Sophie smiled. 'You go, Mrs Fitzhubert. I imagine Colonel Sevenoaks and his wife will escort me back.'

'If you're sure, my dear.' There was more colour in her cheeks now. There'd be tears tonight, but shared tears. A future, and friends finding a future beyond their own loss too.

The crowd thinned. If he didn't come back soon, she'd have to go and find him before Emily came hunting — and humiliate him if he really was relieving himself. Then she heard the footsteps behind her.

He looked embarrassed. She was glad. The short time of quiet had at least brought him back to himself enough to feel embarrassment.

Now to get him out of here. She was sufficiently aware of her own emotions to know that she was not doing this just from empathy for a young man who had done his duty and much more; nor was it from the slight — very, very slight, she told herself — wish to discommode Emily. It was the way he looked into the distance, as well as at what was nearby, the half-instinctive gaze of a countryman, who looked at the whole world, not the small human slice in front of him.

Malcolm looked at the world like that. So did Moonbeam Joe. And strangely, Dolphie, who perhaps truly loved his land, which was both the same as and different from loving his country. I look at the earth and sky like that too, but James does not, she thought as Captain McIntyre glanced longingly at the darkness beyond the pier, then back at the group of top hats and feathers and regimental caps around Emily.

'Would you think me terribly rude, Captain, if I asked you to walk up to the cliffs with me? Just for a few minutes — the crowd makes it so stuffy, even on a pier.'

'Of course Miss Higgs.' The words were automatic.

She took his arm, led him — as she had led thousands of war-scarred men now, letting them feel they were leading her — beyond the pier and onto the seawall.

The lights behind them faded. The path glowed white in the moonlight, and the noise of the crowd eroded into indistinctness. They turned the corner and even that was gone. The waves swished below them, and there was the faint crunch of their shoes on gravel, but that was all.

'My nanny once said you could hear stars sing on a night like this,' he said at last. The night and waves had worked faster than she'd expected. This was the true man speaking, not the polite puppet.

'Your nanny was a wise woman.'

'Sometimes. She had a bit too much faith in prunes and custard.'

'Ah, I've had too much experience with prunes and custard myself. Thank you for this, Captain McIntyre. I've longed to walk these cliffs by night for the past three weeks. You wanted to escape too, didn't you?'

'I couldn't breathe,' he said.

'I know. I'm sorry if I'm embarrassing you. My manners are entirely too forward.'

But he wasn't hoping for kisses in the darkness. Whatever he had done at Ypres, he had shown as much courage, or more, here tonight.

'What did *you* want to escape?' She could hear the effort it took to make polite conversation.

'A feeling of emptiness at having finished helping Mrs Fitzhubert set up her home as a convalescent hospital.'

'You're a nurse?'

'Nothing so well trained. But it seems I have a bit of a talent for organising. I was spending the season under the wing of Her Grace, the Dowager Duchess of Wooten —' Too painful to mention Alison. 'Her Grace has let us use Wooten Abbey as a hospital since the war began.'

'You're related to the family?'

'No. Not grand at all. My father owns corned-beef factories and a property called Thuringa back in Australia. He served long ago with the Earl of Shillings, and the earl's cousin is an old friend of Her Grace. I'm nobody important.' She smiled at him, trying a compliment. 'Yet now I'm walking with a hero.'

'I'm no hero.' His voice was curt.

She glanced at his medal, its edge gleaming in the starlight. How could he wear that and deny his heroism? 'You risked your life. All of you over there risk your lives.'

'I'm not sure we do. No, I haven't lost my marbles, Miss Higgs. For most of us death wasn't real when we enlisted. How many men do you think would ever go to war if they knew they would likely die? Lives are sacrificed, but others have made decisions about that sacrifice, have deliberately moved the pawns into harm's way. And men like me give orders on their behalf.'

She had a sudden image of James, moving pawns on a chessboard in his office, across the Atlantic Ocean. She found Captain McIntyre still staring at her. 'I'm sorry, Captain McIntyre. I shouldn't presume to think I have any idea of what's happening over there. My father bears the scars of war, but I don't know what war was like for him.'

His brown eyes were suddenly far away again. 'He obviously thinks it better that you be spared it. He's right.'

'No. Women may not fight wars but we're part of them.' She had never put this into words before; never even known she felt it. There was something in this young man's gaze that took the world to pieces and put it back in its right shape again. 'You shouldn't keep wars secret. Do you think all those young men who cheered when this war began would have celebrated if they had known the truth? If their mothers had told them, "Your papa went to war and this is what happened to him, to us"?'

His gaze was steady. 'You are the most unusual woman I have ever met.'

'This is an unusual situation.'

'War?'

'War is common, at least according to my governess, who tried to teach me some of the dates. I meant walking in the dark with a man. At least war has removed our chaperones.'

He laughed. It was a good laugh. I'm bringing him back, thought Sophie. She wished she could fly, could carry him back to Thuringa, to the old, twisted red gums along the river.

'How long have they been parading you about?'

'Six weeks, since I got out of hospital ... or sixty years, which is what it feels like.

'Hospital?'

'Shrapnel. Nothing serious.'

Serious enough to keep you hospitalised for months, she thought.

'Captain McIntyre, will you forgive my being blunt? You are on convalescent leave? This ... parading ... isn't part of your duties?'

'I'm on convalescent leave. But it's for a good cause.' He spoke mechanically.

'Then vanish. Forget about The Cause for a week, at least.'

He looked at her with sudden hope. 'I can't.'

'You can. You can scribble your regrets to Mrs Colonel Sevenoaks. Tell them it's a family emergency. Which is quite true. You are part of your family and you need a break. Trust me,' Sophie added, 'I've been nursing men back from the front for over a year. You need quiet now. That's what leave is supposed to be for, not shaking hands at rallies. Walking on the cliffs, eating fish and chips, if there are any to be found.'

'It sounds like paradise!' She caught the flash of a smile in the darkness.

'Why not go home?'

He shook his head. 'It would be more of the same. My father's the agent for Lord Arthur Rothmere, up on the borders. Lady Arthur wrote that she expected me to do my duty to help with the recruiting up there. I pleaded Mrs Colonel Sevenoaks's previous invitation as a way out.'

'From the frying pan into the fire. You must miss home dreadfully.'

He looked out over the waves. 'Yes, though ... I know it sounds strange, but even without Lady Arthur's plans I don't want to be there now. My parents stayed nearby while I was in hospital; my father could only get a few days away but my mother was there the whole time. It was good to be with her. But home ...'

'It hasn't a hold on you?'

'That's the trouble: it has too much. We Scots call it our calf country — the land you were raised on. I love every hill and loch of it. But I have only another ten days' leave, then I'll be posted back to the front. I need to spend the next ten days becoming the Scots captain again, not the Angus McIntyre of home.'

Her heart wept, just a little, for this man who could not bear to see the hills he loved. 'You need to find another place where you can be at peace, then.'

'You don't know Mrs Colonel Sevenoaks. If I'm within fifty miles of here, she'll find me. I'm surprised she hasn't sent out spotter planes already.'

'I do know Mrs Sevenoaks.' And wouldn't you be startled if I told you how well. She watched him watch the waves, an outrageous idea somehow becoming not just possible, but even good.

'I think I can find you a place to stay. Come back with me to Wooten Abbey.'

There — she'd said it. It was the worst of manners to ask a guest to stay when you were a guest yourself, impossibly forward to ask a young man, especially one your hostess had never met.

But the dowager had said that she was family. And there was no way she could leave this man to be paraded about till he left again for France.

'I won't ask you to stay at the Abbey itself.' Too much like the hospital he'd left, she thought. 'But there's a groom's cottage that's empty, if you don't mind two rooms and an outhouse. Her Grace keeps it in readiness in case any of the men from the estate come back on leave, but I'm pretty sure none are expected. I'll have your meals sent down ... It's not the land you're longing for at all, Captain McIntyre. It's flat mostly, all in wheat and barley; even much of the park has been dug up for potatoes. But if you'd like it ...?'

He stared. 'Are you sure?'

Of course not, she thought. If Her Grace doesn't forgive this, I have no refuge in England. 'Yes.'

Again he looked across the sea. 'You can hear the guns from here, on a still night. Can you hear them now?'

She couldn't. 'Don't go back to the pier. I'll write a note explaining that you've been called away, and get Mrs Fitzhubert's kitchen maid to take it to Mrs Sevenoaks. There's a train to Wooten at ten past eleven. It'll be late when we get in, but I'll use the stationmaster's telephone to call Wooten so someone meets us. Don't bother with your luggage,' she added. 'I'll arrange with Mrs Fitzhubert to get it sent to you. I just need to leave her a note in case she worries if I'm not there tonight. I'll tell her it's an emergency back at Wooten.'

'You remind me of a sergeant major,' he said slowly.

She gave him her best Miss Lily smile. 'Most people wouldn't realise that was a compliment.'

'Oh, it is.'

'Then we'll meet in the waiting room,' said Sophie, starting back towards the house.

The wind blew cold on her sweating palms. Please, she thought, please let what I'm doing be right. Let him be the man I think he is. Let Wooten be a refuge, not remind him of the hospital he's left.

She glanced back, but he was looking at the stars again.

Chapter 49

Love at first sight exists. 'First sight' isn't just about beauty, or the lack of it. The quirk of a smile, the lines about the eyes, even the way a uniform is worn — you absorb so much about a person without realising it. Love at first sight may not last, but it exists.

Miss Sophie Higgs, 1918

As soon as she left the house, she began to doubt he'd be at the station. The suggestion must surely have seemed outrageous to him, as soon as he properly considered it. But there he stood in the corner of the waiting room, leaving the seats for the convalescents wearier than himself. The room was a fug of cigarette smoke. He gave a quirk of smile as soon as he saw her, as though he had been wondering if any of this was real.

'Sorry about the crowd,' he said.

'Shall we wait outside?' Her words tripped over his. Again she had to put her hand on his arm before he moved towards the door. He was a captain; you didn't rise to be a captain, even in the Territorials, even in a war, without the ability to act decisively. Yet he had let both her and Emily move him more or less at will. Frighteningly, she felt she might tell him to stand on the train line and he'd obey.

There were fewer soldiers outside, and they were mostly with wives, sisters, mothers, sweethearts. She and the captain walked to the end of the platform, where there was a vacant seat. She sat, then gestured to him to take the seat next to her.

They sat in silence for a while. The wind was cold along the train track. She was warm in her fur coat and wished she could offer him her muff; he had no gloves and couldn't even put his hands in his coat pockets while he was in uniform, or in the presence of a lady. But a muff would push forwardness into eccentricity.

'Miss Higgs, why are you doing this?'

If she'd been him she would have asked the same question — would have guessed her impulse wasn't solely forged by compassion. She tried to give him an honest answer, even if she wasn't sure what the answer was herself. 'Maybe because my job here has been done. I need to go back and ... I've been dreading it. Haven't even admitted to myself how much. You'll be a ... diversion. A treat.'

'Like a box of chocolates?'

'If I can accept a comparison to a sergeant major as a compliment, you can accept being a box of chocolates.'

'A diversion from what?' he asked softly. 'The work? I've watched nurses manage on three hours' sleep, week in, week out. At least we get leave, or time out behind the lines.'

'Not the work. I've been replaced by twenty VADs.'

His face truly relaxed for the first time as he laughed. 'Twenty VADs to replace you!'

She flushed. 'I didn't mean it that way.'

'But I suspect it's true. Go on. What do you dread, then?'

'I don't know.'

'What are your nightmares?' He asked the question as if it was the most normal question in the world. But this was a world of nightmares now.

She glanced at the stillness of his face. 'About people who have left me.'

'Which people?' He might have been soothing a restless horse.

She said nothing.

'Tell me.'

'My mother. A woman who taught me, just before the war. Lost to me, like so many people in a war. Another friend is lost too.' She was telling him the truth, but not the whole truth. She wished she could be honest, but Miss Lily and a German princess could not be mentioned, even to this man. Especially, perhaps, to this man, a mentally exhausted official hero. 'My best friend, Alison, Her Grace's granddaughter — she died in childbirth last year. Her Grace ... Her Grace is dying too, though she won't admit it. My father was middle-aged when I was born, and the war must have aged him too, but I can't even get home to see him, not since the *Lusitania* was torpedoed. Everyone I love ... I'm sorry. Many women have lost far more than I.'

Sophie felt the wetness of tears on her cheeks, felt his hand grip hers through her glove, saw the white of the scar across his fingers ...

'Miss Higgs,' said Emily coldly.

Sophie looked up, trusting the poor light to hide her tears. Further up the platform, Colonel Sevenoaks waited with a small group of men and women. Emily had obviously told them to wait while she collected her errant lamb.

'Emily, how pleasant to see you again. I'm sorry not to have said goodbye properly back at the pier, but I've been called back to Wooten and Captain McIntyre has kindly offered to escort me.'

Emily smiled at Captain McIntyre. Instinctively he smiled back. Step one to Emily, thought Sophie. 'You are feeling quite well, Captain McIntyre?' she asked. 'I was concerned.'

'Yes, I'm right as rain, thank you.'

'It was so kind of you to let Miss Higgs appeal to your better nature.'

Step two, thought Sophie. And a hint that I am manipulating him, which has the advantage of being correct.

'Miss Higgs, could we speak privately?'

Sophie let herself be drawn down the platform.

Emily's smile vanished. 'How dare you?'

'Easily. He's exhausted. He needs rest, not being hung out like a recruiting banner.'

'And you need a husband.'

The attack was so crude she simply stared.

'It wasn't a successful season for you, was it? Alison and I married. Mr Lorrimer did not come up to scratch. No ring on your finger nearly two years later, despite all the eligible men you have been cosseting at Wooten. And now you have found yourself someone who is eligible *and* vulnerable, and you have sneaked him out into the night.'

The assumption was so extraordinary Sophie began to laugh, despite the remnants of tears on her cheeks. 'Emily, it didn't even occur to me he was eligible.'

'I prefer not to be on first-name terms these days, Miss Higgs. The captain's mother is the youngest daughter of Viscount Eldershire. His father is third in line to a baronetcy. No money, of course, but that is of no matter to you, is it? Your father is a war profiteer. And you, of course, know exactly how to charm a man away from his duty.'

All true, thought Sophie. His duty? Doubt chilled her. Was she causing a scandal for this man — this good man — by smuggling him away into the night? She should have encouraged him to simply go home. He'd have done what she suggested, just as he would do what Emily suggested; he'd had his will torn away with his flesh.

'Miss Higgs, I think our train is approaching.' Somehow the captain had followed them down the platform and placed her hand on his arm again. 'Thank you for your kindness, Mrs Sevenoaks, and please do give my apologies to your husband. But as Miss Higgs has said, there is an emergency back at Wooten. Her Grace is an old acquaintance of my mother's ... I'm sure you understand ...'

The train hissed to a halt behind them. The three of them were far enough down the platform to be next to the first-class carriages. The captain had the door open while Emily's mouth still hung agape, her husband suddenly hurrying down the platform.

'Again, so many thanks for all your kindness, and my utmost apologies.' Captain McIntyre shut the door as Sophie sat down next to a well-upholstered woman in blue tweed, then moved up to make room for him. She scrubbed the last of her tears away hurriedly, leaving a soot mark on her glove.

The train creaked, then began to chug. She didn't even bother to watch Emily's face disappear as they pulled away from the platform.

'Thank you, Captain McIntyre,' she managed at last.

'Perhaps you would consider calling me Angus.'

'My name is Sophie. Sophronia.'

'You don't really want to be called Sophronia?'

'No.'

'I presume there is a dowager duchess and a Wooten Abbey waiting for us?'

'Yes, of course, Captain ... Angus.'

'Pity,' he said lightly. 'I hoped you were the adventuress Mrs Sevenoaks was implying, luring me into the unknown.'

Her breath was back in her body. She liked this man. Admired not just what he must have done, to be so decorated, but also the courage it must have taken to pull his spirit back into himself and outface Emily so swiftly. He hadn't been escaping his duty when he'd manoeuvred them into the train. He'd been rescuing Sophie.

Emily would be an enemy now. She might even have the skill — and will — to make it hurt.

'I'll make it up to you, if I can,' she said lightly. 'The next ten days will be good ones.'

'I believe they will be.' His body was warm next to hers.

Chapter 50

Age might wither us, but never love.

Miss Lily, 1916

MAY 1916

'It has been more than seven years,' said the dowager duchess — her glance might even have been flirtatious — 'since I took tea alone with a man. I am speaking of my husband, of course.'

'Except I am here too this time, Your Grace,' said Sophie. She nibbled at a meringue. A miracle: meringues in wartime. She wondered if they were a gift from the kitchen for the wounded hero or for Her Grace, or even for Sophie Higgs. Perhaps all three.

'A widow like myself needs a chaperone,' said Her Grace, winking. Sophie had never imagined that the dowager even knew how to wink. 'Do try a buttered crumpet, Captain. Crumpets should always be eaten hot.' For a moment her voice was Miss Lily's; or perhaps it was a voice they had cultivated together decades earlier.

Angus took a crumpet, licked butter from his lip, then met Sophie's eyes.

He had been at Wooten for eight days. They hadn't kissed yet. Both knew it was a 'yet'.

He slept alone in the groom's cottage. Sophie suspected he slept badly: her bedroom in the pensioners' quarters looked across the courtyard and his lamp was usually still lit when she went to bed.

Her Grace had not suggested that Captain McIntyre breakfast with them, and he used the simple facilities in the cottage to extend his solitude until lunchtime.

At first Sophie had thought that he might want to spend all his time alone, but that first day, after she had checked on baby Sophie and Doris, both blooming, walked the wards and found them running smoothly and professionally under the VADs' charge, she had gone down to his cottage 'to see you have settled in, Captain McIntyre'. She had found him sitting in the cottage's one easy chair, grinning up at her.

She caught her breath. This was the real man, the one whose shadow she had seen the previous night, his eyes bright and head slightly cocked as he heard a lark out the window.

'I believe in the Abbey, and the cottage. Now, where is this duchess? I've never met a duchess,' he added.

'This one is a dowager.'

'All the better.'

The duchess greeted him in Nanny's sitting room, as she might a friend of her granddaughter. She instructed Sophie to show him the old water mill, 'where we used to grind all the wheat from the district, not just the estate', a good hour's walk away.

From that day on it had been their routine: a dutiful checking that there was no urgent work needed (she suspected Her Grace had ordered everyone to hide anything urgent from her), followed by a cup of weak tea with the dowager.

Then a walk into a world of green leaves unfurling and clouds puffing along the sky, and birds she'd heard for the nearly three years she'd been in England, though no one had ever thought to tell her their names.

Luncheon in the VADs' kitchen, where he relaxed as the women flirted with him, and Sophie sat back and let them, for he was hers, and they both knew it. He would talk to some of the men, and she liked that too; even though he had escaped the recruiting drives, duty continued, quiet, personal.

Afternoon tea with Her Grace, delicacies that none of them had bothered with for two years but some of which had miraculously appeared again — maids of honour, the cherished ginger nuts, sponge and teacake — the ingredients hoarded in the locked storeroom for when His Grace returned, but some spared now. Her Grace had dined on a tray in her room since Alison's death, but now she hobbled to the morning room, where the dinner table was set with pre-war formality.

She felt disloyalty to James Lorrimer only once, when a letter arrived from him — short, like all his letters. He was still in the United States; work was going well, but not as well as he would have liked. He was always hers. The letters were a contract of sorts.

I will write when Angus leaves, she thought. I may know what to write then. She had been counting each day and knew Angus had too, although they never mentioned it.

On day nine there were letters for him on the morning-room table: two, one on plain but good stationery; the other in a buff War Office envelope. She carried them over to his cottage.

'Come in.' He waved an egg spoon at her. 'Sorry, late start today.' He stopped as he saw the letters in her hand. 'Sit down. I'll pour you tea.'

'Thank you.' She didn't want tea, but sipping it would give her something to do while he read his letters.

He read the plain one first, smiling, then glanced up. 'It's from my mother. Would you like to read it?'

She nodded, touched, and took it. It was a simple letter: a woman trying to find enough subjects to fill a weekly page when all she really wanted was to send her love and a spell to guarantee his safety.

At the end she had written: *Please do give my very best regards to your friend Miss Higgs. I look forward to meeting her very much. Please give my thanks to Her Grace too, if you think it appropriate. My love always, dear son, Mother.* At the end of the page was scrawled: *Your loving father too. A wild cat has been at the pheasants. Putting the traps out today.*

She could see his flash of homesickness. 'Any regrets about coming here instead?'

'A few.' She liked his honesty. 'But it was the right decision.' He looked at the letter. 'I miss the river most.'

She nodded. 'I think one is either a sea person or a river person.'

'So you're a river person too? Which river?'

'The one on our place, Thuringa. Twists like a pale brown snake in the sand —' She stopped, embarrassed.

'Mine's a brown one, but clear — the peat dyes it. Trout as long as your arm too. Are there trout in yours?'

'I don't think so. There are perch in the deep holes. Our cook bakes them with butter and almonds. My father caught one that was nearly four feet long.'

'Your fish beat my fish, then. The biggest trout I ever caught was a three-pounder. I think I enlisted for that river. I know it seems mad. But the thought of enemy boots marching on that land ...' He shrugged. 'I suppose each of us has our own image of what Britain is. That's mine. And a stretch of moor.' He looked at the buff envelope both of them had been avoiding. 'Better open this one.'

He read it swiftly. He looked back at her. 'I have to report to the medical officer on Friday. I have a feeling he'll say I'm fit for duty again.'

Something cold breathed across her bones. 'Back to France?'

'But with any luck not to the front. I ... I need to be honest with you. I wasn't just with the Sevenoakses out of duty. The colonel has connections. He said he could get me a staff position over in France.'

'And I made you offend them.' What have I done? she thought.

'The staff job is mine anyway. It's confirmed now.'

'Thank goodness. It'll mean less danger.' She hadn't realised she'd said the words aloud.

He looked her straight in the face. 'You deserve the truth. I'm a coward, Sophie. I hear the sound of the guns in my sleep, even when I'm not asleep sometimes.' He tried to smile. 'Don't think I'll ever watch fireworks again. I ... I didn't know if I could face going back. The staff job, well, it's a nothing job. I should be ashamed to take it.' He shrugged. 'I *am* ashamed.'

'That's not cowardice. It's sense.'

'Except I accept the need to fight. Don't you?'

She spoke slowly, trying to articulate what she felt but had never put into words. 'I think so. I didn't, before the war. I thought war was a stupid game men played. Maybe I still do. But something deep inside me says that I'd fight, if I had to, if soldiers were invading. Broom handles, carving knives ...'

'I profoundly hope I never meet you holding a carving knife. If we don't fight this war, we lose it. Losing it would be a horror like this island has never seen. The war may be fought in stupid ways but ...' He shrugged. 'At least the Hun's high command is as dunderheaded as ours.'

A year back she'd have wanted to discuss the quality of their leaders. Now she just watched the man as he looked for words.

'I've become the kind of man who wants others to do the fighting for him.'

'You've earned that.'

'No. I ...'

She had to know. 'Angus ... you really did what they said, didn't you? Rescued those men?'

'Yes.' He said it simply and honestly. 'But it didn't make me a hero.'

'It makes you a man who has earned time away from the front. Besides,' she added lightly, 'you'll raise the ability level of the administration by several notches.'

He almost smiled. 'Thank you for that.'

She gave him the most perfect smile she could, a smile that would bring him back from the war and all that had happened there, all that might happen there. 'I arranged something special for today. One of the maids says there's a badger's set beyond the apple orchard at the Home Farm.'

It was as though she had given him gold and rubies. 'Badgers only come out at night. Dusk is the best time to see them.'

'Wombats too. They're like badgers,' she added. 'Except they aren't. I've ordered a picnic for us too. We can go there late this afternoon and wait. The apple trees are still in bloom.'

'Apple blossom, badgers and Sophie Higgs,' he said. 'I don't think there could be anything more perfect in the world.'

'Your river, perhaps?'

He looked at her, suddenly serious. 'There are other beautiful places in the world. Perhaps I need to learn to love more than a river.'

Chapter 51

The past is never simple, and the future never clear. I learned years ago to live each second as it happens. Even the bad ones can have fragments of beauty at the edges.

Miss Sophie Higgs, 1918

Wooten was still dressed for spring. The apple blossom drifted in the sunlight, as though reluctant to reach the ground. Sophie lay back and watched it: pink petals, white petals, blue sky. Grass tickled her neck. It could have been anywhere, any time, a moment before Eden.

She shut her eyes and felt a petal rest on her cheek, and then another on her nose. She sneezed and sat up, to find Angus looking at her.

'I thought you were going to sleep. I must be poor company.'

Sophie smiled. 'Never.' She opened the basket.

Angus peered over her shoulder. 'Good Lord!'

Cook had done them proud, glad perhaps to be preparing a meal that wasn't stew for three hundred. Cold roast chicken nestled in vine leaves from the succession houses, a loaf of bread, yellow butter oozing moisture in still more vine leaves, a tomato, a chunk of cheddar cheese studded with walnut halves, hothouse peaches cushioned in crumpled napkins.

'I haven't seen anything like that since … well, ever, I suppose.'

Sophie broke open the bread and took up a knife for the butter. Even here, she thought, I move my hands like butterflies.

Suddenly she wanted to be gauche: the old Sophie, the real one. But this is real too, she thought just as suddenly. That me is gone. I'm no longer that Sophie any more than I'm Miss Lily's ideal.

'What's this?'

'Quince paste. Here, try a bit.' She sliced a piece, then felt his fingers, warm on hers, as he took it. She would have liked to put it to his lips herself, but that would shock him.

'It's good. Good Lord,' he repeated, almost reverently. 'This is real bread.'

'Baked this morning, from Cook's precious pre-war larder. Try it with cheese and the quince paste. One day there'll be real bread again everywhere.'

'I suppose.' He leaned against an apple tree, brushing away the lichen that fell onto his shoulders. 'I've never eaten like this at home.'

'Your mother isn't a good cook?' Suddenly she realised she might have insulted him by assuming his mother did her own cooking. But he was smiling.

'Terrible. And somehow she teaches every maid to cook as badly.'

'Miss — A friend of mine says that you need to be able to cook if you're to manage a household, even if you never lift a pan. I can make French bread, and roast chicken with chestnut stuffing too.'

She realised she was trying to impress him with her qualifications as a wife. He must have been aware of it too, for he was silent, even when she passed him a leg of chicken and a napkin. He bit it, wiped his fingers. 'Are *you* a good cook?'

'I like cooking. It's … real. Solid. You can't cheat when you cook. Cooking is something you can depend on.'

'Any good with venison?'

'I know to make sure it's either rare or cooked long and slowly, and it must be well hung if you're going to stew it.' She smiled. 'I want to try the same recipes with kangaroo one day.'

'What's Thuringa like?'

She looked around, at the spring-green trees, the dappled ground. 'Harder. You can see the bones of the land. Sky so blue you can almost reach into it.'

He looked at her with enormous understanding. 'You love it.'

'Yes.' She was shocked at the depth of longing that had shot through her. 'Angus ... I'm not, well, I'm not what I look like.'

'Smudged?'

'What?' She brushed her nose. The blossom had left a gold trail of pollen. 'No. My family aren't top drawer back in Australia. Rich, but that means mixing only with other businessmen and their families. It's almost an accident that I've spent my time in England with the aristocracy. I even had to relearn my accent before I was ... acceptable.' She paused. 'What will you do when the war's over?' The question was spoken before she had considered it, realised it was exactly what it sounded like: an invitation for him to turn to her and say, 'Marry you, if you'll have me.'

Instead he quirked a smile. 'Quietly rot in the soil of France.' He laughed at her shock. 'You don't need to be good at figures to know the odds out there. One in three survives each time we go over the top. And I'm very good at figures.'

'But you'll be in a staff job.'

'War moves around, Sophie,' he said gently. 'And things aren't good. I read yesterday's papers.' He must have seen them in the VADs' sitting room, she realised, while she was in the wards. 'The Dublin uprising will mean more of our troops in Ireland. We're being annihilated out in Mesopotamia — we need conscription just to get more men, but the conscripts will be dead in a year too.'

She inhaled. 'All right. What would you do if you could choose?'

'Tend the land. Like my father, and his father. We may not have land of our own but we know how to love it.' He shrugged. 'Isn't that what we're fighting for?'

'But the Germans don't destroy land. They farm it, like us.' She thought of Dolphie, his face as he spoke of the woods at home. She had tried so hard not to think of him, an enemy soldier. Please let him be safe, she thought. And Hannelore.

'War destroys land. It's dead country over there. Dead trees and mud.'

'But things will grow again when the war is over.'

'When will that be? This year, next year, some time, never? It's destroying this land too, the war.'

'I don't understand.'

'Look around you. No one to mend the fences, clear the drains. Sodden land turning sour, rabbits taking all the grass, the best horses gone to war, and the best timber too. Forests that have been there for thousands of years turned into pit props. It's eating us all, the war.'

'But you're part of it.'

'Because to do nothing would be worse.' He shut his eyes.

'I'm sorry. I should have talked about other things.'

'No. You've made the last nine days worth living.'

She wanted him to kiss her. Needed his warmth against her. Should she subtly move closer, to make a kiss almost inevitable? But a kiss, here, in the gathering dusk, would mean more than the farewell kiss to Malcolm.

This man was too fragile to be allowed to make a commitment. And she did not want commitment even now — the war had not changed that. Marriage meant taking on your husband's life. Who would she even be when all this ended? James Lorrimer saw that, and would not ask. And Dolphie too.

Suddenly Angus moved beside her, but not to kiss her. 'Shh,' he breathed.

Something moved in the growing dusk beyond the apple trees. Black, with a hint of white, a long nose at first and then the whole creature, not wombat-like at all, unless a wombat had bred with a wolf. All at once the badger darted back into its hole. Perhaps it had smelled them.

Then it was back again, pushing and pulling at what looked like a ball of dried bracken.

The shadows were thickening into dimness. Another form appeared, and then another, both smaller, darker. One lunged towards the other, then they were rolling, snapping, bouncing while the large shape went back and forth, cleaning out the bracken.

A mother and her cubs. It was a miracle: two hundred maimed men up at the Abbey, the battlefront so close across the Channel, the anguish of the past two years. Yet here were these animals, untouched by it all. It was so domestic.

'I've never seen it,' he whispered. 'I've watched badgers night upon night, but never seen a mother clean out a burrow or the young ones play like this. You could watch for a hundred years ...'

She glanced at him, saw him watching her, not the badgers. 'Sophie, I don't know how I'll end up in this war. Dead's not the worst of it. I've seen fellows blind, screaming, armless and legless both. I wouldn't ask a woman to share that. I couldn't. But ... when all this is over ... will you share a picnic basket with me again?'

'Yes,' said Sophie.

Chapter 52

I learned many years ago never to make a life decision in times of danger. Your mind and body are so keyed up to 'do what must be done now' that you lack the mental quiet necessary for the choice you need to make.

Sophie, 1958

Angus left. At the high Wooten doorway he hesitated, then kissed Sophie's cheek. She touched her cheek with her fingers absently, feeling the kiss again, for weeks after he left.

She did not write to James of his visit. Her relationship to either man had never been clearly stated. Two years before she had felt too young to make a choice regarding marriage. These days the world was too complex to be able to make a choice.

She still wrote to him, and to Malcolm, and also to Miss Lily, although there had been no more letters from her, nor to the duchess, when Sophie had bluntly asked.

She sent both Angus and Malcolm cakes baked in the Abbey kitchens, socks knitted by Doris that she hoped they'd think had been knitted by her, she told them about the potatoes growing in what had been the lawn, how Her Grace had ordered the longer-haired dogs shorn and the hair spun.

She didn't add that the cloth would make light bandages for the worst of the burns patients, the men who screamed when anything was laid upon their ulcerated flesh. Instead she talked about the two spaniels, suddenly dramatically bare, how one went leaping like a puppy and how the other stalked over to the fire and refused to budge for three days, so that Blaise had to bring its food and serve it in state, and one of the maids had to gather up its 'business' too.

The war went on. The management of Wooten was out of Sophie's hands now, but there was still plenty to do. Women's work. Boring work. She tried to thrust the concept from her mind.

In May German and British fleets met, fought, sank, with both sides claiming the victory that only the sea won. Irish rebels were executed, the rebellion quashed. The Germans had begun a new push at Verdun; the Russian army won a victory at Sokal on the River Styr, a hundred trains of German troops diverted to the Russian front from the trenches of France and Belgium.

Mid-summer brought another battle on the Somme, the great push for victory that gained a few miles — and almost one hundred thousand dead. Sixty per cent of junior officers died ...

And suddenly there was a new Allied weapon, codenamed a 'tank', rolling over the German line and crushing men and trenches.

Sophie held the newspaper with trembling fingers, her tea and porridge forgotten. Was this the weapon Miss Lily had spoken about, so long ago, the one that was so terrible it would change warfare forever? There were only twelve of them, most disabled now, but more would be built and used ...

But she didn't believe in a miracle weapon to end the war any more. The Allies had their tanks; the Germans had the manpower, conscripting Poles and Belgians to do the work back home to free their own men to be soldiers.

That year alone perhaps seven hundred thousand Allies had died at Verdun, and almost as many on the Somme, according to the pamphlets put out by the pacifists, but anyone who could count the casualty lists could work it out. The pacifist lists were right. But their cause? How could you not fight for others when they were being attacked? For yourself? 'Let any man who has not a sword sell his cloak to buy one,' the vicar quoted in a Sunday sermon.

Doris left, taking baby Sophie to live with Alison's cousin Mary and her children, to be part of a normal family — as much as anything could be normal in this land of war. Mary's husband had been repatriated with one eye lost, a 'Blighty one' that would keep him safe in England — as much as England herself was safe.

The little girl was toddling. Sophie held her namesake's hands one last time as she waddled across the nursery, then stood with the impassively weeping dowager as they watched Doris hold the child's hand up to wave goodbye and the car rattled down the driveway.

She would miss them desperately. But Alison's daughter needed a proper home, not a hospital. She needed a permanent mother and father.

And Sophie no longer needed a maid, even if her conscience would spare a woman from the hospital to attend her. She could lace her own much looser stays, put her own washing out for the maids, dress her own hair in the simple style needed for a much simpler life.

The dowager still staggered from her bed to wave each busload of men goodbye. 'Miss Higgs? She's the duchess's companion,' Sophie heard one of the VADs tell a newcomer. 'A good sort. You'll like her.'

That was her. Sophie Higgs, a good sort. An old lady's companion.

Only letters gave a glimpse of the world outside.

1 September 1916
Dear Soapy,

How are you, old thing? This is just to let you know that I'm moving on from Lady Mary's lot — she had the hide to object to my wearing trousers one evening at dinner. I'd taken the bike out for a spin and come back just as the gong went. Well, anyhow, we've had words.

No matter, I'm fixed up even better now with Blinkers and Swatt. They were good chums of mine at school. They brought a van over — used to be a baker's van but they've had it fixed up with stretchers in the back and painted it white with a red cross on it. All unofficial, of course, but no one cares about that over here. We're billeted at a chattow (I still can't spell that) with a nice old duck near Ypres. Her husband and three sons are in the French army. She treats us jolly well. We take turns going out to wherever the shelling has been worst, loading the wounded up and taking them to the first-aid posts.

Two of us take the van out, and the other has a kip back here if possible. We're pretty close to the shelling: just noise and smoke during the day but you should see the sky at night. Like Guy Fawkes — fireworks to the left of us, fireworks to the right of us, into the valley of death rode, well, a collection of carts and vans and ambulances, and even then we are only half enough, or not even that. Most of the poor blighters have to hoof it — carrying their mates or leading them, if they can still walk, five miles or more sometimes, just to get to an aid post or a casualty clearing station, and then sometimes there's a three-day wait before anyone can really check them over.

I picked up one blighter on the bike the other day. He was just wandering down the lane, blood all over his face, no idea where he was going. I cleaned the muck off with my scarf then tied up the wound — shrapnel I think, into his head just above his eye. You wouldn't think anyone could survive that, but I reckon if he was able to get that far on his own two feet he's the sort who'll make it through. Didn't know where he was or who I was, but when I said 'Hold on behind' he did like a good 'un. Took him straight to the Base Hospital — even I could see he needed surgery — which meant I had to ride back by moonlight. Ran over a hare on the way back, which our old duck was VERY pleased about, as we shall have it for dinner. She was even up waiting for me with a log on the fire in her drawing room and a hot brick in my bed, and her maid to bring me potato soup. A real old darling.

Don't think I've ever written as much as this before to anyone, even when I was at school. Give my regards to Her Grace. I almost know her from your letters by now.

Cheers, old girl, and love too,
Dodders

Men came; men left. Two-thirds, perhaps, went back to fight. When had those who were blinded, crippled begun to say they were the lucky ones? A wound that left you lame, with sight lost in only one eye not two, the fingers on one hand blown away — these days they meant only that you would survive.

The local women's group no longer made gas pads. It seemed that too many men had suffocated behind them as they tried to save their lungs from gas. The soldiers now wore flannel bags soaked in chemicals over their heads, with a celluloid panel so that they could see. At least there was enough air in the bags for them to escape the poisonous green clouds, though despite this ever more men were arriving blinded or gasping from gas attacks. There were rumours that clouds of British gas meant for the enemy had blown back on their own men.

But what foundation was there in rumours from men too weak to leave their beds? Nightmares, perhaps; tales strung together from memory and fear.

Sydney
September 1916
My dearest Sophie,

It is so good to get your letters. Your father worries every time a week passes and we do not receive one, but I tell him that mail must be irregular in wartime. We dearly wish you back at home, but with the submarine menace and so many ships sunk, there can be no thought of it.

It has been difficult with Oswald away fighting — we heard from him last week, by the way, from Palestine, and he sent you his best regards. Who would have known that he would become such an accomplished horseman? But your father says that he and his brothers were all grooms, as were Oswald's father and grandfather, so perhaps it is not strange at all. This war has shown us sides of ourselves that we might never have imagined.

I have now taken on much of Oswald's work in an attempt to lessen the burden on your father. I have always enjoyed 'figures' and am finding it strangely enjoyable to work with 'real' sums

*instead of problems in a textbook. Rosalind Millbanks, whom
you may remember as our second housemaid, assists me with the
work. She is an intelligent and capable girl and makes an excellent
assistant. Her 'young man' is in Flanders, and she is glad of the
increased wages to save for the day when this war is over and our
heroes return and the two of them can be married.*

*I must now tell you that your father had a small 'turn' at
the factory last week. Miss Millbanks found him unconscious at
his desk. Dr Weaver says his heart is strong, and that he fainted
from heat and overwork, and a man of his age needs to take it a
little more easily. You can trust me when I say I will make sure
that he does. Please do not worry about your father — it would
worry him far more to know that you were worried! I will make
sure he rests each afternoon and does exactly as Dr Weaver tells
him to.*

*He sends his love — and does not know I have told you about
his 'turn' — and love always from,*
Maria Thwaites

30 September 1916
Dear Soapy,

*Damn, damn and triple damn: Swatt caught it. A stupid,
stupid accident — we had the men packed tight as sardines in the
ambulance. I was sure that the weapons were all unloaded but there
must have been one I missed. A bump in the road and it went off,
took off the back of her head. Sorry, I shouldn't be writing this but
if I don't tell someone I'll go mad. Can't tell her parents, not that
she died like that.*

*It's my fault, all my fault, and don't say it isn't, because I
know it isn't too. It's the bally Kaiser's fault. It's because we'd been
on the road for a day and a night without sleep. It was because —
well, never mind the becauses. She is dead and I had to tell
someone, and you are far enough away not to howl when you read
this. Maybe just a small howl. She was a brick, Soapy. A right
good 'un. She deserves some howling. Maybe howl for me while
you're at it, if you have the time.*

Thank you for listening, old thing. It did help to write this, you know.

 Love,

 Dodders

10 October 1916

Dear Sophie,

 This is just to say that I am safe, and thinking of you, and to thank you for the fruitcake that arrives every week, and for your letters. I am glad you saw the badger again. It seems so far away now.

 I hoped I might get some leave at Christmas, but it will only be two days, not long enough to cross the Channel. May you have a Merry Christmas anyway.

 Yours always,

 Angus

No words of love, not even memories of apple blossom. But he wrote to her every week, on clean, good-quality paper, and that told her he was away from the front line, most of the time at least. She wrote back, trying, as she imagined his mother doing, to find things unstained by war to write about. The spaniel had had puppies by the great Dane: *a terrible misalliance but so sweet.* She had managed to knit bedsocks — so much easier when you didn't have to turn a heel, and would he like a pair? Nothing things, on either side, that said only 'I am here, and you are there.'

She wrote to Sergeant Brandon at the factory too — he sometimes dictated a letter to his female assistant to send to her; and to James Lorrimer, the only letters in which she included opinions, though never queries.

She wrote to her father and Miss Thwaites, helplessly wishing she could take some of the business load herself, despite trusting Miss Thwaites's capability to care for both factory management and her father. Passage to Australia now was almost impossible for civilians.

At two am, waking at a patient's scream in the rooms above her, she longed to write to Dolphie, to ask more about the ancient forests that he loved; and to find out, perhaps, who he truly was. In daylight she knew that it only mattered that he was the enemy. As Hannelore had said, as the horrors in Belgium showed, losing a war was even worse than fighting one.

Most of all, she longed to write to Hannelore, or Miss Lily. They were the only ones left who might understand how she felt her life had vanished, just as she had begun to understand who she might be.

Chapter 53

December 1916
Dear Sophie,

  *I write this just so you do not forget who I am; so that I don't
forget who I am, perhaps, in what might only diplomatically be
called the 'diplomacy' of this war. Privately, I sometimes find our
enemies easier to deal with than our allies.*

  *I have not said this, of course, to you or anyone else. But you
will know the esteem in which I hold you from the fact that you are
someone I have not told it to.*

  I remain, yours always,
  James

The card sat on a silver salver. *Miss Ethel Carryman*, with a
Yorkshire address. Sophie glanced up at the boy in his taken-in
footman's attire. 'She wishes to see me, Jeremy?'

'Yes, miss.' The boy hesitated. 'She's ... she's sort of a lady,
miss. But she came in an army car, with a soldier driver. Will
you see her, miss?'

A proper footman would have been more reticent. 'Of course.
Please, could you bring tea too?' Even if Miss Carryman had
only come from the village, she'd need a cup of restoring tea.

Sophie folded the letter she had been writing, then stood as
the 'sort of a lady' was ushered in.

Tall as a man, broader shoulders than a shearer, a square,
almost ugly face. A red ungloved hand thrust towards her,
a hand that looked like it scrubbed floors. Of course, many
ladies' hands looked like that now, and the suit was well
tailored.

The accent was not.

'Miss Higgs?' Pure Yorkshire. No, not pure. Someone had done their best to graft a good accent onto this young woman but had done a far worse job than Miss Lily would have. 'I'm after your corned beef.'

Sophie collapsed back into her chair in laughter. Impossible not to. All her life everyone had been so ... tactful ... about corned beef. Now this. 'You don't beat about the bush, Miss Carryman.'

Miss Carryman grinned. 'Not in wartime, Miss Higgs.'

'Call me Sophie,' said Sophie.

'Well, then, I'm Ethel. But I didn't expect someone who lives in a place like this to be so chummy.'

'My dear Miss — I mean, Ethel, you are the first person in my life who has spoken frankly to me about what is the only truly interesting thing about me. Now, tell me why you want it. I presume you don't just want a few cans for a jumble sale? Thank you, Higgins,' she said as the maid put down the tea tray. 'Milk, Miss — Ethel?'

'Please. And make it three sugars.'

'You must help yourself to teacake.'

The big woman took two large bites — hungry bites, not just bad manners. She swallowed, then said, 'I need enough corned beef to feed ten thousand men a night. We had a year's contract with your pa's company, but when that came to an end his agent told us that our corned beef was going to the army now.'

'And so it should,' said Sophie.

'Yes. Well. Except our canteen feeds soldiers who need it just as much as them in the trenches. We're on a main route to the battlefields for fresh British troops, the last one they see before Blighty if they're being sent home. Which means they've been shot up, and probably going to —'

'I know what a Blighty one is,' said Sophie. 'We are a convalescent home.'

'*You* see them convalescing,' said Ethel bluntly. '*I* see them with their legs bleeding stumps, or their faces so smashed it takes three hours to spoon a mug of cocoa down them. But if they don't get that cocoa, they'll die all the sooner. We give every man jack of 'em a corned-beef sandwich, a mug of cocoa and two cigarettes. Cocoa is no problem — my dad and brother are Carryman's Cocoa, and with all the white feathers my brother's collected he could cover a whole hen run. Quaker,' she added. 'Not coward. He believes you shouldn't kill another human being.'

'And you?'

Ethel met her eyes. 'And I agree with him. But when a Hun buries a bayonet in a baby I reckon we need to do summat more than pray for his little soul. Cocoa and corned beef save people, they don't kill 'em. *If* we can get that corned beef.'

'Ethel, I'll be frank. I've never had much to do with my father's business. If he could have managed it, Dad would have had me grow up without even knowing the words "corned beef". But I do know that corned beef comes from cattle, and is processed in factories, and I do know my father. If it were possible for him to be producing more corned beef, he'd be doing it. Asking him to find extra cans to feed your ten thousand men a day won't do any good at all. Even he can't magic up more cattle and factories that quickly. Is it really ten thousand?'

'Only on a good day. Or should I say a bad one, after a stoush. On other days we cope with maybe a couple o' hundred.'

'Who is we?'

'Schoolfriends of mine.' The grin again. 'We decided running the canteen was more important than French irregular verbs. Though I reckon some of the verbs we've heard in the last couple o' years aren't especially regular. Midge McPherson, she's a New Zealander. Brother caught it at Gallipoli. Anne is an honourable.'

'Just the three of you?'

'And the young women who used to be our maids. We manage,' said Ethel calmly. 'But not without corned beef.'

'I'm sorry. I —'

'Nay, lass, I didn't come here to ask you to magic that corned beef out of the air. Because I've found the corned beef we need. Only problem is, your pa's sellin' it to someone else. Worthy's Teahouses.'

Worthy's were one of the largest teahouse chains in Britain. 'You want me to ask Dad to divert the corned beef bound for Worthy's to your canteen?'

'You ask that, and your pa will tell you the same thing his agent told Lady George — that's Anne's mother. Thought your pa'd be more willing to go the extra mile for her than me. Your pa's Mr Slithersole says a contract is a contract, and he's right. Even if your pa gave us that corned beef, old Worthy could get the law on him to get it back.'

'Then what would you like me to do?'

'Ask your pa to offer Worthy's summat that'll change their minds. Like cheap corned beef for ten years after the war. Because I'm not feeding my lads fish-paste sandwiches, not after what they've been through.'

'I can do that,' said Sophie.

'There speaks a lass whose pa has always given her her every wish,' said Ethel.

Sophie flushed. Yet it was true. 'I'll send the cable now.'

The reply sat at the breakfast table. Only Sophie and Ethel, who had stayed the night, were breakfasting downstairs, Ethel's chauffeur having headed to the barracks side of the Abbey for more official accommodation. The breakfast salvers contained only porridge these days, the de rigueur sugar on the table, despite rationing but, tactfully, never touched.

Except this morning, by Ethel, who ladled it onto her nearly full bowl. She caught Sophie's stare. 'Sorry, I forget sugar's rationed over here. Back in France we get used to fuelling up.' She nodded at the yellow cable envelope. 'Going to open it?'

'Of course,' said Sophie, a little stunned by so much forthrightness after years of excellent manners. She slid the cable out of its envelope.

'*Dearest Sophie tried but Worthy is not having any stop,*' she read out. '*Would if I could stop who has been pestering you about the business anyway question mark Her Grace should be looking after you better stop Miss Thwaites sends her love your loving father Jeremiah Higgs stop.'*

She looked over at Ethel. 'No go. Sorry.' She watched Ethel spooning up her porridge like a small conveyor belt. 'What are you thinking?'

'About how to turn every cow I've seen in the last two days into corned beef. But then there'd be no cheese or milk, and we need that too.'

Sophie smiled as she helped herself to a much smaller bowl of porridge, sugarless. Excitement trickled like honey. 'Then we'll have to try another weapon.'

'And what's that? One bloke did give me a German Luger, but I left it behind in France.'

'Charm,' said Sophie.

The head office of Worthy's Teahouses was curiously inhospitable: men at desks with ledgers on the ground floor; men and a scattering of women with more ledgers on the second, where a middle-aged woman in severe serge led them to an office as severe as her costume.

Mr Worthy held Sophie's card by one corner, peering at it through his glasses, though the appointment had been made by his secretary.

No tea tray ready to offer us, noted Sophie. 'Stand back and be quiet,' she muttered to Ethel.

The large woman glanced at her from under the brim of her sensible hat, her mouth quirked in a half-smile.

Sophie held out both gloved hands to Mr Worthy, forcing him to stand, which he had clearly not intended to do, and take her hands in a gesture of intimacy. 'Mr Worthy?'

'Yes.'

'Mr Worthy, how truly good of you to give us five minutes of your valuable time. But I knew you would. All England knows how much you do for your nation, Mr Worthy.' She fluttered her eyelashes up at him.

A smile, slightly like Ethel's, quirked his lips. 'Thank you, Miss Higgs. But you are still not getting my corned beef.'

Sophie blinked. A man was supposed to give sufficient time for charm to work ...

Ethel chuckled behind her.

'You may as well sit down,' said Mr Worthy, 'as I doubt I will be able to convince you for at least ten minutes, which is all I can afford in times like these.'

Sophie sat; Ethel sat beside her.

'In ten minutes, then,' she said. 'You won't give the beef for your country, then, Mr Worthy?'

'I *am* giving my country corned beef,' said Mr Worthy. 'Corned beef for men and women in the factories, office girls — they're the ones who eat at Worthy's. Those men and girls keep the war effort going, same as the boys in the trenches. And there's no amount of money your father can offer me that will make me take it from them.'

'Cheese and pickle,' said Sophie. 'We still have eight minutes.'

He pushed his glasses up to stare at her. 'I beg your pardon?'

'Mr Worthy, I will give you my word that my father will provide you with as much cheese as corned beef. Very nutritious, cheese and pickle.' Actually, it had been a later cable from Miss Thwaites that had suggested cheese, and Sophie who had added the pickles and worked out how to organise them. 'The pickles will be made in England by our women volunteers, with Australian sugar and vinegar sent by my father.'

Mr Worthy paused at that, actually considering. 'Already offer cheese and pickle. A mixed assortment is a mixed assortment.'

Sophie tried to find an answer.

'Cut the meat thinner,' said Ethel suddenly. She met Mr Worthy's eye. 'I'll do you a deal.'

'Will you, now?' But he stopped fiddling with his watch, and gazed at Ethel intently. Perhaps there were forms of flirtation beyond Miss Lily's ken ...

'You cut your corned beef thinner, and so will I. We'll go halves in the corned beef. You can put a sign on every plate saying *Half your beef is going to our Tommies in the trenches*. You'll get your extra cheese and pickle, and I'll cut you in on the tomatoes from Lady George and her posh friends' greenhouses. She's a patron of ours and eager to help. Tomato sandwiches will be a treat your customers can't get anywhere else. Four months of them, every summer. Mayhap you can even put the family crest on your pats of margarine.'

'Butter,' said Mr Worthy, meeting Ethel's gaze.

'Butter,' Ethel agreed, with the grin of one who knew it wasn't.

'And the price of the corned beef I don't get ...'

'Will be your donation to our boys,' said Sophie, feeling it was time she put in something useful, beyond getting Ethel the entrée here today through her father's name.

'Done.' Mr Worthy stood again, putting his hand out to shake, realising he was handing it to a woman at the same time as Ethel shook it, hard, then let Sophie grab it too.

'Thanks for your ten minutes,' said Ethel.

Mr Worthy looked at Ethel for a moment. 'If you were a man, I'd offer you a job.'

'Thanks. But I've got one,' said Ethel cheerfully.

I don't, thought Sophie. Would Ethel accept her as a volunteer at her canteen? And yet mixing cocoa and slicing bread would be much like the soup kitchen, if larger and more agonising. Good work, but work anyone could do.

I should be thinking of what *needs* to be done, she thought. Yet who has the luxury of doing what fulfils them most? I've had my head filled with nonsense by Miss Lily, who is probably right now doing ...

What? Her duty, as a VAD? Spying on the German high command, or urging peace?

'Lunch?' asked Mr Worthy, signalling to his secretary.

Ethel beamed. 'I'm right fond of a good cheese sandwich.'

'I'm sure you are,' said Mr Worthy.

Chapter 54

I've just discovered the perfect cure for an overloaded heart: a motorbike. When your heart feels like you can take no more the engine keeps on beating, and the wind in your face hardly smells of guns or blood at all.

Dodders to Soapy, 1917

A flurry of sleet ushered in 1917, sending several men screaming as it rattled on the windows like shrapnel. By March there was a revolt in Russia — two million Russians dead, millions more starving after the Tsar was deposed. Once this would have seemed like a world upended, but the world had been topsy-turvy for so long now.

And the United States entered the war. How much had James Lorrimer helped with this? Perhaps even he did not know the answer, nor could it be asked by mail. 'The world must be made safe for democracy,' said President Woodrow Wilson, though the only woman in Congress had wiped away tears as she said, 'I want to stand by my country but I cannot vote for war.'

But war exists, thought Sophie. Your voting for or against it will make no difference. While men are still willing to fight and to order others to fight, it will go on.

Would the United States army make any real difference? Their entire armed forces were just over one hundred thousand men. A hundred thousand men were hardly more than the losses already incurred on only one of the major battlefields, although hundreds of thousands more men were being mobilised, that useful word that meant tearing a man from one life and thrusting him into uniform in another. And how could they cross an ocean with submarines lurking below?

Perhaps she had given up hope that war would end now. We all have, she thought. Maybe that is why it goes on. We imagined war and got it. We can't imagine peace, and so it vanishes.

James Lorrimer was still in the United States, presumably helping coordinate this new joint war, one country's experience matched with another's energy, and still mobilising resources and securing the major loans the United States government had made to the British, and the fighter aircraft from their vast steel factories.

King George asked his subjects to eat less bread — a quarter less — to aid the war. Even the royal household was on rations now. Potatoes had vanished from the shops. People ate swedes instead, cattle food, and children foraged in the lanes for extra food for cows. Wooten still had potatoes from its home farm, but even now in mid-summer, with the first vegetable crops of the year, it was a stretch to feed the men. At least there was still porridge, and the table still set precisely so; letters were still there no matter what time you managed to stagger down to breakfast.

Including this letter, lying so innocently on the table.

She glanced at the handwriting — unknown — and the postmark — Switzerland — then looked at it more closely.

She took the letter-opener and ripped the envelope. The paper inside was good quality, pre-war. She opened it and stared.

20 June 1917
My dear Sophie,

I am sending this to a friend who will see it reaches you. I sent one similar to Miss Lily also, but have had no reply. Perhaps she is no longer at Shillings, or they no longer forward her mail. I hope only that this one will reach you.

The letters at the bottom of this page are important. I hope you will know who should see them. You will understand why I do not tell you more.

I hope truly that you are well and happy and married perhaps to a very nice man, and that you and he are both safe in all that is

happening. I hope too that Alison and her husband are safe. Please
give her my love, but it would be best if you do not tell anyone else
that you have heard from me, not good for either of us I am thinking.

As for me, I am well, not married, and busy, as we all must be,
I think. I hope to tell you one day. One day we will have teatime
together once again.

I am your friend, always.

H

Hannelore was still safe! The first thought overwhelmed all else.
And then: I have a letter from the enemy. And after that: Her
English sounds so stilted. Is she all right? The newspapers had
said Germany was starving, but surely a prinzessin wouldn't
starve. Hannelore, she thought. My friend.

It was only then that she looked at the bottom of the page.

At first glance it looked like an inkblot, but she found a
magnifying glass in the nurses' closet, then stared at the blot again.

Not just letters, but symbols too. And then a date, and a place.
13 July. Ypres.

Chemistry, she thought. The symbols look like chemistry.
What did they call it? A formula.

What did Hannelore expect her to do with this? Take it to
someone who knew chemistry? But there was no one here — or
if there was, she couldn't take it from officer to officer among the
patients, asking if any understood it.

Nor did she have Miss Lily's contacts — contacts that might
also have been hers, if war had not intervened. If Alison's Philip
had been alive, if she had married James, as Hannelore perhaps
presumed she had, or if there had still been dinners here at
Wooten, something might have been possible. Not now. Nor could
she involve Her Grace in this. She could cable James in America,
but what could she say, when so many eyes would see her words,
and his reply?

This is from the enemy, she thought. If anyone knows I've got
it, they will think I'm a spy. I might even be arrested, imprisoned.
Someone might even link me to Miss Lily and what must now be

thought of as traitorous ideals. If any German spy knows I have this letter, Hannelore might be arrested too.

13 July was just over a week away. If this was to be used, it must be seen, urgently. She should be delicately weeping at the lack of male hands to give it to. Instead she felt life springing up in her veins again, a crack in the closed-in world the war had condemned her to.

Chemistry, she thought.

She found him at Cambridge. It had been surprisingly easy to get there: a lie to Her Grace. 'Dodders is coming over for a few weeks' leave with her parents. I said I'd stay with her.'

Guilt, just a little, at how easily the dowager accepted it. 'Of course, my dear. You have been working so hard. A break will do you good.'

A train, filled with men coming back from leave, or absurdly young new recruits. One gave up his seat for her. She felt even guiltier, sitting when the corridor was crowded with tired soldiers.

Another train and then another. Strange to travel by herself; unthinkable just three years before.

She took a taxicab to his address. It was a hotel, thank goodness, not lodgings. Even under the unwritten social rules of war she'd have hesitated to visit a young man's lodgings.

The waiter showed her to a sitting room, then offered her tea. She accepted just as she heard his footsteps on the stairs.

'Miss Higgs! What are you doing here? Have you heard from Malcolm?'

He wore a uniform, but with a shapeless blue sweater over it. She forced herself not even to glance at his mutilated hand.

'Not since last March. He was well then. Lieutenant Armitage, I know this sounds silly, but I need your help.'

'Of course, Miss Higgs. Anything.' He thinks I'm organising a jumble sale, she realised. Or in need of an escort to the train. She handed him a piece of paper with the mysterious formula freshly written out. 'I received this. I don't know what it means, but it might be important.'

He glanced down at it, then stared. 'It's a formula. A gas, I think ...' His expression changed. He is familiar with this, she thought. Very familiar. 'Miss Higgs, how did you get this?'

No one would believe this was important if she lied. This risk was inevitable. 'A friend sent it to me. A German friend.'

'A Hun? How do you know a Hun?'

'I met several Germans during my season, at parties, even at Windsor Castle. Remember, Their Majesties are of German origin too. A German girl was a visitor at the Earl of Shillings's home while I was a guest there as well.'

'Not a close friend?'

I'm sorry, Hannelore, she thought. 'No. But she ... she was against war. Liked England. Talked of wanting to marry and live here, if she could. I think she might think she can help England with this.' Not quite a lie. Not quite the truth either.

He scrutinised the paper again. 'I'll have to show it to someone,' he said abruptly. 'Will you stay here?'

'Yes. Of course.'

Lieutenant Armitage nodded. He turned again as he left the room. 'You really will stay here?'

'I'll stay,' she said.

She drank the pot of tea, and then another pot; she visited the bathroom, was offered toast and a slice of ham for luncheon, accepted, ate. By late afternoon and a slice of fruitless fruitcake, dyed dark with stewed tea, she had booked a room in the hotel for the night.

Lieutenant Armitage was there at breakfast. He looked tired, stubbled, and was wearing the same clothes, even more rumpled now. Another man accompanied him, older, a blue scar down one cheek, scars on his hands too. No uniform, but official. She came and sat at their table.

'Miss Higgs, this is Major Ericson. Major, this is Miss Higgs.'

'Good morning, Miss Higgs. I say, would you mind coming with us to our facility? We'd be honoured to have you.'

A calm, easy invitation, designed for the ears of the other breakfasting guests.

'Of course, Major Ericson.'

A car waited outside; the driver carefully did not look at her, or them. Lieutenant Armitage sat in the front, the major with Sophie in the back.

No one spoke.

Out of town, between hedges, birds trilling — didn't they know that there was a war? And then a sentry box with an arm like a train crossing. The sentry raised it, saluted as they passed.

'Where are we going?'

'My office, Miss Higgs,' the major said.

There seemed little point in asking more.

The drive wound between rhododendron bushes, untrimmed. It ended in a gravelled courtyard, beside a red-brick Victorian mansion hideous with tiny turrets. The driver opened the door for Sophie before he opened the doors for the others.

At least I don't seem to be under arrest, she thought. Or maybe they are polite to ladies they have arrested.

A woman sat at a desk in the front hall, the first non-nursing woman Sophie had seen in a uniform. Women ran much of the war effort, manned the factories, but not in official uniform. She nodded briefly to the men and looked curiously at their guest.

'This way,' said Major Ericson.

His office was at the back of the building. Once, perhaps, it had been the housekeeper's room. It looked out onto lines of recently built huts.

'Please take a seat, Miss Higgs.'

She sat. The chair was hard. Lieutenant Armitage had vanished.

'This letter: who did you say it was from?'

'I didn't say, Major Ericson.' I have to charm, she thought, but imperceptibly. Play this wrong and I will be arrested. She said confidingly, 'Do please understand, Major. There were German students at a finishing school, in Switzerland. Later, during my London season, there were German visitors too, of course, including guests of Their Majesties at Windsor Castle.' That should stop him, she thought. Even this man would baulk at questioning the royal household about their guests. 'I truly believe that whoever sent this to me must be a friend of England, trying to help. I don't know any more than the formula I gave Lieutenant Armitage, in an envelope sent from Switzerland.' She let him assume there had been no letter with it. 'At least I thought it looked like a formula. The only person I knew who might understand it was Lieutenant Armitage, so I brought it to him at once.'

'Have you shown it to anyone else?'

'No, Major Ericson.'

'Do you know what it is for?'

She shook her head. 'I'm sorry. I don't know anything about ... science or chemicals.'

'I ... see. You are Australian, I believe? Where have you been staying while you have been in England?'

'At Wooten Abbey, with the Dowager Duchess of Wooten. I am a friend of the family. The Abbey is a hospital now — I help with the nursing.'

His expression grew even more respectful than when she had mentioned the royal family, who had tactfully assumed 'Windsor' instead of their German name. But the dowager was as English as a Bramley apple. 'Have you been writing to German friends of yours during the war?'

'No, of course not. I said whoever sent this must be a friend of England's, not of mine. Perhaps they sent it to me rather than implicate a closer friend.' Like one of the royal family was left unsaid. But she saw he understood her meaning.

'I see.' Major Ericson seemed to be wondering what to do with her.

Someone screamed. No, it was an animal scream. Sophie had heard noises like that when a grass fire raced across one of the Thuringa paddocks. She had run to her bedroom and put her pillow over her ears ...

The noise came from one of the sheds outside. Sophie heard Lieutenant Armitage's voice yell something. She was on her feet, running, before the major could stop her.

'Miss Higgs! I insist —!'

The back door was open. She had reached the shed before the major caught up with her. She shook his hand off her arm and opened the door.

A small room, a glass partition. Two officers, on this side, their faces white — Lieutenant Armitage and another man. And beyond them ...

Three sheep. Or they had once been sheep. Their eyes were gone. Blood soaked into the wool. Their mouths were ... no longer mouths. Foam seeped out, and bloody foam from their nostrils too.

'What have you done to them?' She wanted to scream, but it came out as a croak.

'Your formula, Miss Higgs,' said Major Ericson. He seemed comfortable with the sheep and her reaction, but not her disobedience.

She stumbled back to his office. 'Tea,' Major Ericson said to the woman outside, before shutting the door. He sat behind the desk again, waited till the tea was served, then waited until she had drunk half a cup. He seemed less suspicious, as if the shock and violence of her action proved she had no understanding of what she had brought here.

'You are to forget everything you have just seen.' Major Ericson said this as though no other option could be considered. 'Forget you ever saw the paper. Do you understand?'

She nodded. 'I ... I've seen men who have been gassed. It's not like that.'

'No. This is a new formula. More powerful. More ... useful.'

'There was a name too. Ypres. And a date. Do you think that's where and when the Germans plan to use it?'

'Miss Higgs, I must say: do not ask any more questions. Do not even think of this again. Can you undertake not to tell anyone?'

'Of course I won't say anything. But you'll warn the men at Ypres? You'll make sure the men have the right kind of gas masks and other protection in time?'

'No questions, Miss Higgs.' He waited. If he thinks I will talk about this, he will imprison me, she thought. Not in a real prison, of course. Just where I can tell no one what I have seen.

'No questions,' she whispered. 'I ... I am so glad I brought it here, Major Ericson. It is all so ... so awful. I will be glad to forget it entirely. Thank you. Thank you so much.'

He relaxed. 'Armitage will see you back to the train. You will go straight back to the Abbey.'

'Yes. Yes, that's what I want to do.'

Major Ericson nodded. He'd like to keep me here, she thought — keep me somewhere, anyway, to make sure I don't talk. But you can't keep a duchess's guest locked up unless she makes a fuss. If I were a man, just possibly. Not a young woman, not even now.

And what can a young woman do?

Chapter 55

Father, forgive them, for they know not what they do.

Chaplain Merryweather's sermon
the morning he died, 1916

8 JULY 1917

Lieutenant Armitage sat in the back of the car with Sophie this time. The glass was pulled across so the driver couldn't hear their conversation. 'There's a train to Wooten in an hour's time.' Lieutenant Armitage's voice was tired. 'I'll wait with you till it comes.'

'Thank you.' Sophie pretended he offered from courtesy, not mistrust.

'It's the Northern Line. You change at Little Hamnet.'

'I know. It's the way I came before.' She risked a question, now she was away from the immediate threat of arrest. 'Lieutenant Armitage, the major is going to warn the men at Ypres, isn't he?'

He didn't answer.

'Lieutenant Armitage?'

'It's best if we don't talk about it. If you *never* talk about it. This is a German weapon, but it can be ours too. We need time to develop it, make stocks of it, work out how to best attack the enemy without affecting our own lines. We can't let the Germans know that we know about it.'

'But the *men*!'

'Miss Higgs.' Lieutenant Armitage was trying to control himself again. And he is too inexperienced, thought Sophie, to

408

realise how much he is telling me. After all, I'm just a woman ... 'If the Germans can't use the new gas successfully next week, they will simply try again. In the long run, warning our troops on the ground makes no difference.'

'Yes,' she whispered, thinking. 'But in the short run, those men will be dead.'

Lieutenant Armitage stared at her, an inarticulate man trying to find words, an officer who was not allowed the normal military responses of court-martialling, imprisonment or killing someone who might oppose the army that he served. 'We have been butting heads for three years now, Miss Higgs. Them and us. Guns aren't going to end this war. But a weapon like this, one that can wipe out a whole army — this might do it. If the Huns are going to use it, we need to as well.'

We have added submarines, aircraft, mines, steel flechettes, tanks and chlorine gas to war in the past three years, thought Sophie, and still death balances death — weapon for weapon, mud for mud, bloody corpse for bloody corpse ...

The car stopped. It was dusk, the light of the single gas lamp all but crushed by the dimness.

The train came, two hours late. They had hardly spoken, sitting in the first-class waiting room with a man carrying an umbrella, and a woman in a headscarf with a little girl.

Lieutenant Armitage helped her onto the train. Polite, she thought. Minding his manners even if he will let all those men die.

How many men were killed in each gas attack? Hundreds? Thousands? The papers never said. And this gas was so much worse. A weapon that might end the war ...

She knew no one at Ypres, except for Dodders, and there was no way to contact her; nor would the army possibly listen to a woman who drove an unofficial ambulance, rejecting military order. Possibly Malcolm, even the earl, could help her, but she had no way to find out where they were either, much less contact them.

'Thank you, Lieutenant Armitage. You have been very kind.'

At last, 'Thank you, Miss Higgs. If your ... acquaintance writes to you again, you will let us know?'

'Of course. I'm so very glad I came to you. Glad it's all in the right hands. I don't have to worry now.'

She had said the appropriate thing. He smiled and gave her a mock salute. She smiled too, at him, at the soldier who gave up his seat mainly for her — a corner seat where she could look out at the darkness. The train lurched, then began to chug.

She got out at the next station. The train to London wasn't due till morning, so she dozed, sitting in another first-class waiting room. Before the war it would have been shut after the last train. Now there were all too many who had to wait through the night at stations like these. At least in July her feet did not freeze.

The station tearoom opened an hour before the train was due. She washed her face and combed her hair, then ate a boiled egg — from one of the stationmaster's hens, she supposed. She could see them running about. They sensed the train before she heard it, stalking off the lines and into the grass beyond minutes before the engine appeared.

By some miracle first class was half empty. She found another corner seat and dozed again till London.

The gaslights had been lit by the time she arrived at the house — fewer of them in these war years. 'Miss Higgs! Her Grace didn't say you were coming.' Ffoulkes stood aside to let her in.

'I'm sorry, Ffoulkes. She must have forgotten.' A smile, implying that the dowager's mind was failing, not just her body. 'I hope it's not too much of an inconvenience if I stay tonight.'

'No, of course not, Miss Higgs.' Ffoulkes didn't ask where her luggage was. 'Tea, Miss Higgs?'

'I'll clean up, if you don't mind. It's been a long trip down.'

'Of course, Miss Higgs. I'll send Gwendolyn up to you, miss.'

A bath, thought Sophie. And Alison had left some clothes there, though the skirts would not quite fit without some adjusting, of course. It should have hurt, thinking of wearing her dead friend's clothes. Instead it felt as though Alison were with her.

'How long will you be staying, Miss Higgs? I'm sorry to ask,' Ffoulkes added, 'but Cook will want to know. It is difficult to get provisions these days, miss.'

'Whatever you have will be fine. Please, no fuss. I'm just here for the night.'

'Very good, miss,' said Ffoulkes.

The clothes fitted, once Gwendolyn had rapidly hemmed the skirts — she was no lady's maid but her sewing was good. Sophie selected half a dozen garments, from serviceable serge to elegance and dinner dress. She had no idea whom she might have to charm to get a message to Ypres, but the correct clothes must be part of her armoury.

It was good to be clean, well fed, wearing a fresh nightdress. She let Gwendolyn bring her cocoa in bed, sipped it, smiled. 'Leave me a candle.' Since the air raids, the gas had been turned off when the household slept. 'I'll read awhile. You go to bed.'

'Very good, miss. What time would you like to be called?'

'Seven o'clock. I need to catch a train.' The train to Dover didn't go till midday, but she needed to go to the bank first and convince the manager she was indeed the Miss Higgs who should be allowed access to her father's accounts.

She waited till the house was quiet; waited another hour for safety, then lit her candle.

The stairs creaked. But what did it matter if Ffoulkes heard? She was a guest who wanted something to read for a sleepless night. Why shouldn't she go to the library?

The books were still dusted, the desk polished, waiting for the duke to return and sit in that leather chair and call for whisky. His desk drawer was locked, but she found a paper knife and forced it open. Ffoulkes would see what she had done, of course, but by then she'd be gone.

The drawer opened. She picked up the tiny pistol lying inside. Her father had kept a gun in his desk drawer too; so did the villains in a dozen novels, so she'd assumed that it would be a general rule.

It seemed it was.

She put the pistol and ammunition in her — Alison's — dressing-gown pocket, and climbed back up the stairs to bed.

There were scrambled eggs for breakfast. Sophie wondered if they had been sent down from the Home Farm, or were they the house's entire weekly ration? Either way, she ate them and was glad.

'I'm sorry there is no marmalade, Miss Higgs. Cook says she hopes you don't mind plum jam.'

Oranges, like sugar, had to come on ships that were vulnerable to German submarines. Plums were home-grown. 'Of course not, Ffoulkes. Please thank Cook. This is a wonderful breakfast.'

'I will be sure to tell her, Miss Higgs,' he replied coolly.

Ffoulkes knew about the pillaged desk already, she guessed. But what could he say? He couldn't call a constable to arrest Her Grace's friend.

Could he?

'May I make a telephone call, Ffoulkes?'

'Of course, Miss Higgs. May I get the number for you?'

'It's an international one. I'm sorry, I don't even know what it is. It's for a Mr James Lorrimer, at the British Embassy in Washington.'

'I am sure the operator will assist, Miss Higgs. I will fetch you when the call is through.'

'Thank you, Ffoulkes.'

It would be night there. They would have to wake him, but he, of all people, might know someone at Ypres, and a way to contact them. If only she had the address of the Earl of Shillings. But war security had removed his address from the letter he had sent her. Even if she had known it, it might have taken too long for a letter to reach him, and the letter would most certainly have been censored of everything she needed to say. Even his connections might not be high enough to get word to the commanders at Ypres.

She had eaten three slices of toast and plum jam — it was really very good jam, not too sweet, like many pre-war jams had been — before Ffoulkes returned.

She stood, then sat back down when he shook his head. 'I regret that Mr Lorrimer is not available, Miss Higgs.'

'Did you say who was calling?'

'Yes, Miss Higgs. The butler said that he is away inspecting factories, and not contactable until tomorrow, or possibly later.'

And what could she have expected him to do, from the British Embassy? Countermand the War Office here in England? Possible, but unlikely. She'd had to try, and was now grateful that she need not put him in the position of refusing her plea to try to help, nor of risking his career by accepting. 'Thank you, Ffoulkes.'

Deeply, desperately, she wished she could talk to Miss Lily. Miss Lily, who loved her country, even if others might condemn what she had decided was best for it. Miss Lily would have given her courage. Sophie could almost imagine her voice ...

'Could you call me a taxicab please, Ffoulkes?'

'Yes, Miss Higgs,' he said.

Chapter 56

In the words of St Paul, 'I have fought the good fight. I have run the race well.' What more can any of us do, but what we know is right, and pray for courage and strength to keep doing it?

Chaplain Merryweather's final sermon, 1916

10 JULY 1917

The banker had been reluctant to part with so much cash, but had finally agreed. The threat of displeasing the far-off Mr Jeremiah Higgs was evidently greater than the risk of handing over money to his daughter.

Sophie was just pulling on her gloves as she left the jeweller's when her shoulder jostled someone else.

'I'm so sorry,' she said automatically, 'I was looking at my gloves … Emily!'

Emily's swollen eyes peered out under the wisp of black veil without recognition.

'Emily, it's Sophie. Is something wrong?'

A stupid question, with Emily's eyes blinking as if she had been thrown into the village pond. At last Emily said slowly, 'Sophie Higgs.'

For a moment Sophie wondered if Emily simply didn't wish to admit the acquaintance — perhaps Sophie's theft of Angus had made her an enemy forever, as she'd feared. But now Emily's black-gloved hands grasped Sophie's grey ones. 'Sophie?'

'Tea,' said Sophie. She looked around. No acceptable teashop lurked by the jeweller's, but there was a Worthy's Teahouse across the road.

Would Emily accept a Worthy's Teahouse? But she meekly allowed Sophie to shepherd her, to seat her in a corner by the window.

What did one order in a Worthy's Teahouse? She repressed an almost hysterical giggle. Not mixed sandwiches with precious corned beef. 'Tea for two, and Bath buns, please. Emily, is it your husband?'

Emily's eyes seemed almost to see her now. 'He's well. Busy. He's standing for election after the war is over. There is talk of a cabinet position.' Her voice was controlled now. 'It's good to see you. I gather you are doing sterling work up at Wooten.' She reached into her handbag, pulled out a tiny diary. 'Do you have time for dinner before you return? Viscount Shortcliff is dining with us on —'

Sophie had just over an hour before she had to catch a train. 'Emily, you're talking to *me*. A woman who can keep a secret. Something is the matter. Badly the matter.'

'If I tell you, I will cry,' said Emily carefully. 'One doesn't cry in public.'

'All sorts of people cry in public these days.'

'Not our sort.'

'Tell me,' said Sophie. 'Or is there someone else you can tell?'

'No.' The voice was a whisper now.

'If you don't talk about things, they eat at you,' said Sophie. 'I've seen it with the men, the VADs. You see something ... bad, and try to hide it away. But if you talk about it, the monster behind the door is never as dangerous.'

'He's dead,' said Emily simply.

Not husband, not brother. A lover?

'Who is dead?' asked Sophie gently.

Emily — the old Emily — was back now. 'No, he wasn't my lover,' she said quietly. 'His name was James O'Brien and I hardly knew him. He was the only son of a neighbour. He was studying to be a doctor, said he'd enlist — his whole year would enlist — when he graduated. But I ... I didn't wait.'

'I don't understand.'

'I posted him a white feather.' Emily's voice was feather-light too. 'Wars have to be won, Sophie. Most people here have no idea how bad things are over there. Even with the Americans ... we're winning, but only yard by yard. We need more men ...'

'So you gave out white feathers.' Feathers that said, 'You are an able-bodied man who is not in uniform. You are a coward, betraying us all.'

'He enlisted the next day. And now he's dead. Another year and he might have been saving lives. I didn't think ...'

Sophie held the black-gloved hand until Emily took it gently away. 'You know,' she told Emily, 'if the events of this war are ever weighed up, I don't think that ... mistake ... will figure at all.'

'Not exactly a mistake, was it?' Emily was almost wry, and Sophie nodded. 'I think the greatest cause of my guilt isn't his death, but the fact that I let myself be caught up, without thought. Fed by the mob.'

That sounded more like the old Emily.

'Then don't let it happen again,' said Sophie matter-of-factly.

'You still haven't learned tact.'

Sophie considered. There was a pistol in her pocket, English pounds, French francs and jewels that could be converted to cash in her bag and on her person. 'No.'

She could have added that her father had not amassed a fortune with tact; that two opposing armies slugging it out, inch by inch, was as far from tact as could be imagined; that posting a boy a white feather was not tact at all, but cowardice. But Emily looked defeated enough.

The tea arrived, and two Bath buns, sitting sticky-topped on thick white china plates. Sophie poured the hot, dark tea into the cups, added milk, a sugar each, even though Miss Lily had insisted they drink tea with neither milk nor sugar.

Emily sipped. 'It's quite good tea.' She sounded astonished.

'I think we needed it.' Sophie took a bun and pushed the other towards Emily.

The buns were fresh, and Emily looked better when she had eaten hers.

'No more posting white feathers,' said Sophie. 'If you're going to urge a man to war, do it to his face, and without assuming he is a coward.'

'Yes.' Emily chewed her bun. 'Do you hear from Captain McIntyre?'

'Yes.' Sophie wasn't going to discuss Angus with Emily.

'Please give him my regards. Your father's fortune must be growing in leaps and bounds.' A small revenge.

'It is. But he isn't glad of the reason.'

'No. I don't suppose he is. If only there were some way to break the stalemate. Submarines, aircraft — we're too evenly matched.'

For a second Sophie considered asking Emily if her connections could help. Then she had a sudden vision of what Emily might do, if she knew there was another weapon, a weapon more deadly than any currently being used in the war. Was Armitage right? Could the new gas end the war — for the Germans, if the English didn't use it too?

Am I like Emily, she thought, plunging in without knowing what is right or wrong?

She didn't know. You could only do your best.

Sophie stood, then bent and kissed Emily's pale cheek. The netting on Emily's hat scratched her skin. 'You did what you thought was right. I'm glad you're grieving though. I have to catch a train.' Let Emily think she was bound for Wooten. 'We must meet up again soon.'

'Yes, we must.'

Neither of them meant it. Emily stood as Sophie left, but Sophie glanced back to see her sit again and pour another cup of tea. Impossible to guess her thoughts as she sipped it.

Chapter 57

*We manage quite well here, given everything. Surprisingly well.
Sometimes I look at the wives and widows ploughing the fields,
the girls here who should be at dances or tennis parties, and think,
Where was all this ability bottled up before the war? Has anyone
noticed how easily a man's world has become woman's?*

The Dowager Duchess of Wooten to Miss Lily, 1917

11 JULY 1917

Two days until the weapons fell. Paris in 1917 was nothing but
grey skies and soldiers — soldiers drunk; soldiers sitting on
steps, white-faced, hung over or shell shocked or both; soldiers
in British uniforms and French, the occasional slouch hat of an
Australian or a New Zealander and accents that almost made
her cry. Sophie had an absurd impulse to touch one on the
shoulder, to ask for help. But no ordinary soldier could help
her now.

The ferry trip, a night on the train, stopping and starting with
no regular schedule and no buffet car had left her weary, gritty,
and badly in need of a bath, sleep and food that wasn't buns.
There was no time for any of them.

Desperation kept her walking, talking, pleading.

If she could not get a message to Ypres, she must get there
herself. It must be possible, if Dodders and her companions had
managed to drive their ambulances there. She might even find
Dodders's château.

But Dodders had organised her own ambulance.

It was impossible to hire a car in Paris. Impossible to buy one either, even with ready money. The concierge at the Ritz was desolate. 'It is wartime, mademoiselle,' he said, as though she hadn't noticed.

She should have realised that it would be even more difficult to get a car in France than in England. Stupid, sheltered ...

Recriminations wasted time. She had to have a car. A driver too, preferably a military one. No maps were available for civilians.

Thank goodness for French lessons, but if only she knew someone in Paris. A useful countess, perhaps. If there hadn't been a war, she'd have come here with Alison, perhaps, and would have met countesses galore, even the 'Mrs Higgs' whom Miss Lily had mentioned. She wished she could have seen the famous city in peacetime.

The only person she knew anywhere nearby was Ethel Carryman. Miraculous Ethel, who had managed to get a canny businessman to part with half a war's worth of corned beef.

Could Ethel, just possibly, perform a miracle again?

The train from England had passed Ethel's canteen, but not stopped at what was now a purely military destination. Which meant Sophie couldn't get a train there from Paris either, unless she disguised herself as a wounded Tommy. She considered the idea for five-sixths of a second.

The doorman called a cab, a horse-drawn one. The nag looked nearly dead. The cab driver was an elderly woman, dressed in what might be her grandson's trousers and shapeless coat. The woman looked startled when told the address. Sophie held out a handful of notes and the woman flicked the reins.

The horse began to plod.

Sophie could have run faster. But, unlike the horse, she could not have run all night. When they crept into the courtyard of Ethel's village, she looked at the railway station hotel with longing. Hot water. Sleep, in a bed, not curled up on the cab's wooden seat.

No time. She trudged into the station house, then out onto the empty platform.

She stared. She had expected carnage, but there was only an elderly man in a once-white apron sweeping the concrete with a straw broom. Long tables at one end of the station showed what might be, had been, would be, dealt with here, when the next train came in.

The man looked at her curiously, his moustache like straggled cobwebs.

'Mademoiselle Carryman?' she asked.

'Oui.' He gestured to the stationmaster's office, as unsurprised that one young woman might ask for another at this deserted railway station as he obviously was that a woman was commandeering a stationmaster's office.

Sophie went back inside and knocked on the office door.

'Ontray.' The Yorkshire accent was even more pronounced in French. Ethel looked up from scribbling in a ledger when she entered. 'Sophie! Come to give us a hand, old girl? We could do with —'

Sophie held up a hand. No time. No time. 'No time,' she said. 'Ethel, I need a car, a military one if possible, and a driver who knows France. And enough fuel for a day's drive — no, two days' drive, if we are to get back.'

'Why —?'

'Please don't ask me why. It's ... it's desperately urgent.'

'Why is it urgent?'

'I can't tell you.' Ethel's fury at what was due to happen the day after tomorrow might make her indiscreet — and indiscretion put them both at risk of a charge of treason, even a firing squad. 'Just trust me. Please. I must get a car.'

'Ask me for summat easy, like the moon.' Ethel chewed her pencil. 'Can't get you a car. Don't have one myself, not even one I can borrow just now. Most of the wounded come through on farm bullock carts these days. Don't suppose even one of those could be spared, or a woman to drive it.'

A bullock wagon wouldn't get her to Ypres, or not in time. 'You had an army car in England.'

'I'm English. This is France.'

Sophie supposed that made sense.

Ethel looked at her. 'Best I can get you is lunch with a randy French general. Was sniffing round Midge till she gave him the flick. But he's got a car, and a driver, and most of the time they're both just sitting around our hotel finding the best in Madame's wine cellar. You might just be able to persuade the old bastard that he can spare you his car for a few days.'

'How about one of the ambulances?'

Ethel shrugged. 'Those girls will take you to the edge of hell, and give the devil what-for if he tries to stop them. But there's no way to get hold of 'em until they arrive here with a wagonload, and who can tell when that will be? Might be tonight, mightn't be for a week. I can give you an address where some of them stay, but even that's a couple of hours away on foot, or by cart, and chances are they won't be there anyway. And you'd still have to persuade them.'

Sophie was fairly sure that if she showed a woman like Dodders the note, and described the deaths of the sheep, she'd agree to help. But Ethel was right. It might take days, or even a week. Because the women's ambulances were unofficial, they simply waited by the front lines till they had enough wounded to bring to a casualty station.

'I'll risk the general,' she said. If that failed, she'd try to locate some of the ambulance drivers.

Ethel scribbled a note. 'Garsson!' The elderly man peered around the door. 'Pour le général, see voo play.'

'At your service, missy,' said the man, in a London Tommy accent. He vanished.

'I've told the general a young woman from England wants to meet him. You've time to pretty yourself up,' said Ethel. 'Basin and necessaries through there.' She indicated the inner door of the office.

'Do you really think I can persuade the general?'

'Dunno. Reckon he likes fluttering eyelashes better than old Worthy did.' She looked at Sophie, with the knowledge of a young woman who had coped with three years of male bodies, and of the officers who had charge of their lives, and their deaths. 'Might depend on how much you are prepared to convince him. His are the only car and driver around here. I've done all I can. The rest is up to you.'

Sophie had a sudden image of herself pointing the revolver at the général and saying, 'Take me to the front lines.' Which might, just possibly, be an option.

'Thanks.'

She suddenly realised that a French général was exactly who she needed. She would not even need the car and driver, or to try to get to Ypres herself. If she could persuade the général of the danger, he could call the commanders there, tell them to get their troops away ...

She slipped inside, took off her serge suit, unpacked a silk dress with a low, frilled neckline, perfume, soap, comb, rouge for both cheeks and lips, the powder Miss Lily had taught her could be moistened to hide shadows under the eyes, positioned the corset to plump her breasts much further above the neckline than even Alison's married-woman status would have allowed.

'Got a message back! He can see you now!' yelled Ethel from the outer room as Sophie tried to lace herself into a more alluring figure.

'Already? Can you give me a hand? I need to show off my bosom.'

Ethel stared at the reddened lips and low neckline. 'Cripes. You don't mess around.' She pulled severely at the stays. 'There you are. Eighteen-inch waist, and more bosom than the old rooster has seen since the Huns crossed into Belgium.' She hesitated. 'He'll mean business, ducky.'

'So do I.'

Would she sacrifice her ... her virtue ... to stop the unleashing of a worse hell onto the battlefield?

Stupid question. Hannelore had been willing to give her life — not just her death, but decades spent in a marriage of convenience — to stop this war. Miss Lily had made it her life's work to teach girls to at least try. Not to mention the men and women actually already dying for their countries and honour. She owed this to all of them.

A telegraph clattered in the office next door. A young woman's head appeared around the door; she blinked curiously at Sophie. 'Train in two hours, Eth.'

'Which means three or fifteen,' said Ethel, not bothering to introduce them to each other. 'Call the girls. Work stations, everyone.'

The head vanished.

'New troops, going to the front. No need for ambulances yet. The general'll meet you at the hotel dining room,' said Ethel. 'Now.' She hesitated, then hugged her. A bit like being hugged by a friendly gorilla. 'Good luck, lass. And I don't just mean with le général.'

The hotel dining room was a good one: white damask tablecloths, much-mended, but good quality. What looked like genuine silver cutlery, not plate. A waitress cleared empty tables, presumably where Ethel's volunteers had eaten.

One table still set, in a discreet corner. Two chairs. One général, in uniform, wearing enough medals to brocade an entire sofa. He was seventy perhaps, with a trimmed grey moustache. He stood, and bowed over her hand. 'A little English rose. How kind of you to dine with me, mademoiselle. It makes an old man's heart glad, in these hard times ...'

She wanted to plead, on her knees if necessary. Every second mattered. But charm could not be hurried. Or not too much, at any rate. And this old man would know the rituals of charm far too well to skip them.

A shy look down, a more flirtatious look upwards. It was as if Miss Lily's instructions had taken over: all the sessions of her debutante season's practice, just for this.

'An honour, Monsieur le Général, to dine with a hero of France.'

Soup, which she tried not to gulp, her first food since yesterday's hamper on the train. Roast pheasant, celeriac remoulade, red wine, white wine ...

'If I had known in advance of the pleasure this afternoon would bring, mademoiselle, it would have been champagne. But I have brandy in my room, a hundred years old.'

Should she ask him for the car now? Or tell him about the plan, plead with him to contact Ypres, and hope nothing more was necessary?

No. Even a général could not profligately distribute cars and drivers to mesdemoiselles, nor put his career at risk by giving orders or even recommendations to another's command, on the word of a young woman he had only just met. Especially, perhaps, a général so old he had been discarded here, presumably overseeing the transportation of the wounded. She would have to trust that he was a man of honour, would give value for what he received.

She held out her hand to him ... ungloved, flesh on flesh. A hand can be more seductive than a naked houri, said Miss Lily's whisper ... The smallest of caresses of his fingers.

The waitress discreetly looked the other way. Sophie suspected the discretion would last only until they had mounted the stairs; then her reputation would be gone. Though no one except Ethel knew her name. The général had not asked for it.

After their cheese and a last sip of wine, they went upstairs and he opened the bedroom door for her. A corner room: a desk, workmanlike; two brocade chairs; a surprisingly niggardly bed. He made no pretence of offering brandy, but began to strip, shirt, trousers and then ...

A corset. A giant corset, covering him from chest to thigh. She stared as he reached behind to unhook it, fumbled then finally swore.

'Pardon, my little flower. If you wouldn't mind ...?'

She began to fumble at the laces, not sure if she should cry or laugh.

'You will have to help me with mine,' she admitted, trying to keep her voice steady. This was worth it. Had to be worth it. She felt sick, wished she hadn't eaten despite the need for strength for this, and what might follow.

For the rest of her life she would try to burn this day away. This whole month away.

'A prelude to paradise, mademoiselle. But we have not talked about your fee.' He smiled under the weight of his moustache. 'You may not know that a général does not carry money. I must ask my aide de camp later. I say this so you know I do not cheat you.'

She stared at him, still fully dressed. He had taken her for ... a prostitute! But of course he had. Why would a young woman ask to lunch with him if not for money, especially in wartime, when so many needed money so desperately? Even a young woman with her accent, her manner of dress, could be a refugee, saving her good clothes for an occasion such as this. Miss Lily's lessons had been for another type of setting entirely — the salon, dinner parties, not a single table at an obscure hotel. She had been unbelievably naïve. Ethel had even warned her, yet she had not entirely understood ...

'Mademoiselle?'

She took a deep breath, smelled sweat, talcum powder, something simply male. 'I don't want money. I need a car. A driver. Or your help, getting a message to the front lines at Ypres. Monsieur le Général, it is urgent. Vital.' She backed onto the bed, because her legs wouldn't hold her any more. She would not cry.

'Mademoiselle?'

The foolish old lover in a corset had vanished. Instead this was a general, a man who might be her grandfather. He pulled up one of the white brocade chairs and stared at her, absent-mindedly rebuttoning his trousers and shirt. 'Who are you? And what are you doing here, mademoiselle?'

'As I said. Trying to borrow a car, Monsieur le Général. My name is Sophie Higgs.'

'And why would you want a car, or to send this message?'

Only truth would work. And she must risk it. This man could have her sent back to England, even to prison in France. Vaguely she thought of the Code Napoléon: guilty till proven innocent.

'Because the Germans have a new gas. It will be used on our troops at Ypres, the day after tomorrow. It is a horrible gas, far more deadly than anything before. It kills and keeps on killing.'

He stared at her, weighing up whether this was a fantasy, or she had been driven to insanity by the war. At last he said, 'Do your English military know about this gas?'

He believes me, she thought. Or doesn't disbelieve, at least. 'Yes. I was sent the information by a German girl. We met before the war. I don't know if she wants the Allies to win, or if she just doesn't want this weapon to be used because it is so terrible. There is no way I can find out. But I have told the English authorities.'

'Then why are you here?'

'Because they want to use the gas themselves. If they warn the soldiers at the front, the Germans may discover they have the formula. I ... I told them that men would die, and the officer I spoke to said that men always die in war, as if it doesn't matter how they die, or how many ...' Her voice cracked.

The old man stared at her. He might not believe the story of a secret weapon, she thought, but he did believe the story of English perfidy. He patted her hand automatically.

'You are a virgin, then?'

'Yes, monsieur.'

The général sighed. 'A pity. My first true virgin and she is no cocotte.'

'You mean you believe me?'

He smiled. It was a grandfatherly smile. 'Let us say I *choose* to believe you. It is a good afternoon's entertainment. Better than I had expected.'

'I ... I'm sorry you didn't get what you expected, Monsieur le Général.'

His smile grew wider. 'In truth, mademoiselle ... What is your name?'

'Sophie Higgs.'

'May I call you Sophie? In truth, my performance has not been ... admirable ... for some time. But one must keep up the appearance.'

426

Relief turned her legs to jelly. 'I wanted the car to go and warn the troops, the officers in charge. But you can telegraph them and tell the commanders at Ypres what is going to happen.'

'No, mademoiselle.'

'But you said you believed me!'

'You do not understand war, my dear. I am a général.' He shrugged. 'But my country is under the boot of the Bosch as well as of our allies. What do I say to your countrymen, or to my own, or the Belgians? That a girl in a hotel told me of a secret German weapon? If they believe me, they would say your English major was correct. Some things must be kept secret. Your country, my country, Belgium must use this weapon too. Men die in war. That is what war is.'

'They don't have to die this way. Not this time.' She tried to shut out the memory of the sheep.

'It is that bad, mademoiselle?'

'It is that bad.'

'I am desolate. But I cannot help you.'

'You *won't* help me.'

'That too, mademoiselle. But it is you who do not understand. Have you ever fought a war?'

'Of course not.'

'Then let an old man who has explain it to you. How can the troops at Ypres be kept safe from this weapon?'

'I ... I don't know. Masks. Thick clothes and gloves. Or just get them out of there.'

'Exactly, mademoiselle. How do you find masks and thick gloves for ten thousand men, on a battlefront, in one day, or even a week? It cannot be done.'

'Then move them away!'

'In other words, retreat. Months of fighting, tens of thousands dead for every yard of French soil won back, and you ask me to tell the commanders there to move the men back, leaving the ground to the enemy? They would not do it.' He did not add, 'I will not risk what little position I have left on the judgement of a young woman', but she heard the words nonetheless.

No, the English command would not move their troops, not give up an inch of ground, no matter the casualty rate. Nor would the French, and other nationalities serving there. They had not cared about the death of thousands before. Why should it be different now? Especially when they, too, might use the weapon ...

But the men on the ground ... If she could talk to the junior officers who shared the trenches with their men, so when the gas came they'd know enough to give the order, 'Run!'

'Then lend me that car. And a driver who knows how to get there. If anyone finds out, you can say that it was an act of chivalry ... that I was trying to reach my brother who has been wounded.'

'Do you have a brother?' The général sounded merely intrigued.

'No, mon Général.'

'You want a driver too?' The old voice was resigned. He did believe her, had seen enough suffering, perhaps, to do a little — a very little — to stop more.

'I do not know the way,' she said.

'Very well. But I would like to meet you again, mademoiselle. When you have finished with my car and driver, where can I find you?' His smile was the most genuine of the afternoon as he added, 'And I will try to seduce you at luncheon again, and this time you will most properly refuse, and it shall be entertaining for us both and for all who watch us.'

'At the Ritz,' said Sophie. It was the only Paris hotel she knew.

'And your name really is Miss Sophie Higgs?'

'Yes.' It hadn't occurred to her she should have given him a false one. His smile grew as he followed her thought.

'Luncheon after the war, then? With champagne to toast your efforts?' For a moment he looked serious. 'I think you may trust my driver, mademoiselle. He is British, assigned to my staff as my aide de camp, and he should know the area. He is a man of sense. If it is too dangerous, he will not take you further, nor himself, nor my car. You understand that and accept?'

'Yes,' said Sophie. 'You … you are very kind.'

He shrugged. 'In this war I have saved no men's lives, nor cost any. Too eminent to discard, I am put out to graze like a worn-out horse. But this afternoon, perhaps, I may be of use.' He lifted her hand, and kissed it.

'I would love to lunch with you, mon Général. After the war is over.'

'Then let us find my aide, and the car. And a basket of provisions suitable for a young lady.' He opened the door and ushered Sophie into the corridor. 'Venez ici!' he called.

'Mon Général.'

The door to the next room opened. The man wore a British uniform, well pressed. He stared at Sophie, then at the door to the général's bedroom open behind them.

'Hello, Angus,' she said.

Chapter 58

13 JULY 1917

Dawn was a grey smudge beyond the farmhouse.

'So there you were,' Sophie said. 'And there was I. But I didn't ... have relations with him. Truly. Though I would have, if that had been required.'

'Then I will give you the truth too. I wasn't angry with you because I thought you'd slept with a French general — or yes, I was, but it was more than that. I was mostly angry because you put me in danger, and because I was ashamed that I was terrified, but had no power to refuse.' Angus met her eyes in the dimness. 'This is *your* fight, Sophie Higgs. I was as safe as one can be in war, till you seduced the général.'

'I didn't.'

Angus shrugged. 'Whatever you actually did together, you seduced him. And he gave you me, just like he gave you the car, and the picnic basket.'

The sky's black was turning grey. Soon there'd be light, the day, the war. Charlie stirred restlessly in her arms. He peered out towards the chicken, still balanced on the steering wheel of the car.

'No,' she said firmly. 'Good dog.'

Charlie gazed at her as though he didn't care about 'Good dog', even in French. But at least he settled back, a heavy weight on her lap. She suspected the soldiers wouldn't waste ammunition on a dog, but they might mistake something as big as Charlie for a human.

'I was safe. A liaison staffer with the général, which means taking messages to *our* generals, usually about where they are to lunch. It's the safest job in France, and the best-fed. It's all I'm good for. Do you know why I couldn't face going back to the trenches?'

'Because you'd been through too much already. I never blamed you. You're not alone; I've seen what can happen to men who've been there too long —'

'Have you really? You've seen the ones who make it back to England. Most like me don't! I'm not scared of dying. Well, I am, perhaps, but that's not it.' He moved back from her. 'There was a kid in my unit, back in early '16. I do mean a kid — one of the borstal boys.'

'Borstal?'

'The boys' prisons. I don't know what this one had done. Pickpocket, thief … Twelve years old, maybe.'

'*Twelve?* But you can't enlist at twelve.'

'He didn't enlist. The borstal boys had a choice: stay in prison or join the army. If they spent a year in the army, they'd be free, all records wiped away. Money in their pockets, heroes back home — what boy wouldn't join the army after that?

'That's who I was back then. A man who gave orders to a twelve-year-old child. And others, who might have been older in years, but knew no more.

'The lad stood it for three weeks. I found him hunched up crying for his mother in the trench. The other chaps pretended they didn't see him. I gave him my handkerchief, persuaded him to drink some cocoa. Said the usual things, how his mother would be proud of him, England would be proud of him. God knows if any of it was true. Got him to stop crying, though, even to eat a biscuit. Then the orders came. We were to go over the top as soon as the moon rose, try to take a farmhouse pretty much like this one.' He stopped.

'He was killed?'

'No. He ran. Away from the farmhouse, away from the guns. He hadn't gone more than a few yards when a sergeant felled him in a rugby tackle. By the time I got back from the raid they'd already tried him. I had to command the firing squad that shot him. And, heaven help me, I did.'

'You ... you had no choice.' She tried not to let the horror sound in her voice.

'I had a choice. It would have meant a court martial, and maybe they'd have shot me too. But I had a choice.'

She touched him tentatively, then when he didn't reject her put an arm around him. He put his arms around her again too. They sat for a moment.

'Sophie,' he whispered.

'Yes?'

'They didn't kill him. Not quite. I think five of that firing squad deliberately missed. The sixth hadn't quite hit the target. I ... I went up to him, kneeled down. He was dying, blood coming from his mouth. But he knew me. One of the men crouched beside me. I wondered if he was trying to give the lad comfort too, but he must have been the one who shot to kill. He dipped his fingers in the boy's blood and wrote "coward" on his forehead. He stood and spat. And then the boy died.'

'What was his name?'

'Lloyd Biggins.'

'I'm glad you remember. Only a good man would remember.'

'Two nights later we went over the top again. That was when I got that medal you admired, and the leg wound too. But I wasn't brave. I was just past caring. After that boy's death I couldn't give orders — not to send men to their deaths, not to send them to kill other men. Did you know that about one man in three can't shoot the enemy? They fire over their heads, or shut their eyes when they pull the trigger. Did you know that after every advance about half the men have messed their pants or wet themselves? That's who our British heroes are. And they *are* heroes, because they try to stick it.'

She wanted to comfort him, but didn't dare interrupt the flow of speech.

'I ... I vomit if I have to give an order now. If I'm lucky, I make it to privacy before I do. I'll help you through this if I can, but I don't know how much use I'll be. Letting that boy die like that was the greatest act of cowardice I can imagine.'

'You were trapped. Like he was trapped.'

'No. Just playing by the rules. Goddamned inhuman rules. You were right. This war is fought like a rugby match. If enough of us had the guts to break the rules, we might end it all. But most don't even see it, and men like me don't stand firm.'

He looked at her fully now. His face was sooty in the growing light, white where Charlie had licked his cheek. 'I'm a tailor's dummy, useful for wearing a nice uniform with my medal.

'You know why they gave it to me and not some other poor damn sod? Because the lieutenant I saved was a viscount — he'd enlisted under another name. There're men out there who carry stretchers into the heaviest of shelling to bring out the wounded. Men who have died trying to bring a mate back beyond the lines. But this thing,' he flicked the decoration, 'they gave this to a coward for carrying an aristocrat.'

'What if I said I loved you anyway?'

'The truth, Miss Sophie Higgs? I'd feel worse. I can't stand pity.'

'This isn't pity — it's respect.'

He snorted.

For a second she saw herself clearly; saw her choices as vividly as if they were lined up on the skyline for snipers to shoot at. Angus deserved his self-respect, for he had done his duty.

There was one way she could stop him from feeling a coward. Give him another image of himself that would take him once more into the front lines. Just once, to save lives. And then back, to his général and safety — because she wanted him safe, because she did love him, even if she was not sure what kind of love it was.

She carefully shoved Charlie behind her, where he couldn't make a dive outside. She bent to whisper in Angus's ear. Whispers

433

are for secrets, Miss Lily said. And pillow talk is always secrets. 'I have four breasts.'

'What?' Angus stared at her, then began to laugh. 'Sophie, there's no need to seduce me. I'm not the général. I'm here. I'll do my best.'

Sophie kneeled to whisper again. 'Imagine my wedding night when my husband found out I had four breasts. You are the only man I could confess it to.'

'Sophie ...' He sounded torn between desperation and laughter. And something — perhaps — more.

'You don't believe me? You'd better count them, then.' She reached down and undid two buttons on the now-grubby silk dress, showing a whisper of the lace on her stays. Only two, whispered Miss Lily, always let him do the rest.

His hands moved to her dress. She waited anxiously to see if he did up the buttons again. His fingers fumbled another undone, and then another. He looked down at the tops of her breasts in her stays. 'Only two.' His voice was hoarse.

'I have to hide the others. You'll have to untie my stays to find them.' She swivelled, felt the stays loosen behind her as his fingers touched them, trembling. 'Now pull them off,' she whispered.

He reached under her skirt and hauled the stays down: a blessed release, though she had already loosened them while Madame at the hotel prepared the picnic basket. Charlie sniffed them, and began to chew. The whalebone crunched. A doggy grin crossed his face and he crunched some more.

Sophie looked up at Angus. Suddenly she was giggling, leaning on his chest, feeling the rumble of his laughter too. Charlie gave a satisfied growl as another whalebone broke.

'A dog is not supposed to chew your stays in the best seductions.'

'So this *is* a seduction?' he asked, suddenly serious.

'Yes. It may be the only one I ever do successfully, so be quiet and do what you are told. Charlie, you be quiet too.'

'Hrff,' said Charlie, with satisfaction.

'Sophie.' Angus's arms tightened about her. He kissed her hair, lifted her face and kissed that too, eyes, lips. He pulled back. 'Sophie, I love you.'

'Even though I only have two breasts?'

'Maybe you'll grow some more. When we're married I will have to check them, very often —'

A voice muttered just beyond the farmhouse wall. 'I reckon they're in the chimney!'

How had daylight thrust itself into the world so quickly? Angus got her behind him before she knew it was happening. 'We're English,' he called as she hurriedly did up her buttons.

'Are you, now? Prove it! And come out with your hands up!'

'Stay here,' he murmured.

Angus stepped out of the chimney, his hands in the air. Sophie watched as two English army privates faced him, one with a rifle, bayonet fixed. Both had the stunted, narrow-shouldered look of the men she'd seen in London's East End, mud and blood on their uniforms, unshaven faces, and eyes that didn't blink.

Fox eyes, Sophie thought. Foxes who have been hunted by the hounds, who know they will die, and no longer care because they've run too long.

'What do you think, Johnno? Shoot 'im anyway? Probably pinched that uniform from one of our lot.'

Sophie pushed herself out of the chimney, the dog at her heels. 'No! We really are English!'

The smaller of the two men grinned. He had no teeth. 'Knew I'd heard a woman. Prove yer English, ducky.'

'How ...' Suddenly she knew. She began to sing. Words a patient had sung every time she'd changed his dressings; said it lessened the pain if he did. A pre-war music-hall song, with the words changed to fit the rougher time. They seemed particularly fitting now.

'Lottie Collins has no drawers
Will you kindly lend her yours?
She is going far away
To sing "Ta ra ra ra boom de ay" ...'

435

Both soldiers were grinning now. Angus's expression was impossible to read.

'So she *is* English. Right then, love, let's see *your* drawers.'

She'd hoped the music-hall song would make them think of girls at home. But maybe they used girls at home like this too.

Angus stood in front of her, his elbows out to block her from their view. 'Put your weapons down now. That is an order.'

Neither made any sign they had heard him or even noticed his insignia of rank. Charlie growled. Sophie pushed his head to make him sit. The dog might grab one of them before he could use his rifle, but the other could still shoot him.

Angus's hands clenched into fists. 'I gave you an order, soldier!'

'An' I heard it. But I reckon we're gunna be shot anyway, by the firing squad or the Hun, whichever gets us first. An' if you had a pistol handy you'd 'ave it out by now.' The grin grew wider as Angus's hands didn't move towards a weapon. 'I thought as much. We heard what you was doing in there. Officers only, eh?' He glanced back at Sophie. 'Now, lift them skirts and lie down.'

Angus lunged towards them. She grabbed his arm. He stared at her for a brief second.

Please understand, she thought. Please, Angus. Let them try to rape me. Stay still. Look beaten, till both men look only at me. Our only chance is to take them unawares.

Angus met her eyes, then nodded, the smallest of nods. He knew she had her pistol. His eyes said, As soon as I move, you attack them too.

She bent down and slowly gripped the hem of her skirt. Next to her Charlie wagged his tail, as though this were a game.

The men's eyes followed the silk skirt as she slid it almost imperceptibly up her legs, over her ripped stockings, showing her bare thighs. 'I should open my bodice too,' she said softly. 'Don't you think I should open my bodice?'

'We kin do that, missy.'

Don't move, Angus, she thought. She glanced at him; she saw the breath of a nod again. Distract them, she told herself. Lull them so they don't watch him, or my hand when it reaches for the pistol. 'But you might get my bodice dirty. I'll let you watch how it's done.' She undid one button, then another, let the fabric slide down her now-bare breasts before she touched the third.

Both men stared only at her now. She met their eyes, and smiled, looking up at them through her lashes. 'On second thoughts, I should unhook my stockings first. Don't want them to get holes.'

The stockings were mostly holes already, but at least both garters were intact. She pushed down one garter, cream brocade, lifted it to her lips, kissed it, then held it out. 'Which one of you would like my garter? Which one of you wants to take me first? I'm all yours now ...' She moved her hand into her pocket, pulled back the pistol's safety catch ...

The men's mouths were open. Stayed open as four shots ripped four holes in the morning and their backs, even though she hadn't had a chance to shoot.

The men flopped like puppets onto the ground.

Angus must have managed to get one of their weapons! No time to wonder how now. 'The car!' she hissed. 'Come on, you stupid dog, don't sniff them ...'

She bent to pull at Charlie's fur as Angus grabbed her shoulder. 'Sophie, stop.'

She realised Angus hadn't shot the men at all. Couldn't have shot them, not in the back.

'Hände hoch!' The order came from just beyond the wall.

Charlie sat, as though he felt the order was directed at him, not them. His tail thudded on the ground. He looked towards Sophie as though saying, 'See? That's what you need to say. I *am* a good dog.'

Sophie glanced at Angus. Once again he shifted his body to protect her from any shots.

'Do what he says, put your hands up,' he said quietly. 'Prisoner of war is better than being dead. Or so I gather.' He gave her hand a quick squeeze. 'It's good they are asking us to surrender. It means there is someone in charge. Means ...' He hesitated. 'Things will be ... controlled ...'

So the Germans won't rape me, thought Sophie. Possibly. She nodded.

Angus raised his hands in the air. 'I'm not armed.' Sophie gave a fleeting thought to her still half-bare breasts, then raised her hands too. Charlie wagged his tail, as though hoping for a biscuit or a game.

A face peered around the wall, and then advanced, bayonet out. A German private. The soldier patted Angus down, hunting for arms, then, reassured he had no weapon, yelled something. Two more men followed him, in the uniforms of German privates too. Behind them a booted officer leaned on a cane. Red stained one half of his shirt. Fresh blood, dripping onto the mud.

Sophie let her hands fall. She quickly did up her buttons.

'That was quite a show, Miss Higgs.'

'*Dolphie!* What ...? I ...'

'I think the English phrase is "Fancy seeing you here". Sophie, what are you doing in a war zone? Are you a nurse?'

'Yes.' It was the truth. Just not the whole truth. 'Are we in the middle of German territory?'

Beside her, Angus stared at Dolphie, at her, clearly remembering the count from Sophie's story in the night; possibly wondering, as she was, if he too might be here to stop tomorrow's carnage — or to assist it.

She could see Dolphie considering how much to tell her. 'This is held by no one, at this moment. But I am not sure where either force is. My regiment is a long way from here. My men and I are ... on a mission.'

Was such a coincidence possible? *Was* it a coincidence? Given the troop positions this was probably the best, or even only, route possible, for this particular mission, on this particular night. Malcolm will show up next, she thought. And the earl, and possibly Jones, carrying coffee for breakfast.

'Dolphie, your shoulder needs to be bandaged.'

'I hope it will be. May I ask who this gentleman is?'

'He's a friend,' she said shortly. She was blowed if she was going to do drawing-room introductions in a war zone. And

438

besides, Angus's role in what might be treason would need to be kept quiet, whether they landed in a prisoner-of-war camp or escaped. No, when they escaped.

'I ... see.'

'No, you damn well don't. Look, I'm going to rip up my petticoat for bandages. Is that all right? Dolphie, take your shirt off.'

'Ah, Sophie. You will never know how often I have dreamed you would say that to me. But not ... quite like this.' He looked at Angus as he said it, not at her.

'Your men can cover us,' she said impatiently as she tugged the petticoat down from under her skirt. 'I'm armed only with a petticoat.' She pulled at it. The seam held. She looked over at Angus. 'Rip it into pieces, please.'

Angus's look was indecipherable. 'You know,' he said conversationally, 'I dreamed of ripping your underwear, but not quite like this.'

Staking his claim, just as Dolphie had tried to do. Just what she needed: two possessive men in the middle of a battlefield.

'Just rip.'

Two tugs. The seams gave. Angus handed the strip back to her, then glanced infinitesimally at her pocket with the pistol as he began to rip off more petticoat. 'Thank you,' she said, just as conversationally. 'You always know what to do.'

'I hope so,' he said quietly. 'Sit,' he added to Charlie, who had bounced up in case he was invited to rip too, all injury forgotten in a chance to play. Charlie sat, then put his head on his paws, watching to see what the next human game might be.

'Here.' Sophie balled the strip of cloth as a pad and pressed it against the blood that welled from Dolphie's shoulder; Angus handed her another to tie in a rough bandage to keep it there. 'Try not to move.'

Dolphie looked almost amused, despite the black shadows under his eyes. 'I am afraid that will not be possible.'

She looked up from her bandaging. 'Dolphie, please, let us go.'

'You know that I can't. Your friend here must be taken prisoner, you understand?'

'I understand you think it's your duty.'

'Yes. It is my duty. A duty you do *not* understand, and I have no time to explain. And you ...' He paused. 'I will see what I can arrange. When I can make a telephone call I may be able to help you. But that may not be for a week or more.'

She imagined seeing the war out in a cold German castle. 'Dolphie, I have to get somewhere. It's important.'

'As I must get somewhere. And that is important too.'

'Nothing can be as important as what I am trying to do today.' She could not ask if he was attempting to stop the gas attack. His escort might not know his true purpose. 'Dolphie, I give you my word we won't try to hurt you, or any of your men. I give you my word that Germans will not be killed or hurt because you let me go now.'

'Sophie, I regret this deeply. But you do not understand.'

'I regret this too,' she said.

She tilted the gun in her pocket, glad the soldiers were standing so still, trying to follow the exchange in a foreign language; glad of the years of potting rabbits, with no time to raise the gun to her eye to aim.

Two shots. A soldier sank to the ground, red stars appearing, one on his forehead, a second in his neck. Angus threw the petticoat over the soldier next to him, then lunged, bringing him down like a footballer. Sophie fired at the third soldier, before he came to his senses and used his rifle; she saw the red rose bloom on his shoulder, saw him fall, turned her pistol to Dolphie.

His own pistol was in his hand.

'You gave your word,' said Dolphie.

Angus seized some shreds of petticoat, and tied the wrists of the man he'd felled, and then his ankles. One of the other fallen Germans groaned.

'I lied,' said Sophie as Angus efficiently took off the wounded boy's shirt — for he was a boy, she saw, perhaps as young as Angus's borstal boy — to tie his wrists together. Angus glanced at her, then took off the boy's undershirt to pack against the wound in his shoulder, tying it with another strip of petticoat. Sophie watched him. She wanted to sob; to beg the boy's forgiveness; to run and keep running; to close her eyes and vanish back to Thuringa where war was safely across the world.

She could do none of these, not even show her anguish and remorse. Worse: part of her was proud that unlike the men Angus had mentioned, she had been able to shoot when necessary. She had killed a man, wounded a second.

But I am not a soldier, she thought. What am I, then? A murderer?

She managed to give a polite bob. 'I am sorry if I have not followed the correct traditions of a war, or of a gentleman.'

'These are my men. Loyal men, doing their duty.'

She wanted to cry, 'I'm doing my duty too! I am trying to save hundreds. Thousands. And if you are too, then I could not ask you, in case the men with you did not know what you intend. I did what I had to.' And yet she knew that in the years to come — decades, if she lived that long — this one action would slice her nights to nightmares.

Angus reached for the boy's rifle. 'Do not do that, Captain,' added Dolphie, almost casually. 'Not while my pistol is aimed at Miss Higgs. I can shoot both of you.'

'No,' said Angus. 'If you shoot me, Miss Higgs will shoot you before you can shoot her. If you shoot her, I will have my hands around your throat by the time your finger has left the trigger.'

'I do not think so,' said Dolphie.

'Angus.' Sophie didn't look at him, just at Dolphie. 'You know where to go. I don't. The paper is in my bag. You know what you need to say. If Dolphie and I shoot each other, then you'll be free to go. Do it.'

'Sophie ... Yes. I know where to take it. If I have to.'

Dolphie's expression had changed. 'What paper are you talking about? Sophie, why are you here, now? Today? Are you really a nurse?'

Should she tell him that this was what nurses did on their day off, in a silk dress, seducing an officer in a war zone?

'Dolphie,' she said gently. 'You are the enemy. I cannot tell you that. Will you really shoot me? There is no point shooting only one of us. If you can't shoot us both, then why shoot one?'

'Woof,' said Charlie. He looked from person to person, as though making a decision. Suddenly he got up and moved to Sophie, then leaned against her leg. He growled softly, at Dolphie and Angus, at all the world in general, except Sophie.

'See?' she said to Dolphie. 'Charlie will kill you if you hurt me.' She doubted Charlie would do anything of the kind. But at least he looked big and was no longer slobbering. 'You're outnumbered.'

'I can shoot a dog,' Dolphie said, but even as he said it she knew it wasn't true. Knew, too, that he wouldn't shoot her.

He lowered his pistol.

'Put it on the ground.'

He did. And in that moment she knew for sure how Hannelore had got the information, knew why Dolphie was where he was, where she was, in that place, at that time. Not an unlikely coincidence. He had inadvertently set her on his own mission, although it appeared he did not know that Hannelore had sent the information to her. One man, at least, had not a full heart to do what he had been ordered to do.

Two duties. One to his country, and one to the sense of humanity that remained despite the necessities of war.

She looked at the dead German boy, at the white-faced one groaning on the ground. Had she killed a boy of loyalty and integrity, who knew he was risking his life and reputation to help Dolphie stop the gas from being used? Or had the boy merely been following orders?

She couldn't ask. Not now.

Could Dolphie really stop the Germans from using the gas? Possibly, as an officer. At least he might stop them from using it today, tomorrow, this week, until the other side had time to understand the threat, protect themselves in whatever way was possible.

But Dolphie had no car. Presumably he had had one. Presumably he, too, had tried other means to stop this, and had been driven to try to intervene at the last possible moment, just as she was. Presumably, too, he had been attacked, either by the Allies or by his own side. And she had now shot two of the men who might have helped him.

She — or rather, Angus, with his uniform and medal — had more chance of saving lives today than Dolphie. She saw the moment when Dolphie realised that as well. Dolphie always understands, she thought vaguely.

Dolphie stared at her. 'If you tie me up, you are signing death warrants for me and my men.'

She would not cry. Could not cry. Would she ever be able to? Sophie Higgs, murderer and liar. 'So what do I do with you?'

'I give you my word as an officer and a gentleman that we will not try to hinder your escape.'

'Why should I believe you?'

'Because I am an officer and a gentleman.'

'And I am an ignorant colonial?' And liar. Liar. Murderer, she thought.

The pain in his smile was not from what must be the agony of his wound. 'You never did see me, did you, Sophie? I made most sure that you would not. Even now, you see me as an enemy, not a man. But I saw you. And I did love you.'

Did? Something tore. Perhaps her heart. But how could any man, even a soldier — especially a soldier — love a woman who had just shot his men in cold blood? Or not quite cold, perhaps, for she still trembled.

Angus laid his hand on her arm. 'Sophie, you can't trust him.'

'But I do. And I'm the one with the pistol. Dolphie, I'm sorry. Sorry for many things. But you understand why my friend and I need to hurry, why we have the best chance now. I am not injured and have a car and an officer and a letter from a French general. You understand?' She still could not be sure that the wounded boy and the tied-up officer knew what Dolphie's mission was.

'Yes,' said Dolphie, still not mentioning the gas. He reached out to the dog, ruffled his ears.

443

Sophie felt tears prickle. Did Dolphie have dogs, back on his estates? Of course he did.

'Do I have your word that you won't reach for your pistol till our car is out of sight?'

'I will need to hold my pistol to keep the Korporal in line.'

'I have your word you won't use it to stop us?'

Dolphie clicked his heels together. 'You do.' Then, as she turned to the car, 'Sophie.'

'Yes.'

'The reason you are here, you think you may achieve it?'

Ah, she thought. So his men did not know what Dolphie had been trying to do. At least she had not killed a man attempting mercy. A small crumb to succour her in the nights ahead.

'Yes.'

'You think it may help bring peace? Shorten the war?'

She considered, then shook her head. 'No. Saving lives today might make the war longer. But this is what I think I should do.'

His smile was grim, but still a smile. 'I don't think you are lying now.'

'No. Goodbye, Dolphie. Good luck. Give my love to Hannelore. I am sorry. I cannot tell you how sorry I am, and for how much. I hope … I hope we meet again, when this is all over. I hope you still *want* to meet me.'

Dolphie bowed. It looked strange, with his muddy, bloody uniform. 'I will want to see you. Will always want to see you. And Hannelore will wish to see you too.' He glanced at Angus and back at Sophie. 'And I wish you happiness. Always.'

Her heart wrenched again. But he was an enemy and the Korporal was alive and must be guarded till they left. And Angus needed her. And …

And this was war. Not love. 'Take care, Dolphie. Try to find an aid post, even an English one.'

Dolphie reached down and picked up one of the rifles. She felt a faint prickle between her shoulder blades as she seated herself in the front passenger seat. Charlie leaped unsteadily onto her lap, then gazed at the roast chicken impaled on the steering wheel. She tossed it to him absently, heard him crunch it. Angus already had the motor cranked. He grabbed the crank, tossed it onto the back seat, then dived into the driver's seat. The car lurched into first gear. 'I reckon we have ten seconds before he changes his mind.'

The car moved like a startled horse. Angus swerved back and forth so the shots would miss them.

But they never came.

They were going to make it. Warn hundreds, at least, to take cover. Recompense, maybe, for the life she had just taken. Did lives saved really compensate for murder you had done?

They drove into the sunrise, more yellow now than pink, Charlie snuffling as he slept on her lap, dreaming perhaps of more chicken. She had never seen a sunrise like it. A battlefield sunrise, she thought, made of the smoke of guns and bodies shattered till they were suspended in the air. Did every wind carry small drops of death now? Death that she had added to.

'There's a road ahead.' Angus swerved the car across the rutted paddocks towards it, or rather towards the people who lined it, sitting, not walking. Not talking either. A hundred of them, two hundred perhaps.

Angus sounded the horn. A few moved, just enough to get the car onto the road. But still most of them sat unmoving.

Sophie found the voice she had lost hours, miles, a lifetime ago. 'Why are they here? Why are they sitting like this?'

'They probably have nowhere to go. Villages are bombed every night. Soldiers behind. Soldiers ahead. So they sit.'

Black mud, white faces. Adult eyes that glanced up in fear at the sound of their engine, then looked back down. Children who sheltered their faces in their mothers' aprons, their fathers' coats, and didn't even look their way.

Charlie still hadn't managed to eat the cheese or bread, now packed in Sophie's case. How far would bread and cheese stretch among so many? Perhaps if they brought the food out, people would be injured fighting for it.

Perhaps if they stopped, not only the food would be taken.

'Keep going,' she said stiffly, then realised she didn't have to. This was not new to him.

'Welcome to Flanders,' he said. 'The real Flanders.' There had been no border posts. Not in wartime.

'I knew it was bad.' Was that her voice? 'Knew all this. It's not the same as seeing it.'

'Or living it. Do you think any of the men who give the orders — the real orders, back in London or Berlin — do you think they have ever faced this? That they could keep going if they did?'

'Yes,' said Sophie flatly.

Angus gave a skeleton's grin. 'I think you're right.'

They were past the refugees now. They drove along curiously empty roads, a dead land on either side, two trucks ahead and a barricade across the road. Angus slowed down, then handed two Belgian soldiers his pass. Charlie peered at them curiously, his nose pressed to the glass. The soldiers saluted, stared at Charlie, and waved them on.

Sophie glanced back at them. 'I wonder what they think I'm doing here. And Charlie.'

'A nurse. A VAD.'

'Well, I was, sort of.'

'I think I recognise where we are now.' The shadows were back in his voice. 'Ypres hasn't changed much in two years. Nothing but mud and water then. No more now. We'll come to buildings soon.' He hesitated. 'Can you hear something?'

'I don't know. Like birds? Seagulls?'

'Seagulls here? Vultures, maybe. You'd need a thousand seagulls to make a sound like that.'

This was flat land. Endless land. But they were cresting a small rise, of sorts. On the top Angus stopped the car. They stared at the scene before them.

It was another world.

The sound that they had been listening to was screaming.

No buildings. No trenches either. Barbed wire in giant tangles.

Mud. Mud that stretched down this hill and up the other. Mud that moved. Men with eyeless faces; more men, motionless, who looked like mud. Mud that might be men. Men who heaved and gasped. Men who mostly lay and screamed.

The gas.

She was too late.

Charlie whined, his paws against the window.

One hour late? Four? Had the date '13' meant the night of the 12th, so the gas would take effect on the morning of the 13th, not that the attack would take place on the 13th, as she had thought? It didn't matter. Nor did 'what ifs'.

'Sophie, don't look.'

She thought Angus reached for her, but she had slid out of the car before he could hold her back. 'I have to look. Don't let Charlie out.'

She ran to one of the men. His screaming stopped as he tried to look up. The movement made him shriek again. She could see the yellow blisters under the brown mud. He lurched away from her on his knees then began to vomit, yellow muck tinged with red. She tried to hold him, touch him, but he wrenched away from her as though any touch burned, and retched again.

She could still hear the sheep screaming too.

She looked up as Angus joined her. Up on the hill Charlie peered from the car, too scared to venture further. 'It's happened already,' she whispered. Had Hannelore learned of this from Dolphie, or he from her?

The weapon that would end the war — unless both sides had it.

She was too late. Dolphie would have been too late. And now the Allies would use this weapon too.

If horror could have ended the war, it would have done so years ago. This only added another level to its hell.

The man at her feet clawed at his throat. She had seen doctors open the throat to let air past scars and burning; they used rubber tubes too. No tubes here. No knowledge of how to do it if she had them.

A motor rumbled behind her. She looked around. It was a truck, a baker's van perhaps, a clumsy red cross on one side. The doors opened. Two women in grey overalls got out, their heads wrapped in white veils with red crosses on them, tied up like scarves. Not army nurses, not even Red Cross or VADs, possibly not officially qualified at all. But here.

A woman opened the van doors, drew out a stretcher. 'You here to help?' she called.

'I ... I hoped to ...'

'Your car won't be much use in this mud. Watch where you walk. It's some new stuff — gas at first then it drips to the ground. Those oily patches will burn you alive. One of the girls slid and landed in some last night. She's still screaming.' The voice was matter-of-fact.

Sophie stared around. 'Will they send more of it?' It could be nearly on them now.

'If they do, we'll know it. This stuff comes in shells. If you hear a shell coming, get back in that car and drive. Fast. Careful where you put your hands too.'

She and the other woman trod across the mud, using a strip of leather so their hands didn't touch what might be remnants of the gas on the men's skin, the stretcher between them. They put it down and rolled one of the screaming men onto it. His shrieks grew wilder as his back touched the hessian. Sophie watched as one woman held the man while the other strapped him down.

She kneeled down in the mud — the muddy mud, not the oily mud — frantically thinking how they might help the man in front of her. He was young, younger than Angus, brown hair — no, mud hair. His eyes looked stuck together. Could she and Angus carry him to the car without a stretcher? How far away was the aid post? An hour's drive? A day?

'Choking,' the young man whispered.

'Sophie, I need to get you away from here.'

'No. We came to help.'

'Very well.' She wanted to cry at the trust, the acceptance in his voice.

'All we can do is get them to an aid post,' he said as another van drew up behind them.

'Knew we hadn't got them all last night,' said a third woman's voice. 'Damn the darkness. Just what the poor blighters need. Exposure too. Stinkers, I think there's a live one over there … What the blazes? It's Soapy! Soapy Higgs, what in all the world are you doing here?'

'Dodders! I —' Another not-coincidence. For surely the call had gone all down the line to every aid post for every available ambulance to come here.

She couldn't tell Dodders why she was there. Couldn't tell anyone until the Allies began to use the gas too. For Dolphie's sake, for Hannelore's, for her own and Angus's, she could not betray what was now a military secret.

In a few days, a few weeks, Germans would be suffering like this too.

Instead she said, 'When did this happen?' Behind her she was vaguely conscious that Angus was taking the other end of a stretcher with Dodders's companion, carrying a screaming man to their van.

'They say it came in last night. We were far down the line — only got here an hour or so ago. Never seen stuff like it. Nothing like the other gas. Got to get 'em before they choke. These chaps may look bad now, but they'll get worse. The doctors don't know why yet — maybe their lungs dissolve, maybe the blisters just stop 'em breathing. We just don't know.' Dodders was pulling out another stretcher as she spoke. 'It's bad, Soapy. Look, can you take the other end?'

'Yes.'

'Need everyone we can get. Four of us down with septicaemia this month alone.'

Dodders seemed too focused on the job to query Sophie further. How much sleep had she had in the past few days? Any? How long could she keep going?

As long as she has to, thought Sophie.

Already the first two women had carried the man to their truck and were heading back for another. Another man rose from the mud, his fingers tearing at his eyes, his breath rasping, and stumbled towards them with desperate hope. Angus ran to help him, hauling him on his shoulders without a stretcher. Sophie hoped desperately that any residue of the gas would not soak through his uniform, onto his skin.

An hour, perhaps, passed before the van was full. Another van arrived, then a truck, a French bullock cart, the stoic, thin-ribbed animals no longer even nervous at the smell of blood, the screams. Sophie glanced at their car, but there was no sign of Charlie. He must be sleeping — or hiding from the strangeness — on the seat.

The sun rose. Angus touched her arm lightly. His face was white, his uniform stained with soot and blood and mud, but at least he seemed unhurt. 'I think that's the last of them. Sophie, we've done all we can. I'll get you back to Paris.'

Sophie looked at the bodies in the truck; at the dead bodies in the mud that someone, some time, might deal with; at Dodders's white, determined face. She shook her head, then headed to the car and grabbed her bag from the back seat. Charlie slipped down, whimpering. He pressed against her legs. 'I'm staying.' She glanced at Charlie's black furry head. 'Charlie and I are staying.'

Angus gazed around at the wisps of green cloud that still hovered in the trenches, the shattered trees, the tangles of barbed wire. 'Sophie, you can't.'

'I can. I am. This happened because I wasn't fast enough.' I killed a man to get here, she thought. Killed him for nothing. Two more men died because of my arrogance, thinking I could change a war. They might have been cruel men, but perhaps war had stripped their humanity. Perhaps, if they'd survived, they might have regained it, led good, uneventful lives. I wounded another man, left Dolphie helpless and betrayed among the enemy. And Angus ... 'I need to help. Now.'

'I'm not leaving you here.'

'If you don't, you'll be a deserter. Don't do that to either of us. Please, darling Angus, please, don't let them think you have deserted. Tell Monsieur le Général "Merci" from me, that I will indeed have lunch with him when the war is over. Tell him what I am doing now, and why I must be here, not there. I'll be as safe as anyone can be here, with Dodders and Charlie.'

Angus glanced down at Charlie, who was yawning, carefully not looking at bodies, or at Dodders securing the last of the stretchers in the van. 'Charlie will defect to the first person who offers him a biscuit.'

'Charlie is a survivor. So am I. So are you. I'll write as soon as I can, let you know where I am.' She reached up on tiptoe and kissed his lips. 'Thank you,' she added. 'We did our best. Now, go.'

'I love you. And I'm coming back for you.'

'Yes, of course you are, but you must get back now.'

She knew he wouldn't leave while she still watched him. Oh, dear God, she prayed, I can face almost anything, but not Angus shot as a deserter for me. Please keep him safe. Please. She shoved her bag into the front of Dodders's van, then opened the door for Charlie to jump in there too.

Was this new weapon the end of the war, the end of all war, or the beginning of much worse? It didn't matter now.

Behind her she heard the crank of the car's starter lever again. By the time Dodders was at the driver's seat of her van, Angus had gone.

Chapter 59

*Please pass on my love to Sophie. If I survive this, I will tell her
who I am, and why. I think, I hope, that she is one of the few who
may understand, as you do, my dear friend. I love you both.*

Miss Lily to the Dowager Duchess of Wooten, 1917

The house had once been fine: three storeys, broad stairs, a pair
of stone lions either side. Now one lion had lost a paw and the
other was a crumbled ruin no one had thought to take away.
The top floor was blackened, the windows like empty eyes, but
when Sophie climbed the stairway, Charlie panting at her heels,
she found the roof still functioned and the building was sound.
The third-floor windows could be boarded up.

One army, several armies, had camped in the rooms below.
At first perhaps there had been furniture, beds, officers and their
servants. Now the furniture was gone and the floors pimpled
with dried excrement. Whoever had been there in the last few
months had been too weary, wounded, sick, scared or mad to
even go outside — perhaps all at the same time.

Hills rose around the horizon, each eerily the same: a dead
tree on one hill, three on another, black against pale blue sky.
But around the house a French village that still functioned, or
part of a village, at least: a café next door serving beer and soup
and sawdust bread, the bakery that baked the bread, half a dozen
houses. The residents either had refused to leave, even when the
rest of the village was shelled, or had come back.

Buying houses was easy in wartime. Possibly not quite legal:
there was no notary to witness the deal. It was even possible that
Monsieur who took her money was not the owner, although the

flat-faced woman in the café seemed to know him and the baker too.

Perhaps they were all part of a family of scoundrels, squatters who had moved in and would move out again, taking the café and bakery profits and Sophie's money with them.

But the money wasn't much, not to her or her father. It cost more to have beds, tables, chamber pots brought by train and then by cart. The sullen locals were willing to scrub, whitewash and cook in return for pitifully few francs. As the days went by and the house assumed its function as a shelter for humans once again, Sophie grew to understand that the sullenness was shock, similar to hers.

By the end of a fortnight they had begun to exchange smiles.

Her allowance did not stretch to wages. She borrowed Madame-of-the-café's bicycle and cycled through three villages, leaving Charlie sleeping in a basket by Madame's fire, hoping she had judged the noise correctly and that she was cycling away from battle, not towards it — and sent a telegram to her father.

Have bought house for hospital for gas patients France stop urgently need unlimited allowance stop please stop things are bad here stop

As an afterthought, she added: *I am safe stop your loving daughter Sophie stop*

Details might be censored. She sent another telegram to Angus, care of French General Staff, saying briefly where she was and why, and then a third to get to Wooten faster than the letter she had already sent. Unbearably tired, she cycled back, lying without sleeping on a blanket on bare scrubbed boards.

The smell of shit still lingered.

Two days later the beds still hadn't arrived. A telegram had, brought by a small boy with black hair and eyes and a startlingly white shirt. Somewhere a mother had boiled that shirt, starched it and ironed it, perhaps bought him the bicycle, for it was smaller than Madame's, the wheels so small that even his short legs were hunched up around his ears as he rode.

He waited while she read it, till she realised he wanted to be paid and handed him some francs. He grinned, with teeth as white as his shirt, and wheeled away.

Am most worried stop insist return England at once stop your father stop

She called the boy back — he was riding in circles between the houses, as though he had nothing more to do in this war-eroded land than make patterns in the gravel with his wheels. She scribbled a few words on the back of a ticket while he threw a stick for the delighted Charlie.

Insistence futile stop I stay allowance or not stop love Sophie stop

'What is your name?'

'Jean-Marie, mademoiselle. What is your dog called?'

'Charlie.'

He considered. 'That is a silly name.'

'He's a silly dog.'

The boy looked at her, affronted. 'He is the most beautiful dog!'

'Hfff,' said Charlie, sitting at the boy's feet and drooling on his stick. It had been impossible to find meat to feed him, but he was thriving on potato stew.

Sophie handed Jean-Marie more francs. 'Please take this to the telegraph office. If you can take more messages for me, I'll pay you again.'

'May I take Char-lee,' he stumbled over the name, 'to the telegraph office too?'

She managed her first smile in days at that. 'If he wants to go.'

She watched Charlie bound off joyously beside the bicycle.

Another two nights sleeping on the floor, with Charlie for warmth; the sky lit with blooms of red, her dreams filled with red too, and with burning blistered faces. She woke gasping, and didn't try to sleep again.

The next day brought a procession.

A motorcar, red with a canvas roof; behind it Jean-Marie pedalling frantically to keep up, his eyes fixed on the car in ecstasy. Charlie galloped off towards him. Behind Jean-Marie and his bicycle plodded two teams of bullocks dragging wagons, laden with what might be furniture. Possibly hers.

Sophie tried to push her hair back into its pins, then descended the shattered stairs to meet them.

The first to arrive was the car. The driver was small, French, all bows and pomaded hair. He was Monsieur Brun, the French agent for Higgs's Corned Beef; he was at her service. Here was a telegram from her bon Papa.

Sophie glanced down.

Hope soon come to senses stop funds available stop telegraph if you need more stop set up and find manager that is how you do business stop with love your father stop

Find a manager? As likely to find a pastry chef …

Monsieur Brun, the agent, bowed. He was hers to command, every fourth Thursday. Funds could be transferred through his office. Whatever was needed he could arrange.

Sophie doubted it. But this was a start.

Chapter 60

France
December 1917
Dear Duchess,

It was good to get your letter. I am glad you do not think
I am deserting you and Wooten. There is so much to do here.
In a strange way I feel more alive than I ever have before, despite
the death around me. It is as if I have slipped back into the skin
that was so briefly mine as we turned the Abbey into a hospital.
I am my father's daughter, though it has taken a war for us both
to see it. I am an indifferent nurse, an adequate organiser, but a
magnificent creator of hospitals where none existed before. What I
am doing is just beginning, for so much must be done. Does it seem
desperately self-centred to say I have at last acknowledged my true
self amidst so much horror and tragedy?

This new hospital is up and running. At first we mostly took
victims of the mustard gas, but those who might survive need months
or even years to recover, and are usually shipped back to England
as soon as they have been stabilised. 'Stabilised' here means 'they
probably won't die before they get across the Channel'.

It seems the mustard gas was not the weapon that would end
the war after all. Mustard gas hasn't even shortened it by two
feet six inches. It floats here and there and no one can predict
it, except to know that afterwards men will be screaming, dying
or in pain for what is left of their lives. This makes it a far less
useful weapon than I feared, and so many hoped. It takes about
twelve hours for it to take full effect, which makes it particularly
horrible. Or maybe it doesn't. Is it better to know you have, in
effect, been killed, even though you are still standing, or to die
at once? At any rate, the death — or life — is so bad that men

have to be strapped to their beds screaming, or they tear out their eyes and tongues.

Should I not be writing to you of such things? I apologise if I should not. But I believe you will both understand, and forgive, and know how much solace it is to share what sometimes cannot be borne, but must be, even if you spare three minutes to hide in the linen cupboard to cry.

Despite that last sentence, I am well, though I'm writing this under half a ceiling — the house was bombed last night, or rather the café next door was, and we got the aftershocks. One of the shock cases started screaming; the poor man is screaming still every time someone so much as coughs. One of our VADs has taken him down to that so-useful linen cupboard to help her roll bandages. The other men can't hear him as much down there, and she says he's calmer when he has something to do with his hands.

The war circles us. One week our side is closer; the next week it's the Huns. I wish someone would take both away and teach them how to throw a cricket ball, or whatever they do to get soldiers to hit the targets they're aiming at, not us. I suspect last night's bomb was from the Americans, but as it didn't come labelled 'A gift from Uncle Sam' we remain in ignorance of exactly who our benefactor was.

A ten-year-old boy called Jean-Marie is my liaison officer, aided by what I had thought was my dog, but he has deserted me for a small boy who will throw sticks. Jean-Marie rides his bicycle to the aid stations whenever needed to tell them how many we have to pick up. I try to tell myself the dog is guarding him, though Charlie's only talent seems to be catching those sticks.

One day, of course, Jean-Marie will be shot, and that will be my fault. But for now, well, he is saving lives and, better still, he knows it. And perhaps the war will even end with one ten-year-old boy still alive.

So far here we have the local village doctor, Monsieur le Docteur Armoire, who is too old for the army but manages to give us an hour of help and instruction a day; two English VADs, Sylvia and Sloggers, and dear Dodders and the others who bring the cases in their ambulances and now sleep here too, to help when things get bad; Madame Fuchon who cooks and cleans, with the help of her sister's cousin's aunt (no, not really, but a relationship nearly as complex); our small Jean-Marie and Mademoiselle Marie, whom I found one morning changing the bandages of a new patient, a Frenchman judging by his uniform. He died that afternoon — did I tell you they bring the hopeless cases here as well? At least they die surrounded by smiles and clean floors. We are careful about both.

I thought Mademoiselle would leave then too; I think she knew him, because she sat by his body all afternoon. But when the cart came she didn't follow it to the funeral. By suppertime she was checking the dressings as though she had always been here.

We also have Jean-Marie's mother, who does our washing in a copper fuelled by who knows what. Dried bullock manure, I think, from the smell. Our aprons are stained but boiled, and so are we, from the constant steam of the sterilisers, although we at least use coal, not manure. Or the merchant promised it was coal. It looks more like dust.

We all share the three staff beds between us — no point in our having a bed each when we have to sleep in shifts, and anyway, we're hardly in them. I do sleep. Exhaustion is a wonderful drug. There are dreams, of course, but we all have dreams.

Except Dodders, maybe. Did I tell you she brought her motorbike to Flanders and now here to France? Perfectly useless, as some vital part is broken, but it shares our bedroom, oil and all. I was talking to Sylvia last night, said Dodders was a miracle; she alone never has to force a smile. Sylvia said it was because for her the men don't matter. She would cry if they were motorbikes. Instead they are simply a cause, like votes for women or the old-age pension. You don't cry for them, you fight.

Is she right? I don't know. Just thank God for Dodders and Sylvia and Mademoiselle Marie, and if anything happens to Jean-Marie ...

Forgive me once again for writing to you like this. It is strange, but you are now my oldest friend — in both senses of the word *'oldest'. They would be so impressed back home — 'my friend the dowager duchess'.*

I'd like to tell Miss Lily that I have a definite diagnosis for genuine shell shock now: a man who is not interested in THAT has shell shock. All her training, and none of it useful here. I suppose she is still vanished? I wrote to her via Shillings last week — or maybe it was last month. But of course, no reply.

Poor Miss Lily. Charm is no weapon against war, not this kind of war. We are all essentially powerless. No, that's not true. We all have power over small things, and I suppose those who own munitions factories, the Kruppses and the Schneiders, have the power to make more money. My father too, probably, though at least he is feeding people, not killing them.

May I make one request, Your Grace? I expected a letter from Captain McIntyre, but one hasn't arrived yet, and I am worried. The mail from here is so uncertain, so he may write to Wooten. If a letter arrives, could you telephone Mr Slithersole? He will make sure it is couriered safely to me. Mr Slithersole assures me that Captain McIntyre's name has not been on the casualty lists, but I am still most concerned, especially as he may be under French command and so may be missed by both sets of list-makers.

Thank you for reading about my glooms, Your Grace, and thank you for sending me your love. I return you mine, with my most grateful thanks,
    Sophie

'Mademoiselle?' Sophie looked up from writing her letter at the kitchen table. There was too much she could not say to the duchess, nor to anyone else: the guilt at the useless deaths caused by Sophie Higgs; the unknown fates of Angus and Dolphie, her fault as well; the knowledge that saving lives — any number of lives — did not lessen the crime of taking others.

'Oui, Jean-Marie?' The boy danced beside her holding the bucket for the dirty dressings. Charlie peered wistfully from the doorway, banned from the wards. Even a year ago she would have been shocked that a child might see the wounds beneath the bandages; horrified at the thought of sending a ten-year-old bicycling through a war.

'Mademoiselle, why are you beautiful?'

She stared at him. Her hair had not been washed for a week, and that had been six scrubs with carbolic soap to remove lice; her dress was fouled with substances it was best to forget; her soul stained with the deaths of those she had killed, or caused to be killed; and all that for nothing, except, perhaps, to bring her here, where she could do a little good amidst the horror. 'I'm glad you think I am beautiful, Jean-Marie,' she replied at last.

He looked at her critically. 'I do not think you are really beautiful,' he said with a child's candour. 'Your hair should not be messy, no? And your hands?' He shrugged.

That was fair. 'Then why do you ask?'

He shrugged. 'The men do not watch the other mesdemoiselles as they do you. Sometimes they smile at you. It is the only time the men smile, I think. Sometimes I too have a feeling you are beautiful, mademoiselle, just like the men do.'

Sophie looked at him helplessly. What could she tell a child? Her sway, her walk, her glances, the set of her shoulders, how she could seem to smile up at a man even if he was lying in pain below her?

'I was taught how to look at people and smile,' she compromised at last. 'That can make you look beautiful, even if you aren't.'

He accepted that. 'Mademoiselle, I forgot. I came to give you this.'

He held out a crumpled envelope. 'A telegram,' he said importantly. He watched as she opened the envelope. 'May I read it, mademoiselle?'

'You do not read private telegrams, Jean-Marie.'

Saw Captain McIntyre's name listed missing in action stop thought you should know am so sorry stop thank you for your kindness stop love Emily stop

Her body had vanished. No. She looked at her hand holding the telegram and saw that it was still there. Her next thought was, How can I bear this? An almost-wish that he were dead, so she could mourn. One by one they disappear, she thought.

'Missing' could mean so many things. Taken prisoner; injured in some small private hospital less well run than hers, where a man might lie for weeks or even months unaccounted for. It might also mean his body was shattered or under mud, that warm strong body she had loved ...

She who had condemned Emily for sending men to their deaths had done the same, and with the same arrogant self-righteousness.

'Mademoiselle, you are not sick?'

'No. No, I am well, Jean-Marie.'

'Le Docteur, he is waiting for you.'

'I will come now.' Nothing to be done, she thought. Only to wait, like women across the world now. Easier to wait when there was work to do.

'Mademoiselle, may I see the maggots again today?'

'The what?'

'Dr Armoire's maggots,' he said. 'I like to see them wriggle, Mademoiselle, and how they get fat ...'

For a moment she felt dizzy. She had seen maggot-infested wounds, of course; any man who had been lying on the field for more than a couple of days risked having his wounds infested. But they worked so hard to keep the wounds here clean ...

Was Angus lying wounded somewhere, crawling with maggots?

'Jean-Marie, I want you to take a message for me. Could you ask your maman if she knows a reliable woman who can do darning? We will pay, of course,' she added.

'Can I ask her after I have seen the maggots?'

'No,' said Sophie. 'No maggots today.'

Dr Armoire was a small man, his shrunken face sunken in on itself, a moustache hanging above long, yellow teeth.

His patient was a young English lieutenant. He'd been blown up in a mortar attack and had concussion; all you could do for that was keep the patient quiet and still. Worse were the chunks of flesh blown away all along his left side — face, arms, torso, legs. Miraculously he had no broken limbs, no internal injuries. Weirdly his right side had been almost untouched.

One eye watched the doctor, then blinked towards Sophie. The right corner of the mouth edged up.

Jean-Marie is right, she thought with a distant part of her mind. They do smile, even in agony.

Usually she left the doctor to his work. He did not like the 'mesdemoiselles' — women who organised and gave orders, without even the decency to become nuns and wear the veil, with a bishop to oversee them. He was also a man of sense, who saw that the work they were doing was vital. But he made no secret that this was an alliance of necessity.

'Monsieur le Docteur, a million pardons ... I heard that perhaps we are having a problem with,' she lowered her voice, 'maggots.'

'A problem, mademoiselle? On the contrary, the maggots are most useful.' The long teeth peered out from under the moustache in what must be a smile. He held out the box he carried. Small white creatures wriggled on a lump of chicken meat.

At least, Sophie hoped it was chicken.

'The maggots eat the dead flesh. When flesh rots you get gangrene. Not with maggots, mademoiselle. They eat the dead flesh and leave the wound clean.'

But maggots are dirty! she wanted to say. Yet he was a doctor, their only doctor. And, she grasped suddenly, this might be the reason why so many of their patients recovered, even from serious wounds.

'They are only for the experienced to use, of course, mademoiselle.' He watched her carefully in case she or any of the other 'girls' might take a fancy to applying them. 'When a maggot has eaten the dead flesh it starts on the living ...'

Sophie glanced at the man on the bed, thankful he showed no signs of understanding French.

'But I do not permit that, of course. And they must be removed before they grow too big. Which is why I bring my own.' He nodded again at the small box. He shrugged. 'Maggots at least we have no shortage of, eh, mademoiselle? No laudanum, no rose water, no leeches ... but plenty of maggots.'

She didn't want to ask about the leeches.

'But look.' Monsieur le Docteur pointed to the red flesh of the patient's arm. The skin that remained was still puffy, but there was no sign of putrefaction, no smell of gangrene. There was even a faint trace of new tissue growing at the edges of the wound.

'This one I think will live.' Monsieur le Docteur spoke with enormous satisfaction.

As well he might, thought Sophie. We've had no gangrene cases here for weeks. How many wounds became gangrenous at Wooten, despite the English doctor?

'Thank you, monsieur.' She smiled at the patient, then hesitated. 'Monsieur le Docteur ... would you mind if the boy Jean-Marie sees your maggots before you go? I know you are busy, overburdened. But he is a good boy.'

Monsieur le Docteur seemed to find nothing odd in regarding a display of maggots as a gift, either because he held them in such high repute or because he remembered his own childhood almost a century before.

Jean-Marie would have his treat.

A major was waiting for her in the kitchen when she finished her rounds the next morning, trying not to think of Angus, trying to resist the urge to order a car and attempt to search, to find the général and ask for answers. Angus was a captain, decorated with the country's highest honour. If he could be found, he would be found, and not by Sophie Higgs.

The kitchen was the only room in the house that had no beds in it. The major stood up as she entered.

'I'm sorry, I hope you haven't been waiting long. Jean-Marie only just remembered to give me the message.'

'He appeared to be the only one on duty.' He nodded to her abruptly. 'Major Commington, British Medical Corps.'

'Miss Sophie Higgs. I am pleased to meet you, Major Commington.' She had to work on the smile today. 'And we are all on duty — either on duty or asleep. But as you can see, this house was never designed as a hospital. We have no waiting rooms or reception rooms.'

'Nor any trained personnel either, I gather, Miss Higgs.'

'We are all trained, Major.' She tried to make her tone both professional and charming. 'All of us have worked with the wounded for over three years. We also have the good Dr Armoire.'

'A French leech merchant, I'm told. A job done badly does not get any better for being done often. Miss Higgs, it has come to our attention that you have malingerers here.'

'I'm sorry, I don't understand.'

'We have received eight notifications of shell shock from your establishment in the past week. Miss Higgs, apparently you do not realise that the War Office no longer recognises shell shock as a medical condition. It is simply another term for cowardice or lack of moral fibre.'

She closed her eyes for a second. I have two choices, she thought. I can tell him to get out — out of my house, out of our lives. And then I shall find the Military Police inspecting the hospital every few days, hauling men out screaming and trembling ...

She looked up at him and smiled with every ounce of art she had, saw the automatic smile flick back. She fought to dredge up charm, to keep her voice soft. 'It is so hard to keep up with regulations, isn't it, Major Commington? Especially for a woman.'

He gave a pleased huff. 'Yes, indeed, Miss Higgs.'

'You must be so tired of trying to organise so many unofficial hospitals.'

'If you only knew, Miss Higgs.'

Sophie smiled at him again. 'I will do my best not to add to your headaches, Major. From now you will find no more shell shock cases here.'

He bowed. 'Thank you, Miss Higgs.'

Was Angus in some ward, too numb to even speak his own name, the horror of what he had seen that morning of the first mustard-gas attack too much for him to bear? Or had he finally refused to serve, unable to carry on, even as liaison to the général? They wouldn't court-martial a VC, but they could shoot him and say it had been enemy fire, say he was missing, announcing the death long after his family could find out the truth.

No. She wouldn't believe that. He was alive. He must be.

She waited till she heard the clank of the crank as the major's driver started his staff car, then went to find Dodders, who was scrubbing chamber pots in the scullery.

'What's up, old thing?'

'We need a second hospital. And a benign army doctor, who will put "high blood pressure" instead of "shell shock" on medical certificates.'

Dodders nodded, clearly thinking of something else. 'Soapy, you'd better come see this.'

'This' was their back courtyard, full of weeds, broken furniture ... and men in French uniforms. Among them were skeletal children, women with dusty skirts and desperate eyes. As she looked through the window, she saw Madame Fuchon bring out a big black pot of stew, holding it up so that each person could drink a ladleful.

It was surprisingly orderly, terrifyingly silent.

'This is where the potatoes have been going,' said Dodders.

The potatoes came with the corned beef, carrots and cabbage sent weekly by Mr Slithersole. War-ploughed France could hardly feed its own, much less the various armies fighting — and eating — on its fields. Mr Slithersole's supplies came from across the Empire, including Canada, closer than Australia for perishables. Neither France nor England produced enough food to feed her people now. The huge pre-war harvests had become meagre, planted and harvested by women and old men with no machinery or horses to help. But more ships were making their way across the Atlantic: American and Australian. A shipload of flour, potatoes, corned beef could reach them in three weeks ... Sophie almost smiled at the heresy of planning to use other than Higgs's corned beef.

Sophie nodded. 'I'll deal with it.'

'You always do, old thing,' said Dodders.

Sophie waited in the kitchen until Madame had come in with her empty pot. 'Madame, what is this, please?'

Madame looked at her steadily. 'These men, they are soldiers of France, mademoiselle. When they can no longer fight they are let go, to find their way home, and starve while they are doing it. The others,' she shrugged, 'some have a roof, but no food. Others have neither food nor roof. Should I let them go hungry, mademoiselle, while we have food?'

If Angus were staggering dazed in France or Belgium, Sophie hoped he'd find a haven that might feed him too.

'We will feed them,' she promised softly. 'Let them all come.'

Chapter 61

Dear Sophie,

Dodders wrote to her brother about your hospitals. Her brother was at school with mine, and he passed the story on to me as an example of English pluck. I didn't let on you are Australian or maybe New Zealander like your dad. Well done, old girl. Reckon you can organise supplies yourself, but just you remember you don't HAVE to do it all yourself, and it won't take me more than two shakes of a dog's tail to get our suppliers to send stuff your way too.

We've got a baker's dozen of new helpers this month. I'm the only one who started who's still here, and looks like I'll be the only one to finish the war here too — whenever that may be — mostly because dealing with the supply side I don't get my hands wet and cracked and infected like the others. A year on and three months off to recover seem to be what our girls can manage. Midge is in Dover, off looking after her brother, Doug — got his leg blown off. Human beings are designed wrong, in my opinion. We should have fewer appendages to get shot at. Especially men.

Anne writes that she is recovering well from the wounds she recieved when the shell got her. Wish I could get back to see her, but her ma is turning out to be a brick. Thought she'd have pink kittens about a daughter with a scarred face, because she was in a right dither about one with big feet and spots. But it seems a daughter shot up by the Hun isn't the same as one who isn't a fairy princess to be presented during the season. I'll never understand the upper crust. I miss her and Midge more than I can say.

Speaking of crusts, don't you go forgetting to eat either. Keep up your own strength, girl. I speak from experience. It's right easy to get so caught up feeding others you end up looking like a match with the wood shaved off, and about as much use.

One day this war will end and there'll be good times again. I plan to get a motorbike like Dodders's.

Your loving friend,
Ethel

Time had vanished in routine after Alison's death. Now it returned. Every second was pushed to make twenty. Here, in the midst of carnage, Sophie had never felt more alive.

The village café became a canteen, with soup and bread for all. The church became a hostel — Monsieur le Curé had vanished as a chaplain to the army — with two rooms, one for men and the other for women and children, presided over by two nuns with faces as white as their wimples, who kept decency and order. After his initial reluctance, Sophie's father's funds now appeared limited only by her energy to use them.

Worry about Angus had become a small burning sore. She worked, and bore it.

By March she had two hospitals, five canteens and four refugee hostels operating, and an alliance with two American women. They coordinated relief parcels sent from the United States and originally left in a heap on the dock to rot, but now ferried in vans driven by more trousered women up to Belgium from the south of France.

Life was made up of sandwiches of duty: making lists, added to ordering supplies, waiting endlessly for telephone calls to be put through at Monsieur the Stationmaster's, while back in England the dowager duchess had the telephone line extended to her bed, and was calling every friend for volunteers and help.

Men died in her hospitals. They saved many too. They saved women and children who might have starved, or been driven by desperation to acts they would not be able to face if — when — peace returned.

In odd moments between anguish and exhaustion, and in the three seconds before falling over the wall into a few short hours of sleep, Sophie felt the deepest fulfilment she had ever known.

> *The Laurels, Sussex*
> *15 April 1918*
> *Dear Sophie,*
> *I have heard from Her Grace that you have opened not one*
> *but two hospitals in France, and canteens and hostels for refugees*
> *too. I wish you to know that you have whatever support I or my*
> *husband can offer you. I have already organised for six chests*
> *of woollen children's garments to be sent to your Mr Slithersole.*
> *He assures me that whatever one sends to him will find its way*
> *to wherever you need it most. Our St Anne's Ladies' Guild is*
> *collecting old clothes to make patchwork quilts, and they assure me*
> *there will be fifty finished to send to you next week.*
> *Thank you for your support the last time we met. I do truly*
> *hope we will meet again in happier circumstances.*
> *Yours always,*
> *Mrs Colonel Sevenoaks (Emily)*

Chapter 62

Everything ends — us, the war, the world. Take no notice,
my dear Isobel, I am just tired.

Miss Lily, 11 November 1918

11 NOVEMBER 1918 TO JANUARY 1919

The guns stopped.

For an hour, perhaps, Sophie was unaware of it. A man was dying: one of the cases where moving him would be futile, death would only be hastened, pain increased, the end more agonising in a truck or bullock cart. Sophie sat while he coughed up blood and black tissue that could be lung, throat, tongue, from lips bubbled and blistered like boiling water that had somehow set on a living face.

It was the worst of deaths: a man who needed to die, a body that refused to let him do so.

At last the gasping stopped. His eyes stretched wide, his face set in the last moment of pain. His heart had finally stopped, thought Sophie gratefully, the torn lungs no longer having to strain.

She stood up, went to the window and saw Jean-Marie pedalling hard even though he was hurtling down the hill, waving his slouch hat — tattered, with a bullet hole through the brim, a present from an Australian soldier, and Jean-Marie's proudest possession.

'Mesdemoiselles! L'Armistice! L'Armistice!'

Charlie bounded at his side, his leaps even higher than before. Charlie has been listening to the guns, she thought. Now he does not have to hear them any more.

Dodders was already at the front door. The other women gathered around her. Men called from their beds.

'An armistice? Is it true, miss? Is it really true?'

She shrugged, felt dampness on her face and realised she was crying. No, not her. Her body, shedding tears. For her mind could not believe it. Not yet.

The world was war. It had always been war. It would always be war.

Impossible that the war could be over.

It was.

They went back to work: the pans to be emptied, the dressings to be changed, the bodies to be laid out. Men didn't stop dying because the shelling had ceased. But today when Suzie, Pats, Dodo, Tish, Rachel, Blinkers and all the others stopped their trucks, their vans, their ambulances at the hospital that Sophie had made her headquarters, it was to drink a cup of chicory coffee topped up with brandy.

'We're going home,' said Dodders. She shook her head. 'We made it through. We're going home.'

She cares, thought Sophie. Not just about the men. Perhaps they are all one cause to her. She cares about *us*. Me, Sloggers, Blinkers, Stinkers, Ethel, Sylvia, Marie — the army of unofficial women who had borne so much of the war. And Jean-Marie, of course, too.

Sophie glanced out the window at Jean-Marie, riding his bicycle in tighter and tighter circles about the courtyard, around a heap of the rubble from next door, while Charlie chewed a bone that had been twice boiled for soup.

He has survived, she thought. Jean-Marie at least is safe, and Charlie. Angus, are you safe too?

Eight weeks later Jean-Marie was in bed number eighty-six, Charlie lying on the floor beside him, as though to guard him

471

as he had guarded Sophie that long night over a year ago. The winter winds had teeth of ice. Weakened bodies slumped with influenza. Most of the military patients had been moved now, even the shell shock cases, now that there was no war for the authorities to send them back to. The two worst burns cases had been the last to go; the sister of one had arranged a private ambulance, to spare the men the hours on windswept railway platforms and on a boat's deck.

Perhaps it helped Jean-Marie's mother to have Sophie sit with him, all through that night, as the small body coughed and heaved and tried to breathe.

Dodders brought them cocoa at two am, as well as freshly heated bricks to warm the cot. How did I never see how small he is? marvelled Sophie, cuddling Charlie's warmth as she sipped her cocoa. Perhaps because of his energy, burning so brightly as he pedalled from post to post.

'If there were justice in this world, Jean-Marie would have a medal,' she said to Dodders across the bed.

'If there were justice in this world, none of us would be here.' Dodders's face was white behind the glow of candlelight. 'Get some sleep, old thing. I'll wait with him.'

Wait, thought Sophie. Have we accepted death as inevitable now? But then she realised 'wait' could mean so many things: waiting till morning, till his fever broke, till he turned the corner ... it was she who assumed that waiting was for one thing only.

She would have to get used to peace, and hope. There is still hope, she told herself. Hope for Jean-Marie; hope for Angus, in a prison camp perhaps.

Her hands hurt. Her hands always hurt. Like Dodders's, Marie's and Sylvia's, her hands were always red and cracked, always in water after touching infected wounds, always infected themselves. Never so badly that she had to stop working, like some of the girls, who'd had to go back to England to recover. Her work in administration had given her hands some respite. My body is still strong, she thought, looking down as the boy heaved another breath. But I will have to wear gloves now, if I am to be beautiful. Women over forty must always wear gloves, Miss Lily had once said. A smile can be any age. Hands show the years you've known. How many years ago had that been? Literally a lifetime. She was not the Sophie of five years ago, or even two.

One year of war aged more than ten of peace. My hands are old, thought Sophie. My soul is old too. And then, It has been more than a year since I thought of how I looked.

Despite the plague of influenza, peace, true peace, was coming at last.

Whitehall, London
20 January 1919
My dear Sophie,

Thank you for your last letter. You are the one woman in the world who says, 'I hope your work is going well', assuming that I work for my country as devotedly as any man who wears a uniform. It has been perhaps the hardest duty of this war not to wear one.

My work, and that of others, has resulted in a negotiated peace. I may say to you, as I cannot say to others beyond the cabinet and trusted associates, that this is a bad peace. The terms the French demanded are a continuation of the assault on Germany, meant to keep them powerless, starving and in the gutter. Clemenceau has been merciless, vengeful and deeply short-sighted. Germans will look up and see what might have been, what might still be. The terms signed in that train carriage in the forest of Compiègne merely extend the war, though the actual hostilities may not break out for another decade, or even two. Germany will rise again and rearm.

Do we rearm ourselves too, diverting funds that should be put into peace? Or do we beat our swords into ploughshares and hope that without the deadly competition between empires, Germany will stay content within its negotiated borders? My questions are good ones, my dear, but unfortunately for my job and my country, I have no answers.

I have heard of your work from many quarters, by the way.
You have impressed even Whitehall. 'Excellent work,' one private
secretary said to me last night, 'especially for a colonial.' I can see
your smile at that.

I hope I will see you in person soon too, but, you will note,
I do not urge you home to England, much as I wish to see you.
You will do your duty as long as you are needed, nor would I wish
Sophie Higgs to do otherwise.

Yours always,
James

Jean-Marie did not die. Nor did his mother, who went down with the 'flu herself just as her son recovered. Nor did Stinkers, nor Sloggers, who both went down with it as well.

Dodders died, though. Dodders with her grin and motorbike. She would never peel turnips at the Workmen's Friendship Club again; never chain herself to a parliamentary railing for women's suffrage. Dodders died as she had spent her whole adult life: working for others.

It was only when Sophie went to wake her for her shift that they realised.

Her face looked different. Vacant. Some people looked the same in death. Not Dodders.

Sophie did not get the 'flu. Somehow her body resisted the illness, just as it had refused to let the infections in her hands take hold. Jean-Marie's father did not get the 'flu. He returned, thin and still in uniform, on the day they first let Jean-Marie out of bed, his mother recovering, watching from the window, Charlie leaping at his small master's side.

Jean-Marie's father was a farmer, it seemed, though the farm was now mud and trenches. Charlie would be happy on a farm. There might even be sheep, one day. She would like to see Charlie with sheep.

Money from Australia, from her father, sent the family to the seaside for a month. Perhaps when they returned, they would be a family again: a father, not a stranger; a child, not a messenger from aid post to hospital and back; a wife and mother, not a tirelessly, silently scrubbing woman.

The money would build them a house; would keep them for as long as necessary while a battlefield was turned into a farm again. If only one square of battlefield could be returned to cabbages and sheep instead of mud and poppies, Sophie felt she could leave.

At last, finally, leave the land of war.

Chapter 63

When one reads novels one thinks of beginnings and endings. But really there are very few beginnings or endings that are neat. Even death brings complications to those it leaves behind. Was I happier when I thought the world was simpler? I don't think so. Happiness perhaps is overrated, but maybe fulfilment lasts.

Sophie, 1958

FEBRUARY 1919

The letter came on Sophie's last day in the village, in a pile with accounts and letters for other volunteers and staff, now dispersed in all directions, but all going home. She took them from the postmaster, in his postal uniform now, returned from the front. The nuns and the returned Monsieur le Curé would take over the hospital for as long as it was needed, with help from money from Australia. Already the familiar rooms felt no longer hers.

I have been a visitor here, she thought, just as much as the war. Now it is time to go home.

But where was home? Australia? The Abbey? Even Shillings called to her. No, as James said, this was not the end of war, just the cessation of the guns, for now the true work of war must begin: rebuilding lives and the land. She must find out, somehow, what had happened to Angus, see that the dowager and the Abbey were in good hands, try to discover the fates of Dolphie and Hannelore and Miss Lily, find out what had happened to Angus ... She had written the général a discreet letter, but it had not been answered, had probably never reached him.

She leafed through the pile of letters automatically — then stopped. This writing was familiar. It was as if thinking his name had conjured him up.

Her hands, red, work-roughened hands, shook as she opened it.

Dear Sophie,

This is a difficult letter to write. Perhaps you know that I was posted as 'missing in action'. Even if you don't you must be concerned at not having heard from me for so long.

The reason is that a shell hit the car in which the général and I were travelling, the day after I returned to him. The général was killed. I was badly concussed, and unconscious, they say, for several days, with damage to my foot and hand. I was taken for an American at first in the confusion — we had been about to attend a meeting with the Americans — and then I suppose the paperwork was mislaid with so many influenza cases. It was only in the past week that I discovered that no one, not even my poor parents, had been informed that I am safe.

Now for the hardest part: last night I proposed to a dear girl who nurses here, Miss Glenda Quince, and she has done me the honour of accepting me. Her great-uncle, Sir Alan Crabtree, has an estate, and has offered me the job of agent there. It is all I could want in a job, a challenge, but will mean open spaces and peace too after so many years. Glenda and I shall have the Dower House on the estate, and fill it with children — though Glenda would be indignant if she knew I had told you that. It is not a life I think would content you, but it will suit Glenda and me.

You and I have been through so much together, but I feel you are a woman who will be happy for me. Indeed, you are one of the most magnificent women I have known, and I shall always treasure the time we spent together.

I wish you every possible happiness, and a man worthy of you, and a lifetime of all things that are good.

Your friend, always,
Angus McIntyre

Her first response was almost unbearable relief that he was safe; her second, angry pride: if she had gone back with him that day, there'd have been no Miss Glenda Quince. And then the realisation that perhaps she had done exactly what Emily had implied, over two years earlier: taken a vulnerable man and made him love her, for a time.

Now that Angus was no longer with her that charm had lost its hold, and he had found instead a wife who would share his quiet life, content with family and kitchen, rather than one who would demand to take charge and be part of a wider world. A woman who had killed a man in front of him, used him, risked him, in what had been a fruitless, stupid venture, and then abandoned him to drive back alone. Angus had seen her surface charm at Wooten. How could he want the woman she truly was?

I am not Glenda Quince, she thought, and never could be her.

Nor would there be a lunch at the Ritz with the général. She wiped away unexpected tears — for the old gallant général, she realised, not for Angus. An almost forgotten warrior, who had done his best, and treated her with honour. And if neither he nor she had been able to stop the hell of mustard gas, the attempt had at least led her here, where she could truly be of use.

The général had deserved more. Or perhaps, she thought, he had been given what he might have prayed for: an honourable death at the hands of the enemy.

And Angus? She slipped his letter into her bodice. She felt too many conflicting emotions to read it again now, but eventually she would need to.

Outside, the car drew up. She picked up her single bag: no waiting for footmen to carry out her trunks now.

Soon the village, war, and all that had been in them, would be left behind.

The Ritz's chandeliers shone. Sophie nodded to a porter to take her bag, instructed a maid to ask the concierge to send up a dressmaker — the best dressmaker, she must know the one — tomorrow, not a second before eleven, along with croissants, butter, jam, coffee. And after lunch, someone for hats, for shoes, for stockings.

He would arrange it all. Concierges always did, at places called the Ritz, just as the maid would run a bath, all bubbles and hot water, would bring champagne, steak frites, bread with extra butter, salad.

She sat in her bath: endless glorious hot water. Scrubbed her skin over and over, washed her hair four times before she was sure it was nit-free, and thrust her entire bag of clothes at the astonished chambermaid with instructions to boil them, then throw them away.

She wouldn't. The maid, or perhaps her superior, would either sell them or pass them on to sisters, cousins, aunts. Sophie didn't care, as long as she saw none of them again. She reached for a glass of champagne and realised she couldn't drink, just as she couldn't celebrate the peace.

This wasn't peace. Perhaps it never would be. This was only the absence of war.

She was about to pour the champagne away, then looked at the label, repented and called the maid again. She instructed her to share it with the boot boy, or with whomever she wished. She doubted that the top of the hierarchy of servants — whatever it was in a hotel like this — would allow it, but it would give the girl credit of some sort, and the wine would be enjoyed.

It was as close as she could get to that promised lunch with the général.

She dried herself, changed into her nightdress and tried to sleep.

The bed was soft. The sheets smelled of roses, lavender and sunlight. Somewhere music played, and someone laughed, but not too near, or too loud.

She couldn't sleep. At last she got up, dressed, wrapped herself in coat, scarf and hat, and headed down the stairs.

No Angus. Never Angus. No work to do. Experience told her life would be filled again, somehow, some day, but right now she was a shell, the walking dead, like so many of the men still sheltered in her hospitals.

'Mademoiselle?' She shook her head at the night porter. No, she didn't want a car, or carriage. She wanted …

She didn't know.

She walked. The street lamps were lit again — in these streets, at least. A cluster of soldiers, French, drunk, approached her, laughing; they saw her face, then abruptly turned away, as though they hadn't seen.

She kept on walking.

Dawn grey on the horizon. She turned down alleyways now: no need to keep to the gaslit streets. She was lost, but it didn't matter. When you had money there were cabs, people who would help. Dimly she was aware that her coat was good, if darned; that she could be attacked for money, even raped. On the whole, she thought it was unlikely. She walked too stridently. The shadows would beware.

She was among cafés now, the shutters still up, no smell of chicory coffee or even smoke. If she could find a baker's shop, she might buy a loaf of bread, hot from the oven, eat it slowly, tasting every crumb, as she hadn't had time to do for years.

The shop ahead was not a baker's shop, or even a café. It was an art gallery. Its windows were empty but for one small painting. Perhaps it was to show its value; perhaps the rest of the art was still safely stored away in the countryside, and this was all that was left, still on show, to say to any passer-by, 'This was a gallery, and will be again.'

Sophie stopped and stared.

It was square, with a frame of tarnished gold. There was an orchard, a fraction of a house — just a verandah, a table with a cloth, beyond it flowers and trees and fruit. Apples, she thought. I know what apples look like on old trees. Apple blossom with Angus at the Abbey. Ripe apples, bees crowded at the bird-pecked fruit, at Shillings.

Where was Miss Lily now?

A shaft of sunlight shone onto a single piece of fruit.

That is peace, thought Sophie. Somehow she knew that

soon someone would put a pot of coffee and a treat onto that tablecloth, that there'd be fresh bread and laughter.

Somewhere, perhaps, Jean-Marie was dreaming of paddling in the sea, with Charlie sleeping at his side.

It was a shred of peace, no more. But just at that moment it was enough.

She turned towards one of the larger streets, then signalled to a cab with its thin, weary horse to take her back to the hotel.

Madame Pierre showed no astonishment at a client dressed in three of the Ritz's large soft towels. She clucked at the loose skin of too much weight lost around the bust and hips; folded her tape measure and promised a day dress by the next morning, the tailored suits and the evening dresses to arrive day by day over the next month. Sophie didn't intend to stay here a month, but the Ritz would forward them. Nor did she think she could find a passage to Australia on any ship within a month, not with armies to demobilise.

Madame Pierre hesitated as she was leaving. 'Mademoiselle Higgs — you have been in France for some time?'

'For over a year now.'

'So.' To Sophie's shock, the old woman stepped up to her and kissed one cheek then the other twice, three, four times. Madame Pierre stepped back. 'You too have been fighting for my country, mademoiselle. I thank you.'

The door shut quietly behind her.

More letters had arrived. Sophie redirected the business ones to Mr Slithersole. A letter from Her Grace, not written by her arthritic fingers but by those of her new companions, one of the nurses who would stay on at Wooten, moving to the Dower House with the dowager when His Grace returned, bringing his new duchess, the widow of a chaplain he had met in the Middle East. There will be children in the Abbey, she thought, and laughter in the Dower House. As in Angus and his bride's Dower House — but she thrust that thought away.

Letters from James Lorrimer — less personal than the one in which he had admitted to what might, in another man, have been despair — telling her of political manoeuvrings and acquaintances in common. Letters from Miss Thwaites and Sophie's father, one stained with what might have been seawater; strange to never know what peril it might have been through. The letters said little, but that little said it all: five of the men from Thuringa were dead, and one had lost an arm; he would cook for the shearers now. She supposed he'd learn to manage somehow, like Sergeant Brandon, who couldn't see and learned to use an abacus. Her father was managing; he needed his daughter but, man-like, would never say so.

Malcolm's letters were slightly indignant that she had not been in England to meet him; the third was written just before he embarked for home. He'd had a reasonable war. He would have a good peace too, she was sure.

She sat with his last letter, watching the coal fire, remembering: the golden boy with his brown arms, riding beneath the trees ...

She had loved the boy, for a time, even if she didn't love the man. It was because of him that she had come to England; because of him that she was the Sophie Higgs who had now emerged from the war.

Would there ever be a letter from Hannelore again? Germany was perhaps too chaotic for mail still, even sent via Switzerland. I will wait a year, she thought, in case questions from a former enemy might harm her, then ask Mr Slithersole or someone like him to find her in Germany, and Dolphie too.

No, that was not true. She would wait a year, hoping — because she had left Dolphie wounded on a battlefield, stranded between two enemy lines, vulnerable to both. If Dolphie had died there, she had caused his death.

Or had his sense of humanity done that, as he risked both life and reputation on the same grim task as her? He had risked his men, even if she had been the one to pull the trigger. Perhaps her true sin had been the one he had smilingly accused her of. She had not understood him. 'I made most sure that you would not.'

Dolphie had absolved her of that guilt too. He had loved her.

After four years of war and an influenza epidemic, there were many closets in her memory that must remain dark and locked. Dolphie's was the one that needed the strongest chains, at least until she had healed enough to look inside.

There was one final letter, only one. She had kept it till last, deliberately. Now she rang the bell and ordered dinner. A bottle of claret — yes, a whole bottle, please — no, not roast pigeon: she shuddered at the thought of the tiny feathered bodies carrying messages from one post to another. Impossible ever to eat squab after that. Roast turkey, then, potatoes, petit pois; bombe impératrice, coffee. Bring them at the same time, please. She didn't want to be disturbed.

And more towels. At least a dozen towels. She needed to bathe yet again, hunt for any elusive lice once more. How long would it be before that habit left her?

She opened her final letter.

Shillings
February 1919
My very dear Sophie,

   Please excuse the brevity of this. I am here only for a short time, but hope to return soon. I have heard of all you have done from Her Grace, of course, with pride in your courage and your resourcefulness. I expected nothing less. You always had the rare combination of kindness and ability to succeed at all you tried.

   I would very much like to meet you again, to explain much that I was not able to say before. The earl echoes my sentiments. I also deeply wish for you to meet him at last, my dear.

   Her Grace tells me you will pass through Paris on your way to England. I once promised you an address for Mrs Higgs. You will find it on the enclosed card. I also offered you an explanation, which I would prefer to give to you in person.

   Mrs Goodenough sends her very best regards, and Jones too. I would say he sends his love, but of course he has not said that. But from me, most certainly, my love.

   Yours,
   L

Chapter 64

*In novels it is always one big adventure. However, life always has
so many loose stitches to tidy up.*

Miss Lily, 1919

It was a good address. Somehow Sophie had known it would be
a good address. A tree-lined street of houses, not apartments.
Hedges, stone walls, wrought-iron gates and a sign saying
Attention, chien méchant.

She checked the number — two down from le chien méchant —
and knocked. A pale blue door; grey stone; a scent of honeysuckle.

A maid answered the door. Fifty perhaps, in a white cap and
apron over a black dress. Sophie placed her card on the silver tray
and waited as the maid assessed her quickly then said quietly,
'Please come in, Mademoiselle Higgs. Madame is expecting you.'

Sophie allowed her coat to be taken. She could smell cakes
cooking, sweet and buttery. 'If you please, mademoiselle.'

She followed the maid down the hall. Her heels clacked on
the parquet. Good heels. New, like her dress, her silk stockings,
her corset, stifling after a year without one. A blue dress, grey
stockings, grey gloves; her pearls, sent from Wooten. What else
would one wear to meet one's mother, but blue silk and pearls?

My sweet little grey-haired mother, she thought ...

She saw the woman before she saw the room, and not just
because she was looking for her. This was a woman who was
always seen first, who had created the room as a frame for herself.

The woman before her was not grey-haired. Small, yes. Fine-
boned. Her hair was perhaps too evenly mid-brown, the dress
pale yellow silk, softly draped in a style that was not pre-war.

She might have been Sophie's age. This woman still had the face of a child, unlined, and there was something else childlike about her too.

The room was perfect. Off-white silk walls, pale wooden furniture upholstered in yellow brocade, Chinese silk carpets over the parquet, decorated with peacocks and griffons. No clocks. No ornaments at all besides three porcelain vases, each filled with different flowers. At least two must be gifts: a servant or a mistress would have chosen bouquets that matched.

The woman on the sofa held up a hand. Was it to be kissed, or pressed? Sophie handled it lightly, her grey kid gloves touching white lace. I have not yet touched my mother's skin, she thought. Not for over twenty years.

'Please do sit, darling.'

She sat.

The woman looked at Sophie critically. 'Good. You are pretty,' she said. Her voice was light and high.

'Thank you.'

'It would be terrible to think I had a plain daughter. Though no one must know you are my daughter, of course.'

'Why not?'

The woman laughed. 'My dear, I am twenty-nine. Far too young to have a daughter of nineteen.'

'Twenty-four,' said Sophie.

'Oh, so much worse. A cousin perhaps, from Australia? Your accent is good,' she added. 'But one can still hear you are from Sydney. The French are good at sensing these things.'

'What do I call you?'

'Madame Higgs? No, too formal. Cousin Emilia.' She looked at Sophie critically. 'You have my eyes. But you have had too much sun, my dear. You must be careful about the sun.'

Sophie glanced back at the maid. The woman — impossible to think of her as 'mother', much less Cousin Emilia — laughed. 'Oh, she knows everything.'

'And your friends here?' Sophie asked.

485

The woman smiled. 'If they care, they can find out that I was married, that my husband is in Australia. But why should they be interested? Coffee, please. Now,' as the maid left, 'tell me about yourself.'

'I have been running two hospitals and —'

The tiny woman held up a hand. 'No, no, not about the war. I have had too much of war! Tell me about parties. Your father said you were presented. Tell me of your young men.'

'You hear from my father?' The world was cracked.

'But of course. He sends me money, and sometimes a note.'

She had expected ... What had she expected? That her mother was a friend of Gertrude Stein, even an artist. Someone whose very life had been squeezed out of her by Sydney respectability, by life with her father.

My father knows, she thought. Yet never told me. Has he told Miss Thwaites?

'Why did you leave me?'

'Oh, pouff, how boring. How long ago.' It was a child's pout, a child who wanted to be happy, and entertained. 'I left because I was bored. Sydney, after all! It is the end of the world! And your father can afford for me to be happy.'

'But you left in your nightdress. You left your clothes, your jewels ...'

Her mother — no, that word would never fit — looked shocked, then amused. 'Your father drove me to the ship himself. A friend in India had told me that to have fun in England you must have a husband as well as money, but in Paris these things are understood.'

'He knew you weren't coming back?'

She worked out how her father could have hidden a body — yes, she had denied it, denied he could even have considered it, but of course it would have been easy for him. And just as easy to take a living wife to board a ship, with a trunkful of clothes.

'Of course. I promised that if he sent me money I would not contact you,' she said. 'That year I lived with him! It wasn't at all what I had expected when I agreed to go out and marry him.'

486

'I thought you came out as a governess.'

She laughed, a perfectly practised cadenza of sound. 'Oh, how wonderful. Of course I was not. I was not born to teach children! No, the marriage was arranged between your father and the colonel, my employer. I needed a wealthy husband. Your father wanted a wife who knew how things should be done, a beautiful wife to have on his arm to show he was a gentleman now. And I really did think I would stay with him. But no one had said how terribly dull Sydney was. And babies! Oh!' She leaned over and patted Sophie's hand. 'But you are much improved now. That dress is good.'

She sat back, her eyes sparkling. 'I will take you to my dressmaker. We have the same colouring — she will know exactly what you need. You must come again tomorrow — no, on Thursday. Then we will have coffee, and ice cream too. I love ice cream! I know a café where we can have the most divine pineapple ice. I will even take you to my milliner. But not to dine together, or to parties.' A whisper, and a smile. 'It is not good to have a friend ... or even a cousin ... who has the same beauty as oneself.'

'Did Miss Lily teach you that?'

'Miss Lily?'

'The Earl of Shillings's cousin.'

She shook her head. 'There are so many men. But I would have remembered an earl.'

'You never wondered about me?'

'No,' she said frankly. She smiled. 'But you are very nice now. It would be fun to have a daughter, I think — well, a cousin, but you know what I mean.'

The door opened. The maid appeared, but not with tea.

'The Comte de Longueville, madame.'

'My very dear Comte.'

He was fifty, perhaps. He had the wit to clasp his hostess's hand and kiss it before he looked at Sophie.

I could conquer you, Sophie thought. I only need to smile, to hold my head a certain way. My mother pretends to be young, but I *am* young. And I have been trained by Miss Lily.

She couldn't do it. Didn't want to do it. Knew, suddenly, that it might even be a vain attempt. Miss Lily had taught her well, but this woman had lived her whole life on instinctive charm. And her mother *was* younger than she was, after nearly five years of war.

'My darling Comte, this is my cousin, Mademoiselle Sophie Higgs, from Australia. Sophie, darling, this is my very good friend, the Comte de Longueville. Though he has deserted me shamefully far too often.'

He smiled down at her. 'Madame, there has been a war.'

'Pouff.' The gesture was French. 'There is no war in this house. I have forbidden it. And now the war is nowhere, so you have no excuse.'

Sophie stood up, smoothly, elegantly. 'Thank you so much, Cousin Emilia.'

'Must you go?' There was no real reluctance in the voice. 'But we will meet on Thursday? For lunch here first.' The smile this time was for the man, not for her daughter. 'We will tell each other all our secrets.'

Did you ever think of me? thought Sophie. For as much as three minutes at a time?

The realisation that she probably — no, definitely — hadn't was so strong she felt dizzy. Dad kept you secret for *me*, she grasped, endured all the years of gossip and suspicion. A rich man, deserted by the wife he had bought ... The world might snigger, but not for long. But how do you tell your daughter that her mother doesn't care?

She would have to write to him. Saying what? Divorce her, and tell those who snigger to go to hell. Marry Miss Thwaites.

She smiled, the first true smile since she had been in that house. Dear Miss Thwaites. A man as rich as her father would have a wide choice of wives, but Miss Thwaites would always be the woman he felt comfortable with. Of course I had a mother, thought Sophie. Many mothers: Miss Thwaites, Miss Lily, Her Grace, even those hours at Thuringa, the cicadas singing, with Bill. I have been so rich in mothers.

She looked at the woman again, the tiny fascinating woman. I am glad you left me, she thought. If you had stayed, I might have learnt to charm men as you do, without empathy or compassion. My real mothers taught me well.

And now she would see Miss Lily again.

By evening the concierge had booked tickets for the next day's train and ferry to Dover.

Chapter 65

Never weep for lost love, my dear. Weep that more cannot be shared, perhaps. But rejoice that you have had it.

Sophie, 1958

Sophie took a suite at the Ritz in London too. Stinkers had invited her to stay. Emily, too, had sent a card. The duke's town house was still staffed. But she could not face Ffoulkes. Besides, she'd had enough of other people's houses — even of talking, for a while. The Ritz offered her time to think.

James Lorrimer came to tea. He also came to propose, now that his affairs and the world's were partly tidied away, at least until the next crisis. Sophie liked that in him: his sense of place, and duty. They matched hers. And love?

She thought that in a strange way perhaps the war had cured her of wanting love. War was ... passionate. She had had too much of emotion.

She refused him. He nodded, sitting next to her on the sofa in her suite — no bended knee for James Lorrimer. 'Would it have made a difference if I had been Australian?'

She almost did accept him then. She so deeply wanted, needed, her own land again. James understood her. Their political ideas matched. But she would always be an appendage to James's life — a good life, a rich and intelligent life, but still just part of his. She could never be content now with organising his household, so that he could organise England. But she only said, 'Yes. If you had been Australian, it would have been different. But if you had been Australian, you wouldn't be James Lorrimer.'

He lifted her hand and kissed it. It was the first time she had felt his lips. 'I hope we can still be friends, even if it is from across the world.'

She suddenly wondered why he had never kissed her. She was, after all, eminently kissable. What had his first marriage really been like? Was James capable of passion? Did he even wish it, so distracting from one's duty? But today she had refused him. She did not need more than that, today. 'I hope we can be friends too. If I write to you sometimes, will you give me advice?'

'About corned beef?'

'I have yet to convince my father to let me be part of his empire. Nor am I sure that I want to merely inherit something someone else has made. Advice about politics, perhaps. About the world.' She smiled. 'You are an expert on empires. I may need your expertise.'

'Of course.' He looked at her, again with perfect understanding. 'And, just possibly, when you have felt the earth of your homeland beneath your feet, but begun to feel its society confining, I will ask you the question again, and you might answer differently.'

'Perhaps.' They both knew she did not mean it. She might have chosen life with him, if there had been no war. In another world she could have been his lovely lady, charming politicians and bureaucrats, changing governments behind the scenes, and been content.

But that was then and this was now.

Chapter 66

*True duty isn't what you force yourself to do; it is what you accept
with a full heart.*

Miss Lily, 1919

Sophie arrived at Shillings at a quarter to four. Teatime, she
thought as the driveway gravel crunched under the tyres of
the car Mr Slithersole had bought for her in London, which she
could now drive herself.

This time there was no Jones waiting, or even Mrs
Goodnenough. Instead an elderly man dressed like a farmhand
ambled around the corner of the house. 'Luggage, miss?'

'Thank you.' Ah. Samuel was dead.

The man touched his cap to her as she walked up to the door.
It opened as she approached, revealing a maid. The face at least
was familiar, though it was still strange to see a maid, not a
butler, at the front door of a house like this. 'Good afternoon ...
Jane, isn't it?'

'Miss Higgs.' She gave a bob. 'It's good to see you, Miss
Higgs.' Jane took her coat and scarf, hung them up then led the
way to the library. 'They are in here, miss. They said to show
you in when you arrived.'

Who were 'they'? But Jane was already opening the door.
'Miss Higgs,' she announced.

The room smelled the same as the first time she had come
here: apple wood and beeswax. The candles were burning
already, for the day was clouded, although the curtains had not
been drawn.

Sophie looked instinctively at Miss Lily's chair. It was empty.

Someone moved: a slight gesture, but enough to draw her eyes through the dimness to the sofa on the other side of the fire. Two figures sat on it side by side. Jones, she saw with a shock: Jones not as a butler at the front door to greet her, but sitting in a roll-necked fisherman's jersey and grey corduroy trousers. Next to him a slight figure regarded her steadily, though he did not rise either.

The Earl of Shillings.

'Good afternoon, your lordship. I thought I was to meet Miss Lily.'

The earl smiled. 'Hello, Sophie,' said Miss Lily.

Chapter 67

Can you imagine a world in which you cannot kiss the cheek of someone you love, or even hold his hand, without so many false and varied assumptions? Try, and you might catch a glimpse of the world in which I have lived for forty years.

Miss Lily, 1919

'Won't you sit down?'

Sophie sank into the chair — Miss Lily's chair — and stared at the two men. Jones stood. 'I'll fetch tea. It's good to see you, Miss Higgs,' he added.

'It's good to see you too, Jones. Good to see you so well.'

'Old soldiers never die,' said Jones. 'They just complain about the tea. Speaking of which ...' He tactfully left the room.

The figure opposite smiled at Sophie. His face was drawn, grey around the mouth, dark below the eyes. His hair was short, grey at the temples, but the smile was Miss Lily's.

'What do I call you?' asked Sophie.

He nodded, as though he had expected her acceptance. 'At the moment I am the Earl of Shillings, on a fortnight's compassionate leave from the army.'

'Compassionate?'

'A fortnight in which to explain to the parents and wives and children of the men I led away why eighty-seven of them will never return, why nearly two hundred are blind, crippled and beset with screaming nightmares. A most compassionate leave. The war is over,' he added. 'But a mountain of paperwork remains.'

'So I call you "your lordship"?' She should be trembling with shock. But she never could do what was expected. And, at some deep level, she realised she had known ... not this. She never could have known this. But that her relationship with Miss Lily was not quite that of a young woman and an older one.

'Or Colonel, these days. Or Nigel. I would prefer Nigel.' He sat back against the sofa, shutting his eyes briefly. 'So far I have visited thirty-eight families. Another fourteen to go. Some of the men,' he added, 'were brothers. The Smiths lost four sons. The fifth, I profoundly hope, will be back with them in a few weeks.'

'Nigel ...' She tasted the word.

He opened his eyes. 'I'm sorry. This isn't how I hoped you and I would finally meet.' He speaks as if there are two of him, not one, thought Sophie. 'I am ... preoccupied,' he added. 'Explaining death to the living is not easy, especially when the death is useless and tragic. All one can say is, "He didn't suffer." Which is a lie, of course. Eighty-seven deaths and none of them suffered? Yet each parent accepts it, the last vain hope they have, that their son did not die screaming, watching his arm bleed yards away in the mud ...' The soft voice faltered. Still Miss Lily's voice. The hair, the clothes, the faint stubble on the chin were different. But not the voice.

'Why did you go? You were so against the war.'

'The men would have marched anyway. The most I could do for them then was to lead them, to try to make things better. And I didn't. Of course I didn't. Not one thing I did made any difference at all, not in stopping the war, not in lessening the horror once my men were there.' He made a steeple of his hands and peered at her over them, exactly as Miss Lily had done in that room more than five years earlier.

'You did what you could,' said Sophie gently. 'But why on earth did you ever enlist for the North West Frontier? For the same reason that you are a colonel now?'

He shook his head. 'No. I enlisted to outrun Miss Lily. As far back as I can remember, every time I looked into the mirror, it was a shock to see she wasn't there. My duty as my father's second son was to ...' he shrugged '... to do what the first earl was given his lands for. To serve the Crown in battle, not for my glory, but for my people. How many times have you heard the expression "The army will make a man of him"? I thought it would, of me. Does that sound too impossibly naïve?'

'No.'

'Thank you, my dear.'

'I was taught by Miss Lily.'

'Yes, you're right. We are one person, Miss Lily and the earl. I was deluded ever to think that we were two.'

And yet he had seemed to refer to himself as separate. She gazed at him: Miss Lily's grace, but clutching his arms about himself in memory, in a way Miss Lily never would have.

'You said you started your group of women because you were raped yourself. Was that a lie?'

'No. I have never lied to you. Nor told you the whole truth, of course. I was attacked as a young man. For a while I despised myself almost too much to live. It was Jones who convinced me that what had happened to me had nothing to do with who I am, that rape under certain circumstances is as common for boys as girls.'

'Jones?'

'Jones was my batman, as he has been my batman in this war. If he had been another officer, he could have been my friend. An earl, and even the cousin of an earl, cannot have a man like Jones as a friend, so he became my butler. A butler has charge of the entire household, and we arranged it to suit my needs.' He smiled. Miss Lily's smile. '"Friend" is not a euphemism, by the way. I will answer the question you are too kind to ask. I'm not a homosexualist. I am not anything particularly strongly, which is perhaps why I was able to see how others' urges could be used.'

'That sounds so cold. And you're not cold.'

'Thank you, my dear, but don't confuse sexual desire with love.'

Had he shut away his sexuality after the rape? She could not ask. One day, perhaps. Not now.

'I have loved four people deeply in my life,' he added gently. 'One is Jones, the friend of both Nigel and Miss Lily. The second was Misako, a Japanese woman who helped Miss Lily become herself, the year I fled the army. The third is Isobel, the first friend who knew me only as Lily, although she was aware of Nigel too. I taught her the manners of an aristocrat, and the charm that Misako had taught me. Isobel showed me how I might find meaning in my life as a woman.'

Suddenly Sophie was afraid to ask the name of the fourth person he loved. 'And Jones?' she asked instead.

'There was a Mrs Jones. She died bearing their first child.' He met her eyes. 'The rest is his to tell, not mine.' Which implied, perhaps, that Jones might have wished for more than friendship. But as Nigel said, that knowledge belonged to Jones.

'How many know?'

'The whole truth? Only Jones.' The earl smiled. It was Miss Lily's smile. 'Truth can be a burden and a trouble.'

'How many know about Nigel and Miss Lily, then? My father?'

'Your father believes there are two of us — the earl and his cousin. My oldest friends know. Oldest in both senses. Isobel, Hannelore's aunt, some of the servants and tenants. I have never been sure which of the other locals have guessed. But there have been no sneers in church, no bricks thrown through my windows. When I die, Shillings may be inherited by my second cousin. I have never met him, nor have they. The people here have an interest in keeping things as they are.'

'Keeping a generous landlord? I think it's more than that. They like you.'

'This is who I am.' The earl's voice was light. 'I will never leave Shillings, except to do my duty to my people.'

It should have been melodrama. It wasn't. Perhaps because Sophie suddenly understood just how inseparable this man and his land were.

'Will Miss Lily return?'

He shook his head wearily. 'I don't think she can. As soon as we became a world of war, Miss Lily was a traitor, not a peace campaigner. She ... I ... meant well, but her efforts were mistaken. The balance of power kept war away, for a while. But once it happened, England and Germany were too well balanced, and so the war dragged on until the United States joined in. Now it's best for Miss Lily to vanish. To accept that war is something that men do, like playing football, or condemning a village to lung disease so they can make a fortune with a mine.'

Sophie thought of James Lorrimer's words. 'Surely there can't be another war after this?'

'Of course there will. Greed and hatred have grown even fatter in this war, like maggots feeding on dead men's flesh. Have you any idea how many fortunes have been made these last few years? Not by men like your father, who profited accidentally, but by those who make weapons to tempt countries into illusions of invincibility. How many men have tasted the absolute power of war, and want some more? The despair and anger in Germany must lead to war too, unless some other solution can be found. I profoundly hope that won't be Bolshevism. Bolshevism now is the war in different clothes.'

For the first time in three years, Sophie felt truly helpless. 'How can we stop it?'

The voice was soft in the quiet room. 'War? I don't know. I thought I had an answer, but I don't. Maybe there is no answer, and war of some kind inevitable. Perhaps the Earl of Shillings can be more effective than Miss Lily. It is my duty, at any rate, to see what he may achieve.'

'Nigel ... Miss Lily ...'

'Nigel.'

'Nigel ... how much espionage did Miss Lily take part in?'

'Did *I* take part in, you mean? None, myself. But I did urge others to. And perhaps it made no difference whatsoever, for both countries' foreign offices leaked like a sieve. How could they not, when our royal houses are so closely related? That is what I tell myself when I wake at four am and hear men's screams again, and wonder how much of all those years of stalemate in the trenches was due to me.'

'Stop it! Miss Lily was a force for good!'

'She failed,' said Nigel.

'No. She succeeded in doing something she never planned. Miss Lily — you — taught me that women can have power. I've used that power over the last few years. Emily has used it too, and so has every one of your pupils I have met.' Sophie lifted her chin. 'We are the women who won the war. Not just your ladies — we encouraged and led others too. We are the women who fed the soldiers when supply lines failed, who nursed them when there were official hospitals for perhaps one in a thousand wounded, who ferried screaming men in ambulances made from butcher's carts, or men to the front in ox carts because the officers forgot to organise how to get them there.' She stopped, embarrassed. 'I'm sorry. I'm making a speech.'

'And a good one. Thank you, my dear.' To Sophie's horror, tears slid down Nigel's face. But at least his smile had returned. She was glad she had not told him the whole truth. For the last years had been mostly fought with her father's tools: an inherited and learned genius for organisation and enterprise. Charm had helped, and the compassion that was the foundation of that charm. But across Europe women had stopped believing they could only influence the world by influencing their men …

'I wish you could take my place in the House of Lords. I was never able to speak there,' Nigel was saying. 'Miss Lily is articulate. But not Nigel. And yet he must be, if I am to be of use.'

'Perhaps you've underestimated him.'

He gazed at her. Finally he nodded. 'Perhaps. Miss Lily had friends to help her. Nigel has only Jones and Isobel.'

'And me now,' said Sophie gently.

His face twisted. Had she hurt him somehow? She said quickly, to change the subject, 'You said you would tell me about my mother. I met her. I didn't like her.'

He nodded, not surprised. 'Your father asked me if I could help him find a wife who would make his children socially acceptable. He had only begun to make his fortune then, but was already wealthy. I mentioned it to my ex-commanding officer. The poor orphan governess sounded ideal. I'm sorry. I owe both you and your father a great deal for my inadvertent part in that marriage.'

'Would my father ever have told me about my mother himself?'

'I think you must ask him that.'

'I have. I wrote to him yesterday, telling him to divorce her, and marry Miss Thwaites. And I think he will, now that I can't be hurt. It did hurt, just a little, to see her,' she admitted. 'But I've had Miss Thwaites, Bill, Her Grace and you.'

'Thank you for that, my dear. Please do give my best wishes to your father. He and his factories are the saviour of Shillings more than ever now.'

'The war has made you richer?'

'How many millions of cans of corned beef did the war need? Now they can bring Shillings back. Two-thirds of the trees have gone as pit props. Most of the shire horses are almost too old to work, certainly too old to breed.'

'Mechanical harvesters?'

'Of course Miss Sophie Higgs would have the most practical answer! Accept the new and do not try to bring back the old.' He leaned over and tentatively patted her wrist above her glove.

It was the first time they had touched since Sophie had left Miss Lily nearly five years before — the first time Sophie had felt his hand except through cloth. It burned her skin. Perhaps he felt it too, for he drew away. We are man and woman now, she thought with sudden shock.

But he was speaking as though nothing had happened. 'That's not the worst. So many young men lost, and others who'll never work again. Their parents have worn their hearts and their backs out to keep the farms going during the war, so their sons have something to come back to. But now? Half the fences on this estate would fall down if a cow sneezed. It'll take ten years and a lot of money before it will show a profit again.'

Sophie didn't bother asking Nigel if he planned to sell. 'How will you manage?'

'I've put a moratorium on rents for the next five years. I'll put everything I can into fences, machinery. I'll borrow if I have to.'

'From my father?'

'Yes. From your father.'

She sat back in her seat. It was the way she had sat before she had come here, comfortable rather than graceful. It was deliberate, and he knew it.

'Have you heard from Hannelore?' she asked. 'Or the baroness?'

'No, though I've tried. I am afraid that may mean bad news. Things are so confused there. We must keep hoping.'

He must never have received Hannelore's letter. Best that it be forgotten, for Hannelore's sake and so that Sophie need never confess to what she had done on the journey to Ypres.

'Tea.' The door opened and the trolley rumbled in, followed by Jones. 'I'm longing for a cup of char. I swear the stuff we got over there was burned toast and water. There is even cherry cake, especially for Miss Higgs. Thank God for the butter from the Home Farm.'

The voice was Jones's. The accent wasn't, nor the ease of manner, but the authority was the same. Sophie knew where it came from now: it was the voice not of a man who had worked his way up through the servants' hall, but of the man who cared for the owner of the house more than anyone else.

She took her cup from him, milk and — a miracle, this — real sugar already added. That small act, adding the milk and sugar for her, was a declaration of friendship as loud as an announcement in the Houses of Parliament.

'Call me Sophie,' said Sophie.

Jones shook his head. 'Might accidentally call you that outside this room. Bad to get into the habit.' He sipped his tea; it was still strange to see him seated alongside the earl. And she had never seen a butler eat or drink before. 'Have you asked her yet?'

'No. Still filling in the ... background.'

'That's me,' said Jones cheerfully. 'The background. Here's to the war — may we have seen the back of it — and to friends we won't see again.'

There are shadows in your eyes too, thought Sophie. She just hadn't noticed them before. 'Ask me what?'

'To marry me,' said the earl. 'Cherry cake? Mrs Goodenough is expecting you downstairs before dinner,' he added. 'She's stuffed a shoulder of mutton for you. You must have told her once that you used to eat it back in Australia.'

'Dear Mrs Goodenough. Did you say "marry"?'

'Yes.' The earl sipped his tea. His hand trembled. He laid the cup back on its saucer.

'Which one of you? Nigel or Miss Lily?' She hoped she was the only one who heard the slight note of hysteria in her voice.

'Does it matter?' For the first time there was an edge in Nigel's voice. 'You would be the Countess of Shillings.'

'Bearer of the heir?' There was no mistaking the tremor in her voice now. She wasn't sure if it was laughter or shock.

'Stop it. Both of you.'

Sophie blinked at Jones.

'Tell her the truth, you idiot,' Jones ordered.

Nigel stared at him. It was an earl's stare, of power and privilege. Jones ignored it.

'What truth?' asked Sophie quietly.

Jones turned to Sophie. 'He loves you. And I use the word "he" advisedly, because it is the man who loves you, not Miss Lily. He fell in love with you in your first week here. It shocked him so much he planned to propose to you at Christmas time, then panicked and tried to send you away. I told him he was an idiot then too.' Jones grinned. 'But you weren't easy to get rid of.'

At some level she had known it. Known Miss Lily loved her; had assumed the love to be maternal. She loved Miss Lily too, profoundly. She realised, shocked, that she could love Nigel too.

But not like that.

'Countess is the best bit of the bargain.' The earl kept his voice light. 'I know I am old enough to be your father, though not as old as the one you have. Not to mention … other things.'

'And yet you arranged for me to meet other suitors,' said Sophie slowly.

'I didn't say it would be good for you to marry me. I just asked if you would.'

Not for an heir — or not *just* for one. Sophie could hear the words that were not said, would never be said, perhaps, unless she committed herself to him. This man offered her his love: a marriage of true minds, even of challenges she would relish — managing his estate, as he would willingly let her join him in doing; helping the Earl of Shillings establish himself in the House of Lords and wider political world — and the Countess of Shillings too. And with her by his side, Miss Lily could at last emerge, hand in hand with Nigel.

But this was not the same as James Lorrimer's proposal. This was made with love. Her own hands trembled — not from shock, but from this unexpected depth of feeling. Nigel and Miss Lily were so dear, so impossibly sincere. They had been hurt so much; it felt impossible to hurt them further.

'I don't know. I ... I just don't know.'

'Are you sure? Your father would be proud.' The earl was trying to make his voice light. 'He could visit, and your Miss Thwaites too. You could even spend most of each year back in Australia. I would be a ... kind ... husband, my dear.'

So he understood even that. 'Nigel ... Jones — I'm sorry, I don't even know your other name.'

'Just Jones,' he said. 'Now.'

'I would love to say yes. But how could it work? No, I don't mean the marriage; in a funny way I can see that that would work quite well. And I love you. I loved — still love — Miss Lily. It ... it's taken me perhaps five minutes to love Nigel too.'

'Let her think about it, Nigel,' said Jones quietly. 'How many mountains do you expect the poor girl to climb in a day?'

Nigel tried to smile. 'I ... I need you, very much.'

'I know,' said Sophie softly. She suddenly realised how much she needed to be needed, and how much she needed to be loved.

They ate in the library. Impossible to eat in the dining room, with Jones either serving or at the table. Or was it? When the war had finally drained away, would Jones resume his post as butler?

It was the most informal meal that Sophie had ever eaten at Shillings. Nigel ate automatically, slumped in his armchair, a world — or war — away from Miss Lily's grace and posture. Jones ate steadily, a man who had learned to eat what he could and when he could. Mrs Goodenough's efforts deserved more, as Sophie told her when she slipped into the kitchen tactfully after the servants would have finished their own meal: 'A wonder, Mrs Goodenough.'

'The pheasant?'

'Perfection. Crisp potatoes, and those peas! And the apple tart a dream.' She smiled. 'I did dream of your cherry cake, sometimes, in France.'

'If I'd known your address, I'd have sent you some, Miss Higgs.' Mrs Goodenough hesitated. 'How do you find his lordship?'

It could have meant many things, and probably did. This woman was no fool. Her words carefully did not demand that Sophie pretend to have met Nigel/Lily for the first time; could have been a query about her reaction to what Mrs Goodenough must know had been disclosed today, or a simple enquiry about her master's health.

'I think he will be happy when he is back here full-time.'

'Happier if he were married too,' said Mrs Goodenough bluntly.

Sophie swallowed. Did the whole household know? But Jones and Mrs Goodenough must have been colleagues, conspirators, for decades.

'I don't know,' said Sophie softly. And that, too, could mean many things.

To her surprise she slept well, not even waking at her usual three am, listening for shelling, or men screaming. She woke as dawn filtered through the brocade curtains, even before the maid came to refresh the night's fire, if such luxuries still existed with the house so briefly tenanted by its master. She felt — different. Nor was it just the refreshment of the deepest, quietest sleep she'd known for years.

She dressed quickly, longing for Australian sun; left off her corsets altogether, wondering if Nigel would notice with Miss Lily's eyes. But going corsetless had been one of the comforts that had enabled her to work and keep working through the years of war.

Down the stairs, out into the orchard. It was only as the light dappled lichened tree trunks and leafless twigs that she realised this walk was almost an echo of her first morning at Shillings.

But then Jones had not come striding through the dew towards her. He wore the trousers and jumper of yesterday, or similar; army boots, bright with dew and polish. He hadn't yet shaved, which shocked her deeply for three seconds, before she laughed at herself.

'Good. You're smiling.'

'At you. You haven't shaved.'

'I saw you from the window.'

Which would not have been the servants' hall. Did Jones share Nigel's chamber, despite Nigel's claim?

Jones met her eyes. 'I sleep in the dressing room, like a good batman.'

She should feel relief that Nigel was not a homosexualist, just as he had claimed, that any marriage would be a true one. Yet she felt nothing except curiosity answered. She suddenly realised that after five years of seeing men's bodies in intimate agony, she might never see one with pure desire again. And even now, did Nigel truly know who he was? He, too, had been shaped by social expectations, to be solely either man, or woman. He needed time — and friends — to find his true self. And she knew this because, at last, she had woken up knowing who Sophie Higgs should be.

But Jones was waiting for a reply. 'Will you become a good butler again too? I ... I'd be sorry to see it.'

'I was a magnificent butler.'

'Yes. Magnificent. But you used the past tense.'

505

He nodded. 'Probably Nigel's secretary. The war has loosened things. A man of my background could be a secretary now.' He grinned. 'If a Lloyd George can be Prime Minister, a Jones can be an earl's secretary.'

They turned through the apple orchard, the buds a promise of spring. At least spring varied little if you were an apple tree, she thought.

'It must be a shock,' Jones added abruptly.

'Yes. But not as much as it should have been. If Nigel had asked me that first Christmas, I would probably have said yes.'

'You were too young. I told him you were.'

'You were right.'

She did not say that she was tempted to say yes now too, not because of Nigel's rank, or even love of Shillings, but because all she had been through had made her an unconventional woman, although one who understood the need to keep conventions when necessary. Nigel and Jones would understand her. Perhaps no one else ever could.

'I know the answer now,' she said quietly. 'May I tell you both?' She smiled. 'It is really an answer for the two of you.'

He held out his hand. 'Will you come to breakfast, Miss Higgs?'

She took his hand, warm, still hardly calloused. A batman's work was not hard labour. They walked, arm in arm, towards the house.

He sat alone, the sun from the dining-room window upon his face, revealing his features more clearly than Miss Lily ever permitted. It was that, more than any words, that showed Sophie how distant he must feel, after the years of war, from the woman who was still part of him.

He stood as they entered. 'Coffee? Mrs Goodenough has managed kedgeree too.'

'An answer first,' said Sophie. 'Nigel, I just told Jones that if you'd asked me to marry you that first Christmas, I'd have said yes.' She took a breath. 'But I'm not the girl I was before the war.'

Her voice had strength now. 'You made me into something, in those few months at Shillings. Something I would never have been without you. You gave me the courage to be myself, the skills to make others accept me as that too. I'm not going to stop now, nor will ten thousand other women when the war gave us the opportunity to finally be ourselves. I've seen women on the battlefield driving ambulances with no army officers needed to direct them, carrying men across the craters. I've seen girls not out of their teens running canteens. I've seen a nursing sister run an entire first-aid station that had been set up by women, stitching wounds when the surgeon and his table were blown to smithereens. Do you really think those women will be content to be "lovely ladies" after the war? To go back to their drawing rooms or kitchens?'

'They'll demand the vote? Those over thirty have been given it now.'

'More,' said Sophie. 'Much, much more. What use is a vote if you can only vote for men, or have to choose between the differing visions men have for the world? We may not be lovely, we may not even all be ladies, it may take us years, more wars even, but we will be ourselves, not appendages of husbands, not just daughters, servants, mothers, wives.'

'And you?'

She needed to smell gum leaves. She needed deep blue sky. She needed home, and she needed Australia to be her home. It was home she longed for now, more than any man, a place where she instinctively knew she would find who she was, and who she might become, in this world beyond the war.

And that could never happen with Nigel, or Miss Lily. Impossible even to imagine Miss Lily in Sydney, or at Thuringa.

She sat next to him at the table, close enough to smell cologne, not Miss Lily's perfume. 'I belong in Australia. It's why I refused James Lorrimer, though I never loved him, not as I love you. It's not just because I grew up there. I need to go back for the same reason as my father started his empire there.

'England is too rooted in tradition. All women already have the vote in Australia. Maybe I will stand for parliament in our electorate against Mr Overhill. Perhaps my father will accept me as part of Higgs's Corned Beef. Maybe I will start a ... a cheese factory, employing the million women who will never have husbands after this war.'

'Sophie ... I ... I need you.' Nigel attempted a smile. 'Need you to tell me about mechanical harvesters and convince us all they'll work. Need you to ...' His voice vanished. Jones moved to the dining table, took his hand and held it.

'To convince you that Nigel can be as powerful as the young women Miss Lily taught? That you are lovable, as you convinced me that I was, and not just for the money from corned beef? I do love you, Nigel. I'll stay as long as you need me, which won't be forever. And I'll come back if you need me again.' She met his eyes. 'You'd never consider living in Australia, would you?'

'Of course not.' The words were a chorus, Nigel and Jones together. They glanced at each other, smiled, and almost as one person turned to Sophie.

'You will stay, won't you? For a while?' The earl's grip tightened on his friend's hand.

She stood, then bent and kissed his cheek, then Jones's. 'I'll stay as long as you need me,' she repeated. 'And I'll love you till the seas gang dry. You and Miss Lily.' Suddenly she realised she was beginning to love Jones too. She bit back laughter, only slightly hysterical. Was love — deep love — ever convenient? Her father and her poor, silly mother; his illicit love for Miss Thwaites. 'Now I'll go and tidy myself before breakfast, as Miss Lily taught me to do. No,' as Jones began to rise, 'stay there. I can find my way to my room. That's what I've just been saying, I think. It's not all up to you now — not up to men, or earls. It's women's responsibility as well.'

Jones reached out his arm to comfort Nigel as she left the room.

She brushed the tears away. She only had to walk back into that room to find comfort too. But home, and the life of her own she might forge there, called too deeply, and no amount of love could make it different.

Chapter 68

Well, my dear, it seems that we both still continue. But how?
**The Earl of Shillings to the Dowager Duchess
of Wooten, 1919**

10 March 1919
Dear Miss Higgs,

I hope you are in the best of health. I trust you will not mind
my writing to you. My name is Gladys Muff, Miss Higgs. I work
at Brandon's factory. I have been helping to do the accounts there
because George Brandon, he cannot see.

I would like to marry him, Miss Higgs. George says he won't
marry me because of what he looks like. He is worried I do not
know what it will be like. He thinks our children will be ashamed
of him. I say our children will be proud and I will make sure of
that, miss.

George manages very well: you would be glad if you saw him
now. He wears a hat down over his face. It looks a bit strange,
but people do not notice much. It were a shock when I first saw
him, but that is years ago now. I do know what I am doing, miss.
I really do. George has a house just down from the factory. He uses
a cane to get there, and he has the house all worked out so he can
get around. He does not cook much, mostly eats bread and cheese,
but that will change when we are married.

I am writing to you because I think he will do what you tell
him. If you tell George he should marry me, he will. I hope then
you will come to our wedding, miss.

Your most obedient servant,
Gladys Muff

Sophie stayed at Shillings for two weeks, till Nigel's and Jones's leave was over, and then another week to make sure the estate ran smoothly with them gone, then drove herself to Sergeant Brandon's wedding, staying at the duke's London residence, where Ffoulkes never mentioned, nor had quite forgiven, the broken desk.

She returned to Shillings; interviewed a new estate agent and secured a loan for a mechanical harvester from her father through Mr Slithersole, who also organised its purchase and transport from the United States; she talked to surprisingly accepting tenants about not just how the harvester could be used, but also how it could be hired out to other farmers for income; she gave orders about repairing fences and gates. She bought ewes and a most expensive ram, and gently explained why the beloved horses would not be replaced.

The vicar brought her eight men, still white with shell shock, who needed jobs. She put them to work planting trees, quietly, away from the other workers.

She stayed a further month with Nigel and Jones when they returned, to take the weight of lordship from Nigel while he walked his woods and smelled the air of home, as the earl rather than Miss Lily.

Mr Slithersole booked her a passage on the *Cape of Fortune*. She spent a weekend in London, drinking vast amounts of cocoa with Ethel and her suffragette friends; admired Ethel's motorbike and the care Sloggers had taken with Dodders's precious vehicle, but refused a short escape with them to Wales or Scotland; then drove herself up to Wooten for a final fortnight with Her Grace. She spent most of that time sitting by the old woman's bedside, both of them remembering, or in remembering silence. The duke and his new wife treated her as family; Doris and little Sophie visited often, Sophie looking wonderfully and heartbreakingly like Alison. Nanny still dozed and remembered, with Sophie added to that memory jewel box. I am so rich in families now, Sophie thought.

But the future? Ethel and Sloggers had women's equality to fight for, true university degrees and votes for all women, even if some had been granted the vote in the new Act; Nigel, Jones and the dowager had their estates; James had the future of his nation. Only Sophie seemed still adrift. But she must find her place in Australia.

The last afternoon at Wooten she walked in the orchard, and picked bluebells for Alison's grave. A storm was coming, thunder far off, reminding her of the noise of the big guns. It would never leave her now.

She sat under the lichened apple tree, blossom sparkling as if war had never been, where she and Angus had once lain, with the mail in her lap. So many letters these days, so many friends across the world, women she had worked with, friends bound forever by the war and unbreaking chains.

But she opened none of them. Instead she took out Angus's again. She'd kept it. Somehow it reassured her to know that he was safe, that she had not destroyed him with her foolhardiness, even if he no longer loved her, perhaps had never loved her, had just needed her in his time of vulnerability.

She took it out and read it once again.

What did Glenda Quince look like? she wondered. If Angus could fall out of love with Sophie so soon, and into the arms of Glenda, it had been no love on which to base a lifetime together.

Glenda Quince. Quince paste at their picnic, under the apple trees.

Sir Alan Crabtree. Glenda Quince.

She stood up, brushed the grass and leaves from her skirt, then strode back to the house to look up Debrett's, and then to cancel her passage home.

Chapter 69

Love comes in so many flavours, or like waves, perhaps — some cold, some hot, some high and crashing, others sweet and creeping gently to your feet. There is no one kind that suits us all, nor perhaps is there one kind of love that will suit us our whole lives. But luckily, there doesn't have to be, for love changes too.

But this I do know about the happiest couples I have seen: love came unexpectedly, but those who had the strength embraced it anyway, and were fulfilled.

Sophie, writing many decades later
to her granddaughter, undated

The village was worn, as they all were: the gardens still full of vegetables, not sweetpeas; no old men lingering on benches outside the pub — there was still no time for old men to linger; and the young men, those too crippled to work or with their lungs rotted by gas, were still too sensitive to the stares of others to take up the benches in their place.

Sophie stopped at the blacksmith's for fuel and directions, and ignored his raised eyebrows at the sight of a woman driving a car — *her own* car — as well as at her question. 'Captain McIntyre? You'll find him in Simpkin's old cottage, miss. He moved there two weeks ago last Tuesday.' He winked at her. 'Young man wants his own place, don't he, not under his ma's eye. Two miles past the church, miss, then turn right where McMaster's barn used to be.'

'Used to be?'

'You can't miss it, miss.'

She didn't.

It was a small house. She had expected that. One storey. She had expected that too. The ivy had been recently hacked away from the front door and the wisteria trimmed above the windows, which gave her hope.

The door was plain wood, unpainted. She knocked, once faintly, her hand trembling, and then another harder knock, so the door left a dirt smudge on her glove.

'Come in.'

She opened the door. The inside was a single room: a narrow bed against one wall, covered with a grey army blanket; a fireplace, with a tripod and pot; a sliced cabbage on the table; four chops, uncooked, on a plate.

He sat in the room's only easy chair, a blanket over his lap. He stared as she came in. 'Sophie! How did you —?'

'Find you? Mrs Colonel Sevenoaks asked a friend of her husband's.'

Angus flushed. 'Forgive my not getting up. I was just getting changed. Got muddy checking the partridges this morning.'

'Not at Sir Alan's estate with your Miss Quince yet?'

'Next month,' he said easily. 'Filling in down here for a friend.'

'We're lucky to have such good friends.'

He looked at her warily. 'Yes, aren't we? I'm afraid I can only offer you tea.' He nodded at the pot on the fire. 'The water should be about at the boil.'

'Thank you.' She crossed to the table, found a round brown teapot and a canister of tea. One for each person and one for the pot.

'Excuse my not getting up,' he said again.

'Don't worry on my account.' She smiled at him: a perfect smile, moist lips and steady eyes, her fingertips trailing her hair back from her forehead, all the charm Miss Lily had taught her. 'We are past all that sort of awkwardness between us, aren't we? Or we should be, don't you think?'

'Yes.' He sounded awkward, though. Ah, she had made him say yes. Now for a question he can answer ... 'How do you get water from a pot on the fire into a teapot?'

'I use a teacup.'

'Excellent strategy. Your strategies are always superb, Captain McIntyre.'

'If they were excellent, you wouldn't be here. I'm sorry there's no cake.'

'There's a hamper with ginger nuts in the car.'

'No ginger nuts for me, thank you.' His voice was dry. 'I'm sorry, there's no milk or sugar either.'

'I've lost the habit of them too.'

She handed him his cup and saucer and sat on the room's only other chair — a hard one, armless — and sipped her tea. 'I think there is quince paste in the hamper as well. I remember how you like quince paste.'

He looked at her cautiously. 'I've only had it once.'

'Ah. A memorable once, though.'

'Yes.'

He wasn't helping. She put the cup down on the floor, suddenly impatient. 'A coincidence that your fiancée should be called Quince.'

'Perhaps it is.'

'And Sir Alan Crabtree? Quite an orchard.'

'Sophie, what are you saying?'

'There is no Sir Alan Crabtree in Debrett's. No Crabtrees at all, in fact. Or Appletree or Orangetree, just in case you forgot what kind of fruit was employing you. I didn't look up Banana. Though Sir Alan Banana has a ring to it.'

'I did say my strategies aren't the best,' he said. 'Yours were always infinitely superior. But I worked hard on that letter.'

'Yet the truth seeped through it anyway. Why did you try to lie to me?'

His eyes were honest as they looked at her. 'Because it's best.'

'Why? I'd hoped,' she added, 'that I was the one person in the world you could tell the truth to.'

'Sophie, you are the one person in the world I must lie to. I lied to you because you are a woman of courage and compassion.'

'And a woman of courage and compassion doesn't sail back to Australia leaving a man who has lost a leg?'

Silence filled the room. A lark called outside: a long liquid note. Five years ago I didn't know a lark's call from a nightingale's, she thought.

At last he said, 'Exactly.' He looked at her for a moment, then added, 'Don't say it doesn't matter. Don't you dare say that.'

'Of course it matters! It matters you were hurt! It matters I wasn't there! It matters that you are here alone, that you —'

'Sophie, don't cry.'

'I will if I want to.'

He gave a muffled laugh. 'Sophie, I can't wipe away your tears for you. I haven't got my leg ...'

'I know.'

'I don't mean my real leg. I mean my artificial leg. I've been having trouble with it — the damn thing keeps going at the knee. The blacksmith took it this morning to repair it for me. It should be back by now. There must have been an emergency.'

'I called in to ask the way and he was shoeing a horse. Your leg is sitting by the blacksmith's forge while he shoes a horse?'

Suddenly she was laughing too, as well as crying.

'General Sophie, riding to my rescue, just as I was afraid you would.' He looked at her steadily. 'I can't marry you. And not because of my leg.'

'I don't see any such thing. My *father* has only one leg.' She sat back on her hands and knees, then abruptly lifted the blanket.

He drew in his breath, moved to stop her, realised it was too late.

It was better than she had expected. She had expected a bandaged stump. This had healed clean, just above the knee. There was no sign of ulcers or the lingering infections of so many amputees. He had a skilled surgeon, she thought, remembering others she had seen, then grimaced at what 'lucky' meant these days. She would need to make arrangements for him on the ship ...

She held out a hand to him, smiled, waited for him to take it. Instead he took it only briefly, then pressed it back, against her body. 'Sophie, there is no other way I can think of to say this. I can't marry you.'

'But you said that there is no Miss Quince.'

'There isn't. But one day there will be, when I can manage a bit better. I will be happy.'

'And you and I wouldn't be? We would have our own property, in Australia. A large one. You'd love it, the river and the hills ...'

He looked at her steadily. 'You'd look after me, wouldn't you? You'd give me a property, and a life. And I would let you, as I always let you. Sophie Higgs, who shot at two men and outfaced a German officer so we could escape, who seduced a général into lending her a car and driver, who organised a large part of the war effort in France and Belgium for over a year ...'

Cold seeped through her. 'Is that why you don't want me? Because I killed a man and shot another?'

'No. Never think that. I have never admired a woman more. But it is because you shot them, and I could not have, even if I'd had the pistol.'

'Angus —'

'I do love you, Sophie.' But it was offered as consolation. Already he looked as he had that night in France: part overwhelmed, part apprehensive that a woman had overwhelmed him.

'And I love you.' And she did. She loved him with quince blossom and springtime — which she suddenly saw with deep clarity was not enough to build a lifetime on. Though it might be a place where one could begin ...

'I've got a job now, Sophie,' he said softly. 'Assistant to my father, and he'll retire when I've learned the ropes. It's a good job, and land I love.'

A young woman, dressed in sensible navy blue, let herself in, carrying a false leg. 'Angus?'

The melodrama eased. The young woman stared at Sophie.

Sophie smiled back. I would win if I fought you for Angus, she thought. I could persuade him to come to Australia, to manage Thuringa and whatever neighbouring land we buy. I could make him into exactly the husband that I needed.

And that was what Angus was afraid of.

She rose and held out her hand. 'Sophie Higgs. I knew Captain McIntyre in France. I'm so delighted to see him happy now.'

She drove herself back down the flowering lanes, still wondering if she had done the right thing; if Angus's hesitation had been based far more on the loss of his leg, the notion that this made him inadequate to hold his own as her husband, than he would admit even to himself.

Perhaps when he had been back at work, and part of life, for six months or a year, he would feel differently as the mental scars of war faded — and they would fade, in the healing air of trees and streams, the hush of owl wings and indignant protest of nesting plovers. But by then he might be engaged to that young woman, and Sophie back in Australia.

Where to now? Not just in her life, but today? Her suitcase was strapped to the back of the car, though her trunk still waited at the Abbey; she had been so sure she would need to stay with Angus, or at a hotel near him.

If she kept driving and had no flat tyres, and found fuel whenever needed — each as unlikely a proposition as a lasting peace across the world — she would make it back to the Abbey by midnight, which was not a suitable time to arrive anywhere — unfair to the servants, but also all too obviously saying, 'I am crawling back here because I have nowhere else to be just now.'

A hotel. Not in the next town — she needed distance from Angus physically as well as in other ways, for reasons she did not feel like analysing yet. There would be a post office where she could cable Mr Slithersole to book her another passage home. Perhaps she should go to Shillings again until she sailed. Nigel might even help her untangle her feelings about Angus. Nigel of all people knew the complex flavours of love. Two men currently wanted to marry her, but the one man she had asked had refused ...

Did she truly love him? Of course she did. Angus had been the first man whose very breath could make her shiver, and would always be, as well as the man who had heard her story in that war-shredded night, and yet had travelled on with her, despite his terror.

And if she insisted now, he would travel with her once again. She who had been taught so well that a woman could choose her own life must give the man she loved the freedom to choose his. A small life, which was perhaps all he could manage after so large a war, while she longed for empires ...

The hamper was still on the back seat. She thrust her mind away from another back seat, another hamper, and waited till the mossed stone walls gave way to a muddy lane, drove a little way down and parked the car. Too much mud and cattle muck to bother getting out. She hauled the basket into the front seat and poured tea into the cup that was part of the Thermos lid. Ginger nut biscuits. And the mail, still unopened. The housekeeper must have tucked the letters into the basket so that she would not overlook them in what must have seemed her strange haste.

She flicked through the envelopes. One from Miss Thwaites, darling Miss Thwaites. Another from Ethel, probably inviting her on yet another journey somewhere or other in the sidecar of her new motorbike. If the call of home had not been so strong, she might have said yes.

I will come back to England, she thought. There are people I love here. Every few years I will give six months of my life to cross the world and visit.

Nigel, too, would need her. And so would Miss Lily, for if Nigel was to be truly whole, Miss Lily must return, even if in a different incarnation. Besides, Sophie loved Miss Lily too.

She looked at the letters again. Two from women who had nursed at her hospitals and one from Sloggers. We were an army, she thought. An army of women, never mentioned in dispatches. The history books will probably never mention us either. We make the men who write them too uncomfortable.

Another letter, with many German stamps. An unfamiliar hand, the letters shaped slightly differently from all those she knew, except for Hannelore's ...

The small closet she had chained shut was immediately ajar. Hannelore must be safe! And Dolphie?

She put the letter down, unopened, suddenly unable to bear seeing what it held. Angus had accused her, back during that long night, of sacrificing him in her quest to save the English forces from the gas. But it had been Dolphie she had sacrificed. His arm, if the wound had festered. His men. Possibly his life and honour, because by being found there, presumably with no orders, he would be at best a deserter, at worst a traitor. Imprisoned. Shot.

She thought, I cannot bear to open this.

A cow mooed, sadly. Stop wailing, she thought impatiently. At least you are kept for milk, not corned beef.

She opened the envelope.

The writing was not Hannelore's.

Liebe Sophie,

I write to you for Hannelore, who will not write. Do not worry: she is safe and well, or safe for a time and well enough, though far too thin. But then I do not think there is a person of plumpness in the whole of Germany.

Hannelore's estates are in Russian hands now, as are mine. I cannot help her, as I would wish to do, not just because of the loss of fortune, but because of other matters of which I may not write but which, perhaps, you will understand.

I write to you as her friend, knowing that you will still be her friend, and not her enemy, and can offer her a home, a future, in Australia and its sunshine perhaps, as you once promised, far from the starvation and misery of Germany. You may start with the address on this envelope. She is not there, but the people will know where she can be found.

I remain yours faithfully, as I always have been, and will always be,

D

The letter 'D'. Not his title, not even his full nickname. What was Dolphie's position in a defeated Germany? Traitor? Discarded aristocrat? Precarious enough that even this letter might threaten him, and Hannelore, if it were read by others?

... of other matters of which I may not write but which, perhaps, you will understand. But I don't understand, she thought. I don't know Germany, especially not now, in poverty and defeat, its previous similarity to Britain destroyed.

'You never did see me, did you, Sophie?' he had said that terrible grey morning on the French front line. 'I made most sure that you would not.'

But now she did. Saw the man she had trusted not to shoot her.

Was it possible to trust a man more than that? Saw Dolphie, finally, not as a fashionable fool, joker, enemy, but as the man who would forgive her — and in a way that Angus never could — for sacrificing him, just as she would have sacrificed herself, to save an army from a devastating weapon. Saw the man who trusted her to stop the deployment of a weapon, in the middle of a war. A man who had not just forgiven her, but also understood. Even more, for a man like Dolphie, he had forgiven her for shooting his men. Saw the slightest, smallest possibility that an alliance between a German count and an Australian corned-beef heiress might become something good, something better than either of them alone might be.

Above her a lark soared, delicate, beautiful. She longed instead for a wedge-tailed eagle, broad-winged, that owned the sky. It would be months more before she saw that eagle now.

She didn't know if she was right. Couldn't know. Because for that she must go to Germany. Which she must do anyway, to find Hannelore and make her safe, either in Australia or at Shillings, where Nigel would surely welcome her, even if Hannelore was too proud — or too defeated — to ask. Felt she had failed, perhaps — as if one woman could ever keep a world from war, or a nation at war from using every horror weapon it could find.

Sophie sat back upon the leather seat and felt the smile spread across her face. So this was what she must do tomorrow, after an evening in the next hotel. The strategies spread out before her, as they always did.

Yes, she would return to Shillings. She needed its peace to accomplish this, its scent of new-ploughed earth. Nigel and Jones would help. Perhaps in helping, Miss Lily too might emerge again, this time hand in hand with Nigel.

James Lorrimer would know what passports and letters of introduction were needed. She would not marry him, but she could trust him.

Dangerous for a woman unaccompanied. Would Ethel come to Germany? Or Stinkers, or Sloggers? Sloggers's governess had been a Fräulein. Sloggers spoke German well.

Sophie had a feeling that Sloggers, like a million other women now discarded after the work they'd done throughout the war, might welcome a challenge. Nigel or Jones would find a loyal chauffeur who knew how to use a pistol and his fists.

Letters of credit ... Mr Slithersole presumably had contacts even in Germany. Starving Germany must need corned beef, and this was a good opportunity for securing contracts, an excuse even for her father's daughter to head to Berlin ... lovely, innocuous corned beef, a perfect product to take her into the complexity of an enemy country in safety. Or in as much safety as might be achieved. Corned beef might even be a weapon for peace, when offered on reasonable terms to a starving, war-crippled country. Perhaps she should take a truckload of it, for both supplies and advertising. A truck would also be an excuse for the authorities. Ethel might even join in a new enterprise, forging fresh markets for her father's cocoa instead of picketing parliament and riding her motorbike across the moors.

And then? Find Hannelore at the address, which was a street address, not a castle or manorial name. Hug her. Feed her. Take her to love and safety. And Dolphie, who had asked for help for his niece, not for himself? How to persuade him that he could possibly find sunlight and a future in Australia?

She smiled. She had been trained for this, after all. Knew what to do with every heartbeat in her body, for a man who had lost a war, his wealth and estate, even perhaps his own sense of himself. Knew too, now, that even a woman had the power to change the pieces in the patchwork quilt that was the world, and how precious it was to find a man who would let her be herself.

The lark had perched, begun to sing: lovely, though lacking the liquid power of a lyrebird.

Thank you, Miss Lily, she thought.

Author's Note

While this book is based as far as possible on fact and primary sources, from Queen Mary's knitting to the events that led to war, there is no evidence I have read indicating that anyone tried to stop Germany's first use of mustard gas. On the other hand, if anyone *had* tried, the incident is likely to have been carefully forgotten, just as the role of the millions of women who served unofficially in the war has been forgotten, with only the official nurses and VADs celebrated, the smallest fraction of the women without whom the war would not have been won — or even lasted until the first Christmas, when it would have ended with German victory.

No person in this book, apart from the obvious characters like Winston Churchill, is based on any one person, but all are composites of real people. None is based on any person living.

Please forgive the views and some of the terms expressed in this book. The views are not necessarily mine — even the ones you may agree with — but those of the characters of the time. In the next two books in this series, covering the years 1920 to 1946, you may find the opinions of the same characters change.

This book has evolved under the brilliant editorial guidance of Kate O'Donnell, Kate Burnitt, Emma Dowden and Pam Dunne. More thanks than I can say to Lisa Berryman, Cristina Cappelluto and Angela Marshall, without whom this book could not have been written, and also would not. My deepest love and gratitude, always. These books are your creations, at least as much as they are mine.

Jackie French AM is an award-winning writer, wombat negotiator and was the Australian Children's Laureate for 2014–2015 and the 2015 Senior Australian of the Year. In 2016 Jackie became a Member of the Order of Australia for her contribution to children's literature and her advocacy for youth literacy. She is regarded as one of Australia's most popular authors, and writes across all genres — from picture books, history, fantasy, ecology and sci-fi to her much-loved historical fiction. 'Share a Story' was the primary philosophy behind Jackie's two-year term as Laureate.

jackiefrench.com.au
facebook.com/authorjackiefrench